# Vince.

## Book one.

This collection of writings is purely a work of fiction.

One or two of the businesses mentioned, which take no significant or active part in the plot, are genuine, as are similar geographical locations. They are included merely for authenticity.

All characters and events are entirely a figment of my imagination, and as such, bear no intended resemblance to any person, dead, living, or not yet created, or event from the past, present, or future.

Finally - my apologies to the People of Anglesey, for the liberties I have taken with their country, their language, and place names.

I, the writer, retain copyright.

First hand draft, 1999. First processed draft 3, 3, 2004.

Hi, Ian,

I cannot ask you to buy a book
you have already read, so here's a
freebie to start your collection.
One day it might be worth something, as
it is not off the press.

Eric

Chapter One.

Morning.


I struggle up from the depths of deep sleep at the insane chirruping noise made by the alarm clock. As I lie here, gathering the strength to raise an eyelid, I muse at the noise of the latest device. I've tried all the usual wake-up devices, from the Westclox wind-up bell, via radio alarms that blast you with Radio 1, until the wife or neighbours complain, to the old favourite, the Teasmade. That worked 'til one night, when I was turning in with my eyeballs hanging somewhere around my knees, and I forgot to water the beast. The following morning, I snapped awake to the smell of burning plastic! Other devices were too genteel, and therefore ineffective, or worked for a few months, until the brain learned to ignore them. Hence this thing, which chirps like a randy grasshopper calling for a mate!

The bedding next to me heaved about, then a bleary eye

poked out, followed by a bleary voice, which issues the command, "Shut that bloody thing off". Meet the wife.

I struggle to disentangle an arm from the ensnaring bedding, then reach over to flip the switch. Silence returned – for about two seconds. A milk-float crashed to a halt in the street outside, generating a series of internal clashings as the glass bottles independently came to a halt. Bang! The cab door, crash clatter the bottles, crash rattle the gate, clatter crash the empties, rattle crash the gate, clatter crash onto the float's bed with the empties, bang the cab door, then another cacophone of crashes and clatters as the collective conglomerate lurches into motion again. Thankfully, electric milk floats don't have gears to grind! Why, I ponder, do milkmen hate the rest of humanity, to the extent of thinking "If I'm up – you can be up too, and I'll make sure of it! After all, nobody forces them to be milkmen. And after all is said and done, most people, nowadays, get their milk from a Supermarket, in plastic containers that don't clatter.

Three different milkies travel down our street on a daily basis, at different times, and all three only deliver to one house, (different ones, of course), all three are occupied by Old

Codgers, who only take one pint, daily. How can the job be economical, when a single six pint bottle, kept in the 'fridge, would save them the delivery charge, with which they could purchase a second six pint bottle, or something! Ah, well. I roll over, in preparation for extracting myself from the warm bed. The cat, which had sneaked under the bedding during the night, protested at the disturbance, by burying its twenty claws into the tender flesh of my backside! Fully awake, I glance at the time displayed by the clock. Christ! Ten to eight! Where did the hour go? I scramble into my clothes, and dive for the bathroom, only to be beaten, again, by the four-year-old! I swear that he spends hours standing by his bedroom door, just waiting for me. Another day has begun.

Bathroom obstructed, I switch on the stairway light, and about two millionths of a second later, it goes off again with a Ping! when the filament burns out. In the dark, I stumble down the stairs, to encounter the cat, which, having crawled out of our bed, is lying in wait, halfway down. She completes the journey in a short arc, then cannons into the front door, while I perform a combination splits, forward trip, and long jump, the left hand missing the banister rail, and the right gouging grooves in the battle-scarred wallpaper and plaster on the opposite wall with the fingernails. Arriving at the bottom under partial control, I regain balance, then head for the kitchen, opening the front door for the cat, and the curtains for the dim daylight, in passing. I fill the electric kettle from the tap, then plug it in, hopefully to boil, while I rinse out the old vacuum flask, before spooning coffee powder and sugar into both flask and cup, which bears the replica of a cartoon character, and the legend 'The Biggest Mug In Town' (I was never quite certain what the Mother-in-Law was implying!). Take a plate from the rack, the bread knife from the drawer, (no, I don't cut my finger off, stop anticipating!), and open the bread-box, from which I extract - nothing. The loaf is still in the freezer, because the Wife forgot (again) to take one out to thaw. Repeated practice makes slicing frozen bread easy. You just have to remember to not hold on to the loaf for too long a time, or the fingers stick to it. After placing the remainder of the loaf into a plastic bag, then into the bread-box, I reached into the refrigerator for the butter dish, but somebody has moved it from its normal place, on the rack just above the vegetable tray, at the bottom. It is now located just below the freezer box, and the contents prove to be ever so slightly harder than the bread. So - sliced frozen butter on sliced frozen bread. Where's the cheese dish? Ah, there! It was hidden behind the yoghurts, and the poly-unsaturated axle grease. I open the lid, and shut it again, quickly, before the alien life-form within can escape. It appears to have taken the shape of a blue/green hairy cube, from which emanates a horrendous odour. Find an alternative, quickly now, the clock is going faster than I am. Corned beef? Yes, there are two cans of it. And no, I can't use either. As usual she has taken the 'keys' off the cans and placed them somewhere safe, so they won't get lost in storage. This is one of her little quirks and foibles. Where she puts them, I have no idea, but, as yet, I've never found one, (and nor has she, but she won't admit it!). I would use the electric can-opener, but I know from experience that it cannot cope with the tight-radius corners on the almost rectangular cans. Part of my mind notices that the kettle is taking it's time, today. What else is there, I wonder, I don't fancy cold fried eggs for lunch, and cannot be bothered with the mess of hard-boiled ones. So I settle for tomato sauce and lettuce on the butter slices. Into a bag with them, ready. The kettle still hasn't boiled, although it might speed things up if I turned it on, at the wall socket. That done, what's next? Ah, yes, feed the cat, if it ever decides to come back in. I successfully opened the can using the lever-action, hand-powered opener, without sawing off a finger-tip, (I had previously learned the hard way), Spoon out the malodorous mass into the plastic dish, ready for the cat to take a sniff, shudder in disgust, and stalk off to steal someone else's breakfast, by doing so making a liar of the photograph of the white Persian depicted on the label, drooling over the contents. (perhaps it was really being sick?).

The kettle finally reaches boiling temperature and the cut-out pops the switch to the off-position with a snap. Unplug, and pour the water into the cup and flask, onto the slowly congealing waiting mixture. The liquid in the cup looks rather thin, which is no wonder, the glutinous mass stuck to the bottom doesn't want to dissolve, a difficulty which was rectified with vigorous stirring. Down the throat it goes, in several scalding gulps, then tip a splash more water from the kettle into the cup, to hopefully continue the dissolving process, for when I get back, tonight.

Coat, put it on, flask, pick it up, along with the sandwiches. Car keys? Where are they? Ah! In the coat pocket where the four-year-old hopefully can't find them. Yes, they are the car keys, not the ones for the garden shed. I've tried that previously, and they don't fit the car locks, although almost anything else will. (They also lack a front door key, so once outside, with the wrong bunch, I can't get back in to exchange them). Outside, I lock the front door, trip over the cat again, open the drive gates, stepping carefully around the gift left by a passing dog, (or should it be referred to as a passing left by a gift dog?), A quick scrape to remove the dead leaves and bird droppings from the car windscreen, along with the morning dew, and a predatory spider or two. The roof-rack is festooned with glistening webs, but a swift blast down the traffic jam will shift them! Unlock the door, chuck the flask and sandwiches onto the other seat, flinch at the raucous racket of the car alarm, as my movement disturbs the trembler and sets it blaring, and fumble for the hidden switch, before the neighbour complains, (again). Grab the cat by the scruff of its neck, heave it out, then shut the door. How can a cat occupy so much space, have the ability to sneak, undetected, through the tiniest of gaps, yet be so difficult to extract, once in, if it decides to stay? Key, into the ignition, choke out, check for neutral, by wagging the shift-stick, pump the go-faster pedal to inject a squirt of liquid gold, then turn the key. The little red light on the dashboard glows dimly, the starter motor gives off a feeble groan of protest, and then the solenoid goes "clack, clack, clack". I release the key, with a groan. The intermittent fault built into this car has done it again, and leaked away all the battery amps, overnight. I have already replaced the battery, alternator, solenoid, and ignition-wiring loom, but the fault remains un-located. Yes, Henry Ford's company certainly made a reliable car. A body can rely on it to fail to work at the most inopportune moments. If Henry hadn't died, years ago, many would gladly have executed him!

So, I grope underneath the gubbins tray, to find, and pull, the bonnet release catch, skinning the knuckles on a sharp edge, and dislodge the ashtray full of fuses and miscellaneous screws. With a finger dripping blood everywhere, I remove the ignition key, then climb out, and walk around to the back of the car, to the boot, which I open with the same key, (it also fits all the door-locks, and all the locks on Harry's car, and Joe's, and Mike's, there's no danger of being locked out, at work!). From the boot, I extract the battered old battery charger, fitted with an extra-long mains lead, which enables me to plug into the domestic power, without messing around with extension leads. Having untied about half a dozen half-hitches and reef-knots, I amble over to the front door, cracking my shin on the exhaust pipe, in passing, and tripping over the cat then unlock the front door again, not using the car key, that is one lock it won't fit. From inside, I open a window, then go out again, toss the plug-end of the cable in, and go in again, so I can plug it into a wall socket. Back out again, open the bonnet, and connect the crocodile clips to the battery terminals, avoiding banging my head on the protruding bonnet catch, as I stand up again, afterwards. Then go back into the house again, to switch on the wall socket, that action being immediately followed by a bright blue flash, and a sharp crack! as the fuse commits suicide.

After having a good curse, I resort to the telephone, but not to call the A.A. because I forgot to renew the annual subscription, partly because the car has never broken down while away from home and home-starts are extra. No, I call work, to tell them I may be a little late arriving, today. The auto-dial beeps out the last digit, then there is silence, no ring-tone, no engaged, nothing. Finally there is a loud plop, then a strange male voice bellows "Eh, is that you, love?" I press the rest down, leaving a gory smear, then try again. Pause, then a massive splurge of static assails my ear, followed by a loud plop, then the tone we all love to hate, the brrr, brrr, of the engaged signal.

After all the stress, I decide to make another cuppa, while I repair the battery-charger. With the kettle sizzling again, I notice that I'm still leaving sticky red smears everywhere, and it occurs that it might be a good idea to raid the first-aid kit, for a sticking-plaster. After a search in the logical places, I found the carton in Her sewing-kit box, (box? It's a damn Tardis!), then search unsuccessfully for some scissors. Eventually, I use my Stanley knife, from the car toolbox, cutting off two pieces of plaster, one for the original damage, and one for the knife-nick .inflicted while cutting off the first piece. Fingers patched, I try the 'phone again, while the coffee cools, but the works number is still engaged.

With the screwdriver I brought in at the same time as the Stanley knife, I remove the top from the charger-plug, revealing the cremated remains of the fuse shell, a very dead spider, and a small quantity of water. With that dried up, the fuse replaced, and the top back on, I press the plug into the socket, then flick the switch on. It didn't go bang! So I go to the car, and sure enough, the charger is pumping five amps into the drained battery. Back inside, to wait a while, where I trip over the cat, knock a plant off a ledge, and squash it flat as I fall onto it.

After the room had stopped spinning, I picked up the limp, crushed, green thing, and scraped the compost back into the now cracked pot. A few moments of experimenting proved the plant would not accept being propped up on a splint, so I decided the next best option was to hide the evidence in the bin, which I notice now has only one wheel, one having been 'borrowed' by someone. Back in again, I decide to make another cuppa, to pass the time, trying the 'phone again while the kettle boils. The works number is still engaged. O.K. Coffee into the cup, sugar in, when the water boils, slop that in, and swiftly remove the left leg from the proximity, back-heeling the cat, as the water promptly slops out again, and splatters on the floor. Waiting for the coffee to cool, I try the works number again, but it is still engaged. Then I remembered that the stairs light-bulb had failed, and decide to replace that, before someone has an accident, assuming we have a replacement available. I found one in the cubby-hole under the stairs, together with the step-ladders. After clanging them up to the top of the stairs, and spreading the 'legs', I clambered up, gripped the dead bulb, press-twisted it out of the bayonet socket, to allow replacement. I inserted the new one, and was blinded by the light shining into my eyes from three inches distance. Miracles! It works. It's a pity it was a 150 watt bulb, and not a 60, like the one I had just removed, but at least, She won't be able to moan about not being able to see! I folded the steps, and clanged them back downstairs, then shoved them back into the cubbyhole, where I'd found them. The dead bulb joined the dead plant. The coffee was still too hot, the 'phone, still engaged.

When the coffee had cooled, I disposed of it, then had to go and dispose of all the liquid I'd drunk, in the usual manner.

After this, I tried the car again, hoping the charger had put enough 'zap' into the battery to kick the engine into life. I squirmed into the driving seat, threw the cat out, and tried the key. The starter groaned miserably, cranking the engine over a compression or two. One cylinder fired, kicking the bendix out, then it limped unsteadily for a few moments, before expiring. I tried it again, but it doesn't want to play just yet. I climbed out again, and went to check the ammeter on the charger, seeing that it was still pumping five amps in. With nothing to do but wait, I decide the best place to do it is in the armchair in the living room. So in I go again, shutting the door on the draught, and the cat, nearly chopping it in two. I didn't want any more coffee just yet, so turned on the t.v, then grabbed for the remote, so I could reduce the noise level as the speaker blared. I called up the text news, using the key-pad, but there was nothing of interest to read, other than the usual selection of murders, robberies, muggings, nuclear leaks, political leaks, and back-stabbing top Executives and Politicians, who then gave each other enormous pay-rises before going on holiday to St Lucia, or other warm, exotic, locations. I spotted a new report, the Rivers Authority has

19

been caught polluting themselves, giving the lie to their claims it was the Chemicals plant, upstream. Bored with that, I flick to the 'Sit's Vacant' page, to gaze at page after page of 'Nurse wanted', 'Computer programmers desperately needed', 'Secretaries, with shorthand, and three languages, required immediately, for one month, stand-in for maternity leave', etc.

I felt a sudden crushing pain in the right shin, closely followed by multiple punctures in the thighs, as the cat bolts for safety.

"Waah, er, Wossat?" my voice protests.

Thump on the shin, again, then a voice like a circular saw cutting through damp, knotty, wood , "Aren't you going to work today, you lazy sod?"

My voice says "Ah, er," then the eyes take in the message offered by the wall-clock, which indicates that it is 11-15. "Oh, Christ", my voice continues.

"Well, there's no point in rushing, now", the other voice continues, "So where's my breakfast?"

The words read like a request, sort of, but the tone that goes along with them, means- do it now!

Where did the girl I married go? I wonder, as I go to obey, like a good little slave, as she thuds down into the freshly vacated warm chair, confiscates the t.v. remote control, and switches into the first of the many seemingly endless soap-opera series that she watches.

Into the kitchen I go, where I remove the bread from the storage box, a plate from the rack, and the knife, from the drawer, I start slicing the still crunchy bread, and then realize it is still in the plastic bag. So what's a plastic bag between friends? I binned the hacked up bag, put the loaf into a fresh one, then returned it to the bread-box, before peeling the sliced plastic from the sliced bread and binning that in turn. I turned on the gas tap controlling the grille, counted to ten, to allow the stuff to percolate through the pipes, then tried the igniter. My eyebrows disappeared, in a pouf of orange flame.

"Oh, by the way", she calls, "The gas-man called yesterday, and fixed the cooker!"

"Yes, I just found out!" I didn't reply. Her tongue can hurt more than a singed face. I put the bread slices under the grille, until they were golden brown, turned them over, and started the other side. Kettle on, again, cups, spoon, sugar, coffee, milk in hers, stir, Toast from under the grille, gas off. Carefully spread the butter into all the corners, she doesn't like unbuttered corners, then on with the Ginger jam (Yeuk!), hot water into cups, stir, take it through, present it, and stand back, carefully out of arm's reach.

She looks, "Huff, puff!" she sighs, "Not much use, are you?" she sneers, "Ginger jam, indeed, that's for tea! Where's the marmalade?"

"If you recall", I reply, carefully, "You forgot to buy any, last week, and used the last of it yesterday". If looks could kill, I'd be a nuclear devastated area, and I thought it safer to retire, to continue examining the car engine.

Chapter two.

At the Office.

With the developing domestic 'crisis' neatly sidestepped, I examined the car battery, the cells of which were gently fizzing, as the gases escaped, a sure sign that the battery is fully charged, or the cells are duff, decide which for yourself! Guess who had left the key in the ignition? Well - so what, you don't really need keys for a Ford, anyway! Round to the boot, and open it, then, in turn, the toolbox, from which I removed a plug-spanner. Round at the front, again, I unplugged the H.T. leads, then removed the spark-plugs, so that I could check the condition of the electrodes. At the boot again, I give them, and the fingers, a good scrub with a wire brush, then check the gaps with a thumb nail, which is about the right thickness. Fords aren't critical. At the front, again, I insert, and screw home, three plugs. The fourth one I dropped. It fell to the ground in exactly the place it is impossible to reach from either side, or the front. So, off with the hand-brake, and push the car back, until I can reach the plug. Now, of course, the rear-end is so close to the house wall that I can't push the car forward again, and have to pull it, which is not easy, because my feet are in the sump's oil-drip patch. With the brake applied again, I recheck the thumbnail electrode gap, then fit the plug. Next, on go the H.T. Leads before I remove the distributor cap and the rotor arm. With the gearshift in top gear, I release the brake again, and rock the car back and to, until the points are fully open, on the cam, then I can check the gap there, too. Thumbnail again, which is close enough. It's a fiddling job, setting them, because each time you tighten or slacken the locking screw, the gap alters slightly, making the job pretty hit and miss, anyway. From the corner of my eye, I see the Wife watching from the kitchen, through the window, so I give the engine mounting blocks a thorough visual inspection, while discreetly smearing some black muck up my arms from around the sump and oil filler cap. There's nothing to beat looking busy for helping avoid doing any work! After a suitable delay, I rummage around in the toolbox again, remove a handful of assorted items which I dump on the front passenger seat, then walk round, climb into the driver's side, and lean over, so I can rummage under the dash. I unplug various bits of wiring harness, thus enabling me to switch on and off the ignition, and various lights, without anything actually happening. (I used to take the main fuse out, but she's grown wise to that one). After another suitable interval, I put a puzzled expression onto my face, then wander into the house, wiping fresh muck onto my arms from a rag I keep for that purpose.

She's engrossed in an Australian soap-opera now. So I go into the kitchen, fill the kettle, and plug it in, leaving black hand-prints everywhere, then hunt through all the free newspapers and other junk, until I find the car's 'Destroy-It-Yourself' manual, which falls open, through constant reference, at the wiring diagrams page. Armed with the manual, and a freshly charged coffee-cup, and still displaying my baffled expression, I wander back to the car. (On the t.v, someone slams a door, making the flimsy set wall shake and shed one of the obligatory plaster ducks, which the actors pretend to not notice). At the car, I chuck the cat onto the back seat, then plonk myself down again, to study the way the book doesn't even vaguely resemble the actual

25

thing. I re-connect one wire so I can turn on the radio and can hear Cliff Richard droning on about his 'Summer Holiday'. After a minute, I notice an irregular rasping noise, and trace it to the back seat, where the cat is snoring. Now, what was I doing? I drink some coffee, while I think about it, then spy the Wife looming up, so dive back under the dashboard, wielding a screwdriver and a spanner. I have a couple of bolts mounted through convenient holes, holding absolutely nothing in place, but they are handy things for adjusting, in times of crisis, like now!

"When you've finished playing with those dummy bolts," she sneers, "your Boss 'phoned up, to see if you could spare some of your precious time to meet him in his office, at nine a.m. sharp, tomorrow And wear your suit!"

"Yeah, o.k." I replied. "Did you tell him I tried to 'phone, earlier, but couldn't get through?"

"No, I didn't know you had."

"Or that the car had packed up again?"

"Has it?" She asked, "I thought you were just fiddling around, doing nothing, and keeping out of my way!" She leered at me, "So when you have finished tightening up that spare screw, you can plug the wires back together, and take me to the shops, as you seem to be having a day off".

Defeat is a bitter pill to swallow.


Next morning, at almost exactly five to nine, I presented myself, as instructed, in the required suit, to the Boss's secretary's secretary's assistant secretary.

"Ah, yes." The battle-axe sneered, as she glared at me through her tinted spectacles, which were definitely not of the N.H.S. variety, clipped to the tip of her nose. "You are expected, but He's had to pop out to a meeting. He said that you are to wait in there." She pointed a pen at a door. 'In There' proved to be an empty broom cupboard, fitted with a light, and two uncomfortable plastic garden-style chairs which had been designed for looking at, not for sitting on.

I sat for a while, then stood, to massage the blood back into circulation, then stood for a while longer. I tried pacing, one and a half, turn, one and a half, turn, then sat again for a while, thinking that there was no way I could be a sales rep. A professional at waiting, just sitting, being patient, and watching the clock, if there had been one, tracking the passing time. After another while, the blood had given up circulating again, and I was standing, trying to massage the buttocks and thighs into painful life, and relieve the onset of cramp, when the door snapped open, to reveal the battle-axe. As she registered the place I was pummeling myself, her eyebrows disappeared into orbit, and she gave a mighty sniff of disapproval.

"He will see you now." The icy voice snapped, "Through there."

'There' was another office, with knee-deep pile carpet, proper leather chairs, and a huge window overlooking the world outside, just above the roof-line of any passing double-decker buses. After a few seconds, my ears caught a delicate "Ahem!" When I turned in its direction, my eyes saw two deep liquid-green eyes, in a Barbie doll face, topped with a coiffure to match, coloured honey-blonde, with a few dark roots just starting to show, A well-filled white blouse, probably silk, finished off the expensive suit, of top-quality wool. The rest of the heavenly view was blocked by an enormous walnut desk with the pattern of the grain standing out, as only oiled walnut can. My reaction must have been obvious, because a little smile flickered across the cupid lips, painted in pastel pink, then she spoke, but not in the cultured, genteel, accent I anticipated.

"Froo dere, Wacker". A Scouse bandsaw whined, making my ears cringe.

'Froo dere' was through an oak door I hadn't noticed before, a big, solid, wide, oak door that wouldn't look out of place at Blenheim, or Buck House. It had big polished brass hinges, a big, chunky polished brass handle, and a matching polished brass escutcheon plate around the lock. My hand gripped the handle, and turned it. It didn't rattle in tempo with my quaking nerves. Nice and solid, it was. It rotated smoothly drawing the latch back without a grate or a squeak. I pushed. The door didn't move. I pushed harder. The door still didn't move. Barbie-doll giggled at my discomfiture, so I tried pulling the door, instead. It swung massively, and silently, open, the bottom edge chiseling a scar across the toe of my fairly freshly polished right shoe.

"Well, stop dithering, I haven't all day!" A gravelly voice

barked. "Get in here!"

I got in there, squeaking "Good morning, Sir", as perspiration exploded from my pores.

"Never mind the chit-chat", he growled, "You failed to appear yesterday, and didn't bother to telephone. Why?"

"Er", I began, "Er, I, ah, I, er". Why do Bosses strangle my speech processes? All the words are there, all neatly lined up, and ready to use, but one glare from a Boss, and there's a multiple-pileup in the larynx. "Er, I, ah." The perspiration rivuletted down my spine, tickling all the way and making me squirm, while the armpits began to squelch.

"It isn't the first time, either, is it?" he snarled

"I, er, sorry! I, er!"

"Well, if you don't need us, we don't need you, either. Go through there, (another oak door), and sort out the details. Goodbye." He looked down at some papers neatly arranged on the desk that I hadn't noticed, until just, and forgot about me.

"Er, I, er." I spluttered, to no avail. I didn't exist, to him, any more. So, through the door I went, allowing it to latch behind me before I noticed that there was no handle on this side, and into a crummy, dusty old corridor, which was dimly lit, because three of the four fluorescent strip-lights were either switched off, or deceased. The remaining one illuminated a cobwebby 'fire exit' sign, and another door. As I couldn't go back, I could only go onwards, down the corridor, through the door. This door took me into a narrow passage between portable partitions, from behind which came all the usual office noises of keyboards, printers, fax machines, telephones, and the like, an occasional voice commenting on something, and smoking pencils, scratching computers, coffee cups clattering, etc. About two thirds of the way down, there was a window set into a panel in the partition. Above the window was a sign, but because it was flush with the partition, I couldn't read it in the dim light, so I did the obvious and walked towards it. It read 'En-uir-es'. As I stopped by it, the sliding window crashed open, a voice snapped "Wait", and then it crashed shut again.

After about five minutes of inaudible muttering, file flapping, drawer banging, and a typewriter clatter or two, the window slammed open again.

"You Bertwhistle?"

I agreed that that was my surname. A thin, wrinkled arm appeared in the window opening, brandishing a piece of paper.

"Sign that!"

Written on the paper, in faded ink, was a paragraph that said I accepted the form as agreement to full and final settlement.

"Settlement of what?" I asked, baffled.

"Sign it!" The voice snarled.

I signed it, and handed it back. The arm took it, and in exchange, passed an envelope with some papers in it, to me. The window crashed shut. Behind it, the light in the room went off, then a door banged, sounding VERY final.

As there was nothing else to do, I looked at the envelope. It was dirt-cheap, office grade manila, A4 triple-folded, with my name scrawled across the front. One thin wire staple was punched through it, trapping the contents firmly. Inside were two pieces of paper, one was a cheque for last week's wages, the other a duplicate of the form I had just signed. Now what? At the end of the alleyway was a fire-door, clearly marked 'Alarm fitted. Do not open!' I opened it. Nothing happened, no bells, no lights, nothing. The view through it overlooked a panorama of grimy rooftops, chimneys, and television aerials. A ricketty-looking steel fire escape led up, and down. Up led to the top of the block, and down led to the car-park.

"Well, Bugger me!" I thought. "I've been sacked!"


The fire-door was of the kind that can only be opened from the inside, and as I hadn't let it close, unlike the previous door, I made a wedge of the envelope and the letter it contained, then jammed it open, out of spite. As I was doing that it started spitting with rain. There was nothing to be gained by standing there getting wet, so I clanged noisily down the steel treads, making as much noise as I could, and banging on the few windows that were in reach, in a futile attempt to distract the occupants of the rooms within. At the bottom, I went to the old Cortina, unlocked it, and sat inside, out of the wet, while I pondered my next move. With nothing forthcoming, I turned on the radio, which promptly made a nasty fizzing noise, and a funny smell, then expired with a final crackle from the speakers. Ah, well. I tried the engine, which decided to start without any fuss for once, and then drove round to the barrier, where the Gate-man beckoned to me. I had to un-strap again, so I could get out, into the rain, and see what he wanted.

'Gizz yer pass!' The old git, whose sole pleasure was delaying people, demanded. "Yer don't need it no more!"

I had to get back into the car, and remove the sticker from the windscreen, carefully tearing it in two in the process. As I handed the remains to him, a nasty thought occurred – What was I going to tell the wife?

While pondering that monstrous problem, the car took me to the local airport, and parked itself neatly in a bay overlooking the active runway. A little Cessna two-seat trainer was wobbling down 'finals', heading in the general direction of the runway, onto which it arrived with a solid thud! before bouncing back into the air, where it waffled drunkenly, nose high, on the verge of stalling, before sagging tiredly back down again., with another thud, bounce, thud bounce sequence, before the engine blared, and dragged it back into the air, as presumably the Instructor fought to regain control before it converted itself into a pile of smoking scrap at the far end of the strip. I wondered how those poor souls could do that, day after day. I had been a Driving Instructor, once. The job had lasted about a year, but after the third whiplash injury I decided enough was enough, and gave it up for a safer occupation. Another student faltered down, in a series of saw-tooth steps, as though following the contours of a giant corrugated iron sheet that was set on a slope. He, or she, leveled off ten feet too high, dangled there momentarily, then started down again, leveling off fifteen feet lower. The ground shook as the poor tin-foil thing rebounded, engine howling, to stagger off round for another go. Those Cessna's look awfully flimsy, but they must be remarkably resilient to take the battering they suffer without falling to bits as a result. Over by the hangar, a tinny grinding noise, followed by a crackly blare, indicated that someone was starting up another aircraft. The sound was hardly confidence-inspiring, as it sounded like a coffee-grinder chewing on marbles! The engine idled unevenly, sounding like a Volkswagen Beetle running on two pots, coughing and spluttering, for a few moments, until it stopped again. I hoped it was going in for a service, and not coming out, after having received one!

35

One of the Cherokee's wobbled down the approach, and struck the ground with a thud, rebounded, settled again, and stayed down, rumbling and clonking over the bumpy grass, sounding like a wheelbarrow full of bricks, until it slowed then turned off, and headed for the sheds that doubled as a flying school. I imagine that the Instructor had decided that that was enough spinal damage for one day!

With nowhere to go, except home, where I didn't dare go, without a reasonable explanation to offer, I eased the car seat back a few notches, reclined the backrest to a more relaxing angle, and settled down to ponder the problem for an hour or two. Across the fields, a train rumbled past, offering brief glimpses as it passed behind the shrubbery, scrub, and farmland, beyond the far side of the airfield. On the motorway, hidden in a cutting, the two-tone sirens of one of the Emergency services whooped along. The birds chirped and tweeted, the grass grew, the car became rustier, and I drifted off into sleep.

I was jarred from my slumbers by the ear-splitting racket of a mobile disco going BOOM, BOOM, BOOM, SCREECH, BOOM, BLAM, etc. What the hell? I looked around, bewildered. In the next parking bay, a bod in a flash suit, and an equally flash Porsche, was glaring at ME. On the other side of the Cortina, the dolly-bird in the Nissan was also glaring at me. Me? BLAM, BLAM, BOOM, BOOM. Flickering green lights near my left knee drew my attention. BOOM, BOOM, SCREECH! With a start, I realized that my radio had decided to work, and was cranked up to high volume. Hastily, I turned it down, whereupon it promptly quit again with a sharp splat! I carefully and positively turned it off - very firmly off. Mr Porsche gave me a final glare, then went back to filling in what appeared to be an enormous questionnaire, with his gold pen. On the other side, Miss Nissan waggled a finger at me, made a pillow of her two hands, mimicking sleep, then reversed carefully out of the slot, and drove off. In front of me, thirty feet or so distant, a Helicopter that hadn't been there before began starting up, its igniter going tik tik tik tik, then a wheeeEEEE as its turbine engine started. When did THAT arrive, I wondered. I hadn't noticed it. Its navigation and anti-collision strobe lights came on, then the rotors began to turn, making the familiar whoop whoop noise. I could see the pilot flicking switches, and pushing buttons as he tested things, before adjusting the boom microphone on his headset, into which he spoke, talking to the control-tower. The engine noise increased, the whooping giving way to the hard blatting of the blades, until the machine was jigging about on its skids. It lifted a scant inch, slewed round, to face across the field, then leaped into the air, the backwash from the rotors making the Cortina bob and sway on its springs. The helicopter tilted forwards, then slid through the air, disappearing behind the trees on the far side of the field.

I looked at the clock on the dashboard. It read six-thirty. WHAT! I double checked it with my wrist-watch, which agreed, within a couple of minutes. Hastily, I sat up and re-positioned the seat to my normal driving position, before trying the engine. It grunted, groaned, then choked into life on three cylinders, spluttering, and puffing blue exhaust smoke. I still had no idea what to say to Her when I got home. I nursed the car down to the entrance, and the first major decision, turn left, to the motorway, or right, and take the A road, The engine chuffed and popped, as I slowed at the junction, encouraging me to take the A road, where the tow-fees would be cheaper! Luckily the traffic was light, probably because almost everyone else had already gone home, and was sitting with their feet up in front of the goggle-box. After a mile or so of blue-smoke staggering, there was the earsplitting Krack! of a backfire, followed by number four cylinder joining in. Unfortunately, the backfire also split a seam somewhere on the exhaust system, allowing the engine to blatter, unrestricted, into the air. "Well," I decided, as there was nothing I could do about it, "At least - they cannot say they didn't hear me coming down the road!" The copper that pulled me in, ten minutes later, said pretty much the same thing as he presented me with a "Fix it in seven days, or else" ticket, which also required me to present my documents, and myself, at the local Police station, in the same time-span. What really annoyed me was the sneering way the nineteen-year old asked "Is this your car, Sir". As if anyone would bother to steal a Cortina, and the way he put the emphasis on "this", and not "Sir", while posing in front of his shiny new Range Rover. Of course, as he roared throatily away, leaving me to re-start the car, it decided to have only three pots working, again. Which, with the benefit of the split exhaust, I could hear not firing.

We eventually chugged and blared up the home street, and came to a halt by the drive gates, or rather, gate, in the singular. It hung drunkenly from one hinge. The cremated remains of the other gate lay in an untidy heap in the middle of the drive. It had been used in an attempt, during my absence, to roast the crocus, daffodil, and snowdrop bulbs which were planted in the weedy strip between the two lines of concrete flags which the wheels ran on. As I climbed out of the Cortina to open the remaining gate, the fourth cylinder decided to rejoin the party, with a sharp crack! I opened the gate, with difficulty, as it kept trying to fall over, and then allowed it to fall onto the weed-patch which was supposed to be the front garden, when the remaining corroded hinge snapped. I climbed back into the Cortina, maneuvered it into the drive, and switched off the blattering engine, allowing the quiet to return, apart from the steady Psssst! from a fresh puncture that was allowing a tyre to deflate. As I opened the door again so that I could get out, the cat leaped in, appearing from nowhere as they do, and claimed its usual spot on the rear parcel-shelf in the warmth of the evening sunlight. I left the window open, in the forlorn hope that someone would attempt to steal the car, or the radio, thus allowing me to possibly claim on the insurance! With nothing to be gained by further procrastination, I fumbled for the front-door key, and let myself in, waiting for the roof to fall on me, or some similar thing. Nothing did. No blaring soap-opera, no thrown rolling pin, just the droning of a bluebottle, endlessly circling the ceiling light, which was illuminated. I switched it off, releasing the fly, which zoomed off until it splatted into the window, and began trying to head-butt it's way through. I opened the window, letting the fly out, and some fresh air in. Taking my life in my hands, I drew a deep breath, and called, "I'm home, love". Nothing but silence deafened me as I walked through into the kitchen, and fired up the kettle, before nipping upstairs for a minute, while it boiled. She wasn't up there, either, I checked, after I'd flushed. Back downstairs, I made coffee for myself, then turned on the Hi-fi, loaded a cassette into the drive, and started a copy of The Shadows 'Greatest Hits' rolling. It isn't often that I get the opportunity to listen to my kind of music, as if she is in, all she does is moan. Her kind of noise is the modern computer-generated stuff, to which she can stand and twitch, in the current parody of dancing. Her tiny, tinny, trannie cannot compete with my one hundred watts R.M.S. fed into the Wharfdale speakers, but it is noticeable, and annoying, when she turns it up to maximum, making the case rattle and buzz. I had previously tried using headphones, but had to give up, as she incessantly demanded my attention as she nagged on about whatever, and if I carefully didn't hear her, she adopted the knitting-needle-jab technique of attention gaining. I decided not to bother looking for her, just yet, and allowed 'Greatest Hits' to blend into 'Shades of Rock', then Marvin, Welch, and Farrar, with one of my all-time favourite tracks, 'Lady of the Morning'.By then, I was getting hungry, and went to raid the 'fridge, in which I found a few more yoghurt pots. The cheese-dish was cowering in the back corner, but when coaxed out, merely contained the hairy, green, alien life-form that had been there this morning. I scraped it carefully into the bin, just in case the R.S.P.C.A. found out and came looking for me, (I had enough troubles!), What else? The keyless corned beef tins were still there, as were the shredded remains of the lettuce, and the poly-unsaturated axle-grease. In the freezer, I found three loaves. Two 99p special offer chickens, with a sell-by date for January, last year, (I binned them both), lurked next to three sausages in a plastic bag, one egg, (in the freezer?) and two beef-burgers. A barely started tub of mint-flavoured ice-cream, which I recall tasted like toothpaste, next to nine half-pound packs of butter, and the butter-dish, freshly reloaded, why she insisted on freezing butter, I don't know, and finally a letter. I did a double-take, yes, definitely a letter, written in her scrawl, and bearing my name. When I unfolded the sheet, the note it bore read, "I've gone out. Your tea is in the cat." Blue-tacked to it was a corned-beef tin key. This note was typical of her, she could talk for hours, and say nothing, but when it came to writing anything, she would be ultra-brief, almost telegram-ish, and still succeed in saying nothing! It looked as though I would dine alone, again, on a corned beef, tomato sauce and lettuce scrap sandwich. I took the butter-dish out, and left it on the table to thaw out. Was it spite, or awkwardness, which made her put it in there in the first instance, I wondered? I changed my mind, and decided to eat the 'burgers, so went in search of the frying pan. There was no cooking-oil, so I used a slice of frozen butter, instead. The

43

'burgers slowly went black around the edges, while the inner area remained white and frozen. Belatedly, I turned the gas flame down from maximum, and waited impatiently for the things to cook through. When they were apparently done, I turned, to put them onto the waiting plate using a fork, and tripped over the cat, which was waiting for its next meal. The 'burgers, and the pan, skittered across the floor. Cat grabbed one of the burgers, and bolted through the open window, its teeth smouldering.

Chapter three.

Meeting in the Park.


He finally went out. I heard the door bang and his key rattle in the lock. Then followed the daily car-starting ritual, which involved praying to Mecca and the Almighty, plus threatening the use of a large hammer on the more delicate bits, if it didn't perform. He would drag the drive gates open, rather than bend down, and lift the bolt. After that, he would walk around the car, picking off all the dead leaves, spiders, and other overnight detritus, then he would bang the door shut, waggle the gear-shift a few times, and fiddle with the controls, before cranking vigorously on the starter-motor, until the engine caught. Then he would rev. the poor thing like crazy, to "clear the pipes" before crunching into gear, and driving off, assuming I would shut the gates, later.

In the other room, the infant was clattering with the Lego

bricks, creating a fantasy world of tower-blocks, one brick wide, and as many high as they will go without falling over. After breakfast, I dragged the squalling brat to play-school, and deposited it there, out of the way. On the way home, again, I called in at the local shop, and bought a couple of slices of ham, for lunch, and the daily news-rag. I was just reading the juicy bits, about who had been caught doing what, to whom, in whose bedroom, when the 'phone rang. I decided that if it was the 'Heavy-breather' again, I'd set up a meeting, and then beat the sod to a pulp before screaming "rape!" I was wrong, though. It was his works. The Lord God Almighty had designated one of his under-secretary's assistant's flunkeys to call and tell me, in rather better phraseology, "Don't expect any more pay-slips for the lazy git, as they'd given him the boot." While the nonentity was rambling on, the letter-box rattled, signifying the arrival of a fresh batch of junk-mail. I politically-correctly said "Message understood, you smarmy bitch!" then hung the receiver up. The post was all buff window-envelopes, some in red ink, from the Utilities, all politely demanding that they be paid promptly for their services. I added them to the pile on the window-ledge, for

46

later, because I can't spend what I haven't got. Then I went back to the paper until it was time to collect the little brat from school, taking the last few pound coins from the jar with me, although I had no intention of going anywhere to use them. Before I went out, I left a note for the lazy sod, where I knew he'd find it - in the food store. Then I went for the little sod, who eventually appeared, covered in paint as a spin-off from the morning's lesson. For a change of scenery, I took him down to the park to feed the ducks, and let him run around, screaming and yelling, until he was tired out, in the hope that he would play quietly at home, for a while. The park bores me stupid, but the brat seems to enjoy it. By the duck-pond, I saw the Gent I'd christened 'His Lordship', as he was always smartly dressed in a neat three-piece, with shiny shoes, and a brolly. He was walking with, presumably, his child, a nice, quiet, clean specimen, which knew how to behave in public. Today, 'His Lordship' was wearing an expensive, casual, mohair cardigan over his shirt and precisely aligned tie. His hands were neatly manicured, with no snaggly nails, or half-moons of grime. A gold watch glinted from under the shirt cuff, and a chunky gold ring encircled his small finger.

He didn't have a beer-belly hanging over his trouser belt, or eyebrows that met in the middle. I'd never seen him with the slightest hint of a 'four-o-clock shadow' on his chin. It seemed that every time I came around here, he was here, too. We had never spoken, beyond "Nice day" or "Hello again." His disinterested gaze passed over me, as he watched the pedestrian flow around the pond, then he recognized me, and raised a hand in acknowledgement, just as my little sod tripped over his own feet, and fell, full length, into a puddle of mud and duck-muck. The sudden splosh, followed by the howls of rage and fright, drew everyone's attention. Some were sympathetic, some simply avoided getting involved. I heaved the brat upright by the only clean bit I could find, the collar, and surveyed the damage. From the chin to the knees he was covered in a disgusting, greeny-brown sludge, mixed with a trickle of scarlet that came from a bleeding nose. As I watched, the gloop started dripping from the lower edge hems. The brat's face was a purple circle surrounding the open mouth, from which issued the dreadful wailing noise that assaulted everyone's ears.

"Excuse me", a cultured voice, "You seem to have a

problem, there, do you have far to go to get home?"

I dragged my eyes from the screaming brat, and saw –
Him!

"I, er, about five miles, if they will let us on to the bus like
this." I replied.

"Ah, yes. That could possibly cause difficulties." He said,
as he moved upwind of the bellowing, aromatic blob. "Might I
suggest that you avail yourself of the the facilities at my
residence, a short distance across the park, I believe we have
something, there, which will fit your child, and a plentiful supply
of hot water, with which to repair the damage."

I hadn't realised that people really DO speak like that, and
hesitated, uncertainly.

He must have noted my hesitation, because he spoke again,
"I do hope that I am not being too presumptuous, as we have not
been introduced, and there is no chaperone present, but I believe
that this situation could be classified as a minor emergency, thus
allowing etiquette to be temporarily suspended."

I gave in, gracefully. "Thank you, Sir. I think that would be
for the best. I don't really fancy a five mile hike, dragging that!"

I indicated the brat.

"Shall we?" He collected his infant, with the simple crook of a finger.

As his child came around the pond, and got into range of the malodorous mess, he said, in a broad Cockney accent, "Cor, Blahmee, Pooh, Whattapong!"

'His Lordship' winced, as the harsh accent fell upon his cultured ears, then led the way.


By the time we had completed the journey, the brat's bellowing had subsided to a sustained snivelling whine, which was rather less wearing on the ears, but more stressing on the nerves. 'His Lordship' unlocked the door with a peculiar key which was unusually thick, and without the usual key-shaped bits on the other end to the handle. He didn't turn it, though, after inserting it into the aperture in the escutcheon plate, instead, he pressed the doorbell. Some electronic gadget inside bleeped, before there was a sharp clunk from behind the door. He then turned the handle, and withdrew the key, before pressing on the door, to open it.

"As you no doubt noticed," he commented, wryly, "The locks are a bit special. It is my belief that no lock can prevent unauthorized access, as any device that can be created can be by-passed or over-ridden, but a good gadget increases the delay, and hopefully they will conclude that the putative gain is not worth the effort, and the increased risk of discovery."

I agreed with him, while noting that the key, bell, handle, sequence also cancelled the alarm system, part of which gazed glassily at us from a corner of the door-jamb.

"Right-ho, then." He exclaimed, "In we go, then. You will find the bathroom is in there, second door on the left, where you should find everything you need to sort out your child. In the meantime, I will roust out my house-keeper, and send him to find a change of clothing for your child."


I led the brat through the indicated door, and found that we were in a room larger than the whole of the ground floor of my house. The bathroom was tiled, all around, in white porcelain, with strategically placed mirrors. The floor was that non-slip rubberized stuff, like in a swimming pool changing-room. In separate rooms off, were a bath, and a w.c, a pedestal bowl, and a bidet, with all the relevant fittings and cabinets. The end wall had a double-glazed, frosted glass window, with a vertical blind, below it was a towel rail, heated. Another warm cabinet was filled with towels, flannels, sponges, back-scrubbers, and the like, while it's matching partner bore all the bottles and bars that belong in a bathroom, plus a couple of one-time, disposable razors, hygenically sealed in polythene sleeves. The third cabinet, mirror-fronted, held all the first-aid bits, aspirins, paracetamol, codeine, band-aid's, tweezers, scissors, and the rest. Everything appeared to be new, and still sealed. When I had finished drooling, I went to the bath, placed the gold-plated plug in, turned on the gold-plated taps, then stripped the still sniveling brat. For lack of anywhere suitable, I dumped the muddy clothes into the shower-stall, for now, and then checked the water temperature, before dunking him in, with a block of soap, before attending to my own needs. One thing he will do, of his own volition, is play in the bath. After a quick sluice down, I hauled him out again, wrapped him in a towel, then tried to chase the muck down the plug-hole, then re-filled the bath, unwrapped him again, and parked him back in the clean water, while I sought further guidance.

As I exited the bathroom, a late teenager was walking up the passageway, from the far end, bearing an armful of children's clothing

"Excuse me, Madam," he said, "The Master hopes that these will fit your child, and would you kindly place the soiled items in this bag, then I will have them cleaned for you before you leave. When you are ready, there are some sandwiches and coffee for you in the guest room." He indicated a door opposite where I was standing.

"Thank you." I replied, "And would you thank him for me, but I would rather take them home, and wash them there, if I may. I will return the borrowed items tomorrow."

"As Madam wishes." He replied, "Now would you excuse me, I have my regular duties to attend."

"Certainly, and thank you, but before you go, what should I do with the used towels?"

"If Madam will leave them on the side of the bath, I will deal with them later." He handed me the items, turned, and left.

53

I put the clothes just inside the bathroom, where the brat was playing submarines, using a sponge and a toothbrush, before I went to sample the coffee. And what coffee it was. I don't know the brand, but it wasn't Red Mountain, nor was it from the Chateau of Maxwell. It was real coffee, made from top-quality roasted beans, freshly ground, and percolated gently to extract the flavour, without the bitter edge of the cheaper varieties. Next to the percolator was a kettle of steaming water, with which to adjust the coffee strength to that preferred, and a bowl of demarara sugar, with a little jug of real cream. With them were two translucent bone-china cups and saucers, and silver spoons. On a plate with a glass dome over it were some sandwiches. Not the usual dainty triangles, de-crusted, with a hint of grease, and flavouring, but thick whole-meal, with a dish of butter curls, one of salmon, and one of salady bits, plus the implements necessary to apply them, ready for self-assembly. Pleasure and hunger overcame politeness, and I dug in.

I was watching the woman, and her child, playing, as usual, by the duck-pond, wondering, as I often had, whether she was approachable, as I had never seen her with a male companion. Unfortunately, an opportunity had never arisen, and she had never hinted that an approach would be welcomed, so I had kept my distance, as Society required, until the mis-hap, today. The outcome of which was that I invited them into the guest suite to repair the damage, while I attended to some moderately urgent business in my office. Having fired off a few faxes, and juggled the accounts into something approximating the right shape, I toyed with the design I was engaged in devising on my computer, for a while, without reaching a satisfactory stress-bearing arrangement that would fit within the confines of the available space. Aircraft design is so restrictively legislated, nowadays, and rightly so. When I first started, all that was needed was a shed, a hammer and nails, a few planks, a bolt of canvas, an engine, and some poor soul stupid enough to try to get the thing off the ground. If the wings bent when you pulled a tight turn, you didn't turn so tightly, and everyone was happy, more or less. Now, though, the law rightly demanded that the structure would be sufficiently strong to withstand fourteen times the force of gravity, and have sufficient torsional stiffness to resist four times over-speed. Efficiency dictated that it be done in half the depth, while having a large aperture in the bottom skin to allow undercart retraction, plus the strength to absorb the stresses of indifferent piloting skills causing a firm 'arrival' contact with the ground. And all this was for an aircraft that would spend ninety percent of it's life parked at an airfield, unmoving, and eighty percent of it's flying life travelling in straight lines on calm, sunny days, pulling at most, three Gee's, in a standard rate turn, Yet, if the 'Pilot' should flare the landing attempt six feet high, or three feet low, and succeed in bending something, it was the Designer that got the earache about the weak, shoddy, structure. It is akin to the car driver who strikes the gatepost every time they park the car, and then blames the house-builder for putting the post there! Anyway, after doodling for a while, I sent Harry, my house-man, to check on the guests. He reported back as I was clearing the screen, and advised me that the children were playing with the Lego, while the Lady was inhaling the sandwiches. I thanked him, as I loaded another programme, this time it was a novelty item I was working on. I had tentatively entitled it the 'Beginner's Golf-ball', Inside the standard dimension is a small generator, a piezo sounder, and a coiled spring-loaded rod. The idea is that when the ball is struck, its revolving motion in flight, or on the ground, spins the generator. A motion detector decides when the ball has stopped, then switches on the piezo beeper, and releases the spring rod, which extends, bearing on it's free end, a flag marked 'I'm here!', the end result being a ball that can be found in the long grass off the fairway, a location where most novices' balls disappear forever. I know it is a silly idea, but…. After fiddling inconclusively with that, for half an hour, I filed the changes to the data, then shut the P.C. down and went to entertain my guest, only to find her where Harry had left her, having misinterpreted my earlier instruction. That is one of the difficulties of employing staff whose first language is not English.

"Ah, you have finished with your computer, then," she said, "I heard you typing, and know enough to keep out of the way while the keyboard is live, and there might have been something on the screen that you would rather I didn't see."

"Not really, I was merely playing around with a design I have been trying to resolve, would you care to see?"

"If it is nothing secret!"

I took her into the office, and re-started the p.c., then called up the golf-ball. "That's all I was doing."

"It looks like a motorized football!" She exclaimed.

"Remarkably close!" I explained the theory, and indicated the relevant parts of the drawing,

"It is a clever idea," she agreed, "but why so complex, I can see a way to simplify it, and enhance it, at the same time!"

"Really? I've been stuck for weeks, going up blind alleys!" I said, while I thought "Ha, no way, Lady!"

She studies the screen for a minute, "First of all, put the generator plum-bob into a gimbal, then no matter which way the ball revolves, there will be an output from it, which makes the motion-detector redundant. A simple one-shot flip-flop can detect zero volts after volts, and trigger the release of the rod. Now, as it stands, the ball cannot detect which way up it is, and could therefore attempt to extend its flag downwards. So, make it into a, ah, the name escapes me, -- a clap-trap? No, a caltrop, five rods, arranged so that one is always somewhere near vertical, no matter which way up the ball is. The only problem, now, is getting the thing out of the thicket of brambles it has landed in, so that the rods can be re-set!"

"Ah, yes. I nearly did it that way, in the beginning. I had a series of radials around the shell, as a brace, but I missed the gimbal idea. I was fiddling around with a gyroscope, to keep the ball upright, but scrapped that, as too fragile, and energy-consuming. That was when I realized that the ball spun while in flight, and I converted the gyro into a generator. Just allow me a moment, while I make a note on the file." I tapped a couple of keys, used the 'mouse' to 'click' on the required 'button', then typed in the note, keyed 'enter', and cleared back to the golf-ball.

"One day," she commented, "Someone will develop a computer that accepts plain English, and save all the bother of having to learn COBAL, or whatever."

"Yes, but it's not so easy. There are so many words with the same spelling, but with different meanings, depending on usage, and so many words that mean almost the same thing, then dialectic spelling variations, plus mis-hits. The de-bugging routine would occupy more memory space than there is currently available in a moderately-sized machine. Then, if you were French, German, or whatever... each machine would need a multiplicity of pre-installed programmes, so that it would load the appropriate language for the user, so we are stuck with the mess we have now, but at least it means the same in any language! I heard that someone in America taught one to recognize certain spoken words, and then perform pre-set tasks. The problem was, it only understood a Mid-Western American, if a New Yorker, or a Texan tried it, it threw up its little electronic hands, and sulked. The inventor used it as an electronic door-lock, until one day, when he had a heavy cold, it failed to recognize him, and wouldn't let him in!"

"I heard that a British company was trying an idea where all the prompts appear on the screen, and all you have to do is scroll along or down until the cursor is on the one you want, then one key-stroke does the action, but it is painfully slow."

We were still talking, batting ideas about, and knocking down each other's theories, when there was a knock on the door, and Harry came in. "Excuse me, Sir, Madam," he said, "but it is two-thirty in the morning! Will you be requiring my services any more tonight?"

"It's WHAT! My God! Sorry, Harry, I hadn't noticed! Where are the children?"

"I put them down, five hours ago, Sir, They are sound asleep." He looked at me, "I hope that is acceptable, Madam?"

It was a bit late to say "No", but to say "yes" implied that I had intended to stay, and I hadn't, or had I. No, I couldn't. I shouldn't. While I was struggling with the dilemma, my Host acknowledged Harry's action

"That is fine, Harry, is the other room ready?" Then, to me, "We cannot disturb your infant now, it wouldn't be fair to him, and I cannot expect you to leave him here, alone, to make your way home, at this hour. That would be most impolite!"

"Yes Sir, Madam, I have it prepared, with a suitable overnight pack."

I finally got my voice working again, "Thank you, but ah, Yes, I suppose it wouldn't be proper, and I don't wish to impose on you. That was not my intention." As I said it, I wished I'd phrased it differently, because it sounded exactly like it was, to me.

"I assure you there is no problem. I have more rooms than I can ever utilize, nowadays. I hadn't noticed how the time was passing. Harry, you should have reminded me, ages ago!"

"Sir, I apologise, but tonight was the first time I have seen you looking happy since Annabelle left you, and I didn't wish to spoil the mood without good reason."

"As usual, Harry, you are correct. Tonight has zipped past. I lost all track of time, and that isn't like me. Ah, well, it is late, as you say. Would you kindly prepare a night-cap tray for us, then you may retire, yourself, thank-you."

"Certainly, Sir, I presume your usual drink. What would Madam care for?"

"Horlicks, or Hot Chocolate, if I may, please, Harry."

"We have both, Madam."

"In that case, Horlicks, please."

"Certainly. Approximately five minutes, Sir, Madam. In here?"

"If you would, Harry." He said. When Harry had left, he asked if there was anyone I would like to telephone, to say I was safe.

"No thank you, everyone who needs to know, already does!"

"What about your husband, won't he worry?"

"No, he won't even notice, we're separated." It was stretching the truth a little, but so what. It was nearly true. It might wake the dozy swine up. Anyway, he'd be asleep in the chair, as usual, if my guess was correct, with his damn stereo busy amplifying nothing, because the tape had run out.

"Ah, sorry!"

"There's no need to be. We started out with lust, and passion, but as that faded, nothing replaced it, and we sort of drifted apart, because there was nothing in common left to bind us."

A gentle knock on the door warned us, then Harry came in with a tray. "Will there be anything else, Sir, Madam?"

"Thank you, Harry, no, good-night."

"Good-night, Sir, Madam." Harry left, closing the door behind him.

"Ah, I forgot to ask, do you need to be anywhere, later?"

"No, I had intended to do a bit of shopping, but nothing special, with no set time."

We continued chatting, while the drinks cooled, and we ate the biscuits, then it was that time. - Would he try? Should I leave an opening? What was the protocol in these circumstances?

He showed me to my bedroom door, indicating the en-suite facilities, I thanked him. He said I was welcome. I started to say- … He said-…. I looked at him, he looked at me. I said "Goodnight". He said "Goodnight" back. Our eyes met. I said- …. He said-… I asked how long since she had been gone.

"Two years, now."

What to do? I realized we were holding hands. I pulled him gently into the room, or was he pushing me? Who cares? We kissed. He pushed the door to, with his foot. We are inside. You lot, reading, are on the outside. That's all you get to see, the door. Night- night.

Chapter four.

Going Away.

I woke at the god-awful time of yawn-o-clock, sitting in my chair with a hell of a stiff neck, with a full cat and a full bladder to contend with. The cat did not want to get off my lap, so I had to persuade it by the expedient of standing up and tipping it onto the floor. The hi-fi was hissing to itself as the tape had finished ages ago, so I turned it off as I passed. The cat leaped into the warm chair I had just vacated, gave me a baleful stare, had a slow stretch, curled up by walking round in ever-decreasing circles until it caught itself up, then went back to sleep. After a visit to the bathroom, I re-loaded my cup then tried the television, but the programme was rubbish - some Socialite explaining to the world how important he was. B.B.C.2 was showing pages from Teletext news, and channel 4 was a blank screen. I turned it off again, and turned the stereo back on, selected the tuner, and fiddled with the volume knob until radio 2 was just audible. Unfortunately, the item being broadcast was just some M.P. expounding on how big his ego was. It was too late to go to bed, and too early to go to work, had I any work to go to. I decided to go to the car exhaust centre, instead, and then I could drive around quietly to the cop-shop, and prove I'd had it done. I reminded myself to blow the tyre up, too. Then I brewed up again, and made one for her, as it was about time to disturb her, anyway. If I could sneak in without waking her, I would leave it to go cold on the side table, next to her clock.

When the coffee was ready I took hers up, and found the bed empty, unused. Puzzled, I went into the kid's room, but he was missing too. She must have decided to go to her Mother's for a day or so, which gave me a bit of space to sort out some new employment. Then a sneaky thought crept into my mind. As she wasn't around to complain, I could go away for a break, myself. So I dug out the spare battery, and put it on charge while I got everything organized. The meter wasn't showing too high a charge current, so the battery was pretty full. That was one less problem to consider. At the exhaust centre, they fitted a new tin-can system in eleven minutes, charged me a fortnight's income, and advised me I had a badly worn tyre, and would I like them to replace it while I was there. I thought it a good idea, but my wallet had other ideas! I had to decline the offer. I drove down to the police station, letting them smell the new paint burning off the exhaust, showed them my papers, and got signed off the register, then went home again. The one problem with having a new, quiet, exhaust fitted is it allows you to hear all the creaks, groans, and other incidental noises that have faded into the background, and then you start worrying about them. As I turned onto the drive, the brakes decided to start squealing, and I came to a halt in a long-drawn-out screech. I left the Cortina sitting there, smouldering quietly in a cloud of paint-fumes, and went into the house. The old coot next door made some comment about barbequeing it, as he lovingly polished his Fiesta, again. It was a daily ritual, and a total waste of effort. I don't think he's driven the thing more than twenty miles in the three years he's owned it. The last time I can recall it moving was one day when it was raining, so he drove to the Post Office to collect his pension, then spent another fortnight complaining

67

that his plugs had oiled up. It was hardly surprising, as the whole journey, including queueing time in the office, took five minutes. What it needs, I told him, is a good blast up the M6 to Carlisle and back, at a speed not less than seventy miles per hour, it would do them both good. He looked at me as though I was something a dog had left on his garden.

Inside, I started packing, ducking in and out as required, to stuff things into the car. Cheque book, plastic card, etc, then my diving kit, the wet-suit, fins, mask, A.B.L.J. weight-belt, demand valve, cylinder for compressed air, which needed filling, torch, and box of spare parts. Then the tent, a hammer for knocking the pegs in, sleeping bag, camping stove, tin kettle, a couple of plates, and a couple of pans, cutlery, kitchen sink, etc, all the essentials of 'roughing it' under canvas. Not forgetting the most important item, a tin-opener. I usually take two, to make sure I've got one, if you follow that! Before I left, I wrote her a note, saying I was away on business, and would be back in a few days.

Of course, the bloody car wouldn't start, it merely sat

there, with the starter-motor sucking the battery dry. So I gave it a kick, connected up the charger, and clumped it again with my boot, for good measure. It sizzled gently at me, still smelling of hot paint, for a few minutes, and then I gave it another go. It fired up on the first compression, belched a cloud of smuts which drifted over the gleaming Fiesta, then sat there, idling perkily at me as I put the charger away again. I then fitted the second battery into the clamp I'd mounted, on the opposite side of the engine bay to the regular item, and connected the leads up to it. It's an idea of my own that allows me to have lights and volts, if I want them, in the tent, without draining the main battery. Or, alternatively, I can use it to jump-start the car, when it acts stubborn, out in the field. I have a switch on the dash, which allows me to charge the second battery, while I am travelling, or isolate it, when I am parked up.

Carefully, peering around the heap of stuff on the back seat, which was over-spill from the boot, I reversed out, onto the road, where I left the car idling, not risking switching off again. I put food out for the cat, and then locked up, leaving the cat-flap open, so it could come and go as it saw fit. With everything I could think of, done, I set off for Trearddur Bay on Holy Island, just off the Isle of Anglesey, my presently favoured diving spot.

Of course, I got stuck in traffic going through Conwy, but then everybody does. There is talk of building a by-pass, but so far, only talk. Eventually, I reached the traffic-light controlled road junction at the town of Valley. I turned left, bouncing and jolting over the not-very-level level crossing, then bobbed, weaved, and big-dippered down the coast road, over Four Mile Bridge, and on, into Trearddur, where the sandy beach is on the left of the road. Just past the beach, and the hamlet, I turned left again, and trundled carefully along the narrow, twisting road which eventually winds round to South Stack lighthouse, and a few cross-roads, which all lead, indirectly, to Holyhead. By the small beach called Porth Dafarch, which used to be the port of Holyhead, I turned right, onto the road across the end of the island, logically named Porth Dafarch road, and along, for another half-mile, to the Valley of the Rocks campsite. The site is hidden behind a jumble of rocks, hence the name. It is accessed through a narrow gap, on a tarmac surface. Inside, the road forks, left for the tourers and tents, right for the static vans, toilet block, and parking area. I turned left, drove a few yards, and stopped at the 'club-house' to pay my site-fee, for a few days' stay. That done, I walked round to test the plumbing, before going to look for a flat patch big enough for my tent. That's usually the tricky part, unless you come down very early in the week, because all the good patches have already been claimed. This time I was lucky, there were only a few pitches occupied, and I found one, on a slight rise, which is always handy as, if it rains, the water runs away from, and not into, your tent! I had a spot overlooking the clubhouse roof, with a high rocky escarpment behind, which would break any wind from that direction. With long practice, I had the tent erected and lighting installed, in twenty minutes, and then sat back on a folding chair, to watch the kettle get hot, and study my new, temporary, neighbours. I listened to the silence, and breathed the clean air. Somewhere in the surrounding scrub, a pheasant honked its brassy call, and one of the other tents had a radio playing quietly. The intermittent, low moo of the fog-horn was sounding from the Holyhead breakwater, a sure sign of no wind, and a barometric high, creating a horizon-defeating haze. Grasshoppers chirped, birds chirruped, leaves on the trees rustled in the occasional zephyr, and silence, glorious silence. No endless rumble of traffic on a motorway, no blaring engines, no equally blaring ghetto-blasters, or arguing kids, nothing. Just an occasional crack or tick from the Cortina, as the engine cooled. As I savoured my coffee, which always tastes different, al-fresco, I wondered what to have for the late lunch/early supper, from my limited resources of corned-beef, beans, and bread.

After the meal, I checked that I'd not removed the air cylinder, which needed filling, from the car, then drove round to the local compressor station, located in a building at Soldier's Point. You go through Holyhead town, along the seafront, and off to the extreme left side of the harbour, almost up to the old, disused, slate quarry. There, a hotel has been converted into a Diving school, which also has a small shop selling spare parts, magazines, and fills of air. A fill works out at one pound, so once the admittedly expensive equipment is bought, diving is a pretty cheap hobby, really. I mean, where else can you get an hours combined exercise and entertainment, for one pound?

Back at the tent again, I began the challenge of getting into the wet-suit. Finally ready, I drove a mile or so up the road, to a little cove with a sandy beach with a little rivulet of fresh water from a spring crossing it. It had a nice cliff on each side, protecting it from any wind, while providing a good variety of marine habitat and wild-life. It was a short walk from the road, where there just happens to be a nice, one car wide, and three or four long, parking space worn into the grassy verge. The sandy beach makes access and exit from the water easy, while the grassy area in front, or behind, depending on the point of view, means there is plenty of room for wrestling with all the recalcitrent straps and belts which form part of the diving equipment. With the battle of the straps won, I waddled heavily down the beach, picking my way between the scattered, slippery rocks in the rivulet, to the deeper water, where I could sit, waist deep, on the bottom, to fit my fins, then my mask, and finally, my demand valve, so that I could breathe underwater. The water

73

was icy cold, feeling rather like the water drained from a part defrosted freezer. The wet-suit did its job, though, and the thin layer of water trapped between my flesh, and it, rapidly warmed up once I lay face-down in the sea, gasping as an icy rivulet squirted down my spine. After a quick look round, to confirm my direction, I snaked over and round the rocks, in the shallow water, heading out to the deeper area, where I picked up a handy rock to help fine-tune my bouyancy, then drifted down, following the contours of the bottom, and looking around, to see what, if anything, had altered since my last visit, nearly a year ago. About two hundred yards out, in around thirty feet of water, a large, house-sized boulder, which always has some large fish prowling around, as well as the more sedentary creatures that grow on it, is always worth a visit, as a first, loosening-up dive, or for a novice's first 'deep' open water trip. I know that in a crevice, on the off-shore side of the rock, in a scrambled heap of boulders, a large lobster used to live. I had been trying to coax it out and therefore into my cooking-pot, for the previous ten years, with no success, and decided to see if it was still there. A large, purple-coloured Velvet Swimming Crab glared at me, daring me to come within nipping range of its powerful claws. Long and painful experience had taught me that they are belligerent thugs that don't hesitate to grab hold of anything within reach, and they are extremely difficult to detatch, once latched on. A large, yellowish coloured Breadcrumb Sponge, so named because of it's appearance, like a glob of dough stuck to the rock surface, seemed to have grown somewhat, since my last visit, but it is hard to tell without accurately measuring it, because they are such irregular, shapeless creatures. But if memory serves, it had expanded upwards, and is now crowding up against the underside of the overhang, which supports a colony of Dead Man's Fingers, soft corals so called because they take on a tubular form, and when open, are covered in fine hairs, thus looking exactly like mouldy hands, with the fingers outspread.

A flicker of movement, near the bottom, draws my attention, but I cannot see what caused it, at first, so with a gentle flick of my fins I drift down, nearer to the rock-pile. A shaft of sunlight, spearing down through the water, picked up the unnaturally straight line of a long purple antenna, feeling for unexpected water movements. It is my old adversary, now missing one antenna, where some passing creature had taken a brief hold, still lurking in its lair. Hovering, upside down above its crevice, I wait, hoping it will venture out into the clear space, and come within reach of my eager hand, without my hand coming within reach of the Velvet Crab. A young Rainbow Wrasse zipped up, to study this weird fish that is intruding on its domain, and probably hoping that I will disturb some tasty morsel it can snap up. At the last instant, it realized that I am considerably larger than it, and it decides that I might just snap IT up, as a tasty morsel, and disappeared into the distance with an audible 'flick' from it's powerful tail-fin. That 'flick', of course, has told everything else in the area that there is trouble around, rather like the Magpie, up on its tree branch perch, shouting "Kaaat! Kaaat!" when a feline emerges from it's hiding place. Some things don't need translating, the signal transcending any language barrier. A gentle stir of my fins propels me down the rock, to the seabed, which, here, is a mixture of rubble, rocks, and sand. The larger boulders are pretty well permanent, as the major block stops most of the current, but the smaller stuff is always being re-arranged by each passing storm. Even at this depth, the surge from each roller batters everything against everything else, grinding the big rocks down to small rocks, and the small rocks down to pebbles, which eventually become sand, in a never-ending cycle. Because of this, there is always a clear area around the scree-slope, as it is abraded clean at intervals, the churning and grinding preventing any plant, or sedentary growth, from establishing. This is a world-wide phenomenon, which is why long-buried wrecks suddenly appear, overnight, or conversely, disappear. Around Anglesey, there aren't many treasure-wrecks, although there is the well-publicized 'Royal Charter' lying off Moelfre, on the north side of the island, an easy swim from shore, in around fourty feet of water. The difficulty lies in getting down the hundred-foot cliffs to it! The Charter was a steam/sail ship, homeward bound from Australia with it's cargo of gold, and miners, that didn't quite make it to Holyhead, in a storm. The story is that the old village of Moelfre was built on the proceeds of the wreck. The village has grown, now, of course.

Even now, every once in a while, a trinket is uncovered,

keeping the enthusiasts searching for the proverbial pot of gold that the ship might still contain.

A waving antenna caught my attention, so I eased over, to see what was on the other end of it. Peering from a crack was a large Edible Crab, that's the one you see in Fishmonger's shops. The orangey-brown colour was unmistakeable. I reached a tentative hand in, to try to tickle it out, but this crab wasn't playing, it merely used its powerful legs to jam itself immoveably into its crevice, its carapace wedged against the top edge of the rock. That is something a diver has to remember, NEVER reach over the top of something, in a crevice. You can get very thoroughly trapped by an irritated crab, which can stay there for as long as it sees fit, while the diver's time is finite, limited by the amount of air remaining in his cylinder, or, if a schnorkeller, by the length of time he can hold his breath. The more the diver struggles to get free, the harder the crab will jam! Or, of course, it could be a Conger Eel in the crevice, and they bite! A yard away, a baby lobster, looking like a big shrimp, edged along the bottom of a boulder, intent on a morsel it had spotted. I waited until it was mid-way between possible dens, then reached out and tickled its antenna. The lobster performed a visual representation of "AAAARGH!" then bolted for cover, in a cloud of churned-up sand.

Chuckling, I made a quick check on the gauges of my console, on it's length of hose, The depth gauge showed fourty-nine feet, the watch indicated thirty-eight minutes elapsed, and the contents gauge showed that I had just over sixty atmospheres of pressure left. As I had started with three thousand, it was time to go. From this trivial depth, and time period, there was no need for decompression, just a slow ascent, back into the world of the land-creatures.

I returned home, next day, with a hollow feeling of loss, and a happy soreness, below, a legacy of the previous night's activity. As soon as I unlocked the door, I knew he was out. A couple more of those brown envelopes with the acetate windows, peered at me from the floor-mat, just inside the door. The cat hurtled downstairs, and out, barely missing the gate-post, as it departed to patrol its territory, and before I could discover the little pile of excrement it had left, half-buried in the shredded newspaper, in the corner. That was typical of him, too lazy to clean up behind his own menagerie. I picked up the letters, sent by Bill, before they also got deposits on them, and tossed them onto the table, to deal with, later. That is when I saw his note. Good riddance, I thought, a couple of days without him around would do nicely, while I was feeling happy/sad/guilty/pleased.

The telephone started ringing, and when I answered it, it was James, calling to check that I had got home safely. As soon as he spoke, that tingly feeling began again. I told him that the ex-hubby had gone off to Anglesey for a few days, I knew what his idea of a business trip was, so the biggest hurdle was a non-event!

"Anglesey?" he queried."There's nothing there but a few sheep!"

"I know. He's gone scuba-diving, under the pretext of a business trip. He seems to think I don't know! It's pretty obvious, though, when he takes a tent, and his silly rubber suit!"

"Hmm! I thought rubber suits had another inference!"

"When he goes down there, he's usually gone for a week, so there is nothing to prevent our next date, providing nothing crops up."

"Are you positive that is what you want to do? What about him?"

"Oh, YES! It's a long time since I felt so good....so HAPPY....Alive again! He doesn't matter, I merely share the house with him, nowadays, nothing else."

"Right, then. I have to be going, now, to that boring meeting, in Grey Worsted, not rubber!"

"Bye for now, then."

The 'phone went dead. "I think I'm falling in love with you!" I said to the disconnected line.

As I started for the surface, a sparkle from the bottom, caught my eye, so I paused, looking for it to happen again. The slight surge wafted me to, and fro, as I drifted, then there it was, again, I aimed back down, conscious of my limited remaining time. There! A fin-flip took me to the crevice, and I peered in, looking for the object that had reflected the sunlight. A quick check on the contents gauge showed that I was down to fortyfive, There was the glint, again, from the sand floor between the rocks, I reached in an exploring hand, with visions of Percy, the giant Moray in the film 'The Deep' flashing through my mind. There was something thin, small, and hard between my fingers, and I gripped it, and then withdrew the hand. Free of the crevice, I looked at what I'd found, Gripped, in the sand in my glove, was a shiny ring-pull, from someone's drinks can! Everywhere Man goes, his rubbish does, too. The gauge was telling me I had thirty atmospheres left, definitely time I wasn't here! If I didn't go up, NOW, I would have to try breathing water. Some things you can delay, others, you cannot!

·

Chapter five.

Joan.


The two days passed with maddening slowness, while I went about the normal domestic routine of taking the brat to school, doing the laundry, vacuuming, bringing the brat home, feeding it, entertaining it, feeding it again, then bathing it, before putting it to bed, so I could have a little time to myself. I arranged with a neighbour, one of Vince's and my friends, Joan, to be babysitter, for my night out, and finally the taxi arrived to whisk me off to our clandestine meeting. We window-shopped for a while, along the high street, and then went to watch the latest Lloyd-Weber at the theatre, then a meal at the restaurant, where I got giggly on champagne, and we talked. About him, and about me, and James's deceased wife, and my husband, my wants for the future, and whether I thought I might achieve them, and his. Gradually, un-noticed, it stopped being James and me, and became us and we. Vince was left behind, forgotten, unwanted, and rejected, even. Then I noticed that my hand was captive, in his, over the table, while our feet were intertwined, beneath it. He was saying something about the texture of the sweet, when he, too, noticed, and broke off in mid-sentence. We sat, silent, looking at each other.

"You, too?" he queried.

"Yes."

"Then leave him." He came straight out with it, up-front, and bold. "Now, today, while he is away. Pack your bags, and go!"

"But-."

"You have said, yourself, that you bore each other to the edge of fighting .So dump him. Our children get on well together, as do we."

"But –"

"I need you, and I believe that you need me. I know I want you, and suspect that I am falling in love with you, as I think you are me."

"But -."

He smiled, "You are starting to sound like a motor-lawnmower that won't start, going but, but, but." He withdrew his hand, "Perhaps I am too forward, moving too fast for you. I have no wish to pressure you, and maybe scare you off, so let us leave it, for now, but, please think about it, and let me know, when you are ready." He raised an arm, and beckoned for the waiter. "Now, about that bit in the Finale, when the door fell off its hinges and onto the chorus... Ah, Waiter, the bill, please, and two more coffee's, if you will."

"Did you see the stage-hand, hiding behind the set, with a handful of tools?"

We chatted for a little while longer, over the coffee, but I hardly heard a word, my mind was in turmoil over the implications of the invitation. He paid the bill, and we left. Outside, he hailed a taxi, to take me home, my home, where Joan, and the brat, were waiting. He declined the invitation to come in, merely saying, "Call me when you are decided." After a peck on the cheek, and a brush of fingers, he was gone.

Joan had the kettle on. "My!" She exclaimed, "Do I detect

a developing scandal?"

"I don't know, yet, so don't go gossiping, will you?"

"Who? Me? Never! But I'll say one thing, he doesn't look like a four pounds an hour, fourty hour a week man, to me, and I'd snap him up in an instant!"

"Yes, well, you always did have weak elastic in your knickers!" I retorted.

"Ooh, catty! I think I touched on a sore spot, there! Have you, you know, with him?"

"That's none of your business!"

"In my book, that means "Yes", unless you want to argue!"

I didn't. I couldn't! I had!

"C'mon, tell all to little Joanie."


So I did. We've been best of friends ever since we were at school together, way back when, swapping stories, scandals, and even boyfriends. We'd had one going for months, his gonads clanging together, stringing him along, because he didn't know that we knew each other, if you follow that. Each of us accusing him of two-timing us, with another, and hinting that if he dropped the other girl, then perhaps-, then, when he was bursting with frustration, we both dumped him at the same time! Great fun, when we were young, and nearly innocent. Joan listened to my outpourings, thought for a minute, and decided.

"He's right." She said, "Leave the poor sod you're hitched to. Tell him the truth - that he's not your kid's father after all. You needn't say who really is, if you know, like you told me when you got caught - let him go, and get out yourself, while you have the opportunity. I can't see you staying in this brick box with Vince for another fifty or sixty years, and pretending to be happy. Grab the chance with both hands, and GO!"

"I don't know…" I didn't know, then, that she'd told him the same thing, from the other side of the coin!

"I do. Grab this guy, and run! Divorce Vince, or let him divorce you, and be happy! Or, stay here, bored, stressed, miserable, and brain-dead."

"But-"

"Look. It's your choice, but don't wait too long. Jimmy won't. There is nothing here to keep you, apart from habit. Go, while you have a choice! Does he know that your kid is not Vince's?"

"No, that's the only thing I've kept from him I never thought it would go this far, so it wouldn't matter."

"Well, call him, right now, and tell him. If I'm right, he's sitting there, by his 'phone, right now, and waiting for it to ring." (Did I say that Joan thinks she is psychic?) She put the receiver into my hand.


I pressed down on the rest, while I drew breath to argue. The 'phone rang. As I was holding the thing, I could hardly avoid answering it, could I? "Hello?"

"Good morning!" James said, "I suspect that you have been discussing the evening with your baby-sitter friend, and wondering what to do?"

"You win," I admitted defeat, "but there is something I didn't tell you that is important, and might affect your decision…"

"I suspect I already know," he responded, "You talked about everything else, but avoided this one thing. Your child is not by your husband, is it?'

'You've guessed."

"No, I saw it, in your mind. It doesn't matter, to me."

"I told you so!" said Joan, who couldn't possibly hear what he was saying, from across the room.

'But –'

"You're mowing lawns again!" he teased, "But, but, you were about to 'phone me, as I called you. We belong together."

"You are two parts of a jigsaw," Joan said, from the chair, "That fit together, to make a bigger piece."

"Like two cogs in a machine, we mesh perfectly." James added.

It was difficult listening to two independent conversations, both saying the same thing, but with different words.

"That's what Joan just said." I said.

"Well, when three minds think the same thing, there must be some truth in the statement." He said, "Anyway, sleep on it, and let me know. Goodbye, for now, lover." The 'phone went dead, again.

"You see," Joan continued, "We all agree. Do what you

want, and not what you think is right."

"How did you know what he was saying?"

"The question is - how did he know what I was saying to you?" Joan parried, "Not everyone needs a telephone to talk to a person they cannot see."

"But –"

"Outboard motors, to you, too. I could see in your mind what he was saying to you. We've had this conversation before, and you didn't believe me then, either. When you - or whoever I'm tuned to - feels something strongly, I can feel it, too. If you would stop fighting it, forcing it away, you could be very sensitive, possibly a medium, and maybe a healer, too. But you must stop fighting it, and boost it, instead. Tune in to yourself. I will make a prediction, right now. You are pregnant, and the father is James."

"But -."

"Never mind 'but'! I can see it. It is only a few hours old, but it IS, there, inside you."

"No way!" I exclaimed," I've a coil fitted."

"It happens, sometimes. I can tell you that one of his shots hit the target, and you are hatching it, right now."

"I still don't believe you!"

"Time will tell! You had better buy some knitting patterns, ready!"

"What colour?"

"That, I don't know, it's too early to tell, but I think it will have either copper, or bronze, hair."

"Oh, come on, now I KNOW you're pulling my leg!"

"As I said, Time will tell. In three months, you will be certain. No, wait. Hold my hands, a mo." She held her hands out, palms upwards, to me.

Puzzled, I took them, after a moment's hesitation. As we touched, a little tingle, like a static shock, ran through me, making me twitch. Her hands were cold, then suddenly hot, Joan seemed relaxed, but was concentrating hard, on what I don't know - I just sensed quiet, cool, stillness. There was a tiny flicker of something way off, in the back of my mind, but it was gone before I could focus on it.

"Relax, love." Joan commanded, "You are blocking it by straining. Let it float to you. If you chase it, it will go away, and never be seen."

So I tried to think of nothing, watching the dust motes dancing, in a beam of sunlight through the window.

"Hmm, maybe." Joan mused, as a smile flickering on her face.

"What?" for an instant, I got a picture of Vince, in my mind.

"Well, you didn't believe me before, and you won't believe me now, so I'm going to write something on a scrap of note-pad, and seal it in an envelope," she did. "Date it, and get you to write your name across the flap, so you can see it hasn't been altered. Promise to keep it safe, and un-opened, until you have been ultra-sound scanned."

"Yes, alright! I promise. What did Vince have to do with it?"

"Ah, you saw that, then! Nothing, is the answer, as you will see, in nine months, it will be visibly not his child. What I saw then, was something entirely different. He's either got, or is about to get, a new girlfriend!"

"Why, the dirty, two-timing sod! When I get hold—", then

I realized what I was saying, as Joan burst out laughing.

"Why worry about it, anyway," she gasped, "you were contemplating dumping him, anyway!"

"But-"

"Ah, you're off again!"

Chapter six.

Camp-site dispute.


Once I'd dried off, I dumped the gear into the car, then cranked up the engine. It started, but only on three cylinders, as normal. I coughed and popped into Trearddur, where I stopped at the garage, and fuelled up, then went back through Holyhead, to the dive-shop, for a re-fill, and a gossip. As there was a crowd of two people filling the shop, discussing the merits of toe-hole and strap, or full-foot fins, with Fred, the proprietor, I waited outside, feeding coins into a slot machine, in the hope of receiving a can of pop in exchange. At the same time I was holding a rambling, albeit confused, conversation with Fred's two year old daughter, about her pet rabbit, which seemed to enjoy being towed around in her little toy cart. Eventually, the fins discussion was partly resolved, as the customers both rented a pair of each style, and decided to conduct their own practical tests. They wandered off, up the lane, still bickering about something. I went into the shop, carrying my empty cylinder, and asked for a re-fill, then listened as he explained how he had a salvage job to fit in, sometime soon, because some silly sod had dropped his Yamaha outboard motor over the side of his boat. It now lay at the bottom of the harbour. When I asked how that had happened, Fred said that the daft sod had tried to start it without tightening the transom clamps first, and it had leaped up, nearly decapitated the guy, then propelled itself into the depths, bubbling merrily!

"Ha! There's always one! Was it that crew from Salford, with the landing craft?"

"No, these were some anglers, up from Brum for the weekend, with a big inflatable. Is it a 180?" Fred was referring to the bottle's capacity

"No, it's a 200."

He fitted an airline to the pillar valve, opened the bottle valve, then gradually increased the pressure, from his bottle-bank that was fed by a compressor, while he watched a gauge. When it reached 20, he closed the pillar valve, then his own. "Good dive?"

"Not bad, I was just messing around in the shallows off Dafarch"

"Oh yes, there's a few cannon around there, just follow the line of the old wooden slip-way, and go out around two hundred yards, and look in the gullies at around sixty feet."

"I was around the other side of that big house, on the headland, but I know where you mean. It can be tricky round there, without a boat, the current can run at four knots, plus."

"That's the place, there were some seals round there, last week."

I picked up a magazine I'd seen on the counter, which had an article about the 'Royal Charter' in it, getting a touch of déjà vu as I handed over my three pounds fifty for the air, and the magazine. Outside, I said goodbye to the toddler and her rabbit, then put the cylinder into the car, and smoked and spluttered back to the camp-site.


Back at the tent, I struggled out of the still damp inside wet-suit, towelled off, then dragged on my ordinary clothes, again. That done, I wandered over to the camp shop, looking for consumables for lunch.

Back at the tent, again, I dined on cold steak pie, and beans, with a hot coffee, after which I washed my gear off at the stand-pipe, to remove the salt, before draping it all over the car to dry, then settled down to read the magazine,

The background noise of subdued chatter, occasional pheasant honks, and the howl of an occasional passing jet from R.A.F. Valley, just up the coast, its baby pilot off on a cross-country jaunt as he or she learned the skills, barely intruded. I was chuckling at the comic writings in 'Twilley's Twitterings' when a deep-throated, crackling roar distracted me, and I looked skywards to see a McDonnell Phantom fighter, it's re-heats glowing, standing on it's tail as it burned up the sky in a series of steep climbs, and twists, the pilot showing off, whilst climbing until it was out of sight, in the light cloud-cover.

"Noisy show-off." A pleasant female voice declared. The owner was a gorgeous creature, a wingless Angel. The sun shone through her straggly, short, salt-water bleached hair, giving her a halo of gold.

My mouth said "It was, a bit, wasn't it." While my brain said "WOW!"

"Damn noisy showoff."

"It wasn't too bad," I replied, "You want to hear a Vulcan when it does that!"

"I have," she said, then followed that with the big put-down, "From inside, I've flown one!" She wandered off across the site, then ducked into a nearby canvas mansion, in comparison with which - my tent looked like a bin-bag propped on sticks. It took a while to get back into 'Twilley' after that brief encounter, as my mind wouldn't stay focussed on the pages, and kept letting my eyes wander off, in the hope of another glimpse of the beauty queen. I flicked listlessly through the pages, until I got to the article on the 'Charter'. The article didn't impart much new information, but it did give decent bearings to the wreck, which lies in fairly shallow water, quite close to shore. The accompanying map showed a boat slip, just around the headland, by Moelfre village, and indicated a sandy beach. More useful was the road along the coast, that ran behind the 'Charter's' bay, and the Coast-guard watch-tower, providing access, through a static caravan site, via a public footpath. The prints of the photographs and engravings of the wreck, made at the time, showed a rocky headland, and cliff, but didn't reveal enough detail to be meaningful. As the dusk advanced, and the light faded, I swapped the magazine for my portable cassette player, and headphones, and listened to Karen and Richard Carpenter, for a while, until the biting midges emerged, driving me inside. Later, I brewed up again, then went for a wander round to the block-house, and the showers and bogs, to do the necessary, and wash off the salt, before turning in for the night with visions of the Angel floating across my enhanced memory. I lay there, for a while, listening to a mosquito whining shrilly, somewhere near my left ear, until it settled, and was promptly squished before it got chance to dine on me. Something was scuffling in the nearby reeds, it could have been a mouse, or an elephant, or anything in between. A pheasant honked, close by. On second thoughts, I decided that the creature in the reeds was unlikely to be an elephant. Way off, in the distance, the Boom, Boom noise of a mobile disco faded up, as the car containing it drew nearer. Then a tweaked engine, coupled to a 'sports' exhaust, rasped and crackled as the car drew onto the site. Tyres squealed as it swerved to a halt, then the engine died, leaving the Boom, Boom, resonating over the site. A car door banged, there was raucous laughter, then near quiet again, apart from the disco noise. More door-banging followed, then the engine rasped into life again, then the car cruised around the site, headlights dazzling, the radio still blaring. My tent flooded with light, and I thought, "Oh, please, NOT next to me!" I must have been heard, as the new arrivals kept on going, to over near the cliff. "Thank-you" I sighed. The engine stopped, but the boom, boom didn't. If anything, it got louder, as the car's occupants spilled out, and began larking about, chasing around, yelling, tripping over guy-ropes, and generally annoying everyone. Eventually, they gathered around their car, again. Then there was the snap-hiss! of cans being opened.

Now, one thing that divers insist on is a quiet night, as they are often up early for the first dive of the day, before the tourists and beach-blockers arrive. And it wasn't very long before an anonymous voice called, "Turn that bloody boom-box off!"

"Fuck off!" The replier had a Scouse accent.

"You won't be asked again!" anonymous warned

"Go suck your cock, you fucker!" Scouse voice responded.

After a short pause, there came the unmistakable sound of a tent zip being operated, followed by several more, including mine. About a dozen bodies, in various states of undress moved to, and surrounded, a battered Ford Granada, from which the noise was issuing.

"I said, turn it off!" The speaker was about six feet tall, and six feet wide, built like a brick outhouse, and wore a pair of red boxer shorts, decorated with white polka-dots.

Scouse pulled a flick-knife, and snapped the blade open. "Make me!"

Polka-dot shorts reached carefully forwards, Scouse danced sideways, and lashed the knife at him. His knife-hand stopped in mid-arc with a splat, as polka-dots caught it, then squeezed. Scouse tried to jerk his arm back, with no result, then tried the knee at polka-dot's groin. Polka-dot caught the leg in his other hand, smiled, and then applied pressure. Scouse's face went white as pain-sweat erupted from his skin. His hand released the knife, which dropped to the ground. One of polka-dot's pals, from the same group of tents, picked it up, and snapped the blade off as though it were a carrot, before tossing the remnants back into the Granada, then reached in and turned the radio off.

"Thanks, Pete," said polka-dots. "Now, Scouse, you have a choice, be quiet, go away, or be hurt. Which is it to be?"

Scouse, standing on one leg, his free arm waving pathetically, looked around at his companions, for assistance. One took a pace forward.

"I wouldn't!" The one called Pete cautioned.

The other two looked around, saw the obvious, and quietly got into the car. One pace dithered, then followed suit.

"Aw-rite, den, fuckin' leggo me." Scouse capitulated.

Polka-dot released the leg, then the arm, and stepped back.


Scouse rubbed his crushed wrist, then snarled, "Yer shudna' dun tha'." and launched a very fast karate kick at polka-dot's stomach, who made no attempt to block, or avoid it. He let it land with a hard thock, and just stood there waiting, while Scouse blanched with the pain in his foot.

"Oh, dear, now you've annoyed Trev." Pete sighed.

Trev reached forward, and poked an extended finger into Scouse's solar plexus. Scouse said "WHOOP!" went grey, and fell over, curled up.

"What's up, wacker, you can't be tired, already?"

Scouse lay on the grass, slowly going purple, and making glottal clicking noises, as he struggled to draw breath.

One of the others, in the car, said, "Can I get out, and pick 'im up?"

"Very carefully." Pete advised.


After the car had gone, quietly, we all cheerily said "good-night" to each other, and went back to our respective tents. I found mine, slid the zip up, trying to recall when I'd pulled it down after I'd exited, then crawled in. Halfway, I froze, horrified, and began to back out, again, apologising as I went. "I do beg your pardon, I've got the wrong tent in the dark, please forgive me!" Outside, I looked around, to check my location.

That car was definitely my car, and this was definitely my tent. I crawled part-way in again. "No, it's my tent, YOU are in the wrong one!"

The blanket eased down a bit, baring a soft white shoulder below the golden hair, then a slender arm emerged, to crook a 'come here' finger at me.

Wingless Angel smiled provocatively. "I don't think so!"

There are times when it is best to co-operate with the inevitable!

I first saw him, flopped in a ricketty folding chair next to a dinky little tent with a not-quite-square, home-made fly-sheet. Diving kit was scattered around, over the tent and a tatty rot-box of a car, so it could dry in the sun's heat. He was chuckling at something on the page of a magazine he was reading. I was strolling back from the loo-block, wondering what to do with the rest of the evening, when a Phantom blasted past, showing off. He made some trivial comment about the noise, and as I was only a few feet from him, responded, not intending to do anything more complex or involved. Our glances happened to meet, and a thrill ran through me, as I saw him jump, too. I felt that 'POW!' in my stomach, leaving that sweet/sour sense of desire behind. I hadn't felt like that, since – well, since, but my big mouth got in the way before my head could recover, and slapped him down. He just lifted one eyebrow, as if to say, "O.K. if that's your attitude-" and went back to his magazine.

I went into my trailer-tent, made a hot-chocolate night-cap, and watched the portable telly, for a while, but as there was nothing of interest on, I turned it off, and settled down. There was some animal screeching in the shrubbery, just behind my tent, so I threw a used tea-bag at it through the open window, making it squawk and scurry off to serenade somebody else. I lay there, drowsing, for a while, but although tired, it wasn't sleep my body wanted. His battered, lived-in face kept appearing in my mind, and I knew I would have to do something to distract myself. I was contemplating going over, to apologize, when his light went out, and I knew I'd left it too long. That put paid to the possibility of chatting, for an hour or so, but as I had no intention of taking it further... About then, a bunch of yobs arrived, and set about causing havoc and disruption. I hoped they wouldn't start bothering me, a lone female, as it could get complicated. Before too long, they were advised to shut up, or push off, but their foul language indicated other intentions. This caused several of the other campers, who were mostly divers, from what I'd noted earlier, to emerge from their tents, and converge on the trouble-makers. He was one of them, and I noticed that he was wearing a pair of bathers, apparently put on backwards, suggesting that he slept in his skin, and nothing else. One of the yobs squared up to a guy built like a gorilla, complete with body-hair. A knife was pulled, removed from the wielder, destroyed, and tossed into their car, closely followed by the yobs. I decided, on the spur of the moment, to go for broke, and slid from my tent, across the grass, and into his, while nobody was watching. The yobs drove off, and everything went quiet again, as the group dispersed. It seemed like an age, before he came back, as I lay in his sleeping, bag, nerves quaking, all a-tremble at my cheek and daring. When he was half-way into his tent, his eyes registered my presence, and he mumbled some apology about "The wrong one", and backed out again, hesitated, then came back in. "No, you are!" he stated. It was now or never, and I wiggled an inviting finger, drawing him further into his tent, confused, but hopefully willing.

"Hello again!" I said. He just looked embarrassed, and then we both started to speak at the same time. He said, "Is this what…" as I said "I just couldn't…" We both stopped speaking. His skin, and I could see most of it, was going all goose-bumpy in the cold air, and I could see he was shivering, though whether from cold, or nervousness, I couldn't tell.

"You are getting frozen, out there," I said, "come and join me in your bed." I patted the blanket with my exposed arm.

"Is that what you really want?" he gave me room to back out of the invitation.

"I wouldn't be here, otherwise. I want you, do you want me? I think you do. I'm not a mixed-up kid, and I'm not going to shout 'rape' the second you touch me. I came to you, remember, in your space."

He kissed me, then, gently, and cautiously, ready for the

slightest hint of rejection. I almost had to drag him into his own bed. He lay there, next to me, hesitating, still, shivering, so I instigated the proceedings by caressing his chest, making his nipples stand up like mini-mountains.

"You ought to know," he said, "I'm married."

"It doesn't matter," I replied, as I nibbled his ear, "providing she doesn't walk in on us!"

"Not much chance of that!" he admitted, "It's a hell of a walk! I'm here on my own, and I know she's been cheating on me for years."

"You're not alone now," I replied. "I'm single. I was engaged, but he was killed in an accident, and there has been no-one since."

He rummaged one-handed in a box of bits and pieces, "Do I need these?" he held up a little packet in the dim light, "I'm firing blanks." He must have been a good Boy Scout, always prepared!

"No, now stop talking, and DO something!" I kissed him, to shut him up.

He did.

Her yell, that first time, would have roused Beethoven. A subdued cheer came from a nearby tent. The old couple, in a tent on the other side of mine to hers, was "tut-tutting." Then she let out a deep sigh, and wrapped her arms around me, holding us together. As I nibbled her ear, I was wondering just how much noise we'd made.

"I needed that!" she whispered.

"All the camp-site heard!"

"Bugger them!"

"I'd rather not!" then I moved against her, again, long and slow, making her groan with pleasure, then I kissed her neck, as we began again.

Chapter seven.

Holyhead.

I woke as dawn was breaking, disturbed by the brassy shriek of a pheasant. For a moment, I felt around, and then realized that she had gone, leaving only her perfume on my pillow, and the memory of her lithe body. A stray blonde hair lay next to a little note, which read "Be discreet". There was an undecipherable squiggle for a signature. Suddenly feeling lonely, I would have turned over, and gone back to dreaming of her, but my bladder was begging for mercy. I dragged my clothes on, and ambled off round to the block-house, leaving the tent flap carefully open, so that anyone that cared to look could see the tent was empty, thus defeating the old chap who was on the lookout for gossip, and had carefully positioned his camp chair so that he could see inside when the opportunity was presented.

As I walked back to the tent, the first Hawk sortie of the

day whistled overhead, at about two hundred feet altitude, and as my kettle began to boil, I saw her emerge from her tent.

"Good morning," I called. "Would you care to join me in a breakfast cuppa?"

"Love to," she replied, "I've run out of gas for my stove, until the shop opens." She called back, over her shoulder, as she headed for the loo-block. "I'll be back in a few minutes."

When she came back, and saw I had the frying-pan out –

"And I could murder a bacon butty!"

"Coming right up! I'm afraid it will be a bit mean, I'm about out of groceries. I was intending to go into town a bit later, and re-stock."

"Mmm! Me too." She said, round the rim of her cup.

"Well, then, could I offer you a lift in, or would you rather walk, it's only a mile or so."


She eyed the Cortina, "No thanks, I need some gas, first. I'll go in, later."

"Do you know the way?"

She smiled, at that. "Let me guess, out of the gate, turn

right, left at the end, and there it is!"

"Worcester, or tomato sauce?" I knew when to give up.

"Worcester, please."

We made small-talk while we breakfasted, but she declined another coffee with a shake of her head, as she stood. "See you around, later, perhaps?" she said, as she casually wandered off. The brief twitch of a smile, and a raised eyebrow said "Try hiding from me!"

I made another cuppa, anyway, then, while it cooled, took my rubbish to the bin compound, a dozen or so yards away, then re-filled my water-can from the stand-pipe, so I could heat more water, then wash the few pots I'd used. Jobs done, I picked up the magazine again, for a while, listening to the wildlife, and the rest of the camp waking up. Pete and Trevor wandered past, heading for the toilet block. "Someone was having fun, last night, weren't they, Pete?" Trev commented, as they passed.

"Yeah, Trev, and it weren't me! Oh, Hi, pal, you doin' o.k?"

"Fine, thanks. Those pheasants were rather noisy, weren't

they?"

A bit later, on the return journey, carrying a big box of cornflakes, and a bottle of milk, Pete said, "Didn't sound like a pheasant, to me!"

"Welsh pheasants sound different." I suggested.

"Ah, that could be it, especially if it were a Welsh Rare-bit!" They carried on, to their tent.


I eventually worked up the enthusiasm for a shopping trip, so before the day's heat got going, I wandered up the laneand into Holyhead, looking at the gardens of houses I passed, and the hedge-rows, in the forlorn hope of spotting a native orchid. Before I reached the dock wall, and the main trunk road, the A55, I turned off, into the town, down a side road, which I knew would bring me out near the breakwater, on the sea-front. It wound around a bit, and then led me past a novel garden, basically it was an outcropping of rock, with the house perched on top. The face of the rock sloped down to the footpath and road, at an angle of approximately forty-five degrees, and was devoid of the slightest hint of soil, except in the cracks and

113

crevices, where an assortment of colourful heathers clung. I spent about ten minutes admiring it, not for its outstanding beauty, but for its triumph over apparently insurmountable odds. I eventually wandered into town, and browsed in a newsagent's, where I found an 'Invitation to High Tea' card. From there, I did the bit in the supermarket, pondering between frozen steaks or frozen pork chops, knowing they would all taste of propane anyway. Purchases made, and finalized with a frozen black-currant cheesecake, I wandered around for a while, window-shopping, and eventually emerged on the harbour road, where I turned left, and wandered along, looking at the view, before making my way back to camp.

The kind of training I had done develops a sort of extra sense, so I was aware of it coming before it could do any damage. It fizzed over my shoulder as I side-stepped, spanged off a concrete post, and fell to the floor. My next step took me to the wall dividing the higher road from the lower parade, and I jumped over it. With my feet stinging from the drop, I ran towards a small overhang, where there used to be a tunnel through, a blocked-off pedestrian way into the town. As I pressed into the mean shelter, running feet sounded above, then slithered to a halt. A second pair, shod in steel-tipped boots, clattered up, and halted.

"Where de fucks 'e gone?" a familiar scouse accent snarled.

"Dunno, bu' 'e should'a broke 'is fuckin' neck, jumpin' down dere! 'e can't'a gone far!"

"Ay, Sid!" The first scouser shouted, "Sid! Go ter't end of wall, an' cum back along t'uther side, we'll go down steps, ere, an' meet yer in't middle."


So, There were three of them, possibly all four, from last evening. If I went left, to the steps, there would be two of them, the other way, Sid, at least. Who was carrying what, I didn't know. Behind was the brick wall, and in front, the harbour. The only way out was confrontation. So be it. There was no point waiting and being "Piggy-in-the-middle", so I went to meet Sid. He proved to be the short skinny one who had kept out of the way, last night. He was not so shy now, though. The runny nose,

115

and the bloodshot glassy eyes, suggested that he was 'high' on drugs of some sort, and therefore dangerous, because he would be unpredictable. I wandered along, trying to look like a shopper, hoping he wouldn't recognize me with clothes on, but no such luck. He swerved to meet me, an evil grin on his face, and a wicked knife in his left hand. His right held a length of bicycle chain. Someone vaulted over the wall behind me as I faced Sid. This new arrival was too close, so before he could recover his balance, I turned and kicked him in the plumbing, then on the jaw as he doubled up. Sid, in the meantime, had started a charge at my back, the chain hissing through the air as it was lashed at my head - which I moved out of the way by performing a 'no-hands' forward roll, then span round to meet him. Now it was a waiting game, but I couldn't afford to wait for too long, as Scouse would join the party in a minute if the wall-jumper didn't recover first. Sid feinted with the knife, but it was only half-hearted. A coward at heart, he was a team-player, and was waiting for the team to join in. Wall-jumper groaned, and rolled over, but he wasn't ready to take any further part just yet. Sid's chain flicked at my head, inviting me to grab it, but I declined, a

116

wily Glaswegian friend had once taught me about bike chains. It flicked at my head, again, and I countered with a swing of the bag of frozen food. Sid flinched, and backed off a step, so I advanced, and swung again, a plan forming. Gradually, I shepherded him in the direction I wanted, until he was positioned just so. Then I let out an enormous yell, and charged straight at him. He flinched, back-pedalled, and fell down the steps into the harbour, to land with a splat in the mud and slime at the bottom. My two pace charge ended, and I turned, to see where the others were.

Trev had the car-driver in a firm grip on his shoulder 'Is this a private party," he called, "or can anyone join in?"

"There's another one, somewhere." I replied.

"Yeah, Pete's got him, up top. I don't think you needed us, really, you seem to have been doing alright by yourself!"

"It seems that way," I acknowledged, "but thanks, anyway."

"Pete saw this lot following someone, and we thought it might have been Blondie, so we followed THEM, to see what was going on."

"Unlucky for them!" I moved to the steps, and looked down.

"Is he alive?"

"Seems so, just his ego hurts, he chose a soft patch to land in. He won't be sneaking up on anyone, for a while, though."

"Oh, how come?"

"It's pretty ripe down there!"

Pete joined us, then with Scouse in tow, by the scruff of the neck, "Is everyone o.k?"

"Fine, thanks, Pete, I was just saying to Trev that these two were no bother."

"I saw you drop that one," Pete said, "what happened to the other?"

"Our pal said "BOO" to him, and he fell down the steps!" Trevor laughed.

Pete looked over, and then stood back, "Pooh! It reeks like a sewer out-fall!"

"Two questions," Trev said, "What shall we do with these berks, and what's your name?"

"Ah, well, I don't want them as pets! The name's Vinny, or Vince. Did that one give you any grief?"

"What, this dishrag? No." Trevor shook the creature by the well-crushed shoulder, "Good as gold, weren't you, pal?" He turned him face to face," Now listen, pal. When I let go, you will go down those stairs, and join your pal, in the mud. If you don't, you will, anyway - the quick way." Trev gave him a shove in the indicated direction, and released the shoulder.

"And you," Pete said to the other one, "pick up your pal, and follow him down." He leaned over the railing, "Oh dear, I've dropped their car-keys into the mud!" As he let go of them, he contrived to kick them well out from the wall, so they fell into a stinking pool of green slime. The one Pete had been holding on to leaned over the one still grovelling on the floor, and came up with an automatic pistol. He was just too far away to jump on, bad planning, that. We separated, to divide his targets, and attention. A quick glance around revealed that everyone else in the area had just recalled urgent appointments, and vanished, leaving us five.

There are three tactics of use against a pistol, either be behind something very solid, or a long way off, or extremely close, within arms-length. We were all around ten feet away, which makes it tricky, too far to do anything, and too close to be missed.

Wall-jumper was starting to pay attention, again, and squeaked, "Yeah! Go on! Shoot the buggers!"

The gun-wielder was no gunman, he was crushing the thing in a sweaty grip as though it might turn on him and bite him. With luck, when he fired it, he would be shaking so much the first round would miss, and give the others chance to get in close. Then something blurred past my ear with an audible zip, and thunked into his chest. He coughed, in shock and surprise, firing the pistol in reflex. Where the bullet went, I don't know, but I went for him as the recoil drove the pistol up to smack into his face. Before I reached him, he sagged to the pavement, coughed blood, then dropped the gun, panting, Trev got to him, just then, and booted him in the guts, as I kicked the pistol away. Pete didn't move, just stood, white-faced., his eyes starting, and then he looked down at his chest.

"Oh, shit, no!" Trev went to him, "Where'd it get you?"

"Left side, just under the arm." Pete gasped, "Jesus, it burns!"

Trev ripped his shirt off, ready to make a pad, then started to peel Pete's shirt back, just as I reached them. A neat little hole, with singed edges, showed in Pete's shirt. There was no blood showing, yet. Trev pulled Pete's shirt open, pinging a button off, then stopped, with a laugh. "You jammy bugger!" he exclaimed, as he poked a finger through the matching hole in the back of Pete's shirt, "There's a thin red stripe across your ribs, and a matching one on your arm, where it took a layer of skin off!'

'What? It got me! I felt it!'

'No, you aren't even bleeding. All you need is a new shirt!" he paused, "And me, too, now!"

"And a change of underpants" I added.

"Hey, you lot!" A female voice shouted, "If you don't get a move on, the cops'll be here, I can hear the sirens!"

We got a move on. I picked up the pistol, "I'll get rid of this, later."

121

"No." said Trev, "I've a better idea, I'll test its floating ability when we go round to the Skerries, later."

He took it off me, operated the release catch for the magazine, and then pulled the slide back, ejecting the shell in the chamber, which he deftly slid back into the magazine, which went into one pocket, while the rest of the pistol went into another. "Let's make like the shepherds, and get the flock out of here!"

"Are you divers?" I queried, as we walked along the prom, "Because that's pretty much the same idea I had, but I was going to dispose of it more locally."

"Ah, you too, hey! What did you have planned for tomorrow?"

"I was thinking of having a go, on the 'Charter'." I admitted, "You never know! I might just get an expenses-paid holiday, for once!"

"Fat chance! Tell you what, If you fancy it, we can all have a run round, this afternoon, we've been meaning to go for a rummage, ourselves."

"How deep is it?" Pete asked.

"Not much, about ten metres." I replied.

"That's o.k, then, I was thinking of the deep one, tomorrow, but there's fourteen hours in between, so no worries about decompressing, after."

"About that," Trev put in, "Do you fancy coming with us to the Skerries? There's plenty of room in the boat! Share the fuel costs?"

"Er, how deep are you going?" I asked

"The first one's fourty-five metres, if we get the bottom of the tide, the other's about twenty."

"Fourty-five's too deep for me, the deepest I've been is thirty."

"You'll be o.k." Pete interrupted.

"Maybe, but I don't want to chance spoiling it for you, should I get narked. I have a low tolerance for alcohol, and maybe it carries over."

"You can always skip the first one, and just do the second dive." said Trev, "think about it, anyway."

"Yeah, thanks, but if you fancy a run to Moelfre, later today, I'm in. My car?"

123

Trev flinched. "No, we'll go round in the R.I.B. It saves climbing the cliffs!"

"Does about one p.m. suit? Give Pete time to do his laundry!"

"Fine!"

"Funny bugger!" Pete glared at him, as Trev held his nose. "It still bloody burns!"


Two police cars went hurtling past, sirens blaring followed by an ambulance that was displaying a 'Paramedic' sign.

"Hey!" "Trev suddenly realized something, "Who threw the whatsit?"

We paused, for mutual reflection.

"Beats me," I admitted, "and who shouted?"

"No idea, I saw no-one." Pete stated.

"Nor me, what was it that was thrown?"

"I didn't see, although it just missed my ear. Perhaps it was the same thing that was thrown at me, a minute or so earlier."

Another ambulance bustled past, through the growing traffic jam.

"Perhaps we hit him too hard!" Trev suggested.

"Or the other one's caught something from the muck!"

"More likely something in the muck has caught him!"

We were still laughing about it, as we walked past the front of Woolworth's shop.

Chapter eight.

Trearddur Bay.

After I left him, I went back to my trailer-tent, and pottered around for a while, feeling good inside, and naughty on the outside. I hadn't realized how much I'd needed a Man inside me. Chastity might be hygienic, but it isn't fun. He had said he was firing blanks, but I took my little pill, just for insurance. I heard him clattering pots, and then his tent zipper sounded, before he wandered off out of the site, presumably going to Holyhead on his shopping trip. Across the field, a diesel engined Transit coughed into life, then crunched off down the track. All around, the other campers were stirring, starting a new day, while the keener types were drifting back onto the site, following a dawn dive on the slack tide. The theory is, - they get there before the crowds arrive to scare everything off, the end result is - three hundred divers descend on the beaches at six am, and by nine, the beaches are empty, as is the sea! Everything, and everyone, has gone elsewhere.

The shop shutters went up with a crash, announcing that it was open for business, rather belatedly, as the first rush had already been served. I picked up my empty gas bottle and took it for exchange. On the way back, lugging the heavy full one, I began thinking about 'lover-boy'. Is it to be a holiday fling, forgotten in a week, or should I make it just that one night of fun, or should I see where it would lead? Decisions, decisions. What did I really know about him? Nothing, really. I knew how he looked, felt, smelled, and tasted. I knew he was married. I suspected, from the state of his car, that he was no millionaire. I had a suspicion that I was the first time he'd strayed from the marital bed. I knew he'd needed, and enjoyed me, as much as I had, him, so perhaps he was separated. One of his hobbies was the same as mine, diving, or he wouldn't be here. His name? Well, we hadn't got around to that, but then, he didn't know mine, either! Something came up, if you'll forgive the expression! Would he have slept with me, if I hadn't thrown myself at him? I didn't think so, he was too polite. What had he

127

said? His wife had been cheating, for years? Yet he'd stuck with her. Either he's a good man, or he's stuck in a rut, and can't raise the enthusiasm or courage to leave her. (Maybe he had never found a reason to leave!) Would I go to him, again, tonight? I hadn't decided. I think I will, but then, I might not. Anyway, I was back at the tent. I put the gas bottle down with a sigh of relief, then began checking over my dive kit. I checked the contents of my cylinder, then the demand valve, the pony bottle, the octopus valve, then the direct-feed line to the stabilizer jacket, then the battery in the dive computer. I reminded myself, again, to repair that little nick in the left knee of the suit which allowed a trickle of water to sneak in, Mask, schnorkel, knife, fins? Where've I put the bloody fins? Ah! There, in the junk tray, under the bed, I hadn't used the tray very much, this trip. (I also found my tin-opener). What's that in the grey paper bag? I opened it, to see a melted mass of grotty old chocolate Brazils, squashed into a lumpy mess. They went into the bin, as I didn't know how long they'd been lurking. I vaguely recalled him buying them, for our last trip, so they were at least two years old. Funny, I can't recall his face, any more. I must finally be getting over him. Shopping! What was it I wanted, now? Strange, one night of lust and I've a head like a sieve. Ah, yes! Something to eat would be nice! I lurched, mentally, from one subject to another like this, for a while, then cranked up the old Land-Rover and bounced off down the track. We droned into town on the knobbly tyres, then began looking for a place to park, always a problem in Holyhead in the tourist season. This time I dropped lucky, as a Volvo estate pulled out a short way in front and I managed to nip into the vacated space ahead of a mini, mainly because my Landie was bigger! The battered Granada, close behind, stood on it's brakes, blared the horn, then blasted past, at high rev's and in a low gear, intent on finding a space, too. The four youths in it made various digital gestures at me, so I made one back, as I tugged on the hand-brake lever.

After ducking in and out of several shops, I went back to the Landie, and dumped the proceeds into the back, before looking for a chemist's shop. Why? Mind your own business! (A woman's body does what a woman's body does, and I didn't want it to, for a few days, yet, I had other possibilities planned).

As I was wandering down the main (ha!) street, I saw the thick-set guy, and his bean-pole pal, from the campsite. They appeared to be following someone, ducking in and out of doors, and trying to look innocent. Intrigued, I followed them at a safe distance as they worked down towards the harbour. About then, I saw the local Boots shop, and went in to make my purchases. When I came back out, they had disappeared from view, but something drew me, and I made my way towards the sea-front. Well in front of me, someone whistled, and then I saw the thick-set one point the thin one off to the left, then run down some steps. The general crowd movement was in the direction of away, and I suspected trouble, but who was doing what to whom, I couldn't tell. A sudden flicker of movement further away, as though someone was throwing a frizzbee, drew my eye. I saw, another thirty feet or so in front of the thrower, a man with his back to me, plastic bags of something in his hands, casually strolling along the front, surveying the lack of activity in the harbour. He suddenly ducked right, then span to his left, and jumped over a low wall. I suddenly realized it was 'my' man that had been thrown at. The thing struck sparks from a concrete lamp-post as I

130

recognized the thrower and his pal as two of the yobs from the Granada that I had beaten to the parking space, earlier. Thrower shouted something I couldn't catch, and then made a circling gesture to another person further along the front, before he turned and ran to the wall that 'my' man had hurdled. After looking over it, he ran to his left, to where there was a gap, for either steps or a ramp leading down, his skinny pal trailing a short way behind. Seemingly from nowhere, the tall thin guy from the camp-site appeared, and grabbed hold of the lagger, while the thick-set one rocketed down the steps, surprisingly fast on his feet for a big man,

The crowd got in the way, for a few moments, so I didn't see what happened, but when they cleared, the thin yob was firmly gripped by the tall one, and being pushed down the steps or ramp, or whatever, after the others. I had a suspicion that my first-aid training might come in handy, once I'd figured out who were the good and who the bad guys, in this scuffle, so I kept going, rather faster. As I neared the wall, someone else jumped over, further up, towards the station and dockyard wall. Then there was an ear-splitting shriek, followed by a desperate yell of fear, a brief pause, and then a nasty, squelchy splat!

By the time I reached the wall and could see over, it was all over. One of the yobs was curled up on the pavement, clutching his family jewels, and one was held by the tall thin man. 'My' man was looking over the seafront wall, by a gap in the railings, at something below. As he stood upright and turned, the shoulder-held yob got free, somehow, and produced a gun from one of the pockets of the curled-up one. That made it stalemate, as the three 'Good guys' were too far away from him to do anything about it, as was I. Although I was in throwing distance of the gun-man, I had nothing to throw, until I remembered the thrown thing, and that it had fallen somewhere around here. I looked quickly around, on the floor, then saw a metal thing like a cowboy sheriff's badge, a six pointed star, I picked it up, noting that it was surprisingly heavy for its size, and the points were very sharp. I judged the weight, and trajectory, then flung it at the gunman, intending it to distract him. It hit him solidly on the chest. As he staggered from the shock, my man, and the thick-set one moved, the gun fired, and the tall thin one flinched, then stood still. Both the 'good guys' hit the gunman, at the same instant, knocking the gun out of his hand. It, and him, clattered to the floor. The gun must have been a revolver, not an automatic pistol, as the impact with the flags didn't cause it to fire again, luckily. Then both men went to the tall, thin one's aid.

Somebody must have sent for the Police, as I could hear sirens approaching, from in town, somewhere.

"Hey!" I yelled, "Time to go!" then departed myself. I had no wish to get deeper involved in it than I already was. I had enough to worry about, without spending time in clink, and worrying about how to pay the legal fees for a Solicitor. A crimson-faced copper on a pushbike came trundling past, gasping for breath as he pedalled frantically. I wandered casually back into town, via the nearest back-road. After meandering around for a time, I made my way back to the Landie, arriving just in time to see some spotty youth trying to prize the quarter-light open with a screwdriver. I took it off him, then said, "Why break in, it's not locked", before demonstrating that fact, and disabling the alarm before the orange dye canister triggered, liberally spraying everything in range. I tossed the screwdriver into the back, gave the kid a boot up the backside to help him on his way, then climbed in and got the engine going. I drove round to the garage for some fuel, then back to the campsite. Land-Rover's will go just about anywhere, but they are thirsty beasts.

Later on, back at my tent, I was making final preparations, while waiting for Pete and Trev. I'd made a bag of butties, and had my flask filled with coffee. My gear was all checked, and to hand, ready to load, and I was three-quarters of the way into my wet-suit. All I needed to do was zip up the jacket. I'd found the local chatter channel on the two metres amateur radio band, and was listening to the usual stuff about whose computer had blown up, and what was being done about it, interspersed with which pub they were all meeting at, later. Another voice came on, with a comment that made me listen carefully. Apparently the Police were looking for a gang of youths that had been involved in a street brawl, culminating in a fatal stabbing, earlier, on the Holyhead sea-front. I decided to wander over to Trev's place, and spread the gospel.

"Who got stabbed?" He was struggling into his wet-suit pants,

"Didn't say, just a gang-fight of youths."

"Well, it can't have been us, we're not youths!"

"Or a gang," Pete added, as he joined us. "It's on the local radio, too!"

"Plus, we didn't stab anyone. It must be a different bunch, and coincidence."

"Anyway, I'm ready, when you are. My car or yours?"

"Ours is a bit roomier. Bring your stuff over, and chuck it in the back" He indicated their transport, which turned out to be a three-ton, four-wheel-drive ex-army truck "It's better than it looks, because it's fitted out as a mobile home, Fridge, cooker, t.v, the lot."

"And," Trev added, "heater, room to swing a cat, inside, if it's a very small cat, and room for eight, if they're very friendly. Is your girl coming?"

"She did that, last night" Pete jested.

"What girl-friend?" I asked, feigning innocence.

"Oh come on, the Welsh pheasant, which goes: - oh, oh, oh, OH, OH, OH, AAAAaaahh! You might be playing it cool, but she can't keep her eyes off you. Every time she goes past, or you do, she's watching." Pete ducked inside the tent to avoid the flung flip-flop.

Sure enough, when I looked around, she was looking at us, but then so was half the camp-site, after all the noise! Plucking up my courage, clasping it in both hands, and a convenient holdall, I walked casually over to her, watching for the tiny head-shake – 'No'- that would warn me off, deciding that I would casually wander on past, and make a circuit of the site when it came.

"Hello, again!" She said.

So I asked her if she would dare to come with the three of us, if she thought we were trustworthy enough, and just might manage to behave in her presence, and join us on a boat trip and dive. After a moment's hesitation, she agreed, much to my surprise, so I suggested that she change, while I carried her cylinder, and other bits of kit over to the truck for her.

"What was all that racket about, just now?" she asked.

"Oh! That was Pete, doing his Welsh pheasant impression." I replied, as she went inside. I heard her sniggering, as she pulled the flap zip down.

"Is he the big one?" she called, from out of sight, as clothes rustled suggestively, "and I'm not Welsh!"

"No, that's Trev, Trevor, Pete's the taller of the two." I carried her cylinder across. It had one of those new stabilizer jackets fitted to it, rather than the separate 'horse-collar' adjustable buoyancy life jacket I used. Her kit contained all the basic essentials in one strap-on unit, rather than separate cylinder, buoyancy, and weight-belt, with all the buckles and fasteners.


When she emerged she was dressed in a snazzy pink and blue dry-bag. Normally diving suits make women look like a sack of potatoes, but this one must have been tailored for her, as she stuck out in all the right places.

"Oh, Wow!" Pete drooled, as she walked over.

"Ground rules!" She declared. "I don't mind you looking, but it is strictly hands off, or I'll break them off! If you have other ideas, tough!"

"Don't mind us, Darling, Trev and me're - together, - you know!" Pete minced.

"Oh, I - ah,"

"And if you believe that, you will believe the moon is made of Caerphilly cheese!" Trev laughed," he's an idiot, but I think your man can make him behave!"

"Right, Who's going to be dive leader?" Vince asked. "And isn't the moon made of cheese?"

"That depends. It's Trev's truck and boat. Are we diving as a group, or two pairs?"

"I think we'll decide that when we get there. If it's murky, two pairs, then we won't spend the entire dive looking for each other, and it means those two can hold hands!" Trev suggested, with a cheeky grin. "And if it's crystal, a loose group, everyone keeping their eyes open. I've checked the tide-tables, and it will just be low tide when we get there. Is everyone happy with that?"

"Yes, I'd prefer everyone for themselves, though, as I seem to spend all my time looking out for my partner." She said.

"Fine by me." Trev said, "If it's clear. What do we call you, by the way, he seems to have forgotten to introduce us!"

"Ah, er, - ." Vince said.

Pete started laughing again. "I do believe," he gasped, "that the two love-birds were so busy, they forgot that little detail!"

"I'm George." She said. No-one noticed she didn't deny the accusation of the previous night's activity.

"George, he's Vinny, the other bean-pole is Pete, and I'm Trev."

"I'd heard your names mentioned, but I didn't know who was who." George acknowledged.

"Right, then, gang, is all the gear in? If you've forgotten it, you dive without it, because we're not coming back till after!"

Nods all round.

"Right, let's go!"

We all piled into the back of the truck, all two of us. Pete and Trevor got into the front, someone had to drive! Then the engine started with a blare and a cloud of blue smoke, as big diesel truck engines do, then we were off. We drove about four miles, to the Trearddur Bay yacht club marina, where we stopped. The nearside cab door opened, and Pete climbed out.

"Everyone stay put for a minute, while Pete brings the boat round." Trev called through the communications hatch, from his driving seat. Vince leaned out of the back, while I could see, as I was on the other side, and could see anyway, Pete clamber into a wobbly little tin bath-tub of a thing, and began tugging at the dinky engine's starter rope.

"I hope that's not the boat!" George muttered. "If we all get into that, it'll sink, without all the kit, as well!"

Pete got the little engine going, then untied the bow line, and puttered off across the inlet, over to a large, bright orange, inflatable dinghy that I'd mistaken for one of the Inshore Lifeboats the R.N.L.I. use to rescue kids on Li-Lo's that have been blown off-shore. Pete jumped into the big boat, tied the bath-tub's rope to a cleat, and then turned a key, starting the centre one of three big outboards burbling throatily.

"That's more like it!" George exclaimed, "Radio, radar, and a G.P.S. set, by the looks of it."

"What's G.P.S.?" Vince queried.

"It's an American military satellite navigation system," George explained, pleased she knew something Vince didn't. "Global Positioning Satellite, there are a dozen or so geostationary birds in orbit, and they tell a gizmo in the decoder exactly where on the earth's surface it is, to within a few feet."

"I give in, if they're in orbit, how can they be stationary?"

"Ah, tricks of the trade! If they're far enough out, they are travelling at exactly the same speed as the surface of the earth, beneath them, and so stay in exactly the same place, while going round at a zillion miles an hour!"

Pete waved, from the central control console of the boat, and Trev drove us a bit further along the road.

"There's a slip just up here, where Pete can bring the boat right up to the back of the truck," Trev called, from the cab, "It saves a lot of fetching and carrying!"

He threaded a way through all the parked cars and camper-vans, climbing out once to move an empty boat trailer over a bit, and took us to the slip he'd mentioned, then positioned the truck, ready to reverse down the slip.

"Is it wide enough?" I called, "it looks awfully narrow!"

"We've been down it before!" Trev called back. "Don't panic!"

"You're driving!"

Pete seemed to be having difficulty with steering the boat, as he was waltzing around in circles and figure eights, in the middle of the bay. When I commented, Trev said; "Don't worry, he's just exercising the steering and the gearshifts before he comes into the confined area, because they tend to stiffen up when they haven't been used for a while."

When he was satisfied, Pete headed in to the slip, and Trev reversed us straight back into the water, until the waves were slapping at the floorboards and tail-gate. There, he put the brake on, and climbed around the frame of the truck and into the back, without getting his feet wet.

"Practice!" he grinned, as Pete nosed the boat up to the truck. Trev took the bow-rope, and tied it to a handy frame, then hopped over the fat tube. "O.K. start passing the stuff over, please, Vin."

I did, and then George climbed into the inflatable, followed by me. Trev took the dinghy's bow rope, jumped back into the truck, then dragged the bath-tub in behind him when Pete drew the inflatable out of the way. We pottered about, clear of the slip, while Trev moved the truck and parked it, then walked down the slip again. Pete took us in and picked him up, then reversed us out again, until we were clear of all the moored boats. There, he let us drift while he and Trev balanced the boat, fastening the cylinders down along the centre-line, and putting the small stuff into lockers, out of the way.

"O.K. it's like a mill-pond, so you can ride the centre seat, or the side tubes, or stand and hang onto the A frame!" Trev advised. "Whatever suits. Just make sure you are hanging on to something, because we're going to fly, in a minute!" We pottered along. Two of the three engines burbling quietly, the other shut down, until we were clear of all the wind-surfers, canoeists, and

143

other mobile obstructions, then he opened them up.

The two burbling Mercury's bellowed, pressing the stern down, and the bow up, then we leaped up onto the plane and were skimming the surface like an escaped racing car. Trev throttled back to about seventy-five percent, which was plenty to keep us whizzing along, the occasional wave slapping at the tubes, to be flung up as spray. As the bay opened out, Pete called on the radio, telling the Holyhead harbour control who we were, where we were going, and from where, what for, and how many on board. When he received an acknowledgement, he switched to the general calling channel, 16, with the volume set fairly high, in case anyone wanted to speak to us, then sat on a side tube, one hand on a grab-line. George had taken a seat on the centreline fore-and-aft bench seat, so I took the other side tube, to counter-balance Pete's weight, more or less. Trev was finicking with the trim controls, until he had us set at the most efficient angle, and once we were a mile or so out, headed us west, to take us round South Stack light-house, and Holyhead harbour.

144

The big inflatable, with it's hard bottom hull, Trev called it a R.I.B. or Rigid-hulled Inflatable, settled into a rhythm, four or five small pitches, over the long, shallow rollers, then a bigger one, which made it seem to fly through the air for a distance, before splashing down in a puff of spray, and then repeating.

"Is everyone comfortable?" he called, over the roaring wind, and the engine noise.

"How fast are we going?" George asked, a silly grin on her face, as she rode the swoops, hands on her knees.

"About sixty-two knots indicated on the G.P.S." Trev replied with a grin.

"Watch out for traffic cops!"

"Not even the Navy has anything this fast!" Pete said, "Are you putting the radar on?"

"No, what for?"

"True." He started crooning, over the general noise, "My eyes adored you, though I never laid a hand on you, my eyes adored you!" He admired George's curves as he sang tunelessly.

"Is it something he suffers from?" She asked, of nobody in particular.

145

"No, he doesn't suffer, WE do!" Trev responded.

"Heathens, no taste, that's your trouble!"

"And you couldn't carry a tune if it was tied up in a bin-bag, so stop distressing our guests!"

An extra-large roller launched us up into the air, the engines howling as the props came out of the water.

'YEEE-HAAA!" Pete was suspended in mid-air, only his grab-line keeping him in contact with the boat, then he nearly bounced over the side, when we landed, helped by a sharp swerve when Trev put the helm over an inch or so, for fun.

"MYYY EYESSS ADORED YOU…"

"Anyone brought any cotton-wool?"

"Ah, you're still with us then, Vinny, I thought maybe you'd gone looking for Huey, and fallen off!"

"Who'se Huey?" George asked.

"Oh, the innocence of youth," Pete leaned over the side, and mimed vomiting, with sound effects.

"Oh!"

"On second thoughts, who's innocent?" Pete asked, then in time to the pitching of the boat, called, "oh, oh, oh, OH, OH,

AAAAAHHHH!"

"There aren't any pheasants out here, only Cormorants" Vince reminded him.

"Your pheasant, in the pink and blue feathers, is!"

"I don't make that noise!" George argued.

"Notice - she doesn't deny making A noise, and someone was, a female someone, in, or out of, a tent very near to ours, and somehow I can't see it being the old couple in the other tent next to us."

"Perhaps not, but I can say, with a clear conscience, that there was nobody in MY bed, last night!"

"Then you must have been in Vinnie's!"


"Shucks, li'l me wouldn't do a naughty thing like that!" George faked a passable American mid-western accent.

"Two consenting adults, and I can't hear him rushing to defend your honour!"

"Ah, well, if I could get a word in edgeways!"

"Did someone squeak? Squeak now, or forever hold your peace!"

147

"I'd rather hold someone else's, it's more fun!" she exclaimed, then timed a change of seating position between flying leaps, so she was perched on the side tube directly in front of Vinnie, then squirmed backwards against him. He put an arm round her waist as we leaped off another roller.

"My waist is a bit higher up than that!" she repositioned his hand, "And it isn't that high, either!" She said, a few seconds later.

"It's hard to tell through a rubber suit!" Vince claimed.

"Excuses!"

"Are you two having fun, over there?" Pete called across.

"Someone is!' Trev replied.

'Oh, oh, oh," Pete began, timed to coincide with the boat's movements, like before.

"Oh shut up!" George demanded.

"AAAAAAH!" Three male voices chorused.

Chapter Nine.

Wrong Number.

I pottered about all day, half-heartedly going through the domestic routine. The thing at the front of my mind was the decision I had to make, to choose between boring old meat-head, or James, and his child, Joe. My absent husband still hadn't come back, or 'phoned, so I knew he was in no hurry. I was hesitating, ducking the issue, nibbling around the edges of the choice, frightened of losing what I had, for what might be, and scared to go for it. When I realized that I had already vacuumed the living room carpet twice, and was starting again, I threw the contraption into the cupboard, booted the cat out, and made a cuppa. While the kettle boiled, I clicked on the t.v, ready for my favourite soap-opera. The little white dot flashed across the screen, as normal, and then the colours faded in, without the red. He'd promised to fix that. The sound came on with a fizz and a splat, from the speakers as I put the hot water into the cup containing coffee powder and sugar. Taking a few biscuits with me, I sat as the titles rolled, and cursed, as they'd moved the slot forward for bloody cricket. I'd missed finding out what-, well, never mind, I changed channels to B.B.C. 1, but that was showing Thomas Tank Engine. B.B.C. 2 was some politicians waffling on about how the other party messed up. Channel Four was showing the bloody cricket. Sometimes, the set picks up H.T.V., but not today, it just showed a smeary mess of zig-zag lines and snowstorms. The very hissy audio sounded like cricket - in Welsh. I sighed, climbed out of the chair, put the Thornbirds video into the v.c.r, and sat again, switched the t.v. to channel six, where the video was tuned in, then realized I'd left the remote on top of the tape rack. I heaved out of the chair again, and went for it, pressed 'play' as I regained my chair, and nothing happened. I pressed play again. Nothing, fast forward, fast back, eject, nothing! Perhaps, -- I opened the back of the remote, and saw an empty space where the batteries should be, and only then remembered that I had borrowed them for my radio. That, of course, was on the window-ledge. I re-borrowed

150

and re-fitted them into the remote, then tried 'play' again. The video chugged and whirred, the picture steadied, then the bloody 'phone started ringing! I stopped the tape, climbed out of the chair again, and went to the 'phone, on the window-ledge by the radio. I lifted the receiver, just as the person on the other end gave up, and cleared the line. I hung about for a minute or so, in case they tried again, but my feet were aching, so I went back to the chair, and the video, only to find I'd left the remote by the 'phone. I recovered it, pressed 'play' as I returned to my chair, and the bloody thing ejected the tape. I had to get up again, to push it back in. Then I had to chuck the cat off the chair, because I nearly sat on the flea-bitten creature. Finally, I could watch the t.v. I pressed 'play' yet again, and the picture went green. The various trailers and adverts for coming programmes trailed across the screen while the colour came back on again, then as the theme music began, the 'phone rang again.

"Is that the railway station?" A tremulous old male voice asked

"No, it bloody isn't! You've got the last two digits crossed up again, you old duffer!" I snapped, then bashed the receiver

151

down again. Next door's hot water pipe began hammering, in the wall cavity, then the 'phone rang again. "Oh, er, I think I've done it again!" the same old voice, who often got his numbers wrong, said.

I'd just got settled again, when the 'phone rang again.

"No, it's NOT the bloody railway station!" I yelled at the microphone.

"Oh, I'm glad to hear it, maybe it's the bus-station?"

"Oh! Sorry, Joan, I keep getting duff calls, today, and I'm getting weary of it!"

"So I gathered, you sound a bit frayed around the edges!"

"I am a bit, are you coming over?"

"No, I'm going into town to look for a dress, do you fancy coming along, for a change of scenery?"

"No, I'm not in the mood, but you're welcome to drop in, later, if you fancy."

"Perhaps. I really called to see if you've made up your mind, but I sense that you haven't yet admitted to yourself that you have, if you follow that. Shall I pick the brat up from school for you, as I'm already halfway there?"

"It was a bit convoluted, but I get the drift. And, if you don't mind?"

"See you later."

"Bye".

I'd barely put the thing down, when it rang again, and the tremulous voiced old duffer said that he'd called to apologize for calling. Daft old sod. Fancy ringing to apologize for ringing! The cat was eating something on the freshly vacuumed carpet, making a pile of crumbs, and I discovered that it had pinched my biscuits. "I hope they make you sick!" I said, and then realised, if it was, I'd have to clean it up! The animal glared at me, stretched, gulped, heaved, made a series of 'glop' noises, then chucked its guts up, all over the trailing extension socket I'd been using for the cleaner. There was a bright blue flash, and everything electrical went off - just as the door-bell bing-bonged. At least that worked, because it was battery-powered. When I opened the door, He was standing there, with a posy of flowers in one extended hand. The odour of burned cat-puke, and burned cat, drifted out of the doorway past me, where I stood, in tatty clothes, and a very second-hand hair-do.

153

"I do hope I haven't caught you at a bad moment!"He said, after an instant's hesitation.

That did it. I totally lost it, and laughed and cried at the same time. He put his arm round me, and guided me to a chair, then cast a sweeping glance around the room.

"Sit there for a minute, while I get a few things from the car." He said.

When he came back in., with a tool-kit, and a flashlight, he tried the light-switch, but of course, nothing happened. "Alright, then, where's the fuse box?"

I couldn't speak, as I was too busy sobbing, but managed to point at it, and the toasted cat.

"Ah, I see!" He followed the cable for the extension, and unplugged it from the wall socket, then went to the fuse-box, and rummaged about inside. With a pop, the tripped breaker re-set, and the electrical goods woke up again. He switched off the video and the t.v. before inspecting the cat. "No, I suspect that that one was number nine!" he sighed, sadly. "Pussy is no more."

"Not my cat, - his!" I spluttered.

"Then why the tears?"

"It's, - it's, - this, everything, nothing. Oh, I don't know! It just IS!" I wailed.

"Life, The Universe, and Everything!" he quoted. I'd seen the line in one of Vince's daft books, somewhere, and recalled it, as James said it.

"Yes! Oh God, what a mess!"

"What, this? No, it's soon fixed. I'll open a window to let the odour out, it is a little potent, close up."

"And I've spent all morning cleaning, too." I wailed, as the 'phone rang again

"Ello, is that the rail—"

"No, It's me, again, you blithering –!" I put the thing down before I shamed myself with improper use of Anglo-Saxon words.

James had been looking in cupboards, and came up with the dust-pan and brush.

"Oh, leave it!" I said, "I'll sort it out, later! Just throw the bloody cat into the bin!"

"No, I'll sort it out now, before the guck dries into concrete."

155

"But what if – "

"Now, stop fretting. I am capable!"

"I know, - It's just – just--!"

"Well, it's done, now. I cannot do very much about the smell, though. Let me just bring this other chair over to where you are." He did, and sat on it. "Now, what was all that about?"

"Oh, hell! I don't know! Everything just happened at once, and I couldn't cope." I gulped a bit, and fished around for a tissue to mop my streaming eyes with. "I wasn't crying, well, yes I was, but I was laughing, too, because the cat had stolen a biscuit, and I told it to be sick, and it was, and the 'phone rang, and the doorbell rang, and the fuse blew, and the cat blew up and… and…!" I trailed off, with a sob.

"Well," he said, "I was going to invite myself round for tea, but," he sniffed the air, "my appetite has been somewhat suppressed!"

I collapsed again, laughing, this time. "Would you prefer Whiskas, or Kit-e-Kat, on your toast?"

"I have a better idea," he said, "there's a nice-looking café just up the road, so repair your face, and I'll treat you to a sticky bun!"

"I'd like to, but Joe is due home from school, soon."

"Then we'll all go."

"But Joan is collecting him, and bringing him here!"

"Then we will take Joan as well, and make it into a party!"

"But – "


He wasn't going to give in. "This is where we came in! Go and put your face on, and change your top, that blouse has a blotch on it, where your mascara has dripped off your nose."

I looked down, and sure enough, there were some dirty marks on the top of the 'shelf', so I went, and followed orders. I was just adding the finishing touches, when the doorbell bing-bonged, a key rattled in the lock, and Joan let herself in.

"Hello!" She called, "It's only me!" She slammed the door shut, "I thought I'd – ah – er – Oh! Hello! I'm ah –. " That was the first time I've known her to be stuck for words.

"I presume that you are Joan? Delighted. I'm James Lancaster-Smytthe, with a hyphen, and two tee's."

"Off for a round of golf, then?" Joan recovered quickly

157

"Yes, Joan Willis. I'm pleased to meet you, too!" She raised her hand, palm down, and he started to stoop, reaching with his own, intending to raise her hand to his lips, but as they touched, they both jumped, as though electrocuted, reminding me of the damn cat.

"Oh!"

"Ow!"

"You are powerful!"

"You, too! What is your field?"

"Predictions, Medium, and Healer.' Joan stated, 'You?"

"You out-class me, then. I have pretensions of Healing, and Divining."

"There's something else, too. I got a brief flash, but couldn't identify it. It needs bringing forward, and developing."

"Maybe." He seemed guarded, uncertain. Joe was sitting quietly on the floor, listening to them, big-eyed, as though he understood what they were saying.

"You seem to be getting along alright!" I re-entered the room.

"Yes thanks," Joan took his hand again, "but you needn't

158

worry. I'm not about to pinch your boy-friend!"

"Good. I won't need to chase you off with a carving knife, then!" She has a reputation for suffering from round heels.

"Not this time!" It wasn't the first time she'd 'fallen'! "We wouldn't get on - - Ah! I know what it is. You died, about ten years ago, didn't you?"

"You've got it." James acknowledged, "Nine years, eleven months, give or take a day or so. I was sent back, to finish a task. I just haven't found what it is, yet!"

"That sounds like religion." I said.

"No, not the way you mean, sitting in a miserable, draughty shed, for two hours every Sunday, and to hell with the world for the rest of the week. You have no need to be a pulpit-pounder, to believe in something bigger than us."

"That's ambiguous."

"Deliberately! Now, we were going to visit that café, for a sticky bun. Would you care to join us, Joan?"

"No, thanks, I've some shopping outside in my car that I to get into the freezer. Another time, perhaps?"

"Certainly."

"Let me find my key, so I can get back in, later." I said, and went in search of my bag

"Don't forget to close the window, too." He reminded me, as he saw Joan out.

"Yes!" Joan called, from outside, "What did you burn? It's not like you!"

"The cat!"

"What?"

"It's a long story. I'll tell you next time."

"O.K, see you!"

She banged her car door shut, and rattled off.

Chapter ten.

Moelfre.

As we bounced and skittered around the headland with the glass-windowed coastguard lookout on the top, Pete called up on the radio and told the Station that we were in Moelfre bay, would be mooring soon, and would call again when we set off on the return journey. Trev turned us in towards the jagged cliffs, and eased back on the power. As we came off the plane, the R.I.B. slowed sharply, and settled into the rollers. "Its a hundred metres deep here," he called, "It must come up fast, closer in."

"It doesn't look like a nice place to be in an onshore blow." I said, as I studied the jagged rocks. Even now, in these mild conditions, the little rollers were mashing themselves into white foam on them.

"Did anyone survive?" George asked. I'd 'briefed' her on the 'Charter', on the way.

"I can't remember if I read it in the article. I shouldn't think so. Is that the buoy?" I pointed to the left.

"Got it!" Trev swung us round, "Get the hook, Pete."

"Right."


We anchored up above the wreck marked by the buoy, while Trev nursed his engines, letting them cool down gently before switching them off and allowing the silence to descend again. From here we could hear the steady 'crump'- 'crump'- of the waves hitting the rocks. Pete rummaged in a locker, pulled out a few short lines with snap-hooks on both ends, clipped one end of each to one of the 'A' frame rails, then tossed the other ends over the side, allowing them to trail in the water. Then he hauled a light ladder from under the bench seat, and rigged that over, too, so we could get back into the boat after the dive, without a struggle. "When you come up, clip your bottle onto a hook," he responded to George's puzzled look, "Then, when you've climbed aboard, you can pull it up!"

Trev was watching the water, "The current on top looks like about a knot, northwards." He glanced at the Lowrance depth-finder, "and the bottom's about thirteen metres."

Pete clipped the 'A' flag, which means 'Divers in the water', to a line, and hauled it up the stubby mast at the top of the 'A' frame., then started sorting his diving kit out.

George was checking various pipes and hoses on her Stab. Jacket, then turned her pillar-valve on while I was fishing around obscenely between my legs, trying to catch the jock-strap for my A.B.L.J. Trev caught it, and passed it through. "Thanks." I took it, and clipped it into it's receptacle under the inflation cylinder.

"Shit!" Pete swore, "My 'O' ring has a nick in it! Where's the spares box, Trev?"

"Ah! How does, - in the truck, sound?"

"Oh, bugger! This one's leaking!"

"I thought you checked them, earlier?"

"I did. It must have been damaged when we were loading up."

"If you look in my dive-bag," I said, balanced on one knee, with my cylinder half-on, "you'll find some in a plastic butty box, and some neoprene glue, too."

"In here?" Pete held up a box.

163

"No, that's butties! In the smaller one!"

"Ah, got it!"

"Will you – " George asked, so I held her cylinder up for her, while she slipped her arms through the straps, and tugged them tight, then fastened the waist-belt.

"I've got my contents gauge stuck on something, can you reach it?"

She tugged and pulled carefully "No, it's caught under the back-pack, you'll have to take it off, and start again."

Eventually, we were all sorted, and untangled, and sitting on the side-tubes, two each side, waiting for the last bits and pieces to be arranged.

"Is everyone ready?" Trev asked.

We all made O.K. signs, then Trev gave a 3, 2, 1, countdown with his fingers, and we all rolled backwards into the water.

I hung there, three-quarters upside down, while the cloud of bubbles dissipated and the first shock of cold water subsided, and then looked around. Trev and Pete were already on their way down, while George hung in mid-water a few feet away, readjusting a fin which had been dislodged on something. After a moment, she had it fixed, looked around, saw me waiting, and flashed an o.k. which I returned, then pointed down. She rolled forwards and zoomed off, her exhaust bubbles rattling past me in bursts, as she breathed. Either her fins were more efficient, or she was putting more effort in, as I couldn't catch her. I trudged down, behind, yawning and puffing, trying to get a Eustachian tube to clear, my left ear is always a bit slow at first. On the bottom, the visibility was somewhere around twenty feet, in a sort of milky haze of suspended particles. All that was to be seen, apart from George's pert bottom, was a tangled heap of big boulders, all devoid of any marine growth, indicating that every storm churned them all up, thus giving a clue to the strength of the water movement. George was rummaging under a big boulder, with a gap beneath like a door-less car opening - she was pushed in as far as she could reach, her air cylinder jammed up against the rock. I hoped it didn't move, or she would be squashed like an ant with an elephant standing on it. Trev, or was it Pete, loomed up, over the block, saw our bubbles, and came across, to make an arms open, "Where is it?" gesture. I shrugged. Then Pete, or was it Trev, joined us, and made a 'follow me' sign, so I tugged George's leg, until she backed out of her cave, and looked around. I repeated the 'follow me' and when she did, went after the other two, who were disappearing in the gloom. They led us fifty or sixty feet, to a large steel plate that was nearly two inches thick, and curved gently. It looked like a hull-bottom plate, to me. Pete, or Trev, confirmed it, when he prodded it, then slapped his rump. The plate was resting at an angle on more huge boulders, which rested on huge boulders, which rested on huge boulders. It was like a three-dimensional maze of little gaps and crannies, leading down into the tangle, with no bottom ground visible.

The Royal Charter had been carrying Gold, along with the gold-miners, so I envisaged a piece of gold and wormed my way in, under, and through, the gaps, looking for yellow, because nothing grows on gold, and it doesn't discolour, or tarnish. All the rocks were of a yellowish hue, and the smaller they were, the yellower they were! I backed out, and tried another likely looking opening, next to one with a plume of bubbles exiting, at regular intervals. It took me under the edge of the plate, then under a boulder the size of a house, which was heaped up on a pile of boulders like double-decker buses, which were piled on top of cars, which were piled on top of armchairs, which were - -,

That was where I got stuck, and spent ten minutes squirming out again. All the rocks were yellow! I was starting to feel cold, and paused to check my contents gauge. I was down to eighty atmospheres, so it was time to start keeping an eye on it as we weren't very deep. My watch showed we had been down fourty-two minutes already! Time certainly flies when you are having fun. I looked around, and found two plumes of bubbles close by. So I wormed in behind the first one, and grabbed a slim leg, giving it a squeeze, and then backed out, again. When George emerged, I waved my console, and held up seven fingers. She O.K.d and checked her own, then showed me eight and a half before ducking in to where the other bubbles were issuing from. She backed out again, with Pete, or Trev, in tow, and tapped her gauges, then pointed 'up'. He glanced at his, then made a few hand-signs, which when he repeated them a bit more slowly, told me that one had already gone up, leaving us three down. We started the journey up, in a group. I was feeling a bit deflated, having psyched myself up to finding a gold bar! Silly, I know, but - -.

George finned up, a bit faster than us two, watching her dive computer, which would warn her if she needed to stop, or slow down, while us two, with 'steam-powered' pressure gauges, just ambled up, slower than our smallest bubbles, which the BSAC manual states is good procedure.

Pete was already in the boat, and was helping George by lifting her cylinder in while she climbed the ladder, when we surfaced.

"Has either of you got any air left?" Pete asked

"Not much." Trevor replied.

I had about fifty, and said so.

"That'll do, if I can use it. I just need to zip back down for a minute?"

"Sure, I'll leave it on the hook, for when you're ready." I

said, between mouthfuls of seawater. Trev ducked under the boat, threw his fins up, over the tube, and then climbed the ladder, still kitted up.

"My demand valve jammed open!" Pete explained. "So I left my weight-belt on the anchor, I just need to get it, because it isn't fastened on, I didn't have time to hang around!"

I shrugged out of my cylinder and clipped it to a hook, while Pete put his mask and fins on, then rolled over the side, just as I put my weight onto the ladder. The R.I.B. lurched and swayed as his weight left it, and mine came on, tipping Trev off-balance. He fell over the side again, with a mighty splash. George staggered, but clung to the centre console. Pete bobbed to the surface, and swam over to my cylinder.

"Do you want my weight-belt, as well?" I asked him.

"No, I'll get down, with a bit of thrashing." He slipped an arm into my cylinder harness, and then undid the snap-link.

Trevor had a better idea, and when he'd climbed aboard again, gave Pete a lump of concrete, with a line attached, which he kept taut, to stop it crashing to the seabed.

"Use the spare anchor, I'll pull it back up when you come

up again."

"Why didn't I think of that? I was going to climb down the anchor line!" Pete put my demand valve into his mouth, adjusted his lips, took a firm hold of the concrete, and waved bye-bye. Trev let go, and the line whizzed out from the coil by his feet. It took about three seconds to make the journey.

While we were messing about, George had sorted her kit out, bagged it up, and was trying to decide which fins were mine, which Trev's, and which were spares that had been pulled out of the locker. Trev was watching Pete's bubbles. "He's on the way up." He took hold of the 'anchor' rope, and heaved it back up, puffing a little. I helped him heave it up over the tube, and put it onto the deck, then leaned over to take my cylinder off Pete, when he surfaced.

When everyone was settled, I said, "Anyone fancy a sarnie, and a cuppa?"

Three voices chorused an affirmative, so I said, "Ladies first," then offered the box to Pete, for a moment, then to George, who laughed at the tease. She hadn't forgotten the camp-site conversation when we had invited her to accompany

"What were you struggling with, under that rock?" George asked Trev, in between bites of sandwich.

"Glad you asked!" He brandished a corroded lump of something, "What do you make of this?"

"Well, ah – It's not gold!" George picked it up off the deck, and turned it over in her hands, studying it. "Oh! I see! It's a flintlock pistol, or was, anyway!"

"I found these, just now." Pete put three greenish disks onto the seat. "Somebody must have found them, previously, and forgotten to pick them up."

Trev picked one up, peered at it, rubbed it with a thumb, then chuckled, "You've found three two-pence coins!"

"All I found was a pile of rocks, and a well-mashed coke can!" I added. "According to the magazine article, the 'Charter' is on a sand bottom."

"There's no sand around here, that I saw."

"Nor me."

George just shrugged. "I found this. I thought it was an eyelet, at first, but it's too soft." She held up a small yellow

171

circle, with about an eighth of an inch of thickness, and the same in width. Trev took it from her fingers, and studied it, then gave it back, wrapping her hand round it. "That was someone's wedding band! Look after it, it weighs about an ounce!"

"Perhaps I'll have a use for it, later on." George said, her eyes on me.

I reached over, took her hand, kissed it, and said, "Maybe. I can't make any promises, yet."

"Well, kiddies, shall we go, or we'll be out here in the dark." Trev started the engines burbling, and indicated that Pete should bring the ladder, and snap-lines, in. When they were stowed, he took the weight off the anchor line so Pete could haul it up, then puttered us round, while he coiled the line and secured the anchor. Before we set off he called the Holyhead shipping control, and asked if they had co-ordinates for the 'Royal Charter'. They replied by saying that the wreck was buoyed.

"Not any more, the marker has drifted, and is in the middle of no-where!" Trev told them.

In a minute, they called us back, with a bearing from the

Moelfre coast-guard lookout, and a cross-bearing from the Northern headland, which had a well-defined point. When we took a bearing on these two places, we were well away from the supposed position. Trev motored us along one of the invisible lines, until the other one intersected it. The jagged lines of the bottom, on the Lowrance, gradually smoothed out,

"There's the sand!" he said, then circled around the area, until the Lowrance showed a sudden spike, with nothing but flat around it. "That must be it." He looked up. "We were a good two hundred yards north-west of the right place." He positioned us directly above the spike, then noted the readings on the G.P.S. by pressing a 'store' button. "'There! I can go right to it, next time!" He called the control again, and told them how far their buoy was off, and which direction.

While they were fiddling about, George whispered into my ear, "I could do with a pee!"


"Right, then, let's go!" Trev pointed us in the proper direction, and then pushed the throttles up, making the engines roar. Pete claimed his place on the side tube, and began singing –

"Bye, bye, Miss American Pie, drove my dinghy to the whatsit, but the whatsit was dry" - then added a rebel yell, as we became airborne, off the top of a large roller.

"Hmm," Trev mused, "It's getting a mite bumpy!" A minute or so later, we were launched again, then again, forcing him to ease back a little, on the throttles.

"Thanks for that!" George exclaimed, "Another jolt like that, and I'd have got soggy socks!"

"That's the beauty of a wet-suit." I said to her, "You can have a pee, and nobody notices, it just warms you up, and then drains away."

"Dirty sod!"

"But comfortable! Trev, are there any caves or something around here, the lady wants to powder her nose!"

"Ah, right. Hang on a few minutes longer. You want to get a wet-suit, then you can –. "

"I've already heard that one!"

"I know of a rock outcrop, about half a mile away, where we can find the necessary privacy, if you can wait that long." Trev turned us offshore about ten degrees, and peered ahead.

174

"The tide's on the rise, so they'll not be much above the water, sufficient, though, for the lady to hide behind one!"

"Is that it, about five degrees starboard?"

Trev slewed us round a bit more. "That's them." He throttled back, so we came off the plane, causing us to progress in a series of roller-coaster swoops, towards the foaming rocks. "You'll have to swim for it, there's nowhere to anchor, the rocks are the top of a peak, and the bottom is a hundred feet plus, more or less straight down. It might be an idea if Vinny went, too, to give you a hand out, them he can turn his back, or something, while we hold off, here, then when you come back, we can take it in turns to do the same."

"Why take it in turns?" Vince asked, "I can run a boat. Both of you hop over, and I'll pick you up, after."

"You never said!"

"You never asked me!"

Pete and Trevor looked at each other, "We didn't, did we! We just assumed -." Trev brought the R.I.B. to within twenty feet of the rocks, and then throttled back to the idle. "Over you go!"

George rolled backwards over the side tube, while Vince

just flicked his inboard leg over, and slid in, feet first. George was already scrambling out, she'd seen a crevice where she could climb up without assistance, so Vince just floated on his back, waiting for her.

Zips zipped, elastic stretched, then there was the familiar hissing, and sighs of relief. After which, the usual struggling into dry-bag noises, zips zipping, and so forth.

As she tugged the zip up, something attracted her eye, an unnaturally straight line, buried in the bladder-wrack and stringy algae. "Just a minute, Vince, there's something trapped in the rocks up here!" she called, and then cautiously scrambled, to see what it was.

"Are you decent?" Vince shouted back

"Always, come and see for yourself! I'd hardly go mountain-climbing with my pants round my knees!"

He didn't need a second invitation, although he didn't think she would be teasing, not with the other two waiting in the boat, and clambered up the same crevice she had used. From the rocks, he could see Pete in the water, a few feet from the boat, obviously rinsing his wet-suit through, having taken the easy option, and used the 'central heating' method. "What've you found?" he asked George.

"I'm not sure, it's a metal pipe, or something. It's too heavy to move, and it hasn't been here long, it's still clean."

Vince scrambled to where she was poking at something. As she had said, it was a bright metal bar, possibly stainless steel. On closer examination, it wasn't a bar, but a tube, with the end plugged by a screw-cap which required a three-pronged fitting to turn it. "Hey, Pete!" He called, "Come and see what you make of this!"

Pete scrambled up to where they were.

"There's an eye-bolt, here, in the middle, it must be a hoisting point." Vince noted.

George had pushed more of the waterplants aside. "The other end has a screw in it, too."

Pete tried to lift one end, but couldn't shift it an inch.

"Hey, you lot! It's my turn, or do I go off and leave you?" Trev called.

"Yeah, come on, or we'll be out in the dark. It won't wash off before we can come back with some lifting gear." Pete scrambled down the nearest rock, and leaped into the sea. Vince and George followed closely behind, and nearly beat him to the R.I.B.

Back on board, waiting for Trev, Vince said, "I thought you were planning a run to the Skerries, tomorrow."

"We were." Pete agreed, "but if this swell keeps up it will be a bumpy ride, and we might give it a miss."

Trevor clambered back into the R.I.B. making it sway. "Go on then, Vin, you said you could drive, so grab the wheel, we want to go that way!" He pointed in the general direction of West.

"Hold onto your knickers!" Vince took the helm, then selected forward drive, nudged the right throttle up. then turned the wheel to port, so the R.I.B. turned in it's own length, facing away from the rocks, before matching up the throttles and pushing them forward together as he span the wheel straight. The Mercury's roared, as he blasted the R.I.B. onto the plane, then eased back on the power, and then took them round in a big circle, onto course, before thumbing his nose at Trev, who was looking astonished.

"Maybe he CAN drive!" Pete suggested, as he claimed his usual spot on the side tube. Trevor took the opposite side, leaving the centre bench to the couple. George snuggled up to Vince's back, and wrapped her arms round him, before nibbling his ear, and whispering improper suggestions.

"Now behave!" he cautioned, "There isn't much we can do, bundled up in rubber suits!"

"No, but I'm thinking of after!" Her hand began exploring.

"You're wasting your time, the rubber's too thick!" Vince wriggled uncomfortably, showing that it wasn't, albeit very restricting!


When we got back to Trearddur, Trev let Vince take them into the marina, and asked him to ease in to the beach. Just before they grounded, he leaped out and trotted round to the truck, which he unlocked, then climbed in and started the engine, in a haze of blue smoke, then drove down the slipway to meet us. Vince inched the R.I.B. up close, allowing Pete to tie the bow rope to a strong-point, before the used kit was transferred to the back of the truck. Trev clambered round carrying the painter of the pram dinghy, and then when the gear was transferred, he reversed the R.I.B. away from the slip, dragging the dinghy into the water in the process. He then took the boat to its mooring, shut everything down, and puttered back to the slip, sitting in the tin bathtub.

In the back of the truck, Pete had the kettle going, and in a few minutes, everyone had a steaming cup of something in their hands, to help drive out the apres-dive chill, then Pete and Trev got busy, turning out corned-beef wedges for each of us.

"This is the life!" George sighed, as the protein and heat took hold, "Servants to wait on you, hand and foot!"

"Just wait until you get the bill!" Trevor quipped, "Then you might not be quite so pleased!"

"Hey!" Vince had seen something. "On that house gate-post, there's a sign advertising diving air when they get a compressor installed, in the next few days. That could be handy, it'll save a drive all the way round to Soldiers Point every time you want a fill."

"Yes, it would!" George agreed.

"While we're on the subject, would you three like me to

run the empties round, for a re-fill, once we get sorted out?" Vince asked.

"Are you thinking of that tumble-down wooden shed, round the back of the Raven's Point camp shop?" Trev asked

"No, not there. I mean the newish dive centre, round past the Scimitar pub, by the old slate quarry."

"I didn't know about that one! What does he charge for a fill?"

"Pound a fill for a standard bottle, and one-fifty for a giant single, or a twin-set."

"That sounds reasonable." Trev nodded, "I'll charge you the same, and save you the drive round!"

"You have your own compressor?"

"Right here, under the seat! It'll blow four bottles up to 2000 psi, in an hour."

"Tested and o.k.ed three weeks ago." Pete added, with a grin.

"It's a deal. It'll save me a pound in petrol! Two dives for the price of one!"

"I should have said one-fifty a go!" Trev groaned.

"To change the subject," Pete said, "I wonder if that Scouse nasty found his keys?"

"I wouldn't bet on it, not in that sludge!"

"I wouldn't be too worried. If a Granada has locks like a Cortina, anything will work!" Vince added.

"Keep your eyes peeled for a few days, in case he and his pals come looking for revenge."

"If they're up-wind, we'll smell them coming!" Vince said, making them all chuckle.

"Seriously, though, watch out, Scouse is a nasty piece of work, not the kind to meet in a dark alley." Pete warned.

"It might be an idea if we stick together for the duration, in case he's got some more pals. I can't see 'one-arm' getting up to much, for a few weeks." Vince laughed.

"He might hit you with his plaster cast!" George responded.

"Pete and I'll manage, and Vince seems to be handy, but I wouldn't want them to catch you on your own, Blondie." Trev looked perturbed, "He might try for more than carving his initials on your anatomy!" He stood, "and, with that sobering thought, shall we go and see if the camp-site is still there?"

"When we've changed into normal rags, I'll nip over and settle up." Vince said.

"Nie problemo." Pete.demonstrated his linguistic skills.

"Eh?"

"I think he was speaking Russian, showing off again. He means, - no problem!"

"Oh! Nicht sprechen sie Italiano, Monsewer!"

"Oh, god, don't start him off!"

"Seig Heil!" Vince snapped his heels, then gave a 'Harvey Smith' salute.

Pete faked a round-house punch at Vince's midriff, causing him to jump back, miss his footing, and fall out of the back of the truck, with a yell.

George looked out, to see where he had fallen. "Quick, drive on, before he gets back in!"

"Gee thanks, but you're too late." Vince climbed back in, "That rock was hard!"

"They often are!" George shrugged, "especially when you try to fly through one at five hundred miles an hour!"

183

'Who did that?' Vince asked.

"Didn't I say? My ex-fiance."

"Ouch! I suppose that makes him very ex?"

"Very. Until last night, it hurt me to even talk about it, but now, it's funny! It's strange, but all of a sudden I can't think what he looked like. I can't picture his face any more."

"Part of the healing process, I suppose," Vince offered, "Five hundred, there are no civilian planes that can go that fast, are there? So he must have been R.A.F."

"He was." George didn't expand on it.

Chapter eleven.

Mick and Sid.


I didn't know where Harry had gone. I'd seen Sid go skydiving after being frightened by a Tesco bag, the wimp. I was out of it for a while, after a groin-ful of boot. That left Joe on his own, for now. That was when I realized that 'whoozit' wasn't alone after all. I'd thought he would be a pushover, but he had put me down in less than two seconds, while still keeping Sid on the hop. Christ, the sod was fast. As the pain eased a bit, I managed to suck in a bit of air, and then I felt like chucking up. Joe was yelling at someone to let him go, and when I squirmed round a bit, I saw that the gorilla had hold of him by the shoulder. 'Whoozit' was lucky, because Joe's a nasty bastard when he's angry. He was angry now, and high on something, too. He must have got a snort from somewhere. After a bit of chit-chat, the gorilla threw Joe at me. Joe started to pick me up, then changed his mind, and pulled my gun. He stood there, waving it like a flag, instead of using it. I yelled at him, in a whisper, because that's all the air I had available, to shoot the buggers, but someone stuck a knife or something in him, then as the gun fired, 'whoozis' and the gorilla hit him several times, each. After a couple of minutes more, I could sit up, and realized that they had all gone. "C'mon, Joe, give me a hand up, and let's get out of here, before the – too late, they're here."

P.C. Plod glared down his nose at me, from under his conical helmet, then moved over to Joe, took a quick look, felt for a pulse, then got busy on his talking lapel badge.

Horrible slurping and squelching noises came drifting up, from over the sea wall, and then Sid's head appeared. A long, blue-sleeved arm shot out, one finger crooked, and a stentorian Welsh accented voice said "OY! YEW! COME HERE!"

Sid, on the verge of ducking back down, obeyed, squelched up the last few steps, and said "What?"

"What do you know about this 'ere body?"

"Wot body?" He looked, as well as sounded, stupid. "Me?

Nuffin' 'Onest! I dropped me keys, an' I bin lookin' fer 'em." He waved a glob of mud with slivers of metal embedded in it.

P.C. Plod moved quickly to position himself upwind of Sid. "Do you know him?" He pointed at me.

"No, should I?"

"That depends. You'd better stick around, for now."

"Wo'for?"

"Because I said so! And you," he pointed at me again, "You're nicked!" then said all the usual yap about taking things down - which makes you want to say 'knickers', but you never do.


A meat-wagon screeched to a halt a few yards away, then the crew piled out and examined Joe. After a minute, one of them said there wasn't much they could do with him, except take him to the morgue He'd been killed twice, by a broken neck, and some kind of knife, which was still embedded in his chest. Added to which was a broken jaw, and a possible broken wrist, not that they mattered, any more.

"O.K. Leave it there for the Forensics boyo's. There's

nothing else here for you, unless you have a cure for crushed goolies."

"No. Best thing to get for that, is finding a nice, willing, cuddly woman who will gently caress them better!"

"Not much chance of that, where he's going!"

"Well, you can always round up 'Night-shift' Natalie, from her usual patch by the dockyard gates!"

"Now, there's a thought. There's not much SHE doesn't know about men's anatomy, not that this thing is a man!"

The meat-wagon crew moved off, to make room for the mobile cellblock.

"Right. Mud pie! In you get, next to your pal Castrato."

"Oo's 'e?"

"Your pal with no nuts."

"Oh, 'im! Don' know 'im."


A Range-Rover whined up on its knobbly tyres, closely followed by a Transit van, its rear windows blacked out and barred. Out of the Range-Rover climbed a big ego that was attached to a little man, who dusted off his pants, picked a fleck of fluff off his jacket, tweaked his creases, fiddled his tie straight, then perched his cap exactly centrally and level on his head. He carried a thin rattan cane in his hand, which he constantly slapped against his thigh when he spoke, for punctuation and emphasis, as though riding a horse. He listened as P.C. Plod made his report, then strutted over to look at the remains of Joe, then came to examine us. He got one whiff of Sid's perfume, and backed away hastily. P.C. Plod said that I was charged with making lewd gestures in public, namely clutching repeatedly at my genitals, while Sid was accused of offensive behaviour and appearance, until they found something better.

"O.K. Take them away." Brass-hat decided.

P.C. Plod started to climb into the back with us, then changed his mind, banged the doors shut, and got in with the driver instead. We heard the driver grousing that he should have brought the drunk-truck, instead of this one, as it was easier to hose out, after!

We ended up at Bangor nick. Sid was marched off, and I didn't see him again. I was 'escorted', in an arm-lock, to an interview room with bloodstains on the floor and table. There were two chairs on one side of the table, and a wooden bench that was screwed to the floor, on the other. Guess which side I got to sit. And not on the padded chairs, either! A Gestapo gorilla sat in with me, taking one of the padded chairs, from the comfort of which he commenced the 'devastating stare' routine. From time to time, other faces peeked in, but nothing else happened.

"Any chance of a cuppa, I'm gasping?"

"Grunt."

"Mind if I smoke, then?"

"Grunt."

"Give us a fag, then, I aint got any!"

"Grunt."

"Don't say much, do you?"

"Grunt."

"Can you say anything, except 'grunt'?"

"Shaddup."

"Ah, two words!"

Silence and the nuclear devastating stare greeted that.

Later, another face peered in, exited, came back, peered again, displayed an evil grin, then departed.

190

When they peeled Mick off, they took me down a corridor, into a tiled room. Tiles on the floor, tiles on the walls, steel door. There was no furniture. Plod let go, with a grimace.

"What's this, the persuasion room?"

Plod looked surprised, "No, kiddo, it's a shower room. Get that crap off you before you pollute the place. I'll find you an overall, or something, for after."

Sure enough, when I looked properly, a stubby chrome spout stuck out of the wall, just above head height, and there was a mixer tap on the wall below it. He left me to it, while I scraped the worst of the guck off, and flushed it down the drain, then tried to get the rest off me.

Plod came back, and hung an orange boiler-suit on the doorknob. "When you've done, stand outside, and someone will come and get you. Don't even think about wandering off, because you'll be on telly. Leave your clothes there, and we'll bag them up, for you."

"O.K. thanks." After Plod had gone, I realized there was no towel, so wiped myself dry with my hands when I'd finished dripping, and tried the overalls on for size. They proved to be a papery substance which began to dissolve where I was still wet, and they touched, which was not in many places, I think they were size xxxl. I ended up with turn-ups up to the crutch, which hung down to somewhere between my knees. The sleeves I had to roll up, as they wouldn't stay up, otherwise. The neck-hole was almost as wide as my shoulders. As instructed, I left my clothes in a gloopy heap, and then stood outside the door, looking pathetic in the clown-suit. I could hear two bod's having a hell of a row, behind a door somewhere. A drunk was singing incoherently, someone was yelling, over and over, "Lemme out! I din' do it!" A female was shrieking, "Bastard Coppers, I'm only earning a living!" and someone else was snoring. After a few minutes, Plod poked his head round a door, and indicated that I should join him in an adjacent room, which turned out to be a cell with a bench bed, a bog, and a blanket. "We'll have a cuppa for you in a few minutes. And if you don't mind waiting, we'll have your clothes cleaned and dried, then brought back to you."

"Thanks. There's my wallet, and my keys, in a pants pocket."

"Oh, right, we'll get someone to bring them to you, when we've cleaned them, so you can check the contents."

"There's a tenner, and my plastic, that's all."

"Right, then. We'll keep them safe for you."

"Thanks."

The interview room door crashed open and a Himmler lookalike strutted in. After a hard glare at me, he leaned against the wall. Another plod eased in round him, and put a portable cassette recorder onto the table, loaded two tapes in, and pressed the record button. Plod spoke, stating the time and date, identified himself as "P.C. 1437 Jones, Also present are Detective Inspector Jones 380, and P.C. Evans 1537." He must be the gorilla. I was cautioned again, then asked if I understood the caution.

"I'm sayin' nuffin' wivout me brief."

"Did you know, or have acquaintance with, the deceased, who's identity is yet to be established?"

"Nuffin."

"Were you involved with the fracas, which resulted in the

death of the unidentified person, to be known as John Doe, until his, ah, identity can be established?" The plod repeated himself.

"Nuffin, I said."

In that case, they had no option but to detain me, blah blah -.

"Can I have a cuppa tea?"

"Later, maybe."

The cell door crashed open, and a plod came in, bearing a cracked mug filled with some orange stuff, from which steam escaped. "Eere yare, Boyo!" he said. Then banged the door shut again on the way out. I sampled the contents, which proved to be well-stewed tea factory floor-sweepings, with a cob of sugar, and condensed milk. It tasted better than Holyhead harbour mud. It was definitely hotter, and less salty. The flavour, though, like the mud, left a lot to be desired.

Himmler Jones 380 crashed in, and slapped a clear plastic bag onto the table. "Do you recognize that?"

"Yeah, it's a bike chain!"

194

"Is it yours?"

"Nah, I ain't gorra bike."

"We'll see, it's going to forensics, in a minute." He signed to Jones 1437, who got busy with a fingerprint kit, and my fingers, assisted by the gorilla.

When they'd finished trying to unscrew my wrists, I said, "Can I 'ave a cloff, or summat?"

"Later." They left me with the gorilla for company, so I wiped my hands on the table, leaving some more black streaks on it.

Jones 1437 came in again, with a piece of paper, "Sign here!"

"Why?"

"It's a form saying you've asked for legal representation."

"I'm signin' nuffin' wivout me brief's seen it, first."

"You have to sign the form, to get a brief."

"I ain't signin'. Where's me brief."

"When you sign the form, we can get you one."

"Nah!"

P.C. Jones 1437 gave up, and left. While the door was

195

open, I could hear an electric typewriter thing clattering and whirring, then a voice said, "I thought I'd seen his mug-shot before, somewhere!" He sounded happy. Another voice said, "Just look at this lot, would you, boyo!"

First voice said, "He's a nasty bastard, alright!"

The machine started chattering again, then second voice said, "Oh, hell, the Specials want him!"

As the door banged to, behind Jones 1437, I heard someone calling for the Sarge to look at this, "-'cos the boyo we got is -."

Jones 380 poked his head in, nodded to the gorilla, and led us to another room, a cell. I was bundled in, and the door banged behind me. Keys rattled in the lock, and it went quiet. As it looked like I was here for the duration, I tested the plank bed for comfort.

The cell door opened, and a plod came in. "O.K. sonny, let's move to the interview room!" It was a command phrased as a request. We dog-legged across the passage, to a room with a table, two chairs, and a bench, plod and Brass-hat were occupying the chairs, so I got the bench.

"Interview time, date, blah, present are P.C. Jones 1437, Detective Sergeant Jones 380, and-?" he wig-wagged his eyebrows at me.

"Sid Walson, number one!"

"-and Mr Sid Walson." Jones 1437 reminded me that I'd been cautioned, and did I understand the caution? And did I want a legal representative present?

"Nah, I've done nuffin!"

"Right. You were found grovelling in the mud in Holyhead harbour. What were you doing there?"

"Is that a crime? Like I said, I dropped me keys, an' I went to find 'em."

"The marks in the mud were approximately thirty feet out from the base of the wall, you must have long arms!"

"Nah, they bounced funny, off somethin'!"

"Are these your keys? For the tape, I'm displaying item four."

"Looks like me keys, yeah."

"Item four consists of two small keys, similar to padlock or

197

locker keys, and a leatherette fob, on a spring-ring. I doubt if I could throw them thirty feet, yet you say they bounced?"

"Yeah!"

"On what did they bounce?"

"The wall, o' course!"

"The sea wall?"

"Well, there 'int no gardens there."

"At that point, the sea wall has some steps set into it, doesn't it?"

"Tha'ss how I got down, an' up again."

"The sea wall is undercut, along that stretch, to deflect any breakers back out, so there is nothing for the keys to have bounced on, or off."

"Well, they must have bounced on the steps, then."

"Let us get this straight, you are now saying that your keys bounced on the steps?"

"Yeah, they must've"

"Do you recall seeing a railing around the top of the steps?"

"You know there is, one of them pipe things."

198

"A tubular railing, on upright posts?"

"Summick like that, yeah."

"Just one railing?"

"Nah, two, or three, so kids can't fall through."

"And were you leaning on the top railing?"

"Yeah." Well, how do you lean on the bottom one?

"Doing what?"

"Eh? Oh, watchin' a seagull diggin' for worms."

"With your keys in your hand?"

"Yeah."

"And you dropped them?"

"Yeah, I told you."

"Can you explain how, in the mud, there was a deep depression, possibly caused by your body, in the prone position, arms and legs spread apart?"

"I slipped, an' fell."

"From the steps?"

"Yeah. They've got green slime on."

"How far down were you?"

"Near the bottom."

"Can you explain how you managed to fall ten feet out from, and twenty feet along from, the steps?"

"I must'a fell funny!"

"Like the keys bounced funny?

"Yeah."

"Might I suggest that you fell backwards, from near the top step, the location, and depth of the depression indicate such?"

"Nah."

"Or, perhaps, you jumped, because someone was shooting at you?"

"Nah!"

"You said that there are railings at the top of the steps?"

"Er, yeah."

"It is a matter of record that the railings in that area have been removed for repair, following storm damage a fortnight ago. There was a temporary safety fence of plastic mesh tape in position by the steps."

"Yeah, so?"

"You claim to have been leaning on the railings when you dropped your keys."

200

"Yeah."

"So you dropped your keys at least fifteen days ago?"

"Nah, today."

"So you dropped your keys, while leaning on a railing that isn't there! When you came up the steps, this morning, and were told to sit next to another person, in the van, did you drop this item, item six?"

"Nah, not mine. I aint gotta bike."

"You know what it is, then?"

"I'm not fick!"

"Do you mind if we take samples of your fingerprints?"

"Yeah, I do, I aint done nuffin!"

"When you are found to be innocent, they will be destroyed, and not kept on record."

"Nah."

"Earlier, when you were in the van, did you recognize the person next to you?"

"Nah, don' know 'im."

Someone knocked on the door, and D.S. Jones 380 had a brief whispered conversation with someone outside. An object was passed in. "Mr Walson, do you recognize this item?"

"What's the game? It's a cup!"

"Have you seen it before?"

"Looks like the one I had a cuppa in, a bit back, when I were waitin'."

"How did you hold it?"

"Like this, 'cos the 'andle's broke." I picked it up to show them.

Plod 380 held out a plastic bag. "Put it in here, please."

I did, and he wrapped it up, and passed it out through the door.

"Mr Walson, for the tape, I am now showing item three to you. Do you recognize this item, Sid?"

"It's me wallet!"

"Item seven?"

"Looks like me plastic."

"Item eight?"

"It's a tenner. Prob'ly the one from me wallet."

"Item nine?"

"It's a plastic. Not mine, though."

"You say it isn't yours?"

"Nah. I only got one card."

"Can you explain how this card came to be in your wallet, along with the other items?"

"Nah."

There was a knock on the door, and then a hand was poked through the gap, and a thumbs-up sign given. Then the hand was withdrawn.

"Mr Sid Walson, can you explain why the fingerprints on the cup, the wallet, the ten pound note, the two credit cards, one of which is in a different name, the keys, and the bicycle chain, all match. Are they not your fingerprints?"

"Nah, - Hey! Tha's two questions!"

"Mr Sid Walson, I am further charging you with - -."

etc.etc.

Shit!

There was another knock on the door, and then a hand appeared, pointed at Jones 380, then beckoned 'outside'.

Plod said, "For the tape, Detective Superintendent Jones leaves the room."

After some muttering, outside, Himmler came back in, and said, "Mr Walson, Do you recognize this?" He held up another poly bag.

"Looks like a johnny". Shit shit shit!

"This condom was found in the hip pocket of your trousers. It had been knotted near the tip. In the tip was some white powder, which on analysis, was found to be heroin. Do you deny knowledge of it?"

"Course I do, I'm not fick!"

"Can you explain how your fingerprints are on it?"

"Nah!"

"Mr Walson, I am further charging you with possession of a class 'A' prohibited substance, identified as six grammes of 98% pure heroin powder. – "blah blah

Oh fuck!

"-blah blah, I ask you again whether you require legal representation?"

"Fink I'd better, ant I?"

"Do you have your own counsel, or shall we appoint one?"

"Well, I only got a tenner, an' me plastic's overdue, so I

can't pay 'im."

"You HAD a tenner," plod smiled, "It's now evidence, is it!"

"Yeah, well, where I'm goin' money's no good, is it?"

"No."

Himmler Jones asked, "Now, what were you really doing in the harbour mud?"

"Lookin' for me keys. I already told yer that."

"Lock him up, Jones."

"Yes Sir, Mr Jones!"

"And bring in the other one."


He was duly brought in, and poured into a chair.

"Hey, Man! Like wow! Hey, man, it's hey like, wow, hey?"

"Oh God". P.C. Jones 1437 groaned.

Detective Sergeant Jones 380 just grimaced.

P.C. Jones asked, "Can you tell us your name?"

"Hey, man, whassinna name, man?"

"Do you know where you are?"

"Sure, man! Trippin' around the Universe!"

205

Detective Superintendent Jones 380 decided that this one was for the F.M.E. to examine. "Take him back, and keep an eye on him, until he sobers up."

"Drag, man! Hendrix, tha'ss me, man, Jimmy Hendrix, don't play cricket."

"Hendrix? Really? What happened to the suntan?"

Chapter Twelve.

Aprez Dive.

I limped dramatically back to my tent, dumped the gadget-bag on the floor outside, fired up the kettle, then squirmed into the tent, where I began the battle of extracting myself from the clammy wetsuit. Once the jacket was off, I had a preliminary rub-down with a towel, and then started on the pants. Eventually, one leg peeled free, and I sat, steaming gently, for a moment, then battled the other one out. Her voice said, "Knock, knock. Can I come in?

"Sure, I'm still in my bathers, I've just removed the wet-suit."

She ducked inside, her salty hair sticking out like a hedgehog's spines, with a mischievous grin on her face.

"What can I do with you?" I asked.

"Ah, well, I've a few ideas," - -

"Mmm? Well, I've got the kettle on, and as they say, everything stops for tea, well, coffee, anyway."

"Ah, spoilsport! Seriously, though, like Trevor suggested, I don't want to be alone, in case those thugs come back."

"I thought you wanted to be discreet, but if you'd rather, you can move in here, with me, or vice-versa, until the weekend. I haven't thought past that time, yet."

"Why the weekend?"

"I'll have to go back, then. I don't want to leave you, but I have a family to think of. I did tell you."

"I wasn't meaning that.  I don't want you to go, either, because I've not been so happy for years. - - "

"I'm glad, for you."

".--but why this weekend? I thought you said she'd guess you weren't at some meeting, when she saw what clothing you had, and hadn't taken. Can't you 'phone her, and tell her the car's broken, and the garage can't fix it for another week, or something, I've got to go back, myself, next weekend. After that, who knows? I don't want to lose you now I've found you, and I don't want to be the bit on the side, either. That wouldn't suit either of us. If we have to go our separate ways, so be it, but you said you know she's been cheating on you for years, and the child isn't yours, either. So I was sort of hoping you might think about leaving her, for me. - - "

"I have."

"- - and that sounds like sour grapes, or a whingeing, rejected woman, and it isn't supposed to. I'm trying to say I've fallen in love with you, and I want you to be mine, forever! You have what?"

"Eh? Oh, er, I HAVE been thinking of chucking her, even before I met you, but we've been together for a long time, and I couldn't just dump her. It isn't in me to do that. I'd feel guilty, and that would spoil everything else. I, too, have found new happiness, with you, even though I've only known you for one day, -"

"Thirty-six hours and eight minutes."

" - -and I don't want it to end, but what if it is just a holiday romance, a passionate fling that burns out in a few days or weeks. I can't say that I love you, I don't know! I've never loved anyone or anything in the way it is depicted. This feeling I have for you is different to previous times, but is it love? I don't know! The instant I saw you, yesterday, I knew I wanted you, but it could just be lust, and once that is satisfied, - - "

"Oh, you poor, silly man! That is one of the things I like about you, you are so honest, and nice!"

"- - what if it fades away, and all that is left is an empty shell, and two trapped people who used to mean something to each other!" I paused for breath, still with one leg inside the wet-suit.

"Isn't that exactly where you are now, trapped in an empty shell of a marriage?"

That made me think. "Yes, but, ah, - -, I don't want to sound like I'm rejecting you or anything, but I don't want to make promises grounded on mere passion, either. I don't want to hurt you, but I have anyway. I don't want to duck the issue, but I don't want to start something that could end as a double disaster, either! Would you mind turning the gas out, under the kettle, while I get this thing off my leg, or it will boil dry!"

"What, your leg?"

210

She reached over, and turned the tap under the burner, which was steadily turning the tent into a sauna. The Old Codger in the next tent called across, "You two love-birds want to ease off a bit, there's steam coming from your vents!" He ended with an amused cackle.

"Oh, Oh, Aargh!" Called another voice, it sounded remarkably like Trev.

"So much for discretion - all of the bloody campsite knows, now!" She said.

The wet-suit released my leg with a snap, and I fell over backwards as she stuck a hand out of the tent-flap and made a gesture, to a round of cheers and wolf-whistles. "I think they're all waiting to see what happens next!"

"Anyway, as I was saying, if you will leave the decision, for a day or two, and see how we get on. Please don't be offended. If you want to move in, for company, fine, if not, that's fine, too. If you want to use separate sleeping bags, that's fine. If you want company, and keeping warm, that's better, and if you want to carry on like everyone seems to think we are,

211

that's better still. Then, if you still want me to, I'll 'phone up with an excuse, and give us another week, to think and talk about it. But please, please see that I'm not trying to duck out. I'm not just having a quick fling, then disappearing, I promise!" I reached over, picked a tear from her cheek, with a fingertip, and tasted it. "See, I've made you cry, anyway, because I'm too nice to be nasty!"

Another tear trickled down. "Oh, you – stubborn – !"

She stood up, to leave, then faster than I could dodge, her arm lashed out, looped around my chest, her leg slammed into the back of my knees, and over her hip I went, in a basic judo throw. As I hit the floor, she landed on top of me, her knees in my stomach, hands on my chest. It took me by surprise, partly because I didn't think my little tent was big enough for such activities! I said something along the lines of "HUFFFF" as her weight came onto me.

"I know this, you -, you -," she pummeled at me, "you told me before, but you keep beating me over the head with it, over and over." Thump. Punch. "Are you trying to drive me away?" Thump. Jab. "Just say and I'll go. I'll go to my tent, and have a good cry, and in the morning, I'll be gone." Thump. "Is that what you want?"

I tried shaking my head, but as it coincided with her slaps, it wasn't very conclusive. So I struggled to suck in a bit of air, but with her weight on my stomach, it wasn't very successful. Instead, I reached up, dragged her down, forcibly, and then kissed her, hard. As the weight came off her knees, and my stomach, I sucked in a whoop of air, which stopped my lungs from slapping against each other. She was shaking all over, whether with rage, or grief, I don't know, the tears a torrent, now. I pulled her head round a little, and whispered into her ear, "I want you. I want you to stay. I want you to want me, and instead, I've hurt you so badly. Can you forgive me? I'm torn between what I want, and what I should do, and I don't know what to do for best. I'm sorry, really sorry!" I ran out of things to say, so just held her, shaking, on top of me, until the sobbing eased. "You've got a short fuse, haven't you?"

"Hic! Hic! Oh, bloody hic hell! See what hic you've hic done now hic!"

"At least, you are still talking to me."

213

"I hic mean ithic, make that bloody 'phonehiccall, or I'll be gone in the morninghic."

"I will. I'll have to nip over to Pete and Trevor's first, to settle up, then you can listen in while I do it, then you can't say I didn't make the call."

"That'll do. Now let me up!"

"Why? I'm quite comfortable, apart from a pebble sticking into my ribs, from underneath!"

"I'm not! I'm too hot in all this gear. I want to go and change, and have a shower."

"Alright, call for me when you get back, and we'll make that 'phone-call." I let go of her.

She sat up, straddling me.

"Don't stay like that, too long!"

"Why? You can't do anything!" she fingered my face, "I've given you a shiner!" her gaze travelled down my chest, taking in all the bruises, blotches, and scrapes. "I really did lose it, didn't I?"

"I probably deserved it."

"Yes, you did, you big sod! Ah, the hiccoughs have

214

stopped." She wriggled about provocatively, making the old soldier stir. "At least, that still works!" She flowed to her feet, then left.

Of course, the water in the kettle had gone cold, so I had to re-light the gas and re-boil it, while I finished dressing, then made the coffee, before unlocking the car and rummaging under the floor-mat to find my wallet, before wandering over to Trev's truck. Pete was delving into a plastic bin-bag, by one of the wheels.

"Hi, Trev's in the tent. Who did that?"

"I walked into a cupboard door!"

"You haven't got any - - ." Pete trailed off, sheepishly.

I went to the tent, and called, "Trev, it's Vince, Pete said to come in."

"Yeah. Pull up a pew, I'll be out in a minute."

As there weren't any seats in the awning, I sat on the grass, just as he called, "Don't sit on the grass to the right of the doorway, there's a boggy bit where the kettle got spilled!"

"Yeah, I just found out!"

"Ah!"

A zipper zipped, and then Trev stepped out, wearing sawn-off jeans, and a rag that used to be a tee-shirt. "I save my old stuff for going away, then just dump it, to save on the laundry." He shrugged.

"No decent washing machine would let you put that stuff into it!"

"True. Who socked you one?"

"George, she's got a wicked right cross!"

He chuckled, then called, "Hey, Pete, how much fuel did we use?"

"Er, - - about ten gallons, I think, mate."

"Right, so, - half share is five, at one pound twenty, is six, and two, for the air, makes eight. Sound reasonable?"

"Fine." I gave him a tenner. "Oil and diesel?"

"Not worth measuring."

"Wear and tear, then."

"O.K. mate. The offer's still open, for the Skerries, tomorrow?"

216

"No, thanks, like I said, it's too deep for comfort. I know where I'm safe."

"What's on the agenda for tomorrow, then?"

"Oh, I'll probably just potter around, read, and doze. Maybe a dip in the bay, just up the road."

"And have a quick bonk?" interjected Pete, as he ducked in, "I see you found the boggy bit!"

"Yeah, not many places have a concealed pond on the veranda."

"We've settled up," Trev said, "did you find them?"

"Nah, I've a feeling they're still in the shed, at base."

"What were you looking for?" I asked.

"A screwdriver set. They look a bit like six sided cross-heads, only they're more star-shaped, and have a hole up the centre, for 'security' screws."

"I know what you mean. I've a few in the Cortina that might fit. I'll drop them off in a few minutes, but I've a 'phone call to make, first."

"Fine, thanks."

I went back to collect George. "Are you ready, yet?"

217

"No, I'll be out, in a minute."

"O.K. I'll be by my car, or taking a couple of tools to Pete."

"O.K."

I went to the car, opened the boot, and rummaged in the accumulated junk in there, finally finding the drivers I wanted in the space under the spare wheel hub. "Will any of those do?" I dropped them onto a newspaper on the grass, next to where Pete was sitting.

"Yeah, they look perfect. I'll bring them back later."

"No rush, I've never used them since I bought them!"

"I've got some stuff like that, too!"

As I started back, George was coming to meet me. She'd tamed the hedgehog of her hair, and was dressed all over in white.

"Ready?" she asked.

"You want me to duck it?"

"No."

"Then, let's find a 'phone."

There was one in the 'Clubhouse', bolted to the thin plastered lath wall, with a juke-box on the other side of it. I lined up a couple of 10p coins, and then dialled my home number. A few chugs, clicks and whirrs came from the earpiece, then a mechanical female voice said; 'The number you have dialled is not recognized, please check and try again'.

"That's odd!" I said, as I tapped the rest, and cleared the line. George's brow was furrowed. I tried again, with the same result. "I'm not mucking about, honest!" I showed her my little diary, with the number written down next to an abbreviation that said 'ICE', "Try it yourself."

She did, and the frown eased off a few notches.

"Hang on, I think I've got Joan's number, our babysitter, in here."

I flicked pages, and then tried the new number.

After a few rings, Joan's voice said, "If that's a heavy breather, do your best, I'm bored!"

"Hi, Joan, it's me," I said, uncomfortably, "I've been

219

trying to call home, but - -,"

"If you are asking if it is safe to go back," she interrupted, "the answer is yes. She's gone away for a holiday, and taken the rug-rat with her! I don't know why you'd bother, though!"

"Thank heaven for that!" I exclaimed, "But I'm staying for another week, at least. Can you feed the cat, for me, please?"

"Wellll, I can if you want, but I don't think it will really appreciate it!"

"Oh, why not?"

"It had a piddle in the wrong place!"

"And she chucked it out?"

"No! On a mains plug, and it got the shock of its death! Blew all the fuses, too!"

"Oh, well, she wanted the flea-bitten thing, not me. It's no loss."

"Are you staying there, then, with your new passion?"

"Yes. No! What passion?"

George, her ear pressed against the receiver, jabbed a finger into my ribs.

220

"Oh, come on, Vince, I can read you like a book! I -, hang on, I can see boxing gloves! I bet she bopped you one!"

I gave in. "Yes, she's here, listening in, now."

"Let me speak to her." It was a command, not a request, so I handed over the hand-set.

"Hello?" querulously.

"Hello, love, is he good to you?"

"Sometimes."

"Shy? Never mind. I'd like to talk to you, face to face, some time, please?"

"Maybe." George passed the handset back, just as the 10p ran out. Hastily, I jammed in another, "Still there?"

"Hello again, still here. I think she's the one for you. I think you should know that Betty's got a new fellah, and I think she's going to chuck you, for him. I'll tell you all, later. Bring your new girl round, some time, for a reading. Well, got to dash. See you!"

"Hey! Hang on. Why doesn't the 'phone - .'

"Oh! She forgot to pay the bill again. It's been cut off!"

"Oh, right! See you!"

221

"Bye." The 'phone went clop as the line disconnected, then I noticed George had her ear pressed against the receiver again, listening to what was being said.

"Is June a Psychic?"

"Joan, yes. A good one, too."

"Mmmm!"

"Well, that solves one set of problems, anyway. Are you one, too?"

"One what? - - Oh! In flashes, sometimes I just know something, and I'm usually right, but it's random."

"Then, perhaps, if you go to see her, Joan could 'tune you in' better, it takes practice."

"You seem to know what you are talking about, are you one, too?"

"No, not a flicker! I've just been lectured at, at great length, on several occasions, by one who could, and one who wanted to, but couldn't!"

"Your ex-wife, Hetty, was it?"

"Betty, yes. Do you fancy a drink, while we're here?"

"Yes! Why not push the boat out, and celebrate! I'll

have a Bacardi and coke, without the Bacardi."

"Just coke?"

"Yes, I don't drink and dive."

"This licensed bar sells less alcohol than any I know!"

We claimed a dinky table that was not much larger than a dinner-plate, over in the corner, and over the cokes, we discussed us.

"What was that about the cat, I missed it?"

"Oh, not much. Her, the wife's, cat, had a pee into a mains plug."

"Shocking!" George spluttered.

"The cat thought so, it blew all the fuses!"

In between coughs, she gasped, "The cat's, or the house's?"

"Both!" Practically everyone in the place was looking round, trying to see what the joke was.

"Ay! 's th' lovey-doveys! 'ave a drink wi' me!" It was the old coot from the adjacent tent. "They wus steam comin' from they's tent, a while back." He'd had three or four too many.

"Leave 'em alone. Gran'pa!" someone else said, "She looks like she's got a good punch in her!"

"Perhaps it was a mistake, George." I said, quietly, "Shall we move?"

"What was the mistake, coming in here, or the punch?"

I passed her the invitation card I'd bought earlier, in town. After opening it, with a coy smile, she asked for the menu.

"Nothing too exotic, I'm afraid, I couldn't get any caviar, and the Bollinger was corked. So, fillet steak, new spuds, peas, carrots. Cheesecake, for after."

"All from tins, of course?"

"No, not at all. The steak is in a plastic bag, and the cheesecake is in a cardboard box. They should be thawed out, by now. There's a p.s."

"Oh?" She waited for the catch.

"Bring your own eating irons, I'm a bit short of the necessary hardware!"

"How about plates?"

"Them, too." I admitted. "When I came down here, I

only planned on catering for one!"

"Plan 'B', then. Bring it round to my place. I've got a table, and a six-place set!"

"Tin-opener?"

"Somewhere!"

"Such luxury!"

"There's no point roughing it, when you're roughing it. I have a postscript, too."

"Go on."

"Bring your tooth-brush."

"Razor?"

"That, too."

"Do you have plans that I should know about?"

"Who? Little me?" she feigned innocence.


The rest is left to the reader's imagination. Mere words on paper cannot conjure the images as well as the mind. It is sufficient to know that the club-house occupants gave a rousing cheer, at the first kiss, and the steam escaping from the tent vents, later, was not from a boiling kettle.

Chapter thirteen.

Trev and Pete.


"Something has changed between those two!" Pete

observed, as the couple ducked into George's tent.

"It's just holiday lust, with a capital L"

"No, it's more than that! It's like a barrier between them

has gone down."

"Really? That's nice for them. Do you think it will

last?"

"Who knows? How are we for time?"

"Fine. Fifteen minutes, yet. How're you doing, with that

radio?"

"Just about done. It was a blown diode in the synth. I

just need to put the casing back on, and then I can see if it will fire up."

"Good, we've missed two schedules, they'll be wondering!"

"I had to drill one screw out. It was a tiny thing, must have been a sixteen B.A. or something in that area. Just putting the last one in now, and - - Click! "Voila! Eureka, etcetera. Everything lights up, and the frequency display isn't gibberish! Are those bottles full? I'll take them across, with Vinny's screwdrivers, if they are."

"No, I'd leave them until tomorrow. They seem to be rather engrossed in something else at the moment, like each other!" Trevor suggested.

"Ah, yes. I see what you mean! I'll put the aerial up, instead!"

"If I'm right, that's not the only pole being erected this evening!"


"GW3QNH mobile, callingG3QRT on sked, wakey wakey – over!"

"This is G3QRT, where you been, mate, we were

227

getting worried, over."

"GW3QNH, sorry, blew a diode, and I've just got it going again. I've got some gen for you, is your tape ready? Over."

"Qrt, stand by one, - - o.k. rolling, over"

"GW3QNH, here it comes, three, two, one," Pete pressed a button on the radio's console, causing a pre-recorded data burst to be transmitted., "o.k. that's it, copy, over"

"QRT, I think so, I'll let you know in a minute. Anything to add? Over"

"GW3QNH, no. That's it for now, over"

"QRT, rog, keep an ear open."

Two cuppa's later.

"GW3QNH Mobile, this is G3QRT, you copy? Over"

"GW3QNH, on channel."

"3QRT, stand by for a squealer, over."

Pete set the built-in recorder to high speed, then pressed pause, and record. "Go ahead"

"3QRT, three, two, one, -." A high pitched squeal came

from the speaker, and a line of l.e.d. lights flickered. "That's it. Over."

"GW3QNH, got it. Stand by for ten, or so."

"Roger that."

"Everyone's rogering tonight, except us!" Pete quipped to nobody, and then called. "Trev, come here a minute and see what you think of this!"

When Trev appeared, Pete tossed him a similar pair of headphones to the ones he wore. "Ready?"

"As ever."

Pete switched the tape speed to slow, and then played back the recording he'd just made.

The voice of their Controller said there was – 'Nothing on record about any Vince Birtwhistle. He was a nobody. Georgina Winifred Weastey was R.A.F. a pilot on long term leave to allow recovery from an unspecified stress illness, possibly related to her Fiancé attempting to fly a fast jet through one of the Grampians, rather than over or round it, two days before they were due to be wed. The leave was open-ended, and her 'time' was suspended for the duration, although she was on full pay. There was nothing of significance in her past. Now, the interesting bit, - three of the other four are just thugs, muscles, but Mick, he's a nasty piece of work, if it is the same person. The description tallies. He's wanted by Interpol, Our lot, the Bomb squad, the Met, the Guarda, and some others. Real name is Michael O'Shaunessy, a medium size cog in the Sinn Fein. Can you confirm that he is temporarily resident at Bangor nick? We'll take it from there, and you can forget him. The old chap, nothing on him, but agree he could be an observer for the other team. It's a pity Miss Weastey stumbled onto a cache, but it's given us a new place to watch. Don't let those two get involved, if they're innocent. It could get nasty, and the innocent always end up being hurt. Contact next on this frequency at twenty-three-fifty tomorrow. Ends.' After a longish pause, a deep, slow, voice mumbled something indecipherable before Pete pushed the 'stop' button, and then flicked a glance at Trev, who gave a thumbs-up.

"G3QRT this is GW3QNH mobile, confirm party location, and sked, over, and out."

"Out" the radio retorted.

"Something must be brewing, Trev. Is the gear ready?" Pete said quietly, then in a louder voice, deliberately intended to be heard, "Now, look, Mate, I don't mind you using my tapes, but don't keep bloody re-arranging them, and when you've done, put them back in their cases, the proper ones, to keep the muck out!"

"But, Pete, Black Sabbath doesn't go between Abba, and Carpenters, It should go here, before Seekers!' then quietly, 'Yeah, all set."

"It starts with 'B', not 'R', and I want it HERE!"

They carried on squabbling, in a similar fashion, for a time, while Pete stowed the headphones and aerial, shut down the transceiver, and wiped the cassette tape, using a powerful magnet. "It's a bit chancy, using the mast, here, but we're in a 'black hole', and there's no choice. It's a pity that new satellite gear didn't work out in time."

"We'll have to be careful, I think Vinny's into Ham. It looks like that new A.O.R. set, in his car. I've heard it goes up to 1300 Megs, AM. FM, and sidebands, too. I'd like a proper look at it, some time. Perhaps we could be 'real' Ham's, in public, it

231

might be safer."

"It might be tricky if we use the two-way head-sets, they're at twelve hundred and something. He might hear more than he bargained on."

"I'll bear it in mind, but if we try to keep operations to the night, when he's otherwise occupied - !" Pete chuckled. Then yelled "SO BLOODY PACK IT IN, RIGHT!"

"Oh, sod you!" Trev stormed out of the back of the truck, and slammed the door. "You do what you want. You always do! I'm going to bed, ALONE!"

A chorus of 'Shuttup's', and 'Thank God for that's', drifted round the site, after this exchange. Trev headed for the block-house. A couple of other late arrivals, with the same intent, abruptly changed direction and went to find a bush to water, instead.

Pete waited until everyone had settled, then waited a while longer, then another hour, to make sure, before flipping open the hatch in the truck roof, standing on a table, and taking a long, hard, look around, using infra-red light amplifying binoculars. A fox was rummaging in a litter bin. A flicker of movement over near the reeds around a pond held his attention. He watched for long minutes, the binoculars whistling quietly, as the electronics did their work, then the reeds parted, and a square-ish, long, green snout, with a paler long green stripe on either side, appeared, as a badger foraged. Nearby, a pheasant honked, startling it, and it was gone. Pete switched his attention to the rock faces overlooking the site, particularly on an escarpment to the west, as he considered it to be a good position for a sniper or observer. Finally satisfied, he climbed down, shut the hatch, put the binoc's away, then locked up the truck, pee'd on the wheel, then sneaked into the tent where Trevor was waiting.

"I know he's up there, somewhere, but I can't see him!" Pete sighed.

"We'll take him for a tour, tomorrow."

After a while, the dog-fox trotted over, inspected the damp truck wheel, then strained to fire its own jet higher up, in the symbolic gesture of "This is my patch, and I'm bigger than you!"

233

The man, hidden near the crest of the rock-face, carefully aimed his rifle's infra-red sniper-scope at the fox's head, and whispered "Bang!" It would appear that his crevice, with its camouflaged scrim-net, woven through with some ivy purchased at a garden centre, did the trick. He was used to waiting.

Chapter fourteen.

The love birds.

When I woke, with that deep glow inside, indicative of an active night, we were curled up like a pair of spoons. Vince was snoring heavily, his head on the ground-sheet, as I appeared to have claimed the pillows. My left arm was round his chest, and my knees were underneath his buttocks. I sent my hand exploring, a bit further south, to see if anything would happen.

"MMM." He mumbled. So I performed some gentle manipulation. His pelvis rocked a few times, as his 'soldier' stirred.

"You 'wake?" he muttered.

"Yes." I nibbled his ear. "Are you?" I caressed his love-lever again.

"I am, now! Stop that, or suffer the consequences!"

"Who fell asleep first, last ni – this morning?"

"Ah, well, it had been a stressful day." He squirmed over, and kissed me on the nose. His hands were resting in the proper places. "Do you want to, again?"

"It seems a shame to waste it!"


Later, lying face to face, arms and legs entangled, we had been reduced to pecking at each other. I was starting to get sore, and his plunger had finally collapsed beyond revival.

"What are you planning on doing, for the rest of the day?"

"Not a lot. I'd like to stop right here with you, but I seem to be out of ammo, and anyway,--."

He left it unfinished.

"What?"

He gave a lascivious grin, "I'm busting for a pee!"


That started a scramble for clothes, because I had a

similar need. I think we shared the socks between us, because neither of us had a matching pair on our feet. Where he'd thrown my bra, I don't know, but then, I'd hidden his underpants! In our rush out of the tent, we fell over a pair of dive bottles and a bundle of screwdrivers.

"Didn't hear them arrive!" he gasped, as we raced each other to the block-house. He won. I let him, I didn't dare stride out, or I'd have lost control of my bursting bladder.

On the way back, after, I asked who Trev and Pete were.

"Two nice people I met the night before last. Other than that, not a clue. I thought YOU knew them!"

"Me? No. I've never seen them, until yesterday. I can't figure them, but they're not what they seem. There's something else going on."

"Perhaps they think WE'RE someone else?"

"What is this? The intro to a new Jim Bond story?"

"Ha! Some hope! Those characters get paid a heck of a lot more!"

"Talking of money, how're you fixed?"

"I'm not hurting. Are you a bit short?"

"Oh, no! I was thinking of you! If your wife has chucked you, has she taken the bank account with her?"

"Probably. The one she knew about! I had a second one, for emergencies."

"Much in it?"

"Nosey! No, about two hundred, less a car exhaust."

"Oh! Any cash left?"

"About thirty, and some scrap metal."

"So you are starting to feel the pinch, then. You can save next week's site fee. Drop your tent, and stow it, you aren't using it!"

"If that is your choice! What if you decide to chuck me out?"

"Then re-pitch it. Will your gas bottle fit my burners?"

"I didn't see the fitting, so I can't answer that, but if it doesn't, we can use them both, mine for small stuff, and yours for cooking."

"Good idea, Slave. Put the kettle on, while I pretty up."

"Yes Mistress. What do you fancy doing, for the rest of this morning?"

238

"What morning?"

"This - - Oh! It's eleven fifty!"

"O.K. Brunch, then, and after?"

"What's in your larder, I'm starved!"

"We seem to have been diverted, yesterday, so there are two steaks, - "

"Get them going, then, while I go for a shower!"

"Yes Boss, how do you like them, pink, brown or black?"

"Black on the outside, pink in the middle."

"Awkward sod!" He fiddled with my cooking range for a minute, learning how to start it, and where the gears were, and then dug out my old, partly non-stick pans that were reserved for camping trips.


When she came back, with that freshly-scrubbed glow, her hair like a hedgehog, again, I had the meal progressing nicely, and two cups, as I couldn't find glasses, of that alcohol-free wine, you know - the one with the funny–sounding name, filled, and lined up, ready, with the bottle on show, to save

239

unnecessary questions.

"Ah! Luxury!" She pecked me on the cheek, "You need a shave!"

"Give me a chance! I've been slaving over a hot candle while you've been pampering and preening!"

She snagged up the other cup, took a big sip, paused, and looked startled, as the inside of her mouth shrivelled, and then she swallowed, shivered, and gasped, "God, that's sour!"

"Mmm. Cold, too! That's a nice little fridge you have installed in there, is it battery or gas?"

"Oh, electric, battery, or mains, if there is any. That reminds me, I'll have to charge the battery, it must be getting low, by now. I'll have to find a garage."

"That's no problem. Just clip it to mine with jump-leads, and I'll run the engine for a while."

"Have you got some leads?"

"Of course! They're an essential part of the toolkit, for old cars! Jump-leads, rope, and a big hammer!"

"Hammer?"

"Of course! When all else fails, give it a mighty clout!

Seriously, though, bits tend to become stuck with age, and can weld together, so a good bash starts them moving, or breaks the seal."

"Will your car start?"

"Ah, well! - We'll find out in a while! Brunch will be served just as soon as I find the plates I had placed in handy reach." I looked around the area.

"Oh! I just put them away, so that I could sit down!"

"Sabotage!" I cried, with fake outrage.


We probably collected some strange looks, enjoying steaks, three veg, a sweet, and a bottle of fizz for breakfast, but who cares?

Afterwards, belching discreetly, we tossed a coin, to see who washed up, and guess who won. George showed me where her battery was stashed, so I un-hooked it, and staggered over to the Cortina with it, then put it down near the bonnet, ready. I unlocked, put the key in the ignition, pulled the choke lever out, pressed the clutch pedal, applied three pumps of accelerator, to inject some fuel into the carburettor, and then turned the starter.

241

The solenoid made a loud clack, but nothing else happened. So I released the starter, flicked another switch, connecting my two batteries into parallel, and then tried again. The engine grunted over a couple of compressions, then one cylinder fired, and kept on popping, just barely enough to keep the thing going. I nursed it until another one joined in the game, the shock kicking the other two into life with a backfire, then we were up and running. I left it to warm while I untied the snarled knot of thick wire that had been a pair of neatly coiled leads when I had put them away after their last usage, then clipped the alligators to the battery terminals of George's battery, the negative, at the free end, to the negative of my main car battery, but left the positive one off, for now, until the engine was ready. George had disappeared, divorcing herself from the spectacle.

While I was doing this, the Site Manager wandered past, checking tickets, studied my palsied engine, shook his head in dismay, and wandered off again. When the engine began to labour, I pushed the choke lever in, and tickled the accelerator, but it wasn't ready to rev, yet, and began mis-firing, so I left it for another minute or three. When I tried it again, the exhaust belched a cloud of blue-black muck, then cleared, and the engine began behaving as though it had a function beyond that of a pollution generator. I climbed out, knelt on the grass, and pressed the accelerator down a little with my hand, then slid a purpose made wedge under the back of the pedal, to jam it there, then walked round, and connected George's battery via the remaining jump-lead. My engine slowed, labouring under the load, but kept going, so I left it to get on with the task, while I boiled water to wash the dishes in.

Up in his hide, on the rock face, the hidden man choked in the cloud of smog, then added a note to those previously gleaned, saying that the Cortina was NOT a getaway vehicle!

George came back, from wherever, just as I finished putting the crocks away.

"Just in time! Keep an eye on my car, please, while I go and scrape my chin."

"O.K. But I can't see anyone being desperate enough to try and pinch it!"

243

"That wasn't my worry. I was thinking that someone might get too close and the car might assault them, in self-defence, of course!"

He ducked into his own tent, and then re-emerged, clutching a little ditty-bag, and a day-glow orange towel. After a wave to me, he wandered off to the block-house.  His rust-heap was chugging away, puffing occasional blue clouds, as it warmed up, but was generally behaving itself. Otherwise, the site seemed empty. All the hikers had gone hiking, the twitchers were off twitching, and the divers were either blowing bubbles, or shivering on beaches and boats. A gaudy cock-pheasant pushed out of the scrub, then strutted proudly across the site, pecking at tasty morsels, as it went. Its erratic route brought it to my canvas mansion, where it stood peering warily at a packet of crisps I had been nibbling, earlier. I tossed one to it, but it cut loose with a raucous 'HONK' then legged it back to the scrub. I looked at the flavour, printed on the packet, which read, 'Chicken and Stuffing'. Perhaps that is why it didn't like the idea. I'd thought they tasted like slugs on toast, which was why there were some left in the packet. Drowsy in the sun's heat, I pulled out a folding lounger from its storage, assembled it, and then ducked into the bedroom, to change into a tiny two-piece bather that had never seen water, except in the laundry. I only kept it for teasing the guys. I then decorously draped myself on the lounger, with a well-thumbed copy of 'Lord of the Rings'. Someone had told me it was a good book, and I had been ploughing through it for something like two years, in fits and starts. I'd found it good for insomnia, and swatting mosquitos, but not much else, but I was determined to read it, all the way through, just in case it all made sense at the last page. Today was to be no different. I think I made it to the end of the first page, which I'm sure I'd read at least ten times, previously, - then there was a weird searing sensation on my stomach. I leaped from the lounger with a yell, to find Vince waving an ice-cube at me.

"Not much of a security guard, are you?" he teased, "Asleep on the job!"

"I was NOT asleep!" I denied, as I wiped my wet navel with a handy rag. "I was enjoying the sun!"

"You didn't hear me turn the car engine off, or bring your battery back, and re-connect it, you were snoring so hard!"

"I don't snore!"

"What's the time, then?" he demanded.

"Well, we had break-din at about one, so it must be around two, two thirty, now."

"You're way off, it's turned four. You've been asleep for a good hour and a half! I've done as you suggested, and dropped my tent, stuck it into my car, and moved it nearer. This is your last chance to change your mind. Are you certain this is what you want"

"Yes, I'm certain! I've never been more certain in my life. I've decided that I want you, and you aren't getting away." I reclaimed the lounger.

"Good! I'm glad about that, because I feel the same about you." He kissed me, then, as I responded, the sod pressed the ice-cube into my navel again! This time, though, he kissed it warm and dry again, and was starting to move further south, until I protested. I didn't want him displaying me to the camp-site.

"There's no-one here!" he mumbled into my belly, but started working up towards my mouth again.

246

I pushed him off. "Behave yourself! I want a rest!"

"It isn't me wearing three scraps of hankie, and a yard of ribbon!" he protested.

"It's for looking at, not fiddling with!"

"I'm looking!"

"Well, take charge of your wandering fingers!"

Chapter fifteen.

The Man.

The man, concealed in his crevice behind his scrim-net, was looking too. He had watched the blonde girl, lying in the sun, on and off, ever since she had emerged from the tent. At first, he had thought her to be naked, and had taken his 'moonlight' scope from its bag and focused it in at maximum zoom. He was hoping for a cheap thrill, but was disappointed to find she was wearing a skimpy bikini, which only just managed to cover up those parts that society dictated. He had also watched the man as he went about his tasks. It appeared that he was planning on leaving, soon, as he had dismantled his tent, put it away, and was busy cleaning up his 'patch'. Or had he, the watcher, missed something? It was impossible for him to maintain a twenty-four hour surveillance on four people on his own. Unfortunately, he was too far away to be able to hear what was being said. The sudden squeal drew his attention, and his lens snapped into line. He could see the man and the blonde wrestling, the sun bed tipped over on its side . . . No! Not wrestling, he was kissing her stomach. A curl of blonde hair popped out from beneath the triangle of cloth and – Something cold and metallic, forming a circle, touched the back of his neck, then a voice hissed – "FREEZE!" He froze, shock crashing through him.

A thick, hairy arm reached round, and took the lens from him, and then his arms were wrenched back and round behind him, and fastened by something round his wrists, before a sticky pad was pulled onto his eyes, as a blindfold. Something made a 'zwip' noise, tape perhaps, then his ankles were fastened, too, before another length went over his mouth. Almost helpless, he thrashed and squirmed, futilely, until a boot in the ribs made him keep still. He could hear someone searching his stores, then a long zip was pulled, followed by a sharp intake of breath.

"Look at this beauty, bro."

"That's nice. I think this goes with it!"

"Yeah, that's the day scope. There's one in here, too, looks Russian. What's it say? You can read the back-to-front alphabet they use."

"Ah, - it translates as – Do not remove lens covers in bright light or shine with torches into lens!"

"It's an image intensifier, then. We've already got one, but he won't be needing it again."

A cold sweat broke out on the man's skin when he heard that statement.

"What was the crumb looking at?"

"Those two kiddies, having a snogging session."

"O.K. turd. Talky time. Are you going to make it easy, or hard?"


I shook my head, and started to roll over, and sit up. A weight trapped my legs, and another landed on my chest, so I was pinned onto my back, my arms under me.

"Well, easy, or hard?" the voice demanded, before the

tape over my mouth was ripped off.

"Fuck –. " I started to say.

The tape was slapped back on, and then some sort of clip was snapped onto my nostrils, so I couldn't breathe.

"Hard, I think!" I couldn't tell if the speaker was glad, or sad.

They watched, and waited, for a while, as he struggled desperately, slowly going an interesting shade of purple, then one of them peeled off the mouth-patch and let him suck in a desperate whoop of air, before smoothing it on again.

"I don't think he will talk to us, do you?"

"Probably not, but I like watching them twitch and jiggle."

"I enjoy the bit where the diaphragm and the cheeks go in and out, when the body tries to get the air it can't have."

The man was already at this point in his slow suffocation. He managed to blow a bit of air out of his nose, making a 'razz' noise as he struggled to breathe, but of course, the clip prevented him inhaling, so his cheeks, and belly, were pumping in and out as his diaphragm demanded oxygen.

"Hello! There's a diary here, in foreign, - no, it's some sort of code. There's three clips of ammo for the rifle, a nine mil Browning automatic pistol, bog-standard NATO crap, they're always jamming, two clips for it. Cans of grub, opener, fork, torch, gun cleaning kit, bog-roll. Nice knife, good balance, do you want it?"

Something thudded onto his chest, but the blood was roaring, his ears were whistling, and he was seeing sparks and zig-zags as his brain began to die.

The patch over his mouth was ripped off. "Speak!" the voice commanded.

He gulped air, one, two, three huge gasps, "Go fuck –"

The patch stopped him speaking, as it was slapped back on. He heaved and squirmed with all his remaining strength, achieving nothing. Fear was coursing through him, now. These guys meant it. He was dead, it was just a question of how long they kept him on the ragged edge.

"D'you think we could get this rubbish to the boat, unseen?"

"Tricky. Too many tourists about, but we can't leave it here, either. We'd have to wait until the early hours before we could remove it."

"Do you think it will float?"

"No, not with that sack filled with rocks, tied to it."

"What I fancy doing, is taking it down to fifty feet, done up like this, then when it's struggling to breathe, take the patch off, and watch it struggle not to!"

An evil chuckle was the reply. "Better still, take the patch off, and let it go, see if it can make it to the top!"

"But what if it does?"

"Then drag it back down, for an action replay! We can tie the rocks to a rope, and pull it up again."

They watched for a while, as the diaphragm's heaves grew weaker.

"I think it's about done, where's that hypo?"

"Here. Let me at an arm." The drug was injected.

"Do you think it noticed?"

"No, it's too far gone. Ten seconds more, then we can undo it."

The hairy arm tore the sticky gag off, then, after a moment, a faint rattling noise came from the man's throat, the diaphragm spasmed, and drew in some air.

The other person felt its carotid artery, "Still pumping, too fast to count, but it's still with us."

"I thought for a moment we'd left it too long."

"That WOULD be awkward!"

"Yeah. I hate this, but it has to be done."

"It must be awful, knowing that you are dead, and then waking up, in the morning, in the hands of the opposition!"

The man hadn't moved, but the automatic systems had restarted, and he was heaving air in great gulps, his colour returning slowly to normal

"Yes. Knowing that you died, without talking, then finding out you didn't die after all! He's lucky we're the good guys!" Thick hairy arm raised a walkie-talkie, - "Caretaker, Caretaker, this is Grounds-man, Grounds-man, over."

"Crackle – hiss – splat – is Caretaksplat o ahead ovsplat"

254

"This is Grounds-man, we have cleared the log-jam, cleared the log-jam, and need assistance with some debris, some debris, over."

"Splat crackle wet or dry splat 'ver."

"Mostly dry." He chuckled, looking at the wet patch on the victim's trousers.

"Splat again?"

"Cargo is dry, cargo is dry. Over."

"Splatger, on waysplat."

"Roger that, waiting. Out out."

"Hiss splat."


"You'd think they could afford some radios that worked!" he looked in disgust at the walkie-talkie.

"That is Her Majesty's Government, for you. You still haven't told me how you spotted him! Was it smoke or a movement that gave his position away? I studied the area, and I couldn't see him."

"You were looking FOR something, I was just looking, and saw it straight away, it was this ivy." Thick hairy arms said,

255

as he fingered a leaf.

"How so?"

"Shows you aren't a gardener. It's Hedera Goldheart. It wouldn't grow here, the conditions are all wrong for it."

"You jammy sod!"

"O.K. Let's get organized, here, and get him on top, ready for the transport."

"All done, apart from the net. The cans are in the rucksack, and can go with him, as can the code-book, and the pistol. I'll keep the rifle, I fancy a play with it, as it's a special."

"Right. Let's make like climbers, for any spectators."

"Good idea, though, the ivy!"

"It's worth remembering, for another time, but choose a more appropriate species!"

Chapter sixteen.

New start.

"You know, George, I've been thinking!"

"I thought I could smell something burning!"

'That's coming from the old chap in the next tent, he keeps popping out for an eye-ful. Anyway, it's occurred to me that I have nothing to go home for! Betty has gone back to being a Sprockett, the cat's dead, the job went phut last week. The flat's joint owned, and she'll probably sell her half to an Asian, so all I really own is here, in my car!"

"What about the television?"

"She rented it, and the stereo is only a mono since she stuck the vacuum pipe through the speaker grille. We bought it from a junk shop for a tenner, in the first place."

"Bills?"

"Direct debit, mostly. Her account."

"So - what are you saying, Vince?"

"I don't know. I suppose I'm saying that I have nowhere to go!"

"What's wrong with here?"

"Nothing, right now, but it will be bloody cold in winter, if the site is still open!"

"There is that, and your hundred and fifty, or so, won't last very long." He looked at me, with confusion and uncertainty written all over his face, "What did you say her name was?"

"Who?"

"Your – ex-wife."

"Betty, I thought I'd said."

"No, her maiden name, I know she was Betty."

"Sprockett, as in gear-wheel, why?"

"No reason, just delaying tactics."

"You're deliberately confusing the issue."

"Exactly. – you were saying?"

"Was I? – Oh, er, when you decide to go back, where do

you go back to?"

"WRAF barracks. They won't let you in!" I knew I was ducking the issue.

"Yes. No, but where?"

"I've no idea. Wherever they draft me, I suppose." I wanted him to ask me, but I wasn't going to lead him, as the idea took form in my head.

"But where do you go first, I mean, to be sent on from?"

"Oh, somewhere nice and handy. R.A.F. Valley! Medical section. When I think I'm ready, I breeze in, and they decide if I'm mentally fit for flying duties."

"What if you don't go back?"

My pulse-rate went up a notch or two. "Then eventually they will cut off my pay, and invite me to resign my commission."

"And how much longer will they wait?"

"Not much longer. I've been off for six months, now, not all of it spent here!" Was he going to say it?

"You must have been pretty broken up, then!"

"Not as much as him." She smiled wryly. "I must be getting better, I couldn't have said that, a few days ago!"

"Do you want to go back?"

"I can't answer that, yet. I owe it to them to go back, but whether I want to - - ?"

"So what happens, if you go back, and tell them you want to quit?" He was almost there!

"I don't know. I've signed a contract. I suppose they would have me grounded, and I'd serve my time brushing up, or something similarly exotic."

"Hmm."

He still hadn't plucked up the courage to decide, and I couldn't help him with a push in the right direction. A helicopter was thrashing along, just over the boundary of the camp-site. He fiddled with the stove, lit the gas, and then slapped the kettle on top. "Cuppa?"

"Please."

She would let him stew for a while longer. She knew what he wanted to ask, but daren't, and she knew she wanted him to ask her. She thought she knew what she would answer when he did, but it depended on how he asked. Even though she had been got, she was playing hard to get.

The helicopter was closer now, and she glanced idly up at it, wondering what it was doing so close to habitation, in violation of Air Navigation Laws. Then she recognized it as the S.A.R. Wessex, from Valley as it slowed and turned, coming to a hover just above the outcrop of rock that towered above the campsite. The side door was open, with the winch-man leaning out, presumably talking via his headset, to the pilot.

"Who could possibly want rescuing from there?" Vince bellowed, over the reflected noise of the Wessex's rotors. The tent fabric was flogging in the down-draft. "Here's your coffee, but if I put it down, it will blow away!" He grabbed hold of the sun-lounger, as it floated up, and tumbled. "Like the kettle!" Sure enough, it was rolling across the grass, spilling water. George chased after it. Vince had the lounger in one hand, and was hanging on to the awning, which was thrashing like a demented soul, but he had to let go of the lounger, which blew over, and began bowling across the grass, until George trapped it, upside-down, by sitting on it, so he could save the table. The

Wessex finally inched forward, over the top of the escarpment, and the buffetting ceased. George was intrigued, the S.A.R. team wouldn't normally operate so close to a camp-site, either vertically, or horizontally. The winch-man was coming down, on his wire, now, looking like a spider. She couldn't quite see who it was, and then he was going up again, with a stretcher-case. There was the usual tussle getting it in through the door, then the machine dipped its nose, and thrashed away.

"Give me a hand with this, George!" he called, over the diminishing noise. She looked round, and saw he had the table under one foot, and the tent propped up on his shoulder, while he was trying to re-fit the ridge pole to the corner upright, at arm's length, against the tension of the guy-rope. She dragged the lounger back, tasted her coffee, which was cold, drank it in one gulp, then tossed the cup into a corner, out of the way, and went to help, laughing. She took the upright pole so that he could untangle himself, then he drank the unspilled half of his coffee before tossing his cup after hers, with the comment, - "Good job they're plastic!"

They re-assembled the tent, between them, and then

262

went around rescuing stray property.

"Shall we start again, - Would Madam care for a coffee?"

"Please, that last one was instant cold!"

"It looks like Pete and Trev's tent has collapsed. I'll go and see if I can rebuild it for them, in a few minutes. Now, come and sit here!" He slapped his knee. George made a song and dance about it, but capitulated.

"I was trying to ask you something important, before we were interrupted. Now stop wriggling, you're putting me off!"

"Like this?" she demonstrated.

"Exactly! Now stop it, I'm trying to be serious."

She pecked him on the cheek, "Alright, I'm behaving, but hurry up!"

"Well, like I was saying, -. " He swallowed some coffee, stuck for words.

"Yes?"

"Well, like I said – ah."

"You haven't said, yet, I'm still waiting!"

"Ah, er –." He sucked in a desperate breath, then blurted, "Look, I know what you said, before, about wanting me for ever, but did you mean for ever, or just a few weeks or so?"

"How long is a piece of string? Right now, I want you for ever for ever, but who knows about in a few weeks?" This wasn't going right. She was waiting for some commitment from him.

"It's like talking to a politician, I'm getting lots of words, but no answers."

"You haven't asked anything, yet."

"Oh – I wish I knew -, - - Damnit! Marry me! As soon as I can, marry me!"

"Are you asking, or telling? Wish you knew what?" She was caught out, now.

"I'm tellasking you to marry me!"

"But wish you knew what?"

"I wish I knew what love is, what it feels like, so that I could know whether I love you, or just want and need you around, but I don't, and I - -."

"You only met me the day before yesterday. Are you

certain it isn't just infatuation?" George asked, offering him a way out, now.

"No, how can I? But it doesn't feel like that. It's something more!" His arm was round her waist, the other across her thighs, and she was resting her arm on his shoulders, "I want all of you, all the time. I want you to be just for me, for always. I want to say I love you, but I don't know what love IS, so they're just words. I'm trying to explain, but the words are all wrong. I'm talking a load of cock, aren't I"

"Yes, and Yes." She replied.

"You see, I can't even do that right!"

"No, and I said Yes."

"I heard. I said I was talking nonsense, and you agreed with me."

"You asked two questions, and I said Yes, to both." She pointed out.

"So we are agreed, then, that - -."

"Yes. Of course!"

"- - I was talking nonsense, I always do when I try to say something important, it always goes wrong, somehow!"

265

"You still haven't noticed that I said Yes to the other question, have you?"

"What other - - ? Oh, my God! You mean - - you will?"

"Yes, I will be your lawful wedded wife, when the absolute comes through, and until then, I'll be your unlawfully bedded girl!"

"Don't tempt me! That still leaves one question unanswered, even though I've already asked it, - are you going back to flying? If you are, I shall go back to the flat, and start things happening, or if not, do you have a Pied a Terre somewhere, that you'd prefer to use?"

"Questions, questions, questions, always questions. If this, if that, if the other!"

"Then put your mouth over mine, and tangle my tongue, to stop me talking!"

She did, and they did, several times.

"In the meantime, do you fancy a walk, or a swim, or something?"

"We'll save the 'or something' 'til a bit later. Let's go for a poke around the rock pools."

266

"I thought you wanted to save 'it' 'til later! What I usually do, if I don't fancy a dive, is put the suit on, and fins, mask, and schnorkel, and just float about, in the bay, and see where I get washed to by the current and waves. I nodded off, once, and woke up about three miles down, towards South Stack lighthouse. There was a seagull parked on my chest, until it realized I wasn't a log. If you're lucky, you might see a seal, there are some around. I might even show you the little cave where I carved my initials in the rock."

"Yes, alright. That sounds nice, if you promise not to go zooming off anywhere, I want a nice rest!"

"Promise! Just float about, and enjoy. Have you ever tried it?"

"No, I can't say I ever have, we've either been going, diving, or coming back."

"Well, you know how you feel, when you're lying in a warm bath, just drifting, or at that point in bed, when you're not asleep, but not awake, either?"

"Yes."

"Like that, but without the bath, or the bed, to restrict

you. If there's a nice low swell running, and you close your eyes, it's a bit like riding the big dipper."

It seemed rather a silly idea, to me, but what the heck, if it kept him happy and amused for an hour or two, I'd give it a go. So I changed my sun-bathing suit for one of rather more substance, then wriggled into the dry-suit, then tossed fins, mask, and schnork into the Landie, while he was battling into his suit.

"Do I need the weights?"

"No, just fins and mask. Take your knife if you like, for insurance against discarded nets or fishing line."

"Right." I added the knife, and then fired up the Landie engine, which blared and rattled for a moment, then settled into the normal clatter of a Perkins diesel. Vince was halfway to his Ford, so I called him back. After a moment's hesitation, he climbed up, into the shotgun seat, and we bounced off, down the site track. At the Dafarch road, following his directions, we turned left, to the coast at Porth Dafarch, then turned left, and big dippered along the lane to a small cove called Porth y Post. It had a small parking space on the corner of a driveway, which led to a big house on a promontory. According to Vince, everyone called it the 'Haunted House', although he didn't know why. It did look like a miniature craggy castle, perched there on its rock. He said the owner's didn't mind a car or two parked on the verge, providing they were tight against the hedge, thus leaving both the road, and the drive, clear for passing vehicles. I locked the Landie, set the alarm, and followed him, looping the spare door key around my neck on a nylon cord. Vince led us down the driveway a few yards, and then onto a foot-track down to the cove, which had the public road looping around the back of it, on a raised embankment. I noticed he carried two knives, in sheaths, one strapped to his right calf, and a smaller one, on his left upper arm. When I asked, he explained that if he couldn't reach one, he could get the other. When I asked him to clarify that, he replied by saying that I'd obviously never got tangled in a discarded fishing net! True, I hadn't. Seeing that I didn't understand, he added that he hoped I never found out, first hand.

At the water's edge, he waded out, following a zig-zag path. I tried to follow, but everywhere I put my feet there were round, slippery boulders, and I nearly fell twice in the first few moments. When I yelled at him to slow down, he saw that I couldn't find the path, and showed me how a little fresh-water stream flowed into the cove, and there was a meandering narrow area where there was no weed, allowing the sand bottom to show through. When we were knee deep, he said this would do, and sat down. I tried to, but was floating about, supported by my dry-suit. Vince was putting his fins on, so I followed suit, feeling off-balance, until I got the hang of it. I found it easier to put my mask and schnorkel on first, then float face down, curled up, so I could breathe, and see what I was doing, while I put the fins on.

"All set?" He was floating, on his back, arms spread, so I grabbed hold of one, and flipped him over. Vince set off, at an easy pace, so I zoomed up and linked fingers. We trudged along for a while, approximately following the six-foot contour, which kept the bottom in clear view. As we weaved in and out of clumps of bladder-wrack, a few large silver fish shot off into the distance. I lifted my head out, "What were they?"

"Grey Mullet, I think. I didn't see them properly. Have you seen the big Ballan Wrasse that is following us?"

270

I hadn't, so he pointed it out. I looked hard, but couldn't see it, just rocks and weed, and then a rock yawned at me, and blinked! It was about three feet long, and eight inches deep, with fins like soup ladles, and a tail-fin as big as a dinner-plate. Vince slowly extended an arm, and then twiddled his fingers. The wrasse was paying attention, and drifted nearer, Vince paddled gently with his fins, and wiggled his finger again, and for a moment, he was touching the fish, then it seemed to flicker, and was gone, leaving a swirl of bubbles and sand. After a moment I heard him sigh, then he looked round, to check where I was. I made an O.K. sign, which he repeated to me, before lifting his head to check his bearings.

"There's the cave!" he glugged, as a small wave slapped him in the face.

Sure enough, there was a small cave in the rock, with its own little private shingle beach. I body-surfed up to it on a little wave, and drifted there, looking. The cave opening was about seven feet round, and went back into the rock about ten feet. It appeared to have a sand floor. "Nowhere to shelter, in a storm!" I commented.

271

"No, but it keeps the wind off, if you fancy a breather, some time," he agreed, "Just around the corner is a shallow area, full of nooks and crannies where all the juveniles hang about, if you fancy a look. Watch out for the surge, so you don't get bashed on a rock."

"O.K." I set off, with him trailing by a few feet. As I came round a big rock, I found I was finning quite hard, and making no progress, and then I would suddenly shoot forwards several yards, through the gap between rocks, at a break-neck speed. Then I slowed, and was finning hard, and going backwards, until I shot off, as the surge reversed again, propelling me forwards. Next time, as I reversed, finning hard, I saw Vince hanging on to a rock, and just resting, waiting for the next forward surge, and tried to copy him. I missed my hold, and had to fin even harder to catch up, but next time round I was thinking ahead, and chose my rock before the back-surge took me. Now I had time to look around, I could see all the little fish doing the same thing. As the surge ended, they all popped out of holes and cracks, grabbing whatever food morsels were in reach, then took cover again, as the current built, until next time.

Vince looked around, to see if I'd caught on, if you'll pardon the pun, then waved an O.K. with a spare hand. About a dozen surges later, we were spat out between rocks into deeper water again, where the movement was minimal.

"Fun?" he asked.

"Yes, not bad, for free, once I got the idea!"

"Do you want to go round again, or just go for a float about?"

"I'd rather take it easy, for now."

"O.K. This way, then, we'll get about two hundred yards away from the rocks, to avoid accidents."

"After you!"

He led the way into the approximate centre of the little bay we were in. Eventually he stopped, and had a good look round. "O.K. No wind-surfers to run us over! Roll over, face up, feet inshore. And relax. Push your mask up, if you want, just make sure it doesn't fall off!"

I twiddled round, a bit, until I was balanced, feeling rather foolish, and lay there in the water, as instructed, letting the

273

dry-suit support me. At first, I just felt stupid, and then realized my mind was drifting, the realization bringing me back with a jerk.

"See!" he said, "Just let go."

So I lay there, relaxing. There was enough stiffness and buoyancy in my hood to hold my head up,  Gradually, I noticed I could feel the surge of the ocean passing beneath me, lifting my head, then my shoulders, then my hips and finally my feet, as my head tipped down the back of the waves that were rocking me gently. I could hear the water splooshing on the rock face, making a bassy 'Boosh-shhh' sound. There were lots of clicks and whistles I'd never heard before. From far away a faint whining noise, which I recognized as an outboard motor on a boat, was droning away. I was thinking that this was how it must feel, and sound, to a dolphin, when I noticed I was getting cold. It seemed to be getting dark, too! I 'sat' up, and looked for Vince, who was about six feet away, grinning at me.

"I heard you wake up." He chuckled, "You sucked in a great lung-ful of air, and stopped singing."

"Singing?"

"Mm. Sort of! Random, tuneless snatches, and words I couldn't quite catch, something about dolphins, just then."

"I was thinking that this is how it must seem, to them, – but, I'm getting cold, and I'd like to get back."

"No problem. The current has carried us about a quarter of a mile. So do you want to fin back, or we can go around the corner, and walk back. It's not that far to the car, from there."

"That way, then, round the corner." I waved my fins, rolled over, and grabbed his hand again.

He swam with his mask half in, half out of the water, so he could see where he was going, and seeing that I was keeping up, stepped up the pace somewhat. After about ten minutes, I was warm again, and starting to puff a bit, so he eased off, raised his head, and said "Nearly there!" When I looked, we were about a hundred yards out. He kept finning along, even when the bottom came up to meet us, until he was 'porpoising' over the rocks, and could go no further as he was running aground. He rolled over, and sat up.

"Come on." He said, "We don't want to get run over while walking to the car in the dark!"

275

"It's dark, early, tonight!"

"Not really, we've been in the water nearly two hours!"

"Oh!"

"Yes, Oh!  Miss Van Winkel!"

"But I wasn't – "

"Asleep, no, just drifting. Safer than chemicals, and cheaper than booze, with no hang-over, after! How do you feel?" He was leading us up a track in a gulley, with bracken, brambles and other scrub on both sides, then over a stile, and onto the tarmac road. "It's about half a mile from here." We turned right. "It's a good job you have hard soles on your boots!"


He was bending the truth a little over the distance. After half a mile of up and down, and zig-zags, we reached Dafarch, and I knew the car was another mile further on.

"You rat!" I slapped him on the backside with one of my fins.

We slogged along, for a while, passing a few houses, and the Cliff Hotel, perched up on the highest point in the immediate area, hence its name.

276

"One thing they have plenty of, around here," Vince commented, "is white-wash!"

The road made a big curve round to the right, then over another hump, and we could see the 'Haunted House'.

"If you go onto the beach on this side of the house, there are the remains of an old wooden slip-way buried in the shingle. Loads of big logs, with rusted bolts sticking through them, ideal for bursting inflatables on, and an old hand-crank winch, still with the wire rope on the drum. Rusted solid, of course." Vince said.

"I might have a look, tomorrow, if I'm in the mood. What's the beach like?"

"Pebbles and kelp, full of flies and sand-hoppers, last time I looked. It opens out to where I was playing with the Wrasse."

"I saw that, but didn't believe it. You love the wildlife, don't you?"

"I suppose I do."

"I heard you sigh when the fish left."

"To me, it wasn't just a fish, it was another living being,

277

with more right to be there than us."

"No, there was more than that in the sigh."

"Maybe. I was happy/sad when it went. Happy to meet it, as an equal, and sad that it decided not to trust us."

"Well, it is wild!"

"Wild doesn't mean scared. Cautious, yes, but that Wrasse saw me as danger. Man always ruins everything, everywhere, any way he can."

"That's what I said, you love it all. Has anything ever attacked you?"

"Water, or land?"

"Both. Water first."

"Yes. A couple of years ago. I was poking about in some rocks, in about three feet of water, when this enormous great thing took a chunk out of the back of my hand. There's the scar, to prove it!" He displayed a little pink blotch on his right hand, "It must have been about the size of a dessert spoon bowl! Ruined a good glove, too! Aggressive little sod!"

"What was it?"

"A new Typhoon - - Oh, the fish! I don't know, I barely

saw it, it was so fast, silvery-brown, roundish, laterally compressed. If I didn't know better, I'd say it was a piranha, but they're tropical freshwater!"

"Be serious!"

"I am!"

"Alright." She laughed. "What about on land, apart from Scousers?"

"Horses. I am hated by horses. I only have to stand near a paddock fence, and the vicious brutes come thundering up, and attempt to bite me!"

"Go on!"

"It's true! I'll show you, some time." He smiled when she reached down her neck-line for the Land-Rover key. "I've got a similar necklace!"

"I could murder a cup of coffee." She carefully avoided the comparison of chests.

"Stop nattering, then, and let me in!"

"I think I'll make you walk back, in retribution for making me walk half the length of Wales, to the car!"

Chapter seventeen.

Evening Three.


When they trundled back to camp in George's Landie, the Site Warden was doing his daily rounds. "Ah, there you are! I saw that your car was still here, but both you and your tent had disappeared."

"Don't worry about it. I'm in good hands."

"You're leaving us, today, then?"

"No." Vince grinned at me as I climbed out of the Landie, "A change of plans, and accommodation."

"Ah. Two consenting adults, etc. Mine not to reason why, and so forth. Don't annoy the neighbours."

"He hasn't the time!" George put in her penniworth,

"And anyway, the old chap next door is too busy trying to figure out who is doing what to whom, to complain. It would spoil his fun!"

The Warden laughed, waved, and went on his way.

"Come on, Slave, get the kettle fired up, while I dress for dinner."

"Dress? I thought you WERE dinner!"

"Thinking is bad for you!"

As she ducked into the bedroom, he said, "I was hoping you would be bad - with me!"

As he lit the gas under the kettle, Pete and Trevor came crunching up the gravel track in their truck, so Vince held up a cup, waved five fingers, then added more water to the kettle when he saw the 'thumbs up' acknowledgement.

"Pete and Trev will be over in a few minutes." He said.

"I heard. I'm out, and going for a wee while you change."

Pete and Trevor were out of the truck, looking at their tent, then at each other. Trev shrugged, and then they came over to George's tent.

"Before you ask," Vince said, "A big orange bird sat on it, and knocked it flat."

"Eh?"

"The S.A.R. chopper came over, and picked a climber off the rocks, just above, and its downdraft flattened your tent. I put it back up, but I think I put a couple of the poles in the wrong places."

"It seems to have blown your tent away completely." Pete noted.

"Well, I was busy holding this one down at the time!"

"Forever the gallant hero! What was the pretty one doing while you were fighting to save her accommodation?"

"Wetting herself with laughter, mostly!"

"Typical!"

"Did you get out to the Skerries?" Vince asked, as he emerged, dressed in his usual scruffs.

"Yeah, pretty bumpy trip, and when we got there, the visibility underwater was naff, all of two feet, in the clearest parts."

"We were going to dive a wreck in a hundred and

twenty feet, but on one cylinder, that gives us a bottom time of about six minutes, to avoid decompression, and by the time we'd found the damn thing, it was time to come up!" Trev added.

"I heard that!" George joined them, "I don't know why you bothered, really!"

"Nor me," Trev continued, "We didn't even have time to identify which pile of scrap we'd found. I've never known it to be so mucky, way out there."

"I've heard that people are blaming the spoil-dumping from the Conwy by-pass tunnel, but I thought the current went the other way." Vince added.

"It could be coming down Menai, and going round and round, but, like you, Vince, I thought the Skerries would be too far out, to be affected."

"Yeah," Pete added, "But the only other boat out there, today, was that live-aboard, and there was nobody in the water when we went down, so perhaps they'd been using air-lifts, or something."

Vince passed the cups of coffee round, and they chatted amiably, for a while, then Pete said, "Come on, Trev, let's get our hotel reassembled properly, before it goes too dark."

"That won't be for hours – Oh! Yeah, right!" They left.

We watched them partially dismantle, then re-erect their tent, ending with a rather straighter assembly than Vince had left it, then retired inside the 'veranda', because the insects had come out to play, and were hungry. George lit a citronella candle, and after a few minutes spent swatting stray mosquitos, they settled down, well, Vince did. George was pottering about, fiddling and adjusting things that didn't need fiddling with or adjusting. Something was obviously on her mind. When he came within range, Vince caught her, and pulled her down into the facing chair,

"Talk to me. Tell me what it is."

She was looking at the floor, her hands, the window, anywhere but at Vince.

"Tell me, was it something I did?"

A solitary tear trickled down from her left eye, and hung, twinkling, from her chin. "I, - -. "  She began, but couldn't continue.

"What?" he held her hands, gently, their knees

intertwined, as he had turned his chair to face hers. "Have you changed your mind?"

"I had to - - to - ." She broke down completely, her body shaking, tears pouring down, now. She howled, once, causing Pete, who was fiddling with the compressor, to start across, but then he halted, and went back, as it was none of his business.

Vince got to his knees, and held her tight, feeling her shuddering, her ribs heaving as she buried her face in the side of his neck. She wrapped her arms round him, clinging desperately, as she sobbed silently. He waited, and gradually, the sobbing eased, the shaking stopped.

"Hey! Now what was that all about?" He relaxed his grip on her.

"H - -h - -hold me!" She begged, so he gripped her again.

"I should have left my wet-suit on!" he whispered, "My jumper's all soggy, now!"

George made a noise that was part sob, part laugh, and part hiccough, "S - -s - -sorry, it j - -just hit me f - - from nowhere." She sniffled.

He pulled out his hankie, mopped her eyes and face, then kissed it better, before resuming his hold.

In a while, she started again. "I made a 'phone call, earlier. I've to report on Monday, at eight a.m. for assessment. Sorry!"

"It's O.K. You have your duty to fulfill. You did warn me, but you could have said you were going to call in, before you did!"

"It wouldn't have made any difference, and you might have tried to talk me out of it, so I did it while I could."

"It still gives us three nights, and two days, to enjoy. Will they let you out at night?"

"I don't know. Maybe."

"Well, if they do, I'll be here for as long as I can stay. If they won't, you can 'phone the site office, and ask them to pass a message on, then we can arrange a meeting and decide what to do." He paused, "Or would you rather I went home to wait for you, if she hasn't sold the place."

"Mmmm." She replied, non-committal. "Sod the

286

evening meal, take me to bed!"

Pete saw the tent-lights go out. "Something's up!" he mused.

"Do you think she's called time on him, and it's 'once more, for the road'?"

"Maybe, but I don't think so. It's more involved than that."

"Anyway, what's all that about the climber, and the helicopter?"

"That's what we were supposed to see, but I suspect that the 'watcher' has been removed by somebody else."

"Who's team, though? I didn't spot anyone out of place."

"Beats me! There must be another team operating, as well as us, and our paths have crossed. I wonder whether the Boss knows about them? We'd better put it on the tape for tonight's report."

The Boss didn't know, and became most vocal.

287

Fortunately for the system, he didn't have direct access to the radio link, so the base operator was able to filter out most of the expletives and rage. Pete and Trev were advised, unnecessarily, to watch their backs, and that another team would be sent to guard them, but would not make contact unless absolutely essential.

Pete and Trev discussed various possibilities, and then ended up speculating who the second, supporting, team might be, without coming to any conclusions. Everyone they knew was already in the field on active jobs, around the country.

After a while, Pete went to check on the compressor, which was still chugging quietly, as it filled their used cylinders. Trev heard him clunking about, then there was the sharp hiss of released compressed air, as Pete uncoupled the air-lines, then it went suspiciously quiet.

"Pete?"

No response.

"Pete?"

Trev pulled a pistol from its clip, hidden under the table in the truck, then switched off the light, before opening the back

288

flap which had been lowered to keep the moths out, then eased silently out of the truck. "Pete?"

"Shh! Over there, in the scrub." Pete whispered, from the shadows.

Trev could see nothing, his eyes not yet adapted after the internal lighting. "I can't see a damn thing, yet, where?"

"See that scrubby willow, about thirty yards away?"

"No, not yet, but I know it."

"There's something in the scrub, just to the left of it. I can't see what, yet."

"I still can't see a damn thing! We must get red lights fitted!"

They waited, silent, then "Yeah, got it then, about ten feet left of that clump of bulrushes."

"That's it."

"Right then, you go round to the left, and I'll circle round to the right, and pincer it, No! Wait. Let's see what Mr Fox makes of it, first!"

The fox was ghosting along the edge of the scrub,

looking for lunch, a faint, intermittent clucking suggesting the presence of a moor-hen in the ditch. Then it came face-to-face with the mystery creature, leaped back, yapped with alarm, and bolted. The other creature, equally startled, chattered back, and charged after it for a few paces, then realized it was a lost cause.

"It's a bloody badger!"

"I should have remembered! I saw one there, yesterday, when I was looking around."

"Yeah! I saw it too, when I was having a look, after we'd faked the argument."

"We're getting paranoid!"

"Must be! I'll just put this away, and then I'm going for a pee before I turn in."

"Right with you."


Meanwhile, a similar conversation was taking place, on the camp-site at the rear of the Cliff Hotel, between the thin one, and the one with hairy arms, as they sat in their caravan, Their Toyota four wheel drive pick-up was parked outside, providing volts for the light. Their caravan also had a few, non-standard, items tucked away in the fitted cabinets, away from accidental prying eyes. They included a Yaesu Radio Amateur's set that had been worked on by an engineer, so that it worked on non-amateur frequencies, as did the almost identical one in Trev's truck, when called to do so by a key-code. There was, of course, a similar set in the cab of the pick-up, either of which could also be used with the walkie-talkies that had been in use earlier, and also, in a cross-band mode, as a high powered relay station, so that the walkie-talkie user could talk directly to base, if need be. The caravan radio also had a scrambler/de-scrambler unit built in, to foil accidental listeners. The thin one was amusing itself, (it was one of those confused creatures that nature had placed in the wrong gender body), watching a couple of teenagers snogging and having a clumsy fumble, in what they thought was total darkness. He/she was using the image intensifier lens they had acquired earlier, which made everything in its field appear to be various shades of green, but with sufficient detail to allow him/her to see who was doing what, to whom. Thick hairy-arm was fine tuning the transceiver, trying to persuade the scrambler to lock-on to the signal from base, without success. It would hold lock for a few seconds, then 'drop out' again, no matter what he did. Defeated, he reverted to plain language, and managed to make out the instruction to try 'fifteen', through all the howls and beeps of interference. 'Fifteen' meant thirty point oh two five Megahertz. He tuned up to the new frequency, but the noise was worse there, than on the previous frequency, making base totally inaudible. "All the brass they throw about, and they can't get a decent comm's system!" he groused.

In an office, inside another office, a rarely used telephone rang once, twice, and then the answering machine picked up the call.

"Jimmy? It's Fred. That business we were discussing, - just to keep you up to speed, ah, the monitoring station has gone off the air, it could be just an interruption. We're looking into it." Click.

In a basement, somewhere else, a man who had thought he was dead - woke up. He was spread-eagled on a concrete floor. Ropes went from his wrists to big steel eye-bolts set in the concrete, his legs were fastened at the ankles in, presumably, a similar manner. A chair stood next to a table, on which stood a metal box, with wires dangling in loops over the edge. He was very cold, felt like vomiting, and badly needed to pee. Gradually, he realized he was naked. A closed circuit TV camera was mounted high in a corner, staring at him with its glass eye.

'Oh Shit!' he thought.


Group Three Security Services had sent a van to Bangor prison, to pick up three passengers for transport to more appropriate accommodation. Unfortunately, having collected them, the van crew took an unofficial diversion to a nearby Little Chef café, to partake of a light lunch. While the driver and his shotgun mate were ordering their fish and chips to go, an opportunist thief forced the back door open, hoping to 'borrow' a few watches, or something else of saleable value What he didn't expect was a steel toe-capped boot in the teeth, followed by another, two feet lower, as the prisoners made a hasty departure, one of them snatching up the van-breaker's tool-bag in passing, in the hope there would be something contained within that would remove the hand-cuffs the three wore, at some more appropriate moment. When the crew returned, bearing their fish and chips, they were greeted by the sight of an empty van, the back door swinging in the breeze, and a puddle of fresh vomit on the road behind the van. Being resourceful people, and mindful of their future careers, they repositioned the van a mile up the road, before calling in on their radio link, to report that the prisoners had been kidnapped when they were blocked in by a tractor. They then settled down to their lunch while they waited.

Mick 'knew someone' who lived near the castle at Beaumaris, so that is where they all headed, on foot, still handcuffed together.

Chapter eighteen.

Monday.

Saturday and Sunday flew by, as only the last days of a holiday can. Vince and George spent the time talking, walking, schnorkelling, loving. They talked about themselves, each other, plans, ambitions, money, lack of it, and generally put the world to rights. On Sunday, they packed George's gear into her Landie, then re-pitched Vince's tent on the spot, before retiring early. Pete and Trev had 'Got the Message', and kept away. In truth, they were glad, as it gave them time and space to get on with their own business.

Thick hairy arms and the thin one were baffled. The

people they had been sent to watch weren't DOING anything, just ordinary holiday stuff, and now they had changed tents!

At six a.m. George's watch -alarm beeped her into wakefulness. She clung to him for a few minutes more, and then eased out of the bed to dress. When she got back from the loo block he was up and about, and had the al fresco kitchen going. Bacon and eggs were sizzling in the pan. He put a bacon and egg sandwich into her hand, and said "Eat it!"

George reluctantly nibbled a corner, unwilling, and not wanting food, but hunger took over, and she ate it without tasting it. A cup of coffee washed it down, and he fastened it there with a kiss.

He put a picture-postcard of Port Merion into her hand. "That's my home address, and just in case, Joan's, and her telephone number. I'll be here until next Sunday, waiting for you, but then I'll have to go, from lack of finance. Come back to me, somewhere."

"I will. Don't see me off. Don't even watch. I'll just go." A tear trickled down her face.

"O.K. Take care, my lover." Vince husked. He walked slowly to the loo block, and spent half an hour over a two-minute function. When he returned, she had gone. There was a postcard on his kettle, captioned 'Sydney Harbour at Night'. The scene was totally black. On the reverse, she had written – 'I LOVE YOU.   XXX.   G' There was a small water stain accompanying the words.

Sid, Harry, and Mick succeeded in getting to the address Mick knew of, undetected. Unfortunately, the person they wanted had been 'Removed' by the Provo's a few months earlier. The new occupant did not take kindly to being roused at two a.m. by three handcuffed, footsore scruffs, one of which appeared to be wearing a disintegrating paper overall with nothing beneath it. He slammed the door in their faces, and dialled 999. Beaumaris is not a big place, and the three were soon rounded up again. Naturally, their story of how they escaped differed somewhat from that of the Security Guards, and further study revealed the chisel marks on the van door. The van was impounded, and the guards arrested, pending further investigation.

Vince moped around the site for a while, feeling a bit like the pall-bearer that had turned up at a wedding, then gave himself a mental kick, pulled on his wet-suit pants, and his boots, picked up his jacket, mask, fins and schnorkel, then jogged the mile or so to Porth Dafarch, where he paused long enough to pull the jacket on, then set off to swim across the full bay to Raven's Point. He finned along slowly for a while, to loosen up, and then stepped up the pace, so that the water appeared to be boiling in front of his mask. Keeping a wary eye out for wind-surfers, jet-skiers, and other surface craft, he forged away, until he was nearly ashore again, then he slowed down, looking for a good exit point. With his fins, mask, and jacket off, he pounded along the road, round the bay, through the village, past the Post Office, the garage, where he reminded himself to pick up the repaired tyre, and back to the campsite. He was beginning to limp, as a blister had formed on his heel and was making its presence known. He dumped his gear at the entrance to the tent, and flopped into a folding chair, which creaked in protest at the stress, but held. There was something different about the Cortina, and he puzzled about it for a minute, and then realized it had acquired a new windscreen sticker that proclaimed that it 'would rather be diving'. He grinned, and made a mental note to obtain something suitable to attach to George's Land-Rover at the next opportunity, if there was one. He forced his thoughts away from that line. He looked around the site. Pete's tent was there, but the truck was not. The old codger was pottering around his beat-up Austin Maxi. A new couple, who had arrived on Sunday, were chattering away inside their enormous ridge-tent, their car ticking and cracking as the engine cooled after recent use. Most of the others had gone, as the weekend was almost over. A small, orange, pup-tent lurked near a tree, on the far side of the site, its owner/occupier nowhere to be seen, although a motorcycle leaned drunkenly on its side-stand. All the usual country noises were audible, birds cheeping, the occasional Honk of a pheasant, which reminded him of Pete making fun of.George and himself. Now and then, the plaintive MOO of the Holyhead fog-horn drifted cross the site, its mechanical workings not realizing it was a bright sunny

299

day. He sighed, rummaged in the depleted larder, sawed two doorstops off the rather crispy loaf, buttered them, and added a wedge of cheese, after trimming a green furry corner off, and had lunch.

A growly, snarly noise made him look up, to see a Scottish Aviation Bulldog piston trainer chew it's way across the sky, its orange and grey paint-work glinting in the sunlight.

He suddenly realized, that for the first time in days, he was bored! The thought amused him as he gave up cracking his teeth on the bread-crust, and slung it at some sparrows which were squabbling with a starling, near a litter- bin. The starling grabbed one piece, and - wings flogging, it laboured away to the willow tree, where it tried to beat the crust to death. One sparrow, bigger than the rest, tried to lift the other piece, then they all began to fight over possession of it, failing to notice the magpie which stole it while they were pre-occupied. The magpie, in turn lost it to a dive-bombing tern, which lost it to a herring-gull. It is believed that the gull, being as stupid as all of it's kind, tried to swallow the crust whole, and choked to death, in turn providing the fox that had been frightened by the badger, earlier, with an easy meal, thus giving the pheasant chicks another day in which to learn the art of 'evade and escape'.

George turned her Land-Rover into the parking bay indicated by the gate guard, then climbed out while it was inspected for bombs and contraband. Her armful of passes and I.D. cards were scrutinized, and a couple of telephone calls made. With her identity established, she was directed to the medical section, but had to leave her car where it was. She locked it up, set the booby-traps, and began the three mile hike across the base to the wooden shed with the red cross painted on the white background. She found the entrance, and went in. The old Staffer, on the reception desk, took her papers, and then pointed at a chair, with a grunt. Her papers were added to some more from a file, stuffed into the perspex carrier of a pneumatic tube delivery system, and fired off somewhere, with a slurp. A minute later, the sudden hiss-thud announced its return. The Staffer clambered laboriously out of his chair, and went to retrieve it, then beckoned George over, then gave her a wad of

A4 papers. "Fill that in!"

George took them back to the chair, along with a borrowed pen, and sighed, the first question was 'Name' then 'M or F', then they ranged across all possible medical complaints, starting at headlice, and ending with corns, bunions, in-growing toenails, and flat feet. She skimmed rapidly through them all, paused only to write her name rank, and official number, then on the bottom of the last sheet, she wrote 'As before', and signed it. When she passed it back the Staffer sniffed noisily, as he perused all the blank pages, and read the final comment.

"What do you mean, 'As before'?" he asked, annoyed.

"What it says!"

"But you can't do that! You have to fill it all in."

"So that you can read it in your spare time?" She challenged. "Get your fat arse out of that chair, and go and find my file, it's in that cabinet, behind you." She pointed, "You will find my file in the rack, one left of the end, second drawer down, around the middle, which proves that my eyesight is better than yours. Now stop wasting my time."

The Staffer flicked through a desk diary, muttering, then said - "Come back on Friday, at fifteen-hundred. The trick cyclist will see you then."

"No, he won't. I'm here, now, as instructed. He sees me now, or makes a new appointment, some time next year, when it is convenient for me!"

"But you can't - -."

"I have, I did, and I will. I don't want to be here. I was sent for. I have better things to do."

"Look, I don't want to have to pull rank on you, but -."

"Go ahead. See how far it gets you. I shall have to tell someone higher up what there is in the bottom drawer of that green cabinet marked 'First Aid'. It isn't first aid equipment, although I suppose you could call it 'Educational'."

A door clicked open, behind her. "Well, I believe that Commander Weastey has regained her fire!"

"FLIGHT Commander!" She snapped, whirling, then added "Sir" when she saw that the speaker well out-ranked her.

"Quite! Well, we don't worry too much about rank, here. The only labels that concern us are 'Fit', 'Unfit', or

'Further Consultation'! Come through." He held the door for her, and closed it, behind. "How did you know about that bottom drawer?"

"Simple. As I came in, he hastily dropped a magazine into it, and pushed it shut with his foot."

"Yes, so?"

"A full colour photography magazine, with Scandinavian text?"

"Ah!"

"Yes. Ah. I'm certain there is something in Queen's Reg's, about inappropriate publications, that would be applicable!"

"I can tell from this brief conversation that you have passed my tests, anyway. You are back in balance again, not the broken mouse who last came to see me." He paused, looking at her closely, "You don't remember, do you?"

"I recall being brought here, but not you. Sorry, Sir."

"Don't be. It wasn't you who crashed, but it WAS you who broke. Can you talk about it, now?"

"Yes. Something seemed to snap, a few days ago, and

all of a sudden I could discuss it. I told Vince all –"

"Vince? You have a new man?"

"Mm! He put me back together, just by being there. I can't explain it."

"Call it magic, I do! Are you still with him?"

"Up until this morning, yes. I hope so. It depends."

"On what?"

"Me."

"Explain that, if you will."

"Well, ah, - Any chance of a coffee?"

"I don't see why not. Talking is thirsty work." He pressed a button on the intercom, "Corp? Two coffee's, one normal, one – ," he raised an eyebrow.

"Black and one."

"Black and one sugar, please."

"Sah!" A voice on the intercom responded.

"You were saying?" he turned back to George.

"Yes. I'm trying to put it in a frame." She gazed at a framed print of a Sterling bomber above fluffy white clouds, then there was a knock at the door, and the coffees were brought in.

"Thanks, Corp, That's all."

"Sah!" The corporal left, closing the door.

She was silent for a while, thinking, and trying to formulate the words, then sighed. "I suppose it depends on what I want most - him, or my career. He would wait for me, and put up with twice a year visits, but is that fair on him? Is it right that I should ask him?"

He looked at her, as a man, not as a Surgeon, and liked what he saw. "I know what I would do," he said, smiling, "and I'd enjoy every minute, but it has to be YOUR decision!"

"Yes, I know, and I'm stuck on the fence, I can't decide which way to go, whether to resign, and break a contract, or stay, and break two hearts!"

"Like I said, it is not for me to decide, but perhaps I can help clear the fog. Why did you come back in?"

"Because – I have a duty. I signed a contract for ten years. I have three to go. I could have played sick, but that would be cheating the R.A.F, and myself. I would have been signed off as a nutter, and I'm not, - "

"That answer tells me that you know what you want. All you have to do is admit it to yourself. Go for a wander, and think about it, then come back and tell me again. You won't have to bully the Staff again to get in. That was part of your test, to see if you could, or would!"

"Is there a time limit?" She finished the coffee.

"No, couple of minutes, couple of hours! I'll be here. Go and find somewhere quiet, and contemplate your navel, or something."

"I will. Thank you, Sir."

He opened the door for her, "Sar'nt, When Flight Weastey returns, fit her in, I shouldn't think we would need more than five minutes!"

"Sah!"

"Sorry for shouting at you, Sar'nt." She added.

"It's alright, Ma'am, it goes with the job, the bumbling paper-shuffler!"

"You do it well."

"Lot's of practice. See you later, Ma'am."

"Can you point me at the NAAFI canteen?"

"It's quite a hike, across the far side of the compound. I'll run you round in a car."

"No, thanks, I need to think about something."

"Been there, myself, Ma'am, and took this job on, as a result!" He offered a wry grin, "Out of the door, up to the main drag, Turn left, and keep going, follow the Cinema signs, it's next to the Squash courts and gym."

"Thanks." She set off. The Sergeant was right, it was quite a hike, airfields are big, sprawly places, and by the time she got there, she was ready for a break. The canteen was closed, so she fed coins into slot machines, and collected a meat pie, a bar of chocolate, and a can of lemonade. In a far corner was a table beneath a lamp with a blown bulb, giving an illusion of privacy, where she sat mulling over the Psychiatrist's words, and eating the pie and chocolate. When she was burping from the gassy drink, the answer came to her. The answer she had known all the while, and refused to see.

Half a dozen cadets came crashing in through the door, shouting, and jeering each other, chasing about with the exuberance of youth. The noise and disturbance, plus a growing pressure in her bladder, drove her to move.


Vince fired up the Cortina, and left it coughing and choking while he peeled off the wet-suit pants, then dressed in street clothes. Ready, he chugged off, to pick up his tyre and fill the fuel tank at the garage in Trearddur, and grocery-shop. As he went through Valley village, and turned left onto the A55, he noticed that an Austin Maxi seemed to be following him, so led it on a merry dance around the back-streets of Holyhead while he looked for a parking space. He picked one where there was no other in the immediate area, and watched what happened. The Maxi slowed as it passed, the sole occupant giving him the evil eye, so Vince gave a one-finger salute in return. When the Maxi went round the corner, Vince dove out of the Cortina and ran down a back-alley that led to the market hall, where he went in through one entrance, right through, and out of the other. Then he went briskly down the street a short way, before ducking into Woolworths, where he browsed along the bookshelf. One title caught his eye, and he picked up the latest release from Clive Cussler, paid for it using his plastic card, then went grocery shopping, as no-one had come looking for him. Three bulging carrier-bags later, he arrived, back at the Cortina. With his shopping in the boot, he cranked up the smoke generator, then staggered off, up past the railway station, and onto the Porth Dafarch road, then back to the campsite. There was no sign of Mr Maxi.

Later, somewhere about chapter five, he switched on his scanner, and set it listening for interesting activity. A brief, ear-shattering BEEP from close by nearly ruptured his ear-drums, but before he could press the 'pause' button, the scanner had moved off the frequency. Vince activated the 'frequency hold' function, then spent the next few minutes pressing the 'pass' button when the scanner stopped on the various whistles, tweets, chirps, and other weird noises that fill the radio spectrum. BEEP! There! 458.0875 Mhz. BEEP! Whatever it was, it was close. BEEP! Then the penny dropped. It was his car! It was bugged with a tracer. A quick search of the various accessible nooks and crannies found it, a plastic box attached by a powerful magnet, behind the curve of the rear bumper, with about four inches of wire aerial dangling. Satisfied, he stored the frequency in a spare memory of his receiver, then set it to 'pass' on that frequency. Who was responsible? Pete and Trev, or Austin Maxi? With no immediate answer, he went back to Dirk Pitt, and his latest exploit.

Thick hairy arms wandered casually through the site, apparently heading for the bar. He hoped no-one had seen him climb the fence at the far end, nearly falling into a boggy patch when he snagged a toe. Yes, the guy with the tatty Cortina was there, reading something. There was no sign of the blonde woman, or her jeep. She had gone out, early, catching them on the hop. By the time they'd got the Maxi going, she was out of sight. His partner had raced off in pursuit, but failed to catch her, but was back in time to see the thin guy go running off down the road, in his dive kit. He also fooled them, because he came out of the water in a different location, leaving them sitting there, like a pair of right berks, watching the tide come and go, while he did whatever he did. It was just by chance that they found him again when his smoky old car came trundling past, just when thick hairy arms had gone to water the bushes. The usual car-

311

parking dodge threw them off again, but they had left an electronic tracer on the Cortina, for next time, ensuring they could follow it from a distance.

Trev and Pete came rumbling up the track in their truck, and saw Vince sitting there. He waved at them, and went back to his book, not feeling very sociable, at the moment.

"Are you coming over, for a brew?" Trev called, through the cab window.

Vince hefted a half-used can of coke, and replied, "Not now, thanks."

Pete waved, "It must be withdrawal symptoms!" then sniggered at the double entendre as he parked the truck. Trev climbed down, and wandered off towards the block-house. Pete connected up used dive-bottles to the compressor, which he started up, leaving it chugging away, while he brewed up, and made a couple of doorstop sandwiches for when Trev got back.

"No bloody loo paper again!" Trev said, when he returned, drank the coffee in one gulp, then went back again, carrying a roll of pink tissue. Pete ate his sandwich, watching a magpie watching Trev's food and waiting for a chance to steal it.

Trev trudged back again, and picked up his sandwich, "Have you figured out what is going on, yet?"

"You mean the job, or those two?"

"Both, really. She pissed off at about seven thirty. He seems to be waiting for her to come back, without much hope."

"Yeah! They had a row about something, last night, and another on Friday. Perhaps he was getting too demanding?"

"Maybe, but I don't think it was that." Trevor mused, "Because they didn't want to part. I think she had to go back. About the other business – nothing but dead ends everywhere. I suspect that they're on to us, and are leading us round by the nose."

"Have you even spotted any of them, yet?"

"No. I thought that lot in town, last week, were them, but it seems that they were just thugs passing through, and picked on the wrong ones to mug!"

"That's true enough! Who threw the star?"

"Beats me. A mystery third party."

"I thought it was Blondie, at first, but now, I don't think

she could throw a tantrum." Pete sighed.

"I don't know about that! Vinnie copped a good shiner! She was too far away, anyway, and the wrong angle, a foot either side, and she'd have taken one or other of us out."

"That's a cheering thought!" Pete considered it, "So there has to be another person involved, a female, because it was a female that warned us the law was about to arrive."

"Yeah, it was, and it wasn't George's voice, it was higher, with a Brummie accent."

"Leave that for now, - Who do you think took the pipe?"

"Judging by the weight, and the length, it must have been a biggish boat, with a derrick and a winch. I'd say the pipe was the thick end of a hundredweight."

"Could that Wessex lift it?"

"Probably, with the right kit on its winch, but it's too visible, and that is unlikely."

"True."

They both sat there, pondering the matter, and drawing no conclusions.

314

"Then again, Pete, maybe BECAUSE it is too obvious, no-one would think twice about a SAR chopper thrashing about over a pile of rocks!"

"That's a thought, but it means that the R.A.F. must be in on it!"

"Can't be, or can they?"

"If so, it means this thing is bigger than we thought."

"Yeah, maybe it's 'Get your head down' time!" As he spoke, something went 'thock!' on the tent. Then something went 'Spang!' on the truck, Trev looked at Vince, in case he was fooling about, but he was glaring at them! Then something hit him on the head, with a wet 'splat!' "Hell! It's bloody raining!"


They grabbed the various bits and pieces that were lying around, and slung them into the tent, noticing Vince was doing the same, as they dove into the flimsy shelter.

"Are these raindrops, or golf-balls?" Pete dashed out, and tossed a tarp over the still-chugging compressor, as he was still wearing his wet-suit.

"Whatever. We're in for a soaking!"

The rain was battering down, now, flattening the grass, and converting the site into a bog. A juvenile river cascaded down the central track.

"Quick! Grab a couple of those cans!" Pete was holding up the ground-sheet, just left of centre, thwarting a rivulet that sought entry. Trev slid them under the sheet, making a temporary bridge that would hopefully divert the water underneath, and out at the other side.

Vince dove into his tent, and dragged the end zip down. The rain was a constant roar, now. Had he closed the Cortina windows, he wondered, Sod it! The rain would leak out through the hole in the floor. He shook the water from his hair, and wiped ineffectually at his sodden tee-shirt. The pages of his book were stuck together, so he hung it on the bit of string he used as a clothes-line, to drip-dry, then looked at the inch or so of drinking-water in his barrel, wondering which would last longer, his fresh water, or the rain. With a resigned shrug, he poured half his water into the kettle, and lit the burner. Busy with the coffee, he didn't hear the zip go up. Then a very wet girl was in his arms, laughing, crying, clinging to him, and kissing him. After a comprehensive snogging session, he said "You're wet!"

"So are you, now!"

"I noticed. How did you get on?"

"It's a long story, how long have you got?"

"The rest of my life, how about you?" The hairs on the back of his neck prickled, as he said it.

"That might just be long enough. Did I see you with some coffee?"

"I'll have to start again, someone has dripped into this one!" He ruefully studied the glutinous mess in the bottom of the cup.

Over coffee and damp biscuits, she told him the gist of the first interview.

"And?"

"I think it has stopped raining. I'll get some dry clothes." She left him cliff-hanging.

While she was changing, in his little tent, Vince squelched over to the stand-pipe, with his depleted water-barrel, and re-filled it.

"And then?" he insisted, on his return.

"I've to go back on Wednesday, for a decision." She answered, without answering.

"On what?"

"Oh! I didn't say, did I?" she teased him.

"No."

"Well, the trick cyclist thinks I'm sane, again, -,"

"I never doubted it!"

"– so I've passed his tests, but as I've been out for so long, I've to go through re-training, and refreshers."

"Yes, so?"

"So they have to decide if I'm worth it, as the budget cuts are forcing them to eliminate surplus aircrews."

"And you told the Medic you didn't want to be chopped."

"No, the opposite. I told the Psycho that I'd gone back because it was my duty, etcetera."

"Yes, that's what you said to me."

"What I didn't say I went back for, is - -?"

He thought about it, replaying the earlier conversation,

in his mind. "Flying?" He ventured.

"You've got it! That side of my life is finished. I don't want it any more. So it all depends on if they want to keep me for shuffling paper, or whether they think it would be cheaper to pension me off, and be rid of a surplus body." She shrugged, "They asked me if I was living locally, and I said yes, so they said to go home, and return on Wednesday for their decision. So, here I am."

"Are you sure that is what you want? Out?"

"Yes. I'm sure. I've had enough of it, and if they give me the chance, I'll take it."

"But, if they don't, what then?"

"Then I'll be a very bored, very bad, paper shuffler, until my time is up."

"O.K. then, turn it round. If they boot you out on Wednesday, what will you do, where will you go?"

"That sounds like you are trying to duck out from under! I will do what I want, and go where I want to go. Simple as that! And if you don't like it - -." She was getting angry.

"No, no, no! You've got the wrong end of the stick! I

319

meant - do you want to stay with me? I was trying to avoid trapping you, or pressuring you into something you might not want."

She sat there, looking at him, breathing hard, as her anger faded. "I do wish that you would say what you mean, instead of circling all around it!"

"Alright! Straight out, and blunt. If they turf you out, will you come home with me, assuming I have a home to go to?"

"We have two cars, well, one and a half, and two tents, to live in, if you don't."

"Yes, and no income, next to nothing in the bank, and no employment, as yet."

"So we'll be broke, and happy! Anyway, speak for yourself. I have a fair amount salted away. You can always 'phone whats'ername, June? First, and get an up-to-date sitrep."

"Joan. Yes, that's an idea. She'd know if the flat is still there, as she has a key."

"Right, then, that's settled. What shall we do, now?"

"It's too soon to go to bed, and I'm not hungry, so I don't want to eat, yet. The weather's a bit dodgy for diving,

320

without surface cover, so do you fancy a simple wander round?"

"Yes, fine. But feed me, first! I've only had a meat pie and a mars-bar since breakfast!"

"One doorstop coming up, I've got some fresh bread. Do you fancy egg, cheese, or sardine?"

"Sardine is for cats. What cans have you, in there?"

"Ah, well, the cans got rained on, and the labels have come off! It might be beans, stewing steak, or pears, or there's peanut butter, chocolate spread, or, ah, either marmite or treacle, the label's off that, too."

"Eeny-meeny, that one!" She pointed at a can, "On toast."

"Right, you have chosen, ah -." He opened the can, "– aha! Pear halves in syrup, on toast!"

"Sod the toast. Give me a spoon!"

Later, wandering along a track that undulated along the cliff-top, lost in each other, and oblivious to their surroundings, they totally failed to notice the drama that was unfolding behind them.

Pete paused in his dive through the rain to check the compressor. "She's back!" he called.

"Who? Oh!"

The man with the thick, hairy arms was on watch, and cursing his rotten luck. He'd got badly sun-burned, yesterday, during his 'stint', and today, he was a stand-in for a fish! He saw the Land-Rover splash up the flooded track, and grabbed for his binoculars, but all he could see through them was the fogged-up lenses, so he abandoned them. The four-wheel pulled up by the man's tent, and then its lights went off. For a minute, nothing happened, then the blonde woman made a scrambling dive for the tent, let herself in, and shut the flap. He could vaguely see them embracing, in the glow of a dim lamp hung in the tent apex, but the rain noise drowned any sound. He picked up the walkie-talkie, pressed the transmit button, and said, "She's back."

"What? You're very muffled, say again."

He could barely hear the reply, for the noise of the rain battering on his tarp cover. "Repeat that?"

"That's what I said!"

"What?"

"Eh?"

"Oh, sod it!"

"What?"

"Come up here!"

"Pardon? I can't hear what you're saying for the noise!"

"I'll come down there, then!"

"What?"

"Bloody gadgets!" He glared at the saturated radio, then wormed back from the edge, from which he could survey the site, then stood. He scraped off the worst of the mud, and slithered down the rear of the ridge, to where the thin one lounged in the Maxi, in a mess of chip papers, crisp packets, and pop cans.

"What'cha want?"

"I said, the woman has come back!"

"Oh?"

"So effin get up there, and give me a chance to get dry, and warm up a bit!"

323

"Why? You're already soaked."

"Because I said so!"

Muttering darkly, the thin one got out of the car, wrapped a large oilskin around itself, and then squished off up the muddy slope.


Neither of them registered the two men in the XR4I parked a few yards up the road, in a lay-by.

"Did you get both their ugly mugs, Geordie?"

"Aye." Geordie lowered the camera, with its long lens, "I don't know 'em."


The other man lifted a microphone connected to a radio transmitter, and said;- "GW3QNH, this is GW3QTH Mobile, calling on sked. You in there? GW3QTH, over."

"Hiss-splat QNH mob-hiss, -ot you stren-crackle-woo, where are – whistle."

"Three QNH, I'm in the back of a housing estate, just up the coast road, where are you, over."

"Hiss-crack- NH, in the splat-uck, on the cracklesite,

pop-ver."

"Three QTH, Sorry, missed that, you are very broken, Try the seventy centimeter repeater, the seventy repeater, over."

"Hiss-kay-crackle."

Geordie's mate flicked a few switches, then changed microphones, "GW3QTH this is GW3QNH mobile, how copy now, over."

"3QNH this is 3QTH, five by, now. Where did you say you were, over?"

"3QNH, we're in the truck, on the Valley campsite, over."

"3QTH, in that case, we're about a mile away! We're eye-balling a weird pair in an orange Maxi, who seem to be watching you. Have you made them? Over."

"No, mate, they must be another mob. Has the Boss fed you the gen, over?"

"3QTH, that's affirm, we know about the bod on the cliff, the ones in the tent, and the camouflage you've picked up. My mate's just nipping out, to see what or who these guys are watching, so if you've nothing to add, keep an ear on this freq.

Over."

"Roger, mate. Just one question, what do these two look like, over."

"3QTH, One's a good likeness of a silver-back, all he needs are a few bananas, the other one's a stick insect on an L.S.D. trip, he's got fluorescent green hair, a yellow shirt, and skin-tight pink pants on!"

"Oh my God, he'll definitely blend into the background. In Soho!"

"Yeah!"

"Catch you later! GW3QNH mobile."

"3QRT."

"GW3QNH, GW3QTH, this is GW3OTX, you guys finished your rag-chew, 'cos I've a sked on here in a minute, over."

"3OTX, this is 3QTH, finished, bud. It's all yours, out."

"Thanks, 3OTX, break, break," - -. (the rest of this conversation is irrelevant).


Geordie had drifted up the slope, shadowing the self-

326

propelled traffic light, and was concealed in a clump of dripping wet bracken in a manner indicative of training and long practice. Once green-top had settled, he eased along a fissure in the rock until he could see what green-top was watching. Cautiously easing one eye over a boulder, he looked down on Trev's truck, and the camp-site. Warily checking that he was out of green-top's line of sight, he studied the area, noting the tatty Cortina, with the Land-Rover parked next to it, and the tent with the slightly off-square fly-sheet, he now knew belonged to Vince and George, the orange pup-tent, with the motor-bike, and the old canvas trailer tent he knew was occupied by the old chap. A couple came out of Vince's tent, a tall, thin man, and a slender, but curvy, blonde girl. They set off, on foot, down the puddle-strewn central track, hand in hand. He heard green-top curse, as it watched them go out of sight, then scramble down the hill, sliding in the mud, and dove into the Maxi, which coughed into life, and set off down the road. As soon as they were out of sight, Geordie shot down the hill, into the XR4I

"Well?"

"You'll never believe it! The other side's the camp-site,

and these two were watching Vince and George, Pete and Trev's cover."

"How can you tell?"

"Easy. Just after we got to the top, Vince and George went for a wander up the road, and green-top came shooting back down here, into the car, and they set off, after them! She's a looker, by the way!"

"Right. Let's follow them, too, and see what happens!" The XR4I's Cosworth engine roared into life, and with a brief 'squid' of tyre-slip, chased off in pursuit. They caught odd glimpses of the orange Maxi as the road twisted and turned its way along, over, and round, ridges of rock. With one hand on the wheel, the driver picked up the radio's microphone again, pressed the 'audio up' button, bringing the set to life again, still tuned to the repeater. GW3OTX was yakking on about some computer programme, and when he paused for breath,

"Break, break!" the recognized 'can I interrupt' call.

"Break, go ahead, GW3OTX"

"GW3QTH, thanks, can I give my mate a call? I'll be on about half a minute, over."

328

"3OTX, sure, go ahead, I'm on the side."

"Thanks, GW3QTH calling GW3QNH, GW3QNH, urgent. Over!"

"3QNH, got-cha, go."

"3QTH, heads up! Your pals could do with a hand, coast road, on foot, over!"

'Er, ah, roger, copied. On the way, out.'

"GW3OTX, this is 3QTH, thanks for that. The freq's all yours, again, over."

"3OTX, roger. Intriguing message! Now, where were we? Ah, yes, if you go into BIOS, and reset -."


Pete and Trevor ambled casually along the track, out of the site, turned left and along the road. As soon as they were out of sight of any possible spectators from the site, they ran, hard. They both had special headset radios that left the hands free, operating in the 500 Meg's band. "You up?" Pete asked, of his headset, as they pounded along.

"Yeah. Your party's on the front, walking towards Tee-bay along a track. Day-glow is trailing them, with a hand-held.

The gorilla's in the Maxi, keeping pace along the road. Geordie is on foot, following day-glow. Neither of the parties has realized they're being followed."

Trev made a thumbs-up, as he gasped for air.

"Kay, Keep us posted." Pete acknowledged. Running wasn't his forte either.

Geordie's accent came back to them, over the radio, "They're on the left headland of Dafarch. Vince and George are snogging, Green-top is poking in a rock pool, and I'm in a crevice, out of his sight."

"Kay!" Trev was flagging, now, and Pete was beginning to gasp. They pounded round the final bend in the road, to where the vista opened out onto the bay. Pete leaned against a gate-post, sucking air, while he waited for Trev to catch up. "We're about a hundred yards from the coast road." He gasped to the microphone.

"Right. Onto the coast road, turn left, and keep going. Your party's on the move again. Greenie's still paddling. I'm up on a pinnacle, now, admiring the view."

Trev lumbered up, red-faced, whooping, "I'm too --

330

bloody big -- for this – game!" he gasped.

"I told you to go on a diet, last time we met!" Geordie commented, acidly.

"I'm a clearance diver – not a -- marathon runner!"

"And can't we tell! Hello, what are they up to?"

Green-top was baffled. These two were behaving exactly like a courting couple. They were wandering along, looking at the view, grabbing a kiss, and now and then a quick feel, and chattering about the bloody flowers. She was watching a seagull, floating along the cliff edge without flapping its wings. Then she seemed to be trying to explain something to the man, who seemed uncomprehending. She explained again, he asked questions, she answered, and then began drawing in the loose dirt, with a stick, while he watched.

Green-top heard odd words, as the breeze carried them to him, - 'cliff, - updraft, - speed, - stalling, - lift, greater than descent, - gain height'. None of it made any sense to him. They moved on and green-top drifted over to the patch of earth, studied the drawing, copied it into a note-pad, while keeping an

331

eye on the couple so they didn't get too far away, then followed at a moderate distance. Geordie moved in, glanced at the doodles, a double right-angle making a big 'Z', two elongated esses, and a few scattered arrows. The penny dropped, George had been explaining the principle of hill-soaring. The right-angles were the cliff, the wavy lines the air-flow over it, and the arrows were, well, something. Geordie chuckled, at the thought of the other team, using expensive computer time, trying to decode the secret message! Then he set off in pursuit, again. "Right, then!" he said to his radio, "They're swinging back towards the road, now, as the track follows the edge. Hello, they've stopped, suddenly. I can't – ah! They can see the Maxi. Maybe one of them's had a run-in with it, earlier. They're looking back this way, but can't see me. Oh, heck. They've seen green-top! Vince's leading her down a steep track, onto the beach."

"Contact with the Maxi!" Pete puffed.

"Can you get past, without being spotted?"

"No, but if the gorilla doesn't know us, we can just wander, - No, hang on, it's moving off."

"That's the car that was following me, earlier, in town!" Vince said. "I saw the driver then, and he had green hair, so it's not this guy." He looked around, "More like that one, behind us! I don't like this. Come on, down this way. We'll go down and across the beach, to see if they ARE following us, or just happened to be in the same place as me, twice on the same day."

George took it all in, in one fast sweep. This place was no good for a scrap, if it came to that, so she plunged down the indicated track, with Vince right behind.

Green-top paused, at the top, and raised his walkie-talkie.

The orange Maxi moved round to the other side of the little cove, then stopped again, the driver noticing the cruising XR4 that ducked into his freshly vacated spot. There was one person in the car, apparently studying the view. From this spot, the gorilla could see his partner's green hair bobbing down the track, as the man and woman hurried across the sand, watching the chaser. A glance in his mirror showed that the XR driver was sitting on his car roof, legs dangling through the sun-hatch, gazing out to sea. He decided that he was no threat, just a tourist, probably the father of the two kids chasing about on the beach, with a matronly woman lying on a towel close by, watching them.

Green-top reached the other side of the cove. There were too many people around here, for his liking, but he followed the footsteps of the couple, in the sand. They led off the sand, onto a rocky area, at the head of the promontory, and appeared to be going around it, close in to the cliff. The rocks were extremely slippery with green slimy stuff, and weeds were piled deeply in places, which made the footing treacherous. This stuff must be under water when the tide came in. He lifted the walkie-talkie. "They've gone round the cliff, on the rocks."

"Kay."

Green-top set off in their wake, slipping, and wobbling about, precariously, catching occasional glimpses of them, ahead. They seemed to be making better time, as he was falling back.

334

Vince and George were picking their way, their walking boots giving a fair grip, despite the algae and bladder wrack on the rocks.

"Yes, he's definitely following us!" Vince had glanced back, and then changed their direction, slightly, onto a flat, sandy area beneath a few inches of water, which they splashed quickly through. "Ah, up that way, I think, or we'll have to swim for it, soon."

George studied the cliff face. "I think I'd rather swim, I'm not a climber!"

"Alright, then, up to that triangular rock, with the seagull perched on it, then down that sandy area."

"O.K."

Pete's head appeared over the cliff-edge, saw their predicament, and whistled sharply, before calling, - "Over here, Vince!"

When Vince looked round, Pete tossed the end of a light rope down to where they could reach. Vince changed his mind, caught it, tied a rapid bowline round George, and said "Up!"

She went, steadied and supported by Pete on the other end.

Green-top spoke into his radio, then came at Vince, his eyes oddly glassy.

"Back off, pretty-boy. I don't know what your gripe is, but -."

Green-top flicked a knife out of a spring-loaded sleeve holster, and it slashed through the air, into the space where Vince's head had been. This was no place for fancy footwork, it was too slippery, and uneven. The knife hissed again, slashing at Vince's neck.

The thick-armed one cursed, when he heard that the others had help, and started to get out of the Maxi, until a cold metal ring pressed against his neck.

"I wouldn't!" Trev warned.

Thick-arms turned slowly, then smiled, because he could see that the thing was not a fire-arm, but a mere scrap of metal pipe the other guy had picked up from somewhere. He reached round, and crushed it flat, like a child would a drinking straw, then folded the end over, and flattened that, and again.

"Good job it wasn't mine!" Trev tossed the scrap pipe aside, and stood waiting.

"George is O.K. She's on top, with me!" Pete called down, as he untied the rope from around her. Then, to George, "I hope Vince can handle that creature, it looks nasty!"

"So do I!" She was seething with fury - and worried for Vince.

Green-top tossed the knife from hand to hand, inviting an attack, but Vince was too wily, the knife was what this person lived for - and by. This moment wasn't the one. He waited.

Green-top chuckled, talking to himself. This one was a piece of cake, scared rigid. He'd give  him a few lessons first, drawing some blood, then the fun part! Another hissing slash, making Vince jump back, and green-top shuffled forward, trying to stay in range. Then a sudden dancing step in, for a stab, but his foot slipped on a rounded ball of slime, throwing him off-balance, and robbing the thrust of its power. Vince struck, an axe-like hand smashing into the wrist, making the knife-holding fingers open as the bones of the wrist shattered. Vince's other hand arced round at green-top's solar plexus, but he scrabbled out of reach as his knife fell with a clatter onto the rocks. Vince backed off, waiting, as he was on better footing, here. Green-top scooped up the knife with his other hand, glanced at his damaged, already swelling, wrist, then grinned evilly.

Thick arms looked at Trevor. "I don't know who you are, so why don't you just sod off, and save us both a load of hassle?"

"Sorry! Can't do that. It's my pal your pal is chasing!"

"Ah!" Thick-arms accepted the simple statement.

"What is he to you?" Trev asked, as he studied the bulk of the man.

"A job, that's all."

"I think you've got the wrong guy. He's just a holiday-maker, who came down for a few dives."

"That's not what I was told!"

"Then what you were told was wrong." Trevor paused, listening, Thick arms suddenly realized that the headset wasn't from a tape-player. "Your green-top pal is trying to fillet Vincent, down on the beach."

"Vincent? That's not his - Oh, Jeez. He's the wrong guy! And there was supposed to be no violence, just take them in for questioning!"

"Someone needs to tell your pal that! And take them where?"

"Will you let me try to call him off, on my radio?"

"Very carefully!"

Thick arms slowly raised the walkie-talkie, "Pash, Pash? Knock it off, it's the wrong guy! Answer me, over."

The radio hissed and popped to itself.

"Pash, Pash, answer me, damn it!"

Nothing

"The cliff must be blocking the signal. Will you let me go nearer?"

Trev looked at him. "One wrong move and I'll break your arms off!"

"Look. I'm on a loser, here. If we fight, and I win, I lose, because he's the wrong one. We look a good match, so one or both of us will be well mauled at the end, for nothing!"

Trev studied the man, who seemed sincere. "Come on, then, but be very careful!"

The big man climbed out of the Maxi, its hydrolastic suspension hissing with relief, then ran, hastily, along the path to the cliff-top, with Trev right behind.Pete heard them coming, and whirled, hands ready to attack or block, then saw Trev's hand-sign. "Stay clear, Fellah!" he warned.

"Don't worry about me, it's a cock-up! Wrong people! We're the good guys!" The man arrived at the cliff-edge, and raised his radio, just in time to see the final moments, too late to stop it happening.


Green-top flicked a glance at the ground, looking where best to place his feet. Vince took the opportunity, and smashed a hand into greenie's sternum. Green-top staggered backwards, arms flung wide for balance, then an axe-hand slammed into the side of his neck, smashing the collar-bone. He screamed with pain, reeling back, then regained balance, and came in again, the knife slashing. Vince blocked, then gripped and twisted the arm,

340

forcing the man to drop the knife again or stab himself. Green-top was twisted around, until he was facing the sea, one arm trapped, the other useless, with two different broken bone groups. Desperately, he flailed backwards with a boot, but hit nothing. Vince pulled sharply on the arm, dragging greenie off-balance again, then released the arm before hooking his hand round greenie's jaw. His other hand went to the occiput, and pushed sharply.

The wailing "NOOO!" was punctuated by a sharp crunch, and then greenie went limp.

"Oh Jeez!" The gorilla sighed.

"It's over!" Pete turned to George. "Vince looks alright."

Vince dropped green-top. He then stood there for a while, looking at his hands, before slumping onto a rock, holding his head.

George, white with rage, turned on the big man, her hand slashed across his face with a loud 'splat', leaving a developing blotch. "Why?" She demanded.

He stood there, her hand-print on his cheek. "I can't tell

341

you!"

"You will! You spy on us, you follow us around, you chase us, and you try to kill us, and you say you can't say why! Talk, or go down there, the quick way!" To Pete, she said, "Lower me back down to Vince, he needs help!"

"Right." Pete picked up the rope.

"No! Wait." Said the big man, "Let me lower you down, fellah. Your pal might need some muscle to get him going. No tricks, I promise. It's over."

Trev and Pete looked at each other. Trev nodded, "Go on, I can cope up here."

Pete went down the cliff, lowered on the rope, by the big man, with Trev watching his every move, alert for silly tricks, but there were none. Pete's feet splashed down into a few inches of water, and he waded to the rock where Vince was still sitting, slumped. Cautiously, he worked round to in front of Vince, and then said, clearly, and quietly, "Hey Vince, how're you doing?"

No blood showed, anywhere, but Vince just sat, his head in his hands, visibly shaking. "Hey, Vince. Come on, mate,

342

you can't stop here!" Warily, Pete moved in close, expecting an attack if Vince was still in fighting mood, either deliberate, or reflexive. While he was catatonic, he was unpredictable, and that made him very dangerous. "Vince, come on, pal! The tide's coming in!" Pete reached out, and took one of Vince's wrists, then the other. Holding both arms, he squatted, getting a wet backside for his trouble, as a little wave splashed in, a fore-runner of the rising tide. "Come on. Vince, it's time to go!" The tendons in Vince's wrists were tight as wire ropes. A bigger wave rushed in, splashing their faces. Vince flinched, struggled against Pete's grip for a moment, and then his eyes focussed.

"Pete?"

"Yeah, it's me. Come on now, the tide's coming in, and George is waiting for you on the top."

"George. – Is he, - Did I. – "

"Unless he's learned to breathe water, and cope with a broken neck as well, yes, he's dead. You had no choice, mate, I saw that." Pete felt for the carotid artery without much hope, Green-top's head flopped back and to in the water surge.

"What was it about?" Vince asked, confused.

"This one's not going to tell us anything! Come on up top, and we'll talk to the other one. Your George packs a wicked right hook!" Pete hauled Vince to his feet, and tied the rope round him, then said, to the radio, "O.K. Trev, he's on, take it dead slow, he's not in gear, yet!"

"Right." After a moment, the rope tightened, Vince stumbled onto the first rock, then stuck there. "Hey! Wakey wakey, Vince, up you go!" Pete coaxed. He didn't move, just dangled there, his knees slowly buckling.

"Trev, can you manage a dead lift, or we'll be here all day?"

"Hang on!" The rope slackened slightly, then Vince was hauled up, a couple of feet at a time, like a broken marionette.

"Do you want me to bring green-top up, or shall I let him go?"

After a short pause, "Let him go! Better that way."

"O.K."


Vince was dragged over the top of the cliff like a sack of spuds, then after a short pause while the rope was untied, it came splashing down for Pete, who went back up the rock face like a mountain goat, with the sea chasing him half-way. As he scrambled over the lip at the top, the big man, his shirt black with sweat, was slumped on the ground, gasping, while Trevor continued to hold the rope. Pete untied himself. George was sitting on the floor, her arm round Vince, who still wasn't aware of what was going on.  While Pete and Trevor were disentangling themselves, she snaked out a hand, then plucked a pistol from its holster in the big man's jacket.  The snick! as she cocked it drew their attention.

"Right, you bastards! You can see this pocket cannon is pointing at you! I don't know who are the good guys, and who are the bad ones, and I'm sick of being a mushroom. You need to know I can use this thing, and I will. I placed second at Bisley, last year, beaten by two and a half points. I know this is a powerful weapon, and if I shoot you in the little finger, your arm will fall off.  I am an R.A.F. fighter pilot, on sabbattical. My name is Flight Lieutenant Georgina Weastey.  You first. Who and what are you?" The Magnum pointed at the big man. "Pete and Trev, sit down where you are, and don't twitch!"

"Pete and Trevor!" The big man flinched, "We were told Pat and Trevor! But, like I said, I can't tell you."

George sighed, centred the sights on his chest, and began to squeeze the trigger. "Only you know what the trip pressure is!"

"She means it, man, speak!" Pete warned.

"I can't! Official Secrets Act, and all that. It would cost me my career!"

"Career, or life, which is more important to you?" George shifted aim a fraction, then the gun slammed, and was back on aim before anyone could move. The big man jerked reflexively as a fraction of his earlobe vanished in a spray of blood. "The next one goes dead centre."

The man stared down the barrel, which looked like a tunnel from where he was, the next shell winking brassily at him from its depths.

"Three seconds, I won't count."

He swallowed, sweat pouring off him. "Alright! I'm S.A.S."

"I.D. card?" George snapped.

346

"Don't carry it in the field."

"Give me one reason for not blowing your head off, right now!"

"I can't!"

Pete stirred, easing a cramped leg. The Magnum snapped into line, and he froze. "Move again, and you'll be wearing a hole for decoration! Now, who are you?"

"Customs and Excise. Undercover drugs squad. Me and Trev, they're our real names."

The big man stared, "The other end of the same stick!"

"Tell your other pal, up on the knoll, there, to come down and join the party, and bring his rifle, not pointing at me!" George said to Pete.

"Geordie, come down here, really careful. She's not fooling around." Pete said to the radio.

George eased round a little, to keep them all in view. Vince didn't move, but seemed to be aware now, and listening.

With the pistol still aimed at Pete, George snapped, "And who are you, really, Vince?"

"Vincent Bertwhistle, unemployed sales rep. I told you

347

that before." He muttered, baffled.

Geordie came clumping up, carefully making a lot of noise. George lined the Magnum up on him. "Stop there. Take the magazine out!" He did, "Drop it onto the floor, then work the action." He did, and the round in the breech flicked out in a twinkling arc. He worked the action several times, to show the weapon was empty.

"Kick the magazine over to Vince." He did. "Now, put the rifle down, where you are, then carefully walk round, and sit next to Pete and Trevor." He did as instructed, the muzzle of the Magnum following him every inch of the way.

"I've no argument with you, love. I called Pete and Trev out to back you up, when I saw the other lot was following you."

"Flight, or Miss Weastey, to you!" She glared at him. "Right, the three of you, take your electric headbands off, and toss them over here."

Pete and Trev complied, Geordie did not.

"Do it, man!" Pete hissed at him.

Reluctantly, staring at the yellow glint in the black tube,

Geordie did as instructed.

George scooped one up, and said to the microphone, "O.K. Pal, you too, come out with your hands empty. I know where you are!"

Nothing happened.

"Last chance to come out walking!"

There was no movement, so George shifted aim, and fired a round into some scrub, thirty-five yards away. That drew an agonized yell, then a long groan they didn't need a radio to hear.

"You were warned. Out! Now!"

"O.K. O.K. Don't shoot again. You hit me!"

"I know I did! Now, I'm not an idiot. There are five of you, and only four rounds left, so I won't waste any more on warnings. No more games! Pete. What was it all about?"

"Drugs."

"You thought I was carrying them!"

"No, we were just using you and Vince as camouflage. We didn't, and still don't, know who - just where."

"That pipe I found!" She was putting it together.

349

"And when." Trev added, "Yes, that pipe was part of it, and you took us to it!"

"And you!" The Magnum gestured at the S.A.S. man. "What was your part in it?"

"Like I said, just now, we had two names, Pat and Trevor, and the place, the camp-site. There were no other couples, and it all seemed to fit. Sorry!"

The shot Excise man crawled up. "There's a gun in my belt."

"Take it out, carefully, and pass it to me, by the barrel, I don't trust thrown pistols, they tend to go off, and the bullet can go anywhere." He did. "Another Magnum, that's nice! Now I have ten bullets! You, over there, next to Pete. Pete, Patch him up as best you can, keep all your hands where I can see them, all the time!"

Pete said, "I'm taking a knife out, to cut his trouser leg."

"Carefully."

The trouser leg revealed a ragged gash across the back of the calf. "It's messy, but there'll be no lasting damage." Pete said, "This is going to hurt!" He made a compress from his hankerchief, and a strap from the trouser leg.

"It already is!" The man gasped, white-faced from shock and pain. "K'inell! How did you know where I was?"

"You all seem to operate in pairs, so I just waited for you to show yourself." George replied

"Was it a lucky shot?"

"No. I could see your trainer. There are no native plants with size twelve white leaves with the Nike logo on them."

"K'inell!"

"You are no Indian! So, your lot thought I was running drugs, and your lot was looking for the runners, while hiding behind us, in plain view. Where do you think the other lot came into it?" A rather confused question, but they all knew what she meant.

"We were backing up Pete and Trev, because we knew someone else was watching them." Said Geordie, "But someone removed him before we arrived!"

"Who?"

"Er, I rather think that was us!" The S.A.S. man said. "He's under lock and key at a place in Hereford, now!"

Vince jerked into life. "I killed him!" he exclaimed.

"Yes, but it doesn't matter, now." George said, soothingly.

"It wasn't -." The big man subsided.

"Wasn't what?" George demanded.

"Later, please." He glanced at Vince.

"Anyway, you were all following each other, thinking that you were watching the runners. Someone has been playing you all off against each other, and a right bunch of Patsy's you are! You," she pointed at the S.A.S. man, "Your car keys."

He removed them from a pocket, and tossed them to her feet.

"You, Hopalong, have you a car?"

"Yes." He tossed the keys over.

"What and where is it?"

"XR4, behind the Maxi."

"That'll do. You lot stay here, and I mean here! For one

hour. Then you can send Pete for the truck. Just get into it, and drive off. Leave anything that isn't already in it." She picked up another headset radio. "That's a souvenir, like these pop-guns. The keys will be by the truck's wheel, I'm not a thief! If I ever see any of you again, you can say goodbye to the world - if you are quick enough! You, S.A.S. pick up that rifle, put its barrel on that rock and jump on it, so it bends, then smash the stock, before throwing the bits over the cliff."

He did, and the spare radios followed the broken rifle.

"Come on. Vince. Let's go home!"

George and Vince walked off. After ten minutes, Pete stirred, but froze again when a Magnum 'slammed' and a slug whined off a rock near his foot, making it jump over the cliff. "An hour, I said!" George's voice warned.

"O.K." Trev was resigned to his fate. "We've got an hour to sort out who is doing what, and why! We were sent by the brass-hats, how about you!"

"The same," The S.A.S. man agreed, "So it would seem that we were also being set up."

"Where did your brass get the gen?"

"Don't know, yours?"

"I don't know, either. I suggest we wait a while longer, and then try to move off, before it gets too dark to see the floor."

"Can I suggest we go to my place, on the Cliff Hotel camp-site?"

"Seems reasonable. When we get our truck back, we can call in, and find out what the hell's going on!"

"Firey little vixen, isn't she!"

"I can't say I blame her. Do you think she would have shot us?"

"I wasn't prepared to find out!"

"Oh, she meant it." Pete said, wryly, looking at a nick in the heel of his shoe, and the gouge in the peat. "That slug ricocheted off that rock, came up between my thighs and over my head. An inch either way and I'd have been crippled, or singing falsetto!"

"She must have been fifty yards away, so it was a brilliant shot, in the half-light."

"That, or I'm lucky. People keep shooting at me,

354

recently, and missing!"

"How so?"

Pete told the big man about Scouse, and Co.


George unlocked the XR4I, and they climbed in. Vince had regained control of himself, although he still had the shakes.

"Are you keeping those pocket cannons?" he asked.

"One of them. The other can go for a swim, later."

"Then take the ammo out first, in case there's no more available."

"I was going to. I'll search the car, too, to see what else there is stashed away that we could use." She fiddled with the seat adjusters, until it suited her, then turned the key in the ignition. The engine started instantly, with a throaty 'woofle' before settling to a rumbling idle. "That's not a two litre Ford engine under the lid!" She blipped the throttle, listening to the snarl, and the exhaust crackle, "More like a race-tuned three and a half, big valves, gas-flowed, and all the bells and whistles!" She cranked the window down, adjusted the door mirror, then selected reverse, which snicked in positively. "Sports box, too!"

355

She released the hand-brake, and maneuvered them out of the bay, feeling for where the clutch bit, and the brakes gripped. She left the lights off as she trundled them sedately away. "No point in telling them we've gone!" She commented. She took them a way up the road to a lay-by, where the road had been re-shaped at some time in the past, leaving a loop of tarmac which was hidden behind some bushes. She pulled in, switched off, and began searching the car. In a short while, she had turned up an electronic gadget she didn't recognize, another Magnum, and a dismantled rifle in a case, which used the same shells. It was fitted with a huge telescopic sight which could pick out a gnat's whiskers at half a mile. There was a new, sealed, box of shells, and an open one, part-used. She fiddled with the rifle for a minute, then something made a 'snick' noise, and she withdrew a long bar with a cranked handle at one end, and a stubby spike at the other, "The bolt!" She said. It didn't look like a bolt to Vince, who envisioned a hex head, and a threaded shaft. A further fiddle separated it into its component parts, which she scattered around the area, after mangling the springs, thus rendering the weapon useless.

356

Back at the site, they parked the XR4 just outside the gateway, blocking a farmer's field entry, then clanked up the track, feeling like an army platoon. Vince had a Magnum in each pocket, and the ammo in his hands, while George had the other one, the electronic gadget, some papers, and the head-set radios she'd confiscated. Vince dumped his 'trophies' into the Cortina's boot, then fished around under the rear bumper, and removed something, after which George's Landie was searched, externally. He showed her the two bugs he held, then tossed one onto the top of Pete's truck, where it stuck with a sharp click. The other, he attached to the underside of the motorbike, which still leaned on its stand. The owner was back, snoring noisily in the pup-tent. When Vince got back to the tent, George had dissembled the two surplus Magnums, and had put most of the parts into a plastic bag. Some springs and small bits lay in a cup. "They'll go down the loo, in a bit. The guns are useless without them, anyway."

"You seem to be the armaments expert. I couldn't hit a barn with a gun if I was standing inside it, with the door shut! Do

357

you want to find another site, until Wednesday, or stay here?"

"We may as well stay here.' George shrugged, 'They won't bother us now, they've got bigger problems, like who it was that set them up!"

"There's someone coming down the track!" Vince sat up, listening hard.

"It could be Pete, the timing's about right." As the person came nearer, they could see, in the gloomy light, that it was. "Pete, come here a minute!" It was a command, not a request. He stopped a few feet away. She tossed him the keys, and the bag of gun components. "They're minus a few important parts!" she commented.

"I expected that."

"Did that last one bounce?"

"Yeah, the rock must be shallow, there. It missed my nuts by a – sorry! – by an inch, and nearly took my head off, too."

"Sorry. That wasn't meant to happen, but you WERE pushing your luck!"

"Yeah, I said the same thing, back there. I've got a shirt

with holes in, and shoes with a unique tread pattern, as souvenirs! Why didn't you shoot us?"

"What for? I was mad enough to, and sane enough not to. Your pal in the bush should have come out, when he was told, and then he wouldn't be needing some new pants. Is he hit badly?"

"In the circumstances, no. He won't be playing football for a while! I suppose you could have topped him?"

"Yes, I could see his foot, and tell where the rest of him was. If I'd put a couple of rounds further along, one or the other would have got him. Anyway, that's incidental. In case you are thinking of prosecuting me, I didn't know you were C and E, then, just some people with guns who were following me, so it is justifiable force for self-defence, at best. A Judge would throw it out as a waste of time, and anyway, you lot will be in deeper shit for losing all your fire-arms! I called you over to tell you to watch the big guy. I don't care what he says he is, I don't believe him. Since when did the Army go at civilians with a knife? Green-top wasn't defending himself, he was attacking! Right. Take your keys, and the truck and car, and go. Don't come back

359

without a damn good reason. To save you spying on us, we're staying here until Wednesday, then it all depends. Oh! And thanks for the rope! That's one reason why you're still walking, not hopping."

"Lucky, again, hey?"

"It seems so."

"Can I pick up the air bottles? They're mine, not the company's?"

"I suppose so. And the tent, if you are quick, just drop it, and bundle it into the back, you can sort it out later. If you haven't gone in half an hour, that's," she looked at her watch, "twenty-two-fifteen, look out!"

"Is that wise?" Vince asked her.

"I think so, it saves them sneaking back for it all when we're not watching!"

"Good point. Would you have shot them?"

"I was that far from it!" she held up a finger and thumb, barely apart.

"Remind me not to cross you!"

"Likewise, and you did it with your bare hands! Where

360

did you learn that?"

"Believe it or not, the local chip-shop!"

"Oh, come on! What did you say, six penn-orth of chips, and a lesson in killing nasties?"

"It's true! Tommy's a Japanese, who only teaches his friends."

"He sounds a handy person to know!"

"We don't bother with the fancy arm-waving stuff, and pretty dancing, that's all crap. His philosophy is, the most direct line from the hand, or the foot, to the target is a straight line."

"It usually is, but I don't – Oh, yes! I think I do!"

"And if somebody is looking for trouble, it is simpler to be elsewhere!"

George flopped into a camp chair, yelped, and stood again hastily, rubbing a buttock. "Who put that there?"

"You did!"

She picked up the Magnum she had kept, un-cocked it, and put the safety on. 'It was loaded, too!'

"You're lucky you didn't put one up YOUR spout!"

"That reminds me. I'm going for a pee!' Put the kettle

on for when I get back!"

"I'll come with you, on a similar mission. We'd best keep together for the next few days. Where are those electric headbands?"

"Here." She passed him one, and put the other on, "Testing, one, two, three? I never know what to say!"

"Loud and squeaky!"

"Likewise!"

They walked round, and did the necessary, Vince getting funny looks from another occupant, because he was apparently having a conversation with himself!

Chapter nineteen.

Tuesday.


When we got back, Pete, the tent, and the truck, had gone,
leaving a pale green patch on the grass which was visible in the
remaining light, testimony to the length of their stay. On Vince's
tent-pole a note was attached by a scrap of sticky-tape. "Will be
at the Cliff Hotel site if needed." It was signed P.

"I doubt it!" George was disparaging. "What's left in the
larder?"

"Those cans, with the labels off!"

After a lucky-dip meal, they sat around, listening to Vince's
scanner, which had the volume turned low. He had tuned in to
Radio 2, following a brief demonstration of what else it could
do. They chatted about this and that, swatted mossies, and

enjoyed the silence. After a particularly heavy raid, Vince said "Sod this! I'm going to bed before I get eaten alive!" He turned the radio off, and locked the Cortina. "Are you coming?"

"Not yet!" She grinned wickedly, and followed him into the tent, pulling the zip down behind her. They were asleep in less than a minute.

Some time later, at around Oh-god-o-clock, she heard the zip go up, then the sound of water splashing. Vince came back in, starkers. "Oh, sorry, didn't mean to disturb you, but I was busting!"

"Where did you go?"

"Left rear wheel of my car, why?"

"Because I'm going, too."

"Skinny?"

"Who's to see?" She ducked out, went, and came back, shivering. "Christ, its cold! You could have said it was drizzling!"

"Yep. Come here!" He pulled her in close, and wrapped his arms around her, sharing his warmth. "Stop wriggling, you're causing an agitation!"

"Who's wriggling?" she pressed against him, and writhed some more.

"You were warned!"

Later, that pheasant was heard calling, again.


Vince was first up, driven by the usual need. The air in the tent was bitterly cold, and a few drops of condensation wavered unsteadily on the ridge-pole as he dressed. He added a wooly, and his anorak, before dashing to the loo-block. When he got back, George was still in bed, apparently asleep, although he suspected she was faking it. He lit the gas, then put the kettle on, before getting two pans, adding a small amount of water to one, then, next to her ear, poured the water slowly from one to the other, then repeated it.

"You rat!" She sat up, hastily dragged on some clothes, then dashed off. Halfway to the loos she registered that there had been a night frost, and she was only wearing flip-flops on her feet, which were now freezing! She had a choice, go back to the tent, put on more suitable footwear, and burst, or freeze in comfort! When she got back, she had a good moan about the unfairness of nature. "It's all right for you! You've got a little hose-pipe to stick outside. I've got to unwrap, and let it all freeze, and those loo seats are bloody freezing, too!" In between moans, she found time to surround a plate of eggs, bacon, and beans, and the last of the bread, which she used to soak up the juice, as it was now too hard to be worth buttering, had there had been any left. When she'd chased the last bean round the plate until it capitulated, she said, "That coffee was cold, too. The service here is abominable. If I don't get a fresh, hot one, I won't speak to you for hours and hours!"

"Good! It will give my ears a rest! They'll be bleeding, soon!"

She tossed an icy flip-flop at him. It landed on his plate, splattering his bean juice everywhere. Vince faked slicing a piece off, then chewing it. "Hmm, not too bad, rather like the octopus I tried, once."

"You can't have cooked it properly."

"It wasn't my cooking. I paid for it, in a restaurant. It was bloody expensive rubbish."

"Did you leave a tip?"

"You must be joking!"

"Skinflint!"

He removed the flip-flop from the congealed mess on his plate, and tossed it over to the tent entrance. "I wonder if bean juice works on athlete's foot?"

"I shouldn't think so, but it might improve the smell!"

"At least, I don't fumigate the bed with my surplus gas production!"

"You were squashing me, at the time. It wasn't my fault!"

"I warned you to stop wriggling about!"

"I was just getting myself comfortable. You didn't need to hold me down!"

"Ah, but I did! With all that gas - one spark and you'd have been in orbit, and on the way to Mars!"

"That's your rotten cooking!"

"You don't have to eat it!"

"I do, it's better than mine!"

They continued in the same vein, as couples do, for a while, then –

"What shall we do, today?"

"Well, Vince, I might fancy a dive, later, if it warms up. But, I'm not sure about going anywhere with you, because every time you go out, people chase you, and try to stick knives into you!"

"All the more reason to go out, they're less likely to ruin the tent!"

"There is that! Let's drive around the place, and do the tourist bit, for a look-see, and get some food, on the way, for later!"

"O.K. Your car or mine?"

She sniggered, and picked up the Landie keys. "Two guesses, get the wrong one, and you can run behind!"

"I thought the man with the red flag went in front!"

"How fast can you run?"


As it turned out, despite her R.A.F. training, her roadmap-reading skills left a lot to be desired, as instead of arriving at her intended destination, Llyn Alaw, they found themselves on the top of a hill, near a radio mast.

"Ah, well, In a Jaguar, or a Tornado, you can't mistake a D road for a cart track!" she offered a feeble excuse. "We must have taken the wrong fork, at that three-way split, back there."

"We? You have the map, and the steering wheel is on your side!"

"I haven't got a steering wheel on my side!" she put on a comic voice, and looked at her flanks. After messing with the map, and lot's of muttering, she had to admit she was lost.

"Well, just drive straight towards the sun, until we go splash! Anglesey isn't that big!"

She turned the Landie round, and headed southish, as the track wound around, until she saw a road-sign. "Tell you what! Let's go to – ah, - Am- ul –wooch, instead!"

"Where?" Vince hadn't seen the road-sign.

"Am-el-wooch, it was on that sign, behind."

"Oh! Amlwch! That's North! Which way are you heading? I thought we were going South!"

"The way we're going. What is there, at this Armlock?"

"We'll find out, if we get there! I thought you said you'd been to Anglesey before?"

"Yes, I have, dozens of times, in Hawks, a couple of times in a Phantom, once in the back seat of a Tornado, Twice in an

369

Andover, and once in a Vulcan, -."

"Alright, alright!"

"And once on the train!" She finished off, with a flourish.

"I suppose you went to Valley in a taxi."

"No. The back of a three-ton rag-top truck, painted blue!"

At Amlwch, we drove in, straight through, and out of the other side, without seeing a parking space. As a result, we ended up at Bull Bay, where the road turned right, heading inland from the bay, then up a hill. Near the top, a patch of rough ground had cars parked on it, so George pulled in, collecting a yell from an aggrieved pedal-cyclist who was hurtling down the hill, his brakes smoking. There, she found a flattish patch, and stopped. "This must be the car-park!"

"That's sight-seeing, the hard way!" Vince commented.

"What is?" She claimed she hadn't seen any cyclist.

They locked up, and then wandered into the nearby arcade. There were an assortment of those new electronic arcade games, all making booms, bleeps, and other weird noises, as the few users operated them, zapping aliens, or whatever. The gift shop sold the usual tacky tourist junk, bits of coral, seashell

370

ornaments, slates with desk clocks installed, and the other 'Made in Hong Kong' tat. George riffled through the picture post-cards in a rack, then pulled one out. "I wonder how old this one is?"

Vince glanced at the picture of the bay, with a few cars scattered along the road, the most recent one recognizable was a Morris Minor. "It could have been taken during a Vintage Car Rally!" he ventured.

"No-one would risk their vintage clutch, to come here!" She slotted the card back into the rack, evaded his clutching hand, and looked at the lead crystal ornaments. She smiled at a little green frog, sitting on a lily, and admiring its own reflection in the pond. "I like that one!"

Vince looked, "Eighty-six quid! Maybe next time!"

"Oh!" George read the price label herself, and flinched.

That had taken them full-circle around the shop, so they wandered, arm-in-arm, down the hill. At the bottom, a small cluster of shops, and a couple of market stalls invited exploration. Slurping on fast-melting ice-creams, they leaned on the railings overlooking the beach, watching a water-ski-er repeatedly falling off, and a lone yachtsman standing on the keel of his overturned craft, trying to de-capsize it, if that's the word. He leaned back, pulling on a rope, his feet against the keel's root, until the sail lifted from the water, but he let go of the rope too soon, fell backwards with a splash, and watched his boat re-capsize. He scrambled back onto the bottom, found his rope, and leaned back again. This time, he waited too long, and the mast came up, over, and back down on the other side, dragged down by the weight of water in the sodden cloth. George chuckled, because they could hear his curses from there! Eventually, the rescue boat puttered up, after completing another job. One of the crew leaned over the side, heaved the mast up, by its top end, and held it while most of the water drained off the sails, allowing the boat to roll right-side up on its own, the sails flopping about and scattering rainbows of water everywhere. The man scrambled back in, waved his thanks, and began bailing the sea out, while the rescue boat went off to aid another keel-dancer.

Bored with that spectacle, they moved on to the market stalls. One was displaying the usual tourist junk, the other, locally crafted leather goods, belts, wallets, purses, credit-card folders, and the like. At one end, on the floor, was a tea-chest,

372

which had a notice taped to it. – 'Find a pair, take them for two quid!' In it was a scrambled heap of sandals.

"I could do with a pair!" George delved into the tangle. After ten minutes, exasperated, she gave up. "All the left shoes are size seven, down, and all the rights are size eight, upwards!"

The stall-holder chuckled, "I bought one of two crates, as a job-lot. My competition in Camaes Bay got the other. I think he's got the matching ones! If you fancy your chances, get a couple of these, then go over there, and see if you can make a pair up!"

"No, thanks!" George dumped an armful of sandals back into the chest.

We wandered on a bit further, but there was nothing to see except houses, so we made our way back to the Landie.

"If we go that way," she pointed up the road, "Where does it go?"

"All roads lead to Menai, and Bangor, or Holyhead."

"Well, my stomach says its lunchtime. Let's go that way, and look for a food shop!"

"You're driving!"

"No, I'm not, I'm sitting here, talking!"

"Then start the engine!"

"What a good idea!"

She bullied her way into the stream of traffic that had materialized, the little tin boxes giving way to the tank of a Landie to avoid mortal damage. She converted a 'thank you' wave into a 'V' sign at the outraged blare of a horn, as an old codger who believed he owned all the carriage-way was forced to retreat to the proper side of the white line painted down the centre of the road.

"I bet he's a local farmer!" she commented, looking at a pile of hay-bales lashed to a sagging roof-rack

"It's great fun in the spring, until it dawns on the locals that they aren't driving the only vehicle on the road!" Vince responded.

"How so?"

"Well, from October until the Easter Bank Holiday, the place is nearly deserted. There are just the residents, and they all forget. Then, on Good Friday, about twenty million people descend on the place, just as the locals have got used to having six months of empty roads!"

374

"Then they get six months of traffic jam. Why do they always dig up the roads in summer?" We were slowing to a halt, behind a line of cars that had stopped at temporary traffic lights.

"That's simple! In winter, nobody bothers stopping for red lights, and the petrol stations don't make any profit from it!"

The lights changed, allowing two cars through, before they changed back. It took four more cycles before we got through. Nobody come the other way, except a cyclist who ignored the lights anyway, and weaved unsteadily between the cones and bits of machinery. There was nobody using them. We whined along, the knobbly tyres singing on the tarmac, until we came to a cross-road.

"Did you see any signs?"

"No."

We went straight across, into a tree-lined lane, which suddenly turned sharp left, then narrowed, until the mirrors on both doors were rattling in the hedgerows. Then we burst into a farm-yard, startling the body who was wandering across it, carrying a bucket of something that attracted lots of flies.

"OOPS! Sorry!" George called, then made a three-pointer

375

turn, and rattled us back to the cross-roads. "Left or right?"

I looked for the sun, when it peeked from behind the clouds. "Right for Bangor, left for Holyhead."

"And straight on is where we have already been!" George took us left. After passing through a couple of Hamlets, of the blink and you miss it type, with lots of 'WLL's and 'G's in the names, we came to a dog-leg cross-roads. George zig-zagged us across, then suddenly jammed on the brakes, making the assorted junk in the back crash forwards until it hit the bulkhead. She shifted into reverse, backed into someone's drive, then took us back to the cross, and turned right. About fifty yards along was a sign which read 'Home Baking'. She parked up, outside, and switched the engine off, said "Wait here." Then she made sure, by taking the keys with her.

She was back in about ten minutes, a cat with the cream smile on her face, and an armful of delicious-smelling paper bags, which she carefully stowed in various cubby-holes. "Lunch in about ten minutes!" She declared, "When I find a nice place to stop!" We trundled off again.

"This is roughly west." Vince said.

376

"Who cares? We're in no rush to go anywhere!"

"True."

We rumbled on for a mile or two, until, as we topped a rise, there was a nice panorama of the Irish Sea a few miles ahead, and a surrounding of nothing but fields. "This'll do!" she bounced us up onto the grass verge, at a place where there was room between the dry-stone wall, and the road, then switched off the engine. She un-strapped, and pushed her seat back a few notches, with a sigh. "I'd like to live somewhere like this."

"There's nothing here."

"Exactly! No pubs, no clubs, no discos, cinemas, or neighbours. Listen to the silence!"

I listened. Cows were mooing, sheep barked, dogs chirped, etc.

"That tractor, over there, sounds like your Cortina!"

"How so?"

"It's only got three cylinders!"

"I'll have you know my car has four! They just take it in turns resting! At least, I don't need a ladder to get into it!"

"I always fancied a go in one of those – what-cha-callums?"

"What's one of those?"

"Those monster trucks, you know, thingys!"

"Oh, the Big-foot's. Pickup trucks on tractor tyres, with big engines."

"That's 'em."

"I believe they do about three hundred yards to the gallon, of methanol!"

"Then I wouldn't be going very far!"

"No, about two miles, starting with a full fuel tank!"

She opened paper bags, and then passed me a foam-plastic cup, with a cap on it.

"Soup!" She opened another, and was soon wearing a tomato-coloured moustache. The soup was followed by buttered fruit scones, then some crispy sponge biscuits, with chocolate bits, that she called "Brownies".

"I suppose that one has the 'Boy Scouts in it!" I suggested, indicating the last bag.

"No, silly! That's a fruit- cake, for later!"

"That's what I said, full of nuts, and fruity!"

She caught on, eventually.

378

The tractor spluttered up, and came to a halt, on the other side of the wall, and then the driver said something in Welsh.

"Sorry, I missed that?" Vince said, as he cranked his window down.

"Ar. Oi said, has you folk broken down?"

"Oh, no, we're fine, thanks. We've stopped to enjoy the view, and have a snack, that's all!"

"That's alright then, Boyo, because the nearest telephone is in Llanrhyddlad!" He pointed behind.

"No, we're fine, thanks."

"I'll be getting along, then, or the Woman will murder me, wasting time gossiping!" He chugged off.

"It was decent of him to check!" Vince commented, receiving no reply. He looked across and saw that George was asleep, her head resting on the side window. Vince sighed, content, and went back to watching the world go by.


Vince came to, with a start, some time later. He looked around, vaguely, for a minute, while his brain got into gear, and then gave George a prod. She snorted, but didn't wake, so he

379

took hold of her shoulder, and shook it. She grunted, then bleared at him, through a half-open eye.

"Wassamarrah?"

"Come on, Sleeping Beauty! Time to go!"

"Where?"

"Home. If we stop here much longer, we'll be charged rent!"

"Huh? Oh, yeah! "She sat up, squirmed about, then got out, for a stretch. "What time is it?"

Vince looked at his wrist, and saw an empty space where his watch usually was. "Er." He looked for the sun, "About two hours later than before."

"Before what?"

"Before we stopped. My watch is still in the tent!"

"Oh. Remind me where we are."

"Well, er, Clan-diddle-dad is that way!" He pointed behind.

"Oh, yeah, and we were going THAT way, whichever way that is!"

"That's it, unless the Landie has turned itself round!"

George did a couple of knees-bend, arm stretchers, then a couple of touch-toes, before climbing back in, and sliding her seat forward to its usual position on the rails. Satisfied, she got the map out, and studied it. "We came from Amlwch, which is on the coast, so it's – there! – and we came through Bull Bay, We stopped at the cake-shop in - in, yes - Neuadd, and now something-diddledad is behind us - what looks like something diddledad? Ah, Llanrhyddlad, perhaps! So we're not really very far from the camp-site. Do you want to go back, or off on a jolly, somewhere else?"

"I'm easy. Do you want to keep looking around, or go for a dive?"

"I'm not bothered about a dive, really, today. I'd rather just mess about, getting lost!"

"Well, kick the horse, and whip the buggy-wheels, or something. Would you like me to drive, for a while, so you can gaze at the scenery?"

"Yes, but you can't. It's insured for me, only. Let's have a look, then." She fussed with the map, "What's a big green patch mean?" She hunted for the key that was printed down the margin, "Oh, it's a wood. Trees are trees, what else is there? Ah! Somewhere called Carmel. What is there, there?"

"Clint Eastwood's house?"

"Give over! That's a different Carmel, I hope! Fancy meeting 'Dirty Harry' when you're lugging a Magnum around! D'you feel lucky, punk? Well, do ya!"

"Not a lot, I don't think." I answered the first part of the question. "I've not been there. Cliffs and rocks! We went past it, in the boat, the other day."

"Was that where the gulls used us for target practice!"

"That's the place."

"I'm not going there, then. It's too messy! So – if we go left, left, right, and left, we should end up in the place I meant to go in the first place!"

"Llyn Alaw?"

"Yes, we should end up at Llanbabo, or Clan y goes." She turned the key, the engine churned over a couple of compressions, then started, with a clatter.

We bounced off the verge, onto the tarmac, and whined off down the road, took the next left, left, right, and – "Funny!" She said, "This looks familiar!" We trundled on for a mile, and then came to a signpost for Cemaes bay, straight on.

"We've gone round in a circle!" Vince said.

George stopped the Landie, and studied the map. "This thing tells lies!" she declared, in disgust.

"Can I see?"

She threw it at him, in a tangle. He spent a minute re-folding it into order, then studied it, tracking their route through the towns. "Ah! I see what has happened. You've turned left, the first time, too soon, so we've gone round three sides of a triangle! See." He showed her, "Sooo, go up here a couple of miles, to Bwlch, then Tregele, where we turn right, onto the Llanfechell road." They set off again.


"There was Belch!"

"I blinked, and missed it."

A mile or so later, "Right at Tree-jelly, you said?"

"Yes, this must be it, there's the sign." They screeched round a sharp right hander, about fifteen miles an hour too fast for comfort "Now, just keep going straight, until we get to a tee-junction, with Rhosgoch to the left. We go right!"

"O.K." They whined on, past dry-stone walled fields of

383

sheep, cows, green things, yellow things, and countryside things, and past occasional lonely cottages which were soon left behind. George spent half her time looking at the scenery, and the other half guessing where the twists and turns of the road would take her, next. We were somewhere between Clegyrog Blas and Tyddyn-Pandy when she jammed the brakes on, bringing us to a halt.

"What the –?" Vince, startled, looked up from the map.

"Hang on a mo. I've seen something!" George selected reverse, and took them about sixty yards back. "Look!" She turned the Landie down a dis-used side-road.

"This goes to a little lake called Hafodol, and a bog!"

"That's not it, look!" She indicated a tumble-down, derelict cottage, built of native stone, with the remnants of a slate roof. A stone wall marked off a twenty by thirty foot front garden, full of weeds, and there was about half an acre behind, similarly marked off. There was a narrow strip of land down the south side, and a slightly wider one on the other side.

"It's a falling-down old cottage. What of it?"

George didn't answer, just killed the engine and got out,

then walked up to the broken gate, which hung drunkenly from a rusty hinge. She studied the place for a moment, said "Hello, house!" then sat on the wall, just staring. "Oh, come here, and look!" she insisted.

Vince tucked the map into the glove-box, un-strapped, and got out, then walked, stiff from long inactivity, to where she was sitting. "It's still just a tumble-down – Oh!" The aura of the place reached out and caught him. They sat there for a minute, listening, and looking.

"Just look at the view!"

"It'll be pretty bleak, in winter!" Vince cautioned.

"Maybe, but I bet those little hills, behind, break the wind! The land rises slowly to them, only a few dozen feet, but it's enough to shelter it from storms. There's a bit of a breeze blowing, back there, but can you feel any wind here?"

Vince had to admit that he couldn't.

George climbed down off the wall, then walked hesitantly to the front door, which badly needed paint. She reached for the knocker, then dropped her hand. "This door hasn't been opened in years!" She walked round to the filthy window, and peered in.

385

"Empty. It's just a shell. It's been abandoned for years. There's a sign, here." She pointed at an Estate Agent's sign, the post rotten and fallen over, in the grass, peered at the faded lettering, muttering to herself, then went round the back of the cottage, picking a careful route through the weeds. She was out of sight for a time, and then Vince saw her, inside, through the dirty window.

"You'll get us arrested!" he called.

Eventually, she came out again, covered in smuts and spider-webs. "It seems sound enough. It's got water, and there's an ancient electric meter. There's no gas that I could see."

"No neighbours to borrow a cup of sugar from, either!" Vince teased, "apart from that cottage, way down there, with the smoking chimney."

George went to the Landie, and rummaged in the junk tray. "Have you got a pen?"

"No, sorry! What for?"

She found a scrap of pencil, barely big enough to hold, then wrote something in the margin of the map.

"I must admit I like the place." Vince admitted, "It needs a lot of work, and its miles from anywhere, but it has character!"

"I'd like to live here, if I can get it. It feels happy."

"Yeah!" He had to agree. There WAS something about the place that called to him.

"You like it? Really? You're not just agreeing with me?"

"Yeah, yeah, and no! I like it. It's big enough for two, and like I said, it has character, a sort of quaint charm. Slap in some clematis and climbing roses, to break up the hard lines, and it will look better. There's room for a veggie plot, the sea's less than ten miles in most directions. All we need is pots of money to throw at it, and that is something we haven't got!"

"That's the least of our worries!"

"Oh? Can you see the Law coming, hot-foot, to evict the trespassers? Or is it something else?"

"Now, don't get mad. You did ask. There's no easy way to put it, - ah, -."

"I get it… Do I really love you? Do I want you forever and ever, or am I just along for the ride, and in a – I didn't mean that the way it came out! In a week or two, will I move on? Is that it?"

"Yes." Blunt as the back of a truck.

"I told you before! I don't know what love is! If this feeling I have for you is love, then Yes! I do. I want you to stay with me. When I can, I'll ask you to marry me, there's just a question of paperwork to sort out, first. I've found my soul-mate. Someone I feel I belong with, and who belongs with me." He had his arms round her, now, as he spoke, drawing her close. "This bit is nice!" he moved against her, "And these bits are nice, and this, and that." He kissed her nose, eyes and cheeks, "but I'm a jealous sod, and I want it all, just for me! I've – I've – run out of words! Where's that scrap of pencil?"

She picked it up, and passed it to him. Vince picked up the map, turned it over, and wrote on the back:- 'I, Vince Bertwistle, hereby bequeath all my wordly possessions, remaining after my ex-wife Betty had taken her cut, to my Fiance, Georgina Winifred Weastey. Signed this day:-' He signed and dated it.

George read it. "You've written wordly, not worldly!"

"Well, that's all I might have left, when it's all over! Just words!" He picked a little tear from the corner of her eye, and kissed it away.

388

She read it again, then took the pencil scrap from him, and wrote beneath his words, 'I, G.W.W. as above, after his div'ce, as above, leave all, etc. to Vince Birtwistl-.' The sliver of lead pinged out of the wood, and was lost. "Damn!" She rummaged in the junk-tray again, and found a tiny ball-point pen, like those in Bookies shops, and tried to write with it, but it was dry. "Damn, again!"

"Never mind. If you press hard, it will bruise the paper, and it might show up enough."

George added the missing letters, and then signed her name to it, pressing hard.

They celebrated with a slice of the fruit-cake, and a shared can of coke they found under some rags in the back of the Landie.

"And I thought MY car was full of junk!" he ventured.

"Haven't you noticed? I'm a squirrel."

"I knew there was something about you . . . "

They sat on the wall for a while, arms round each other's waists, while they admired the view, and listened to the total lack of noise. Only one car passed, on the 'main' road.

389

"Hmm! One passing car in an hour, and it's the peak tourist season. It must be really quiet, in the autumn!"

"Two!" George indicated a tractor, weaving drunkenly along in front of a huge trailer, which swayed from side to side, on the verge of toppling over, under its load of hay-bales.

"Well, let's go and see this lake, before it goes dark."

"Lake? What lake?" George asked, playing the fool again.

"Llyn Alaw, where we meant to go in the first place."

"Is it a lake?"

"Yep. Blue bits are water, and Llyn means lake."

"Ah, er!"

"I did wonder why you wanted to go there! What did you think it was?"

"Wellll, -"

"I do believe that my lovely blonde fighter pilot cannot read an Ordnance Survey map!"

"The Ordnance I'm familiar with - is made of metal, and goes bang! R.A.F. maps just show things to avoid bumping into, like hills and masts, and airfields, of course!"

"There are not many of those about, now!"

"You'd be surprised! Anyway, I don't want to look at a lake, so where shall we go, now?"

"Well-," Vince flapped the map, "from here, on the right is the lake you don't want to go to, To the left is Amlwch, then along the coast a bit, is Moelfre, where the 'Charter' is, Then it's Lligwy Bay, Further up is Benllech, then Red Wharf Bay, then Beaumaris, where there's an old castle, and finally Bangor. How's the fuel?"

George glanced at the gauge. "There's about forty-five miles in the tank."

"Don't forget you have to go to Valley, tomorrow, so do you want to fill up, now, or leave it 'til then?"

"I think I'd better put some in today, and then it's one less thing to think about. What's at Moelfre, apart from the wreck?"

Vince studied the map. "Well, there's a road in, a road out, and a wet bit, a dry bit, which has a Coast-guard lookout, a life-boat station, and a burial chamber. Not much else."

"Um. Is there anything interesting, a bit nearer?"

"Yes, she's blonde, with – Ouch! There's a hill with a disused windmill, a cemetary, some standing stones, or a couple of boggy bits, and lot's of little hamlets with unpronounceable names. Which do you fancy?"

"A hot cup of coffee, and a meal, really. Let's go back to the tent, and stop if we see anything interesting!"

"Don't forget, we want some groceries."

"You might, I'll dine, courtesy of the Government, tomorrow!"

"What about tonight, though! All we have left is some Marmite, and three soggy crackers."

"I'd forgotten that."

"O.K. I'll just nip round the back of the cottage and water the weeds."

They took it in turns.

"Right, then. Turn right, on the road, and right at the tee, then just keep going." Vince had the map untangled again.

They droned along, down the side of the lake, with George verbally mutilating the town names, as they passed through them. At Llanbabo, they took the right fork, to Llanddeusant, then Llanfachraeth, where George spotted a petrol station, and pulled in. The tank seemed to take forever to fill.

"The pump's a bit slow!" commented the attendant, in a broad Scouse accent, as he stood there, with the nozzle in place in the Landie's filler pipe. From there, it wasn't far, across the causeway, to Holyhead, where they shopped, hastily, as everywhere was closing, then took the Porth Dafarch road, back to the camp-site.

Chapter twenty.

Wednesday.


Flight Commander Georgina Weastey drove her Land-Rover in between the opened gates of R.A.F. Valley, and parked it in the indicated space, almost the same spot as last time, then walked to the reception block to sign in. The W.R.A.F. Sergeant flicked through the rolodex until she found the reference she wanted, and then went to the wall-full of filing cabinets, where she started clanging drawers, until she found the file she wanted. Eventually she found, and extracted it, clanged the drawer shut, then slapped the file onto the desk. A dehydrated spider fell out.

"Take this down to room Two Charlie, Ma'am." She said. "Someone will be down, shortly."

George blew the dust off the file, making the Sergeant

cough, then took it to Two Charlie, which was second left, down the passage.

The room was empty, apart from a battle-scarred table and two dodgy-looking chairs. She dumped the file on the desk, then tested the better-looking of the two chairs for stability before sitting in it.

After a few minutes, a portly old soul who was wearing Wing-Co badges, shuffled in, and sagged wearily into the other chair, which protested bitterly, but held.

"Mornin', and what have we, here?" he asked, bored stupid by the endless paperwork.

"Flight Commander Weastey, Sir, for consideration of Termination of Contract."

"Hrrrumph!" He leaned back in the chair, which creaked ominously, while peering at her over his half-moon glasses, "What is it, man-trouble?"

"No, Sir, if you would read the resume -."

"It's always man-trouble with you bits of girls! I think it's the uniform that gets you going!"

"With respect, Sir, I am NOT a bit of a girl, and if you

395

would take the trouble to read -."

"No need, I already have! Just testing! He flew a Harrier through a stuffed cloud -."

"Jaguar, Sir."

"–and you went on compassionate leave, with delayed shock syndrome. Now, here you are, wanting to pack it in! Do you realize your contract hasn't gone full term?"

"Yes, Sir, but -."

He launched into the standard speech about how it had cost the country a quadrillion pounds to train her to drive a jet plane, then went on to the bit about re-paying the debt, and loyalty to the Crown etc, ad nauseum. All this was old hat, and was followed by the usual bribe of consideration for advancement to the next rank, should she agree to re-sign. George sat through all the standard bull in silence. When the Wing-Co finally ran down, he asked her if she had carefully considered all the implications of leaving, should it be approved.

She had.

"Like I said," Annnounced Wing-Co, "Man trouble! If he hadn't topped himself, you would be happily howling down valleys, knocking people's telly aerials off, and frightening sheep and hikers. When I was a Flying Officer, and your best mate bought it, you picked up the pieces, and got on with the job."

"That was in nineteen thirty-nine, Sir." George replied, carefully. "We were at war. All the flying I did was to the ranges for the obligatory minimum hours, the permitted one hundred rounds, one twenty-five pound live bomb, and one dummy thousand-pounder, per year, and one live missile every five years. That is hardly vital work. The rest of the time, I shot cine film, lines of bullshit, and shuffled paper. I've been passed over six times for a Q.W.I. course, six! because I don't have certain physical attributes. I scored higher than the Officers that were accepted, in the paper-work, the medicals, the fitness, the psycho's, and the flying. I'm sick of the 'old boy' network, and 'jobs for the boys'. I'm sick of having to be better than everyone else, just to get a menial task a raw recruit could do. I can't be bothered any more. You say it cost a fortune to train me. It probably did, and it was wasted by not letting me do what I was good at! It will cost another fortune to re-train me, and bring me back up to standard. It isn't necessary, but that is procedure - by the book. And for what purpose? To let me sit around, getting a fat behind, while I'm waiting for an occasional flying slot because the weather is bad, or it's a holiday period, and nobody else wants to fly. Or maybe to make a ferry run to somewhere, then have to cadge a lift back, when a male pilot goes sick and the 'plane is needed elsewhere in a hurry? I don't want the hassle. I don't need it. I also know that the Government budget cuts mean that some aircrew, as well as others, will have to go. I'm an obvious choice. The R.A.F. no longer needs me, and I don't need it. Sign that piece of paper, and let us both stop wasting time and money!"

Wing-Co sat, staring at her, surprised by her forceful argument. He didn't like being told what to do, not even politely. "I believe," he said, eventually, "that you really mean it! Has the Force really been that hard on you?"

"You say you have read my file. Tell me why I am still just a Flight. There isn't a blemish in there. The scores are well above average in everything, yet I keep being passed over. I applied for Qualified Weapons Instructor six times, Tactical Nuke Strike three times. I was qualified for every aircraft on the U.K.

inventory, some of the Yankee ones, and even a Soviet Mig! I'm licensed for several helicopters, I've flown P1 on a Dakota, I have six hours in a Mirage, and I've flown one of those Argie things we captured after the dust-up, I forget its name, a spindly twin-prop thing. Yes, the Falklands! When my squadron went down there, where was I sent? Lynham! So I could chug around in a Hercules, ferrying stores to Gibraltar. That's the nearest I got! They wouldn't even post me to Germany, to fly camera combat. I am surplus to requirements, and I can't be bothered fighting them any more. Sign the paper, and let me go home!"

"That could be your trouble, you have been too aggressive! Perhaps -."

"Perhaps nothing! A fighter pilot who isn't aggressive may as well go and drive Boeings for B.A. or somebody. Anyway, I tried that. If I don't push, nothing happens, and the harder I push, the harder nothing happens. I have been offered nice, soft, lady-like jobs, flying filing cabinets and typewriters. They wouldn't even give me a Radar Interceptor course, either as pilot, or controller. Sign the paper!"

Wing-Co had to admit that she was right. He could also see

that she was determined. He sighed, picked up his pen, and wrote – 'Discharge approved. Honourable. S.N.L.R.' signed it, date-stamped it, three times, three bits of paper. Then he pushed it all over to her. "Now it's your turn."

George read all three copies, checking for discrepancies, then signed, and pushed them back.

"That one's yours." Wing-co separated the papers, and put his pen away. "Now the details, First of all, your I.D. card, please."

George fished it out of her purse, which was in her bag, "I'll have a receipt for it, please."

"Of course, later."

"No. Now, or I keep it!"

Wing-Co sighed, "You really are a stubborn cuss, aren't you!"

"I've had to be!"

He made out a receipt, and she passed her I.D. over, in exchange, after cutting it into quarters, with her nail-scissors. "That is to prevent mistakes!"

"You weren't supposed to do that!"

"Do you throw your out-of-date credit cards into the bin?"

"What has that to do – Oh! I see! Now, your uniform and kit."

"All the Government issue is bagged up, in the stores. Here's the ticket." She produced it.

"I suppose you want a receipt for that, too."

"Of course!"

"Should something be missing?"

"It is all itemised. Here's a copy. If I have missed something, let me know, and I'll send it, or bill me for it."

"Back pay, etcetera?"

"I don't think there is any. You have my bank account number on file."

"Discharge medical?"

"Last Monday. I'm fitter now than I was when I took leave. I was suffering from too much sitting around waiting."

"I think that's it, then. Do we have an address for you?"

"I doubt it. I'm not going to settle anywhere for a while. I'm going here, there, and everywhere, until I find a place I like." She lied. She had already decided on that! It just needed some work doing, to make it habitable.

"And what if we need to contact you, to send on your documents, and such?"

"Care of my bank, for now. Is there anything else?"

"No, that's all I can think of. You have cut all the corners, and chopped up the red tape, of course, by not going through the proper channels."

"If you think I am going to live in a communal telephone box for six months, while you all have committee meetings, forget it!"

"Alright, alright! You can go, for the sake of my peace and quiet! Just remember, you cannot return!"

"I don't want to! I just need one more thing from you."

"What is that?" He sighed.

"A temporary gate-pass, so I can get out!"

"Oh, yes! That might be a good idea!" Wing-Co delved into a drawer, and came up blank, "Are there any on that side?"

George had a quick look, "Three Playboy magazines, one bottle of Bell's, half used, and a glass, packet of cigarettes, no – I can't see any!"

"Damn!" He heaved up from his chair, went to the door, opened it, and called, "Melissa?"

"Ello?"

"Bring me some Temp'ry Gate Passes, will you?"

"What's the form number?"

"How the hell do I know? You're I.C. stationery! I'm the Officer, though you wouldn't know it!"

Melissa clattered up, in high heels, and jangly metal ornaments, "Are these them?"

"No, but they'll do." He sat down again, "It's not the same, now the paper factory is run by civvies, if you shout at them they go home!" He crossed out the bit that read – 'The bearer is entitled to enter the base for (write in reason), and wrote in 'Temporary gate pass, for purpose of Exit, after discharge' stamped and signed it, and passed it over to her. "Hand it in, as you leave, the guard will keep it."

"Thank you, Sir."

"Between you and I, off the record, you have probably done the right thing. I wish I had the guts to! Good luck, Lass." He held out a hand.

403

George shook it, "Thank you, Sir. Some people feel safer under the Military umbrella."

"Probably." He acknowledged, wryly.

As George passed through reception, on the way out, Melissa was engrossed in re-painting a chipped fingernail, oblivious to everything else.

"It hasn't changed," George mused, "once you get past the gate, you can go anywhere, and nobody notices! Security is a joke!"

Melissa looked up. "Eh?"

"Nothing."

"Oh, right, you got an appointment?"

"No, I'm just passing through, to save walking all the way round."

"Yeah!" Melissa concentrated on the tricky bit around the tip, her tongue sticking out of her mouth with the effort.

George wandered up to the NAAFI canteen, which was either still shut, or shut again, she couldn't tell, so fed coins to the dispenser, again, pressed the buttons for chicken soup, and got a plastic cup of pale brown liquid with tiny green bits floating on top, in exchange. The pie machine was empty, so she selected crisps, and the fail-safe kit-kat bar. Then she perched on a window-ledge, watching a cleaner wiping the tables with a grey cloth.

After a minute, she tasted the 'soup', grimacing at the peculiar flavour.

"The coffee's no better," the cleaner offered, "I prefer the chocolate, but it's too sweet for me, really."

"Yes, thanks, I tried the coffee on Monday. I think that's my cup, still on that table, where I left it."

"I wasn't on, yesterday." The cleaner ducked the issue.

George turned, and looked out of the window. As usual, the base was a hive of activity, with absolutely nothing moving, apart from the 'bedstead' radar array, which rotated constantly.

"Not much happening!" She observed, to nobody in particular.

"It's the cut-backs, there's only one class in, this month, and they're three short, already. They don't need pilots, because there are no planes for them to play with!"

"I know. That's why I'm leaving. In ten minutes, I'll be a

civvy."

"You got somewhere to go?" The cleaner wiped crumbs onto the floor with the grubby grey cloth.

"I'm going touring, until I find a place I like."

"Nice. Good hunting! Can I get there, then I'm done?"

Vince watched George drive off, then washed up the few pots, and bits, before pottering around, tidying up the area around his tent, collecting stray paper scraps, and a discarded crisp packet, to fill the time. When he'd done that, he coaxed the Cortina into palsied life, and left it spluttering, smoking, and battery-charging. After it settled down, he dug out his abandoned book, peeled the stuck pages apart, carefully, and carried on reading the get-me-out-of-here exploits of Dirk Pitt and Al Giordino.

A while later, the Site Manager made his rounds, and paused by Vince's chair, "Are you stopping much longer,' he asked, 'because I've got the grass-cutter coming on Friday?"

"No, we're here tonight, but probably leaving at around noon, tomorrow."

"That's O.K. then. I was going to ask if you would mind moving over a few feet, give this patch a chance to dry out and green up, but it won't matter as you're leaving. Will you be back again, this year?"

"I shouldn't think so, it depends on how the finances work out, and anyway, it's getting a bit late, now. I'll be back next year, though."

"See you, then!" The Manager wandered off, intent his own affairs.

Across the site, the biker poked his head out through his tent opening, looked blearily about, and then went back to nursing his hangover. It was the end result of too much beer, and a curry he couldn't recall eating, although he had the wrappers and the polystyrene trays in his bed as mute testimony of their consumption. He also had a green army surplus holdall in the tent, the contents of which were his purpose in being in this god-forsaken dump in the first place.

Vince put his book down, then wandered over to the loo block to make room for a re-fill, then telephoned Joan to get a sit-rep, and to ascertain whether he had a flat to go back to. After saying he'd see her in a day or so, he ambled back to his tent, where he found a couple in a VW camper-van had arrived, and were clattering poles, as they assembled an awning. The man called across, "What's it like, here?"

"Quiet, mid-week, it gets busy at weekends, with all the divers. It's the end of the season, now, though, so there won't be very many arriving."

"Good! See you around, perhaps?"

"Maybe, we're leaving, tomorrow."

"Don't leave on account of us!" The woman called, as she clambered into the van in search of something.


Pete was sitting in his truck on the other camp-site, trying to find the source of the irritating 'BEEP' that was interfering with his radio reception. The man with the ragged ear was sitting in his Toyota pickup, cursing his tracking device, which was swinging around in all directions, refusing to settle. It was as though he was only yards from the bug! He decided he would have to go for a drive, and try again from a different location, if he could get rid of the guys in the truck who seemed to be following him everywhere.

Geordie and his temporarily one-legged pal were sitting in their XR4I, in a parking area, near the head of Trearddur Bay, watching the mum's and their kids getting sunburned while the teenagers suffered from hormonal confusion, and frustration, because Mum and/or Dad were watching their every move. Their bug-tracker was pointing steadily at the campsite, as it had, un-moving, for the last two days.

"Fancy an ice-cream?"

"Nah, if I eat any more of it, I'll chuck up!"

"Hotdog?"

"Bugger off!"

"How about a burger, then?" Geordie tried, hopefully.


Georgina drove her Landie along the track, halted next to his chugging Cortina, and switched her engine off. Vince looked up, put his book down, and stood, waiting for her to climb down, then grabbed her by the waist, kissed her, then kissed her again, and kissed her some more. When they paused for breath, he asked, "Am I kissing a pilot, or my future wife?"

"Both!" she replied. "I'm still a licensed aviator, unemployed, as of an hour ago, and I intend to be your wife, if you still want me, now that I'm poor."

"We can be broke and happy, together!" He told her about the 'phone call, and that he still had a flat to go to. "So, do you want to pack up, and go now, or stay until tomorrow?"

"I'd like some food first, the canteen was shut, what's on offer?"

"I was considering chuck-it-all-in stew."

"Pick some tins, open them, and chuck the contents into a pan, then light the gas under it?"

"That's it."

"Right, we'll have the stew, then a last dive, and a wander round, then we'll push off when the traffic has died down."

"Right, I'll get it started."

They dined on stewing steak, peas, and pineapple cubes - a rather odd mix, but that was the random selection, and it added to the fun.

After coffee, and the last of the fruit-cake, they lounged around for an hour, doing nothing much, but not wanting the holiday to end, either. Finally, they stripped the tent out, and put the bedding and surplus kit into Vince's Cortina, to make room for two lots of diving kit in the Landie. When everything was away, except the kettle, coffee, and the gas burner, they squeezed into Vince's empty tent to change into their wet-suits. Comments like "Hey, that's not a handle!" and "Keep doing that, and I'll make you get the bedding out again!" could be heard. When they'd finished larking about, and emerged, Vince checked the cylinders and valves, then made sure he had all the small bits necessary, ready for the short drive down to the cove by the 'Haunted House' at Porth y Post.

They finished kitting-up at the water's edge, then slipped and stumbled over the slimy rocks in the shallows, until they were about knee-deep. George sat on a rock while she fitted her fins to her feet. Vince merely dangled in the water, breathing through his schnorkel, while he did the same, curled up like a shrimp as he wrestled with the strong elastic heel-straps. George fell off her rock as she laughed at his antics, which was what he

411

had intended. She came up, spluttering, and then made a back-flip in the water, so that her demand valve came into reach over her shoulder, purged it to blow out the water, then positioned it between her teeth so that she could breathe before she drowned herself. The air seemed to taste a bit odd, but she assumed it was because of the mouthful of seawater she's just spat out, and forgot about it. Vince put his other fin on, then gave George an O.K., received one in reply, changed over to his demand valve, then lifted his head to check the direction, to find himself looking at the beach, because they'd got turned around as they messed about. He caught George's hand, and they finned easily out in the direction of a large rock, which protruded above the water in the centre of the cove. A few small fish dodged about, as they passed, but there was nothing of any size on display. George spotted a movement amongst the rocks, and they ducked down for a look. Two long, slender, black-and-white ringed antennae waved cautiously at them. Vince tapped George on the arm, then held his hands up about four inches apart. The lobster was too small. A green Ballan Wrasse zoomed in for a closer look at these funny creatures invading its territory, then having decided

412

they were too slow and clumsy to be a threat, zoomed off again on its own errands. From a cranny, a juvenile Rock Cook peeked at them, then slowly reversed out of sight into its den. Vince drifted on, listening to his valve click as he breathed in, followed by the hiss of air, then the gurgling, as he exhaled. He was feeling relaxed and vaguely disconnected, but presumed it was because he was happy. George was a few feet away, playing with a starfish that was trying to walk along a rock. Every time it started off, she would gently touch the advancing arm, causing it to pause, then start off again in a different direction. He found a pretty pink rock, and was holding it in his hand, turning it so the light caught it. He saw George offering her demand valve to the starfish, which was an odd thing to do because . . . . because . . . . something. He couldn't think what he was trying to think about! That was funny-peculiar!

He looked again at the pink rock, but he seemed to have dropped it. That was a pity. He was going to show it to Betty, - No, not Betty, Joan, No, not Joan, either! Joan couldn't - what was it Joan couldn't? His head was all fuzzy. George! That was him. Her! Vince looked for George, who waved happily at him,

413

so he waved back, glad she was, was, what was? He looked for his pink rock, and saw that all the rocks were pink. He could hear a fire-engine siren, too. Perhaps the rocks were on – thingy - drugs! Silly! Not drugs, fire! Fire! Where? He looked about, looking for smoke. He looked for whoozits, George, to see if he, she! had heard it too, but she was pretending to be a starfish, lying on her back on the rocks, blowing a thin stream of bubbles from her mouth. He had better warn her that the rocks were on fire, and they might burn her. He waved his legs randomly, wishing that siren would shut up. He could hear it! What was it he wanted to tell - thingy? Danger! Fire! That damn siren was blaring down his ear, now, so he couldn't concentrate on - what was it he was, was - The rocks were flashing on and off, like a traffic policeman, Red! Stop! Danger! Get out, stop out, and call them out! Why wouldn't his brain - thingy. Bloody bell! "Shut up!" He yelled, losing his demand valve. Somehow he got over to her "Get out!" he shouted, shaking her violently. She couldn't get up. There was a belt round her, what was it holding her down for? He had to undo it. How did it work? His hand fumbled with it. Why couldn't he breathe? It must be the smoke. Don't

414

breathe, then. A lumpy, roundish, metal thing on a hose pipe dangled in front of him, getting in his way, but then the belt fell off. George started blowing away on the wind. He grabbed a dangling strap. Don't let go! Go! Go! Go up! Which way was up? Tired, sleepy. Let me rest for a minute! No! Go up! Which way? Up, you stupid --! Go! Can't! Must! His other hand fumbled vaguely with his own weight belt, and then found a knob. "Turn it!" Something bellowed into his ear. He did. Air hissed. Black. Can't see. Hissing. Pain in his - something. Breathe! Can't! Must! Mustn't! That way, a red spot, going away. Don't go! The last thought, crashing through his failing brain, was 'GEORGE, I LOVE YOU!!!!!'

415

Chapter twenty-one.

Search and Rescue.


The resident of the house came back, and saw that the Land-Rover was still parked there. Perhaps the two divers he'd seen earlier had gone for a walk, because there was nobody on the beach, and they couldn't still be down - could they? He'd check again, later. He put on his old boots, and went for a wander along the shoreline, to see what the tide had washed up, usually it was just rubbish, but you never knew! When he got back, having seen nobody about, the Land-Rover was still there. Unhappy, and feeling uneasy, he phoned for the Coastguard.

A short while later, the helicopter was thrashing about, while a lifeboat chugged along, close in, one of the crew studying the rocks through binoculars. The police arrived, and he told the story, what little there was of it. The police examined the Land-Rover, found the camp-site ticket in the windscreen, and went to check. They found the Cortina, and the empty tent, In the Cortina, they found all the missing camping gear, which indicated that the owner was preparing to leave. The car-keys were under the carpet, along with a set with a Land-Rover fob. The couple in the camper-van could only give a vague description, as they had only arrived yesterday, and had hardly seen the people. As the police left, the man called "Hey, Pat, Where did you put the . . ."

The Land-Rover keys fitted the seemingly abandoned Land-Rover. The Sergeant hesitated before climbing in to examine the contents, some well-honed sixth sense warning him off. The Officer, who had just arrived in his chauffeur driven Granada, tugged his tunic straight, pushed brusquely past, and climbed in, picking a fleck of fluff from his jacket as he did so. He didn't notice the red l.e.d. begin flashing at one second intervals. An ear-splitting siren sounded inside the cab, then the door-locks snapped down, and a choking cloud of orange dye and tear gas

417

belched into his face, as George's thief-deterrent system triggered. The Officer struggled with the door, then dragged the window down and squirmed through, to fall in a choking, dye splattered heap on the gravel surface. The Sergeant and his P.C. tried to not laugh at the sight of the Martinet, choking and gasping, on the floor.

Following up another – different - report of an abandoned car, the police found a tatty old red Austin Maxi, dumped by the slate quarry at Soldier's Point. In the boot was the body of a big man, hands handcuffed behind his back, and wearing a plastic bag over his head. It was tied around his neck with fishing line threaded through it as a drawstring. He also had an unusual injury to one ear, as though a piece had been snipped off. When his identity was established, panic and shockwaves ran through the force, as he had been S.A.S. His partner wasn't found for several weeks. His cause of death couldn't be ascertained, as the body had been immersed in sea-water for an indeterminate period, and it had been run over, at least once, by the Holyhead to Dun Laughaire ferry. The investigation proceeded very slowly, as there appeared to be nothing to connect the events, and no clues to give the police a start.

Another abandoned car turned up, this time a Toyota pickup, parked next to a tent on the camp-site behind the Cliff Hotel, at Trearddur. Another camper said the occupant had been a big guy with a nick in one ear.

Part two.


Chapter twenty-two.

In the beginning-.



In the beginning, there was darkness, soft, warm, velvet

darkness, with no form, or sound, or sensation. The man slept.


Later, still in darkness, there was a tiny – regular -

sound. Beep. Beep. Beep. On and on it went, endlessly. He

slept on.


Much later, he saw a tiny dot of white light, way off in the

distance, and walked towards it for a while, until he tired, then he slept again.

A few thin green lines on a monitor that had shown no variation in their regular pattern for many months, wiggled briefly, then subsided again to their previous stasis. Nobody noticed, because they had been waiting for so long they had almost stopped looking, the paper print-out of the tracer had long since been discontinued.

Later, after resting, he walked some more, getting nearer to the light, but it was still a long way off. The green lines wiggled, and the beep, beep, increased its tempo slightly, from 43 to 45. He slept, and walked, several more times, until the numbers on the monitor read 62.

The plump woman, with the peroxide blonde hair, frizzy from a gone-wrong home perm, was the first to notice. She had spent some time, almost every day, holding the man's hand and talking everyday nothings to him in a rambling monologue, for

421

as long as the staff cared to remember. She called the Nurse, who bustled over, all efficiency, and no soul.

The Nurse made the usual observations, and then called the Doctor. The Doctor, who had long since given up hope on this one, wandered in when he found a few minutes in his busy schedule, then found himself telephoning around, cancelling appointments.

The frizzy-haired woman said, - "I'll be back in a few minutes, I'm just going to the 'phone."

The Doctor and the Nurse hardly noticed. They were busy running a series of complex tests and checks on the man, and his monitors.

Vaguely, distantly, he felt the sting of a needle, but it was far, far away, and he had to keep walking. The white dot was now a tiny circle of light.

The 'phone in the lounge began ringing. In the kitchen, the slim, natural blonde woman was washing pots. She cursed at the intrusive noise, but went to answer it, dripping bubbles. She lifted the hand-set. "Hello?"

"George? It's Joan. He's waking up! You'd better pack a bag, and get over here, ready for him! "

There was no coherent answer, just a sort of sniffly, gulpy, sob, then the crash of the hand-set being dropped. There was no further sound, although the line was still connected. Georgina had dashed into the bedroom, and was sobbing into the pillows on the bed on which she had slept, alone, for so long.

Joan sighed, and hung up. She knew that George owed her life to Vince's determination to survive, his total refusal to drown, after their diving gear had been sabotaged before their pre-honeymoon, and had somehow dragged them both to the surface.


Vince was still walking. He could now see that the light was a tunnel, leading upwards. Why did his right hand hurt? He thought about it, as he walked. It was gripping something. Let go! His hand began to relax. NO! DON'T! MUSTN'T! NOT EVER! DO NOT LET GO! His grip tightened again.

The Nurse saw the sinews in the wrist move, rising like wire ropes, as they had been for all this time, and noted it, and the time, on the log-sheet. The heart-beat was now 67, and the body temperature had risen by two degrees. Occasionally, the eyes moved, behind the closed lids, as though the man was looking around, and the breathing was deeper. It was either the beginning of the end, or the end of the beginning, for this one, and only the Almighty knew which it would be.

Chapter twenty-three.

Awakening.

His face was wet! Memory returned. Drowning! Don't breathe! He held his breath, and swam for the surface. The water went away. Scraping. More water. Then dry again.

"Stop fighting me! I'm shaving you, so you'll be pretty for your girlfriend!" the Nurse chided, chattily, as she patted his face dry with a fluffy towel, and noted that the skin colour was improving. He was no longer the grey of living death. His pale white flesh showed up the black of his hair. For the first time, she really looked at him, at his emaciated body. The man was a pile of bones with skin on, and a deep-down determination to

425

live. The iron will that - with the help of the woman called George, who came to visit, a few days every month, and the other woman called Joan, who came nearly every day, either or both of them sitting there, telling him about the house George had bought. Telling him about the trials and tribulations of having it renovated, until it was habitable again. About the problems she battled with, the builders, the plumbers, the decorators, the money she had to spend, and how she was looking for work to help pay for it all, somehow kept the man alive, against all odds.

The nurse thought the Doctor fancied Joan. She knew he had made a pass at George, on her first visit after he took the patient over, and had been slapped down hard, and literally, as well! That had given rise to some good gossip, for a while, so long ago.

Vince was still walking. He was in the tunnel, now. He had walked, and rested, several times more, and was walking again. The tunnel was getting steeper, and walking up the hill was exhausting work. This time, when he stopped to rest, there was an Angel waiting for him. She had long golden hair which was floating around her head as though she was in free-fall in a space-ship. She had orange wings, which were folded round under her arms, and across her chest.

"After this rest," She told him, "I cannot help you any more. This is as far as I can go. You have to keep on, right to the end, on the next walk, without stopping, or you will slide all the way back to the beginning. You can stay here as long as you wish, but once you start, you must not stop. Do you understand?"

"Yes, Nan, up the ladder, or down the snake!" he replied, although nobody heard him.

"Rest, now, and build your strength."

He rested, and slept.


Georgina parked her Land-Rover in a vacant space, placed her parking permit on the ledge where it was visible through the windscreen, and locked up. Her pants had picked up some more of the orange dye from the seat upholstery. Despite several

427

thorough and determined vacuuming sessions, it still worked out of the fabric and stained everything. As she trekked along corridors and up stairwells, to the back of the hospital, along passages familiar from long use, she wondered vaguely whether the Police Officer who had tripped the alarms and deterrent had ever managed to get his uniform clean, or had abandoned it to the rag-bag.

As she entered the room, where the body of her lover lay, barely clinging to the thread of life, Joan looked up. "He's really coming back! Look!"

George looked at the gaunt, pallid frame lying on the bed, seeing the blood pulsing under the translucent skin, the almost total wasting of the muscles, making the limbs thin, emphasizing the knobbles of the joints. Vince was definitely a different colour. She glanced at the monitors, registering the increased body temperature, heart rate, breathing, and the occasional flicks of brain activity.

"If you watch the monitor, while I'm speaking you can see a change in the patterns. He's hearing, and starting to respond." Joan exclaimed.

"Yes, I saw---." George broke off, as a line of spikes marched across the screen. "Did you see that?" A few more spikes paraded across the monitor.

"Yes, I saw, but he doesn't do that for me!" Joan sounded disappointed - and pleased - at the same time. "Talk to him!"

The nurse came in, to see what all the fuss was about on the normally silent ward. "See what?" She asked.

"Watch the screen!" Joan said, "Talk to him, George!"

George picked up the thin hand, pressed it to her cheek, as she had fallen into the habit of doing, and started. "Hello, Vince! I'm here again." She told him the latest news about the cottage, the plants she was thinking of putting where, all the mundane stuff that people talk about. Lines of spikes marched across the screen.

Joan, a medium, and a healer, was holding his other, clenched hand, and willing him to get well with all the strength she possessed. The Nurse, who didn't believe in all that nonsense, made notes on his chart, and went to call the Doctor.

429

When Vince awoke, the Angel was still there, waiting with him. "It is time to go, now. They're waiting for you at the top. Remember! You must not stop to rest, not for an instant. I cannot help you any further. You have to do the last bit on your own." She led him to a ladder, which disappeared upwards, out of sight. Next to it, a fat rope, bearing a zig-zag pattern, writhed gently, as it led ever downwards.

"Up the ladder or down the snake. I remember. Thank you for your help."

"Good luck." She vanished.


Vince hesitated, and then took a firm hold of the first rung, before starting climbing. He climbed until he ached all over, but kept on climbing, the Angel's parting words in his ears.

"Ressst!" the snake called, "Resssst!"

"No, I mustn't!" Vince kept climbing, trembling with fatigue, now. Something was pulling him upwards, gently, but getting stronger as he climbed, urging him on.

The Doctor poked his head around the door, taking in the information from the monitors in a sweeping glance. "Yes, he's coming out of it, at last!" The one called Joan was sitting in her usual corner, holding one of his hands, and apparently dozing. The other one, George, the blonde, who had slapped him when his hand had strayed, one day, was holding the patient's other hand, talking the usual nonsense that relatives say to non-responsive invalids.

George interrupted her monologue. "How long?"

The Doctor thought about his answer for a minute, not wishing to give her false hopes.

"Who knows?" he settled for the blunt truth, "This has never happened before, for me. Ten minutes, ten days, ten months, - he should never have lived at all!"

The man in the bed stirred feebly, as though he were trying to roll over. "That's a good sign! He's showing signs of co-ordination, that wasn't a random twitch." The Doctor paused again, "Forget the ten months. I'll be nearby when I'm needed." He left, and the nurse slid back in, to perch in a corner on a spare chair, watching her patient like a hawk. She wasn't going to lose him now!

Vince was still climbing his seemingly endless ladder. He didn't dare look up, in case he still couldn't see the top

"Ressst!" the snake kept calling, but there was a car coming. Vince could hear its horn, going "beep, beep, beep." He had to get to the top, to get out of the way. The horn was louder, now, and he could hear its wheels as they rolled across the joins in the concrete slabs, "Thum-bump, beep, thum-bump, beep. "Alright!" he shouted, "I'm going as fast as I can!"

The body, in the bed, mumbled something. George bent over, listening hard.

"What is it, Vince? Say it again, please."

Nurse made a note, "Patient mumbled inaudibly."

Vince was still climbing. God, he was thirsty, his throat was parched. "I could do with a drink!" he said, to the ladder, and the snake.

"Waa-er." The body lying in the bed mumbled.

"What was that, Vince? You want water?" George looked

at the nurse, who shrugged, then held up a hand finger and thumb barely separated, before noting it on the chart.

"Yer."

George picked up a glass, dribbled a few drops of water into it from a jug which had been provided by the kitchens, for either Joan or George to use, and then held it to his lips, allowing a tiny dribble to pass into his mouth. Vince's epiglottis bobbed, as he swallowed, so George tipped in another dribble, then a third, which emptied the glass.

Nurse wrote, 'took approximately 1cc of water by mouth.' on her notepad.

"Koo." Vince mumbled.


Vince felt someone pass him a drink, even though there was no-one in sight, just the ladder he was climbing, and the still hissing snake. He contrived to drink, without pausing in his climb - presuming he must have spilled some, as there wasn't much left in the glass, but it was enough for now. He passed the glass back to the invisible someone, as he climbed.

433

The body in the bed was making tiny squirming motions, now, the heart-beat up to ninety-five, the monitors filled with spikes and ripples. The nurse studied the movements, trying to decide what the patient was doing. "You know, I think he's walking!" She made another note.

George whispered into Vince's ear, "Come on, Vince. Wake up, now! I've been waiting for so long!" A lone tear trickled down from her eye, and dripped onto his face, making his eyelids flutter. "Come on, Vince! You're nearly there. Wake up now, please."

Vince was still climbing, reaching up with his hands, pulling himself up, stepping up, reaching up, stepping up, on and on and on. The snake was getting more and more agitated, thrashing about, brushing against him, looping it's coils across the rungs of the ladder, trying to trick him into gripping it, and not the next rung, but Vince kept pushing it away. Then his hand missed the next rung! He wobbled, his momentum broken.

"Yesss!" The snake looped around him as he teetered, then a disembodied hand appeared to reach down from above,

434

grabbed him by the collar, and dragged him upwards, out of its clutches.

Joan suddenly groaned; sweat breaking out on her brow, as though she was abruptly carrying a heavy weight.

Vince flinched, then cried "No, you don't!" He opened his eyes. Light stabbed into them, and he very nearly closed them again.

"Vince! Stay awake! Look at me!" George put all the force she could command into her voice.

Who was that? Vince knew that voice. It was a good voice, one he could trust, so he kept his eyes open. Everything was blurry, and something was dripping on him. Was it rain? More drips, then the voice, again.

"Oh Vince! Welcome back. I've been so lonely!"

Lonely? Was that George? "Where are you? I can't see you!" He croaked. Everything was still a swimmy mess of light and dark.

"I'm right here!" She leaned over, close to him, and then kissed him. He saw a black shadow, with a golden halo. The kiss was over before his lips had time to pucker.

The nurse made her notes, then went to check on Joan, who had suddenly slumped, drenched in sweat, in her chair, panting as though she had just run a marathon.

Joan waved her off. "'M' alright! Give me a minute. See to Vince!"

George suddenly realized that Joan was distressed. "What's up?"

"Tell you later." Joan had released Vince's hand, and was recovering.

The Nurse sent a passing student for the Doctor, at a run, and then went back to her note-taking, monitor watching, and patient watching, while also trying to keep an eye on Joan. Something beyond her understanding, and probably not possible in conventional medical science, had happened in her presence. Once before, she had seen a deep-coma patient like this one begin to recover, then that delicate thread of life had snapped, and the patient had gone in that instant.

The Doctor came pounding along the passageway, burst into the room, and took a sweeping glance at Vince, the monitors, Joan, George, and the nurse. Funny, he thought. Miss ice-cold, rock-steady Nurse is crying! "What happened?" he asked.

""I'm buggered if I know!" the nurse swore for the first time in her life. "It looked like Joan, there, picked up Vince by the scruff of his - life, and dragged him back into this world. But that's impossible!"

The Doctor took Joan's wrist, and checked her pulse. "Jesus said, "Pick up thy bed, and walk" - according to the Good Book. When the impossible happens, call it a miracle." He kissed Joan's fingers, then released her hand. "Take it easy for a few minutes, you'll be o.k."

"That's what I said to the nurse!" Joan waved him off.

"I take it that you are an expert?"

"Hardly, - it just happened!" Joan sounded as bewildered as the nurse.

"Yes, well! Let us see the wood for the trees, hey?" He

took Vince's jaw between gentle fingers, and turned his head sideways, so Vince was looking at him. "Can you hear me alright?"

"Yeah. Who are you?" Vince's voice was weak, but clear.

"How about your eyes, can you see me?"

"Not properly. Everything's blurry, shadows and halos. The light is too bright."

"Ah, we can easily fix that. Nurse, turn the main light off, please." The Doctor turned on a small reading lamp, on the desk, "How's that?"

"Out for a duck! Better. I can see features, now, still fuzzy, though. Where am I?"

"We'll tell you that, in a minute. Let me just do a few checks, first, then I will leave you alone, to catch up. Your girls can fill in the blanks."

"O.K. Can I have some water, I'm parched?"

"In a minute, as much as you want, in small quantities. Some soup, too."

"Soup? I could eat a horse!"

"I doubt it, let's start with soup, and see how it goes. I'm

438

Doctor Jones, by the way."

"Jones? Do I know you?"

"No reason why you should! Now, shut up a minute, and let me listen to your chest!" Dr Jones applied a stethoscope, poked, and prodded. "How do you feel?"

"Tired and confused. Why am I tied down?"

"You aren't, look." The Doctor picked up a thin arm, and held it where Vince could see.

"Shit! What happened?"

"You've been here a long time, son. I don't think there is much wrong with you that time and exercise won't cure."

"Why does my right hand hurt?"

The Doctor held it up, showing that it was still clenched tightly. "Let go!"

"No! I mustn't!"

"Why not?"

Vince thought about it, for several minutes. "I can't remember. I just know that I mustn't."

"What is it that you are holding?"

Another long pause. "I don't know."

George interrupted, "Let me see, please."

Dr Jones moved aside, to leave room for her to examine the clenched hand. A small cluster of frayed black threads showed on either side of the fist. George felt them. "It feels like nylon, and it looks as though it was woven - Oh!"

"What?" Both Vince and Dr Jones asked, simultaneously.

"Vince, my love, you CAN let go, now. Really! It doesn't need to be held any longer. It is the remains of a strap from my bouyancy jacket. I recall the Lifeboat-man saying he had to cut us apart, as Vince would not let go. He wouldn't breathe, either. Even though he was effectively dead, his will was so powerful he wouldn't breathe water, or let go of me. That's the only reason I'm still on this planet. The Lifeboat crew had an awful job getting him to breathe when they fished us out. They had me pumped out and going again in a couple of minutes, but not Vince. They had to take it in turns, pumping, all the way back, then the Ambulance crew took over the problem, and had to keep him going, all the way to hospital. There was another month of it, on the ward, with the machines doing all the work, because every time he started to wake up, he held his breath again. It should be in the records."

Dr Jones was flipping to the front of the fat file, peering in the dim light. "Yes, it's here. I'd forgotten. Black webbing strap clenched in right hand, tendons locked immovably. Strap cut to free - blah blah, Trachea closed by muscular spasm, intubated. No water in lungs. Diaphragm in spasm, would not respond to reflexive breathing. Etc, etc. E.A.R used. Heart beating. No apparent brain functions as indicated by normal reaction tests. Yak yak. It's all here. And that's how you've been, for the last year. Lying there, breathing, pumping blood, and not a flicker."

"A year?" Vince muttered, his mind churning sluggishly as he tried to understand. "Oh, George, I'm sorry!"

"For what? You saved me. The debt is repaid, in full, with interest!" Her eyes were still leaking, but with joy, now.

"What debt?" Vince was trying hard to catch up. "Oh, I get it, I think! I might still be dozy, but I'm certain I recall someone promising me a steak soup!"

"Yes, we did!" Said Nurse. "I'll raid our little kitchen, and heat it myself, because if we send to the hospital kitchens for it, by the time it finds it's way up here, it'll be next week!" She made a last scan of the monitors, and left George and Joan alone, with Vince. They had a lot to catch up on.

"Well!" Dr Jones said, "I can't envisage you absconding, so I think I can leave you alone, too, We'll leave everything plugged in, for now, then tomorrow, we can start giving you your body back, o.k?"

"Plugged in? You mean -?"

"Plumbing, as in body wastes, as well as the electronic oracle, there."

"I don't think I'm up to the hundred yard dash, yet, anyway!" Vince agreed, "even if I knew where the loo was!"

"There is that! I won't be far away, so if you need me, just open the door, and yell!" Doctor Jones left, going to his office to contemplate miracles.

"A year!" Vince muttered, as his brain gradually caught up.

"Yes, my love. A year." George held his hand. "So, come on, let go now. It's alright, really."

"Let go." Vince looked at his hand, which George was holding up. "Let go!" Very gradually, the tendons relaxed, but the fingers didn't move.

442

"Yes, let go, now. It's alright to let go. It doesn't matter, any more."

"I have, I think. My fingers seem to be stuck!"

George worked her fingertips under his, and gently prized his hand open a little. He groaned with pain as the fingers moved. George gave the remnant of strap a tug, but it was still gripped, so she eased his fingers out a little more, then it came free, followed by a ragged piece of crushed neoprene rubber. The hand was badly discoloured, inside. "We'll let the nurse see that, when she comes back. There's the strap, see. Do you want to hold it in your other hand, for a while?"

"No, but keep it. I think I'll frame it, later." He stopped speaking, puzzled, thinking hard.

"What?"

"I'm trying to remember something. Something I told you, or wanted to, or - Oh God!"

"What? Tell me now."

"It just came back!"

So did the nurse, with the soup.

"Wait a minute!" He struggled to remember, suddenly

going pale as memory returned. "We were diving? Yes! You were playing with - with a starfish, and then you gave it your demand valve! I was holding a magic rock, or something. There was something special about it, anyway, or I thought there was. Then you waved at me, and when I looked again, you were a starfish, too, blowing bubbles. I suppose you were in the middle of drowning, really, and I had this damned rock, then I dropped it, because it, and all the others, were red-hot. I could hear a fire-engine siren. Then I was shouting at you to get off the rocks, before they burned you, but you didn't, then I couldn't breathe. I must have lost my demand valve. I grabbed you, then ditched your weight belt, but I couldn't get your life-jacket to inflate -."

"You wouldn't. I was told, later, that the cylinder was empty."

"Then I tried to dump my weights, but I couldn't find the release, so I blew my a.b.l.j. up, to take us up. That was when it hit me."

"What, the Holyhead ferry?" George tried a feeble joke.

"No, silly! I told you, then, I had found something out. Something I hadn't been able to say, before."

"What?" George asked, baffled.

"I love you! I really do! For the first time, I really love someone, You!"

Joan said, to the Nurse, "There are too many people in here. Let us leave the love-birds together, alone, for a while."

"Don't feel pushed out, Joan, we owe you a lot." George responded.

"Good idea!" the nurse agreed, "I'll be just outside, if you need me."

"Before you leave, just have a look at his hand, please, now that he's let go of the strap." George asked.

The nurse lifted his right hand, and studied it. "Hmm, a touch of rigour, but the physio can fix that. It looks like deep bruising, dermatitis, and muck. I think its o.k, but I'll get Dr Jones to check it, a bit later. Come on, Joan, let us leave them to it. George can feed him the soup." They both left.

Vince was moving, struggling to sit up. "Help me up, please! I can't seem to move!"

"I don't think your wires are long enough, lover, so leave it for now. You will be very weak, because your muscles haven't been working. They should start to come back, pretty quickly, now that you're awake. Let me feed you with this soup."

"God, I feel so helpless!"

"You are!"


When the nurse came back, an hour or so later to check on Vince, she found them both asleep on the narrow bed. George was balanced on the edge, one arm under his shoulders, with Vince's arm draped across her. She checked the monitors, and, satisfied that all was well, took a chair, and sat guard outside.


Some time after that, just before the shift-change, Dr Jones called by to check on his patient. He found the nurse, drowsing on a chair outside. She snapped alert when he approached, and asked him to avoid disturbing them, if he could, but to look at Vince's right hand. She explained what she'd seen, and what they were both doing, now.

"Good! It will give his brain time to catch up, and hers some time to unwind. All the signs showed she was getting pretty close to the end of her tether. It isn't hospital policy for two people to share the same bed, but as nobody comes up here, who's to know, except us! I'd rather break a few petty rules, than admit a new patient with a nervous breakdown!" He eased the door open, smiled at the couple, checked the monitors, carefully examined Vince's hand, and then crept out again, bringing the empty soup dish which he gave to the nurse to dispose of. "There's nothing to worry about, there. Put him onto half-hourly checks for the rest of today, hourlies tomorrow, then probably twice dailies, I think he's back in this world to stay."

"Yes, Doctor."

"Just being with his girl is all the medicine he needs right now, and I suspect that goes both ways. That, and lots of t.l.c."

"Yes, Doctor."

The shifts changed. The fresh nurse looked in on her charge, hesitating at the breach of the rules, but did nothing about it. If a Doctor had said it was alright, then who was she to argue? She was just piqued that she'd missed all the fun!

Several half-hours later, when she went in, the patient was awake. He had turned his head, and was trying to command his arm to put his hand onto George's hair. The nurse started to reach out, to help him, but he told her "No!" and to let him struggle. She knew he was right, the sooner he could get himself mobile, the better it would be, for him.

Vince concentrated, building up the energy, and managed to move his arm a few more inches. Then it slid down the curve of her shoulder, and onto her neck. George's eyes snapped open, to see him smiling at her.

"Sorry, love. I was trying to stroke you, not knock you out!" he apologized. "It got away from me!"

"It's alright." George saw the nurse watching, and started to get up.

"No, stay there, if you're comfortable! You've been there so long, a few more minutes won't hurt. It's against the rules, but then it isn't every day a coma patient wakes up!"

"Where's the other nurse, - Eagles?"

"Nancy? Her shift finished hours ago!"

"Have we met before?" George asked, failing to recognize the nurse.

"You didn't notice me before. I've been on the team for six months!"

"Oh, my. I'm sorry."

"It doesn't matter. You had other things on your mind. I'm Mary O'Flaherty, and the ginger-haired one, on the third shift, is Jill. She married a Pole a few months back, and no-one can pronounce her surname now, including her, so she's Ginger Jill, as there are three Jill's on this floor!"

"Hello, Mary. If you didn't already know, I'm Vince, and this is my fiance, Georgina. Thank you for looking after me."

"Oh. We did nothing much. The work starts now. Before, the machines did it all."

"Should I be sorry? Only joking!"

"That depends on whether you're a good patient, or not. If not, we'll make you sorry! Anyway, in a day or so you won't be on this ward. You'll be moved off our patch, as you aren't really one of ours any more!"

"That sounds like a threat!"

"No, it's a promise! Now, come on, George. Out of here, while I pretty him up for the -." The door opened. "- too late. I was about to say - the Doctor."

"That's me. How do you feel, Vince?"

449

"Like a well wrung out dish-rag. As limp as last week's lettuce."

"Ah! Do I detect humour? I think you are doing well, considering. Do you have any complaints?"

"Yes! This damn bed is too narrow, and too hard!"

"Well, they aren't intended for two, sharing! Once you put some flesh onto those bones, it will seem like a feather bed."

"They tickle, and the quills prickle!"

"While you are awake, we'll do a few checks"" The Doctor poked, prodded, and scratched for the reflexes. "Well, everything seems to be connected. It's all up to you, and the physio, now."

George asked, "How long before I can take him home?"

"That depends on a few details, have you got -."

She interrupted him. "To save a lengthy question and answer session, I have a G.P. arranged for daily visits, I've got a dietician, and a physio arranged. I've got a small gym. I have a special bed on order, pending confirmation if I, or rather, if he, needs it. I've arranged for a home help, I have a wheel-chair, a telephone, and lots of peace and quiet. Fresh air, and me! What else will he need?"

"Lots of determination and patience, from both of you. Time, good food, exercise, and love, are what he really needs. All the stuff you have will help. If he keeps picking up, as he has over these last few hours, we can let him go in maybe a week. I'm not promising, it's too soon, and it isn't my speciality. There is nothing much radically wrong, now, but we need to be ready for the unexpected. He will tend to wake for a while, and then sleep a lot, for the next few days, like a new baby, which, in a way, he is. You organized all that, before you came, today?" He turned to Vince, "Can you remember what happened?"

"Sort of. I don't know what caused it, but I think the air we were breathing had been got at.'

'That's it." The Doctor flicked to the front page. "It makes interesting reading, to a lab-rat. Er, yes, here we are, page eight. Lab analysis of the contents, blah, blah, ten to fifteen percent nitrous oxide, three parts per million of carbon monoxide. Trace of water, er - "

"Nitrous - that's laughing gas, isn't it, anaesthetic? Ten percent? That accounts for the hallucinations."

451

"Yes. There was plenty there to put you under, slowly, but not enough to notice on a quick test. It seems that someone didn't like you! In a day or so, I shall have to tell the Law that you are awake and talking sense, because they have been waiting to interview you about that."

"Yeah, they would. I would like legal representation present, too, when you think I'm ready."

"That would be wise! Right, I will allow you ten more minutes with the Beauty-Queen, and then I'm going to throw her out. She can revert to normal visiting hours, after this, and that goes for miracle-worker Joan, too!"

"Yes, Doc, thanks."

Chapter twenty-four.

Homecoming.

George spent the next few days at Joan's place when she wasn't with Vince, finalizing arrangements for the loan of various bits of equipment that would be needed until Vince was self-propelled. She also arranged one or two surprises for him once he was home again, a Solicitor who would be present at the police interview, and to help finalize a few other documents that had been hanging in limbo. She achieved it all with a unique mixture of charm, aggression, and downright bullying, while all the time keeping a tight hold on the reins of her dwindling funds. They weren't at danger levels, yet, but her Bank Manager was getting distinctly nervous.

Vince was repeatedly worked on by the hospital Physio's, who had previously been limited to keeping the joints mobile, but now had a mostly co-operating patient, so were able to exercise the musculature, as well. Three sessions a day left him gasping, and shaking with exhaustion, all his muscles, including some he didn't know he had, screaming in protest at the unaccustomed strain after their long rest. By the end of the first day, he could raise either hand from the mattress, pick up objects, and lift his head from the pillows. Once the medics were happy, he was unplugged from the monitors, which were rolled back, out of the way, and all the wires removed, except the heart-beat connectors, the sticky pads for which were left in place, for when he was exercising. Vince discovered that he could roll over on his own, but had to be careful not to go too far, because he got stuck, or his legs got tangled up in the plumbing, which was still necessary, just yet.

On the third day, when George called in at visiting time, she found him sitting up in the bed, propped by cushions strategically wedged around. He had a large bump, and an angry bruise, on his forehead. When she asked, he laughed, and admitted to falling out of bed, because he rolled over twice in the same direction!

They discussed the routine goings-on, and then he asked, "Did Betty ever come to visit?"

"Not that I'm aware of. Her legal rep. telephoned, to see if you were still around."

"Oh. Do you know where to get in touch with them, there are some things that need to be sorted."

"No, I don't, but my legal rep. does." Now came the tricky bit. "I've had to make certain decisions for you, while you were out of it. What I've done is legal, I've checked, but I don't know whether you will like it, or agree - - "

"Is it bad?"

"Not really, but I've had to cover a lot of expenses." She paused, unwilling to continue, while he was so weak.

"Just tell me. Don't dress it up with a load of waffle. My body might be weak, my head isn't!"

"She took a deep breath. "O.K, I've had to sell your flat."

"Is that all?"

"No, your car, and your tent had to go, too. I didn't get

much for them."

"Did you keep my radios?"

"Yes, and your stereo, your records, and personal stuff."

"That's alright, then. Half the flat was Betty's, anyway. No doubt she took her cut?"

"Yes, she took half. That was flat, contents, and furnishings. That left you with about twelve grand. I got two-fifty for the car."

"Twelve grand. Take out unpaid bills, they're paid now? So most, if not all, of it went on this place. I know it's not National Health. How much of your money have you spent on me?"

"Yes, your bills were paid, and the accounts closed. All your money has gone, bar a few pounds. I drew the last out for this month's treatment, so we should get, sorry, you should get a bit back. My money, not a lot, directly, but I have a lot held in abeyance, on equipment loans, commencing when you come home, I can get a bit back, because I can now cancel the box, and the ceremony."

"Box? Oh, yeah! Did you choose cardboard or plastic?

And as far as I'm concerned, you were right the first time, when you said "we". You've stuck by me for all this time, from choice, not knowing if I would wake up, or what or when the end would be. I can see that it has cost you, emotionally, and I don't know if I can ever repay that. What was going to happen, next month, if I hadn't woken up? Do I want to know? Anyway, we can talk about that any time. The cops are going to interview me tomorrow. What did you tell them?"

"Ah, well, I was economical with the truth. I said nothing about the fights, or Trev and Pete, or their pals, I just said you had the cylinders filled, and we went diving. It's caused a lot of bother, because all the dive shops were raided, and their compressors tested, trying to find the source. A couple of private compressors were impounded, too, because they sold a few fills. No-one knows where our air came from."

"Trev and Pete! I want to talk to them, when I'm able. There are some unanswered questions!"

"More than you know. It's nearly chucking-out time. Are your eyes working properly, yet?"

"Yes, they woke up this morning, and I can focus again,

457

why?"

"I'll leave you to read this, then. There's a document you might want to sign, and some news-paper clippings you might find interesting." She passed him two envelopes, one an A4 Manila, the other, a normal letter envelope. They spent the last few minutes, until the Nurse evicted her, in a clinch, kissing and cuddling.

Ginger Jill prized them apart. "Come on Kiddies, time to kiss and tell, or in other words, if he doesn't kiss me "thank-you" for letting you have five minutes extra, I'll tell the Doc he's getting too frisky for his own good!"

They parted, reluctantly.

"Out, George! The physio is due, in a few minutes!"

Vince groaned. "More torture!"

"Maybe, but it's doing you some good! The Doctor has seen your notes, and he says, if you keep up the progress, you can go home in a few days, if everything is in place and ready."

"You ought to know, you've bed-bathed me often enough!" Vince teased.

"Yes, everything is set up, I just need a start date." George

458

responded.

"There is just one minor point." Vince interrupted, "As you've sold the flat, where IS home?"

"You'll see, when you are ready. It'll give you a target to aim for."

The Physio arrived, then, bouncing around the room like a ball of surplus energy. "Come on. Everybody out! Not you, sonny! I've got a task for you!"

"How's he doing?" George asked.

"Terrible. He's a lazy-bones who won't keep at his exercises. Now, go on, OUT! Let me at the patient."

George retired, defeated, and went to arrange for her private physio/dietician/assistant to be at the house, starting in three days, so that various bits of equipment could be delivered, and set up, on the fourth

She had met Tommy in his flat above the restaurant, which his family now ran. They were slowly easing him into retirement, against his wishes, despite the fact that he knew they were right. The business had been stagnating, but was now beginning to boom again as they broke away from the formal traditions which only served to keep his clientele restricted.

When Joan had introduced Tommy to Georgina, he had been coldly polite, not wishing to pick up the threads of one of his previous occupations, but when she explained who she was asking for, and what had happened, his attitude changed.

This time, when George called on him, to finalize the arrangements, bringing him a map so that he could find the house, and a spare door key, he was waiting with the traditional greeting. His daughter, dressed formally, performed the tea ceremony, and then served a small meal, this being a business meeting.

After the meal, George stumbled through the proper acknowledgement in Japanese, (she'd sought guidance from an acquaintance, who had coached her), the girl stifled a giggle, while Tommy gave a wry smile.

"You use wrong phrase!" he explained, "Thirty years ago, maybe, it could happen, but time has taken its toll! I thank you for the invitation, though. I would have been honoured!" He bowed, then waved his daughter away. "I accept your speech in the manner it was intended, and not for what you actually said. Few British would have made the attempt."

"What should I have said?" George asked, knowing they could now talk freely, as equals.

He told her, and she attempted to repeat it. After coaching, and several repeated efforts, she nearly had it.

"And what DID I say?"

Tommy smiled again, "You offered to accompany me to my sleeping quarters, etcetera!"

"Ah!"

"Ah, so, even!" He laughed at himself.

"And that brings us to the reason for my visit. Vince will be leaving the hospital in a few days, they haven't exactly said when, so I'd like you to move to the cottage, and prepare for our arrival. There will be some deliveries made - of a wheel-chair, and a few other things, on loan, if you could be there to receive them."

"Yes, I said I would do this for my great friend, Vincent." He paused, "As this is a business discussion, I have to ask you this. I imagine that the hospital where he is staying is very expensive?"

"It is, but I am not asking for money. I have enough, just." She had briefly explained her financial arrangements to him during a previous visit.

"So you have a little left, but not very much?"

"I have enough to live for another year, with no earned income, if I am careful. The cost of some things cannot be estimated, like the final legal costs, but I've been trying to find work. There are some things I will not do, and others only if I absolutely have no choice, but it hasn't come to that, yet!"

"One thing I do not understand, why do you ask this of me. There are properly qualified people out there," Tommy gestured through the window, "who would do this work for you, for less money. Why do you not ask them?"

""Money is not the issue, or rather, it is. The others would be doing it for the money, but I believe, to you, the monetary aspect is insignificant. I hope you will do it for the love of the work, and for Vince and for myself."

"That is so, but what if I ask for more, to do this task?" He pressed.

"Then I would argue, but in the end, I would give in to you."

Tommy considered it. He still hadn't found the commitment, within her, that he was looking for. "Perhaps you have less money than you think, for one reason or another, and I ask for more than you have left."

"Then I would find work, somewhere, and eventually have enough, if you would wait."

"But, should there be no work?"

George hesitated for a fraction of a second, and then said "Then I would have to do one of the things I said I would not do. I made the offer earlier, in error, by mis-pronouncing some of your language. If that is what you will accept as payment, I will do it. I only ask that the debt is paid in a time and place that does not hurt Vince, and that he never finds out."

She was looking straight into his eyes as she spoke, and deep down, he could see the fire of her will, and knew that if he asked, she would do this thing. They sat, like that, for a long moment, eyes locked, across the small table, and then Tommy sighed. "I will not ask. I had to know whether this was for

Vincent, or yourself, - if you would pay the ultimate price. I know now. I will leave in the morning, if you will provide directions."

"I would still do it, if you asked, and do it well! I have a spare door key, and a map." She took them from her hand-bag, and unfolded the map. "The main road comes in, here, at Menai, and you need to go along here, to the A5025," she traced the route with her finger, "follow it round, and down here. The cottage is here. Or, if you'd rather, you can pick your own way across, on the minor roads. I've written the address there, if you need to ask."

"I can find it from that. I will need to purchase some supplies."

George opened her purse, and passed him a thin wad of notes. "That's a hundred pounds, in tens, to start you off. If you need more, let me know when we meet again, at the cottage. There is a telephone, if you need it. I will call when we are ready to leave the hospital, so you can be prepared. If you need to speak to me, I will be here." She indicated a number written on the margin of the map, "Or the hospital." She indicated another number.

"I think that is everything."

"You said you had to know if I would pay the ultimate price. Do you really think I would still be here after all this time, looking after his affairs, with my money, if I was not doing it for Vince?"

"I do not know you. We have met, briefly, twice. Vincent has not been able to vouch for you. I had no time to learn your intentions. In my country, a woman does not negotiate these things. It is a man's work, while the woman makes the tea. I am beginning to know you, and have no reason to doubt you, but I have no reason to trust you, either. There is more to this than you have said. This 'accident' would not normally happen to Vincent, he is too careful."

"Perhaps Vince will fill in the details, if he believes that you should know. It is not for me to do so, at this time."

Tommy gave a little bow of acceptance. "It is traditional to end a meeting with a glass of sake, but I suspect your police would not take kindly to the resulting drunken driving! Will you accept a glass of fruit juice, as a substitute?"

"I thank you for your kindness, but will refuse, if I may do so without causing offence, I have a lot to do, and little time to do it."

"Then we will meet again, in a few days." Tommy clapped his hands, once, sharply, calling the 'geisha' daughter.

"Oki will see you to the door."

George stood, then bowed to Tommy in the proper manner, received an acknowledgement, then followed Oki.

Out of earshot, Oki said, "Thank god that stuff is over! He's a stickler for the proper traditions. Would you like a coffee before you leave?"

"No, thanks, Oki, I really do have things to attend to."

"So! Ladies room is through there, and the exit is here. The door will latch behind you."

"Thanks, I could do with a quick visit to the plumbing!"

"Sayonara."

"Thank you. Goodbye, for now."

On Saturday, when George called at the hospital, Vince was waiting for her, fully dressed, sitting in a wheel-chair. His clothes looked about ten sizes too large on his gaunt frame.

"Don't sit down!" was his greeting, "We're outta here!" He passed her three manila envelopes, "One for my G.P. One for the physio, and one for you. What to do in emergencies, I suppose."

"I already know that-. Clasp hands to head, scream, and run round in tiny circles like a headless chicken!"

"That's about it! If you will bring your car to the main entrance, I will get a Porter to wheel me down to wherever it is."

"Right. See you again in a few minutes." She gave him a peck on the cheek.

George halted her Land-Rover outside the main entrance, and switched off the engine, just as a Porter rushed over, shouting, "OY! You can't park that, there! It's for Ambulances, only!"

He cringed at her stare, and the reply of, - "This IS an ambulance! Can't you see the blue strobe-light? I'm picking up a disabled person."

The Porter was drawing breath for a fresh attack, when Ginger Jill wheeled Vince out of the doorway. "Ah, there you are!" Jill fussed around with the blanket draped over Vince's

467

legs.

"Give over fussing!" he kicked it off again. "You're making me feel ill! Let the stick-insect feel the fresh breeze! Bloody hell, it's cold!"

"See! You're complaining again!" Jill retorted, "Always moaning about something!" She picked up the blanket. "We'll be glad to see the back of you! Have you got everything?"

"Nothing fell off on the way down. It doesn't help, not knowing what I had, or didn't, when I was wheeled into the place!"

Jill looked around. "Hey, Megger, give the patient a hand into the car!"

"Megger?" George inquired. She vaguely recalled electricians using them.

"Yes, short for Megalomaniac. He thinks he owns the forecourt. Last week he wheel-clamped the Senior Registrar's car, when he came on an emergency call-out. There was a hell of a row about that!"

While everyone was chattering, Vince was studying the Landie, a puzzled look on his face.

George noticed. "What is it?"

"It looks like the one I remember from last week, last year, rather, but I don't recall the orange seats and head-lining."

"There's a story behind that! I'll tell you later. Climb in, or do you want me to tow you, behind?"

"We want the chair back!" Jill exclaimed, as she opened the near-side door for him.

Vince levered himself out of the wheel-chair, then with some careful hand-swapping, and a few pushes and shoves, got into the Land-Rover, settled into the seat, and relaxed, panting. "I'm glad you didn't get one of those 'Bigfoot's' we were talking about last w - year."

George went quiet for a moment. Jill sensed it, and put on her artificial bonhomie. "Well, chop chop! We might decide to keep him for a pet, or Megger might find a clamp big enough!"

George came back with a snap. "Yes." She reached under the seat below Vince, pulled out a bag, and handed it to Jill, "A token of appreciation from us both. Share them round, please."

"Bang goes the diet, again! I'd better get back to my work. I have to clean up the mess he's left behind him, now."

Vince reached for her, and nearly fell out of his seat

"Steady!" Jill caught him, "Don't go and break something, now!"

Vince kissed her cheek. "That's for Mary, that's for Nancy" he kissed the other cheek, "and that" he kissed her on the lips, "Is for you!"

"Oh, take him away!" Jill sniffed "before I take him home myself!" She backed off, collected the wheel-chair and blanket, and went to the entrance.

George strapped Vince in with the seat-belt, positioned a few strategically placed towels where the webbing pressed against his un-padded bones, then walked round and climbed in herself, to start the engine. She drove them round to Joan's place, where she'd been staying while the cottage was re-built. "Two minutes, while I pick up my stuff, most of it's packed already, then I'll take you to our home."

"O.K. Say goodbye to - don't bother, she's coming out."

"They threw you out, then, for being a right pain in the rear?"

"Forgive me for not getting out, but it would take another

470

week to get back in again! I wanted to thank you for looking after me, and George, for all this time."

"I had nothing better to do."

"Pull the other one, but not too hard, it might come off!"

George came out, carrying a hold-all which she tossed casually into the back of the Landie. It landed with a solid thud. "Thanks for everything, Joan. Come and visit us, when you wish. You know where we are."

Once they were rolling, Vince asked, "Is that the cannon, still in your bag?"

"The Magnum? Yes, I thought it might come in handy, one day. There are still some scores to settle."

He was quiet, then, letting her concentrate on her driving. He was amazed at how much the traffic level had increased over the last week - year, since he was last outside. Buildings he knew of, as land-marks, had disappeared, and roads had moved, been widened, or become by-passes, but most of the time, he knew where he was, although he still didn't know their destination. Where-ever they were going, he was with George. That was all that mattered.

471

The next time George looked over, at him, he had slumped down in the seat, as far as the belt would allow, and was asleep. She tried to adjust her driving to give a smoother ride, but the stiffly sprung short-wheel-base Land-Rover is no luxury saloon car, and it bounced, jolted, and nodded just as energetically as ever.

There wasn't too much of a delay in the traffic through Conwy, and just over two hours from the start of the journey, they were pulling up by the cottage.

The cessation of noise and motion woke him, and he struggled up in the seat, looking around, puzzled. "Is this home? It looks familiar, but I don't recognize it."

"Yes, this is home. It was the tumble-down cottage at Llyn Hafodol that we stopped at, that day, when we were just riding around."

"Oh yes! I recognize it now! You've put a lot of time and effort into renovating it. I keep forgetting that last week, to me, is a year for you."

"Stay there a minute, while I get the door open."

"No need, it's either magic, or you've got burglars!"

The cottage door opened, and an old Japanese man, wearing a kimono, stood there. He bowed briefly to George, and then turned to look at Vince. Shock and horror flashed momentarily across his face, then was gone, as he regained control.

Vince made the salute from pupil to Master which can be made from the seated position, when it is impractical, or impossible to rise. "Tommy! What are you doing here?"

"I would have thought that was obvious! I am here to try to repair your body. I can see it will not be an easy task, for you! You are very undernourished."

"I called myself a stick-insect, earlier! I presume you have met Georgina?"

"She is a very hard-headed business-woman. It was she that found me, and persuaded me to come. I can see now that her decision was the correct one. The task is not one for a professional keep-fitter. It will need care, and dedication. When you greeted me, I was not thinking of a stick-insect, but of a preying mantis."

Vince was struggling with the seat-belt release. "I can't

even manage to press this damn thing," he muttered, "my thumb isn't strong enough!"

"May I assist?" Tommy reached in, pressed the release, allowing the latch to spring out, then took Vince's hands, looked into his eyes, saw the things in there, and flinched as he sensed the aura. "You have looked upon, and done, things that a mortal man should have no need for. You are much more, now, than last time we trained together, but are you strong enough to complete the journey, I wonder?"

"The journey I am more concerned with, right now, is the one from here to the bathroom. Those muscles are weak, too, and are becoming distressed! If you would help me down, with support, I think I can make it!"

Between the three of them, they half-carried Vince to the required room. George went back to the Land-Rover for the bags and documents, then locked it up. When she came back into the cottage, the cistern was gurgling, and Vince, propped up by Tommy, was struggling with his zips and buttons.

Half an hour, and a cup of coffee for George and Vince, tea for Tommy, later, his notes accepted, read, and discarded, Vince was performing a series of gentle exercises while Tommy learned what he was capable of in his present physical state, In between the groans, gasps, and protests, Vince was filling in some of the gaps in his story.

"You, like your lady, are not telling me all the things that happened. Until you are able, there will be a barrier between us, not of my making, that may be un-surmountable."

"Please do not misunderstand, Tommy, it is not that I do not want to tell you, I cannot, for your own safety."

"Then there is all the more reason for you to tell me, for my own safety. You could not protect me from an angry green-fly, right now!"

Vince started giggling, then chuckling, then laughing, great gulping sounds, with tears streaming down his face, and then he was crying. Tommy allowed him three or four great gulping sobs, then a hand flicked out, landing with a sharp "splat!" on Vince's cheek. There was stunned silence, for a moment, then Vince's eyes closed, and he slept.

George crashed into the room. "You hit him!"

"It was necessary. The healing can begin, now. He reached

a catharsis point."

Vince sighed, and then smiled, still asleep.

"See, he is not hurt, he is released! I do not think he will even remember it when he wakes, in a few minutes. Permit an old man a silly question, - why did you come in?"

"Because you hit him!"

"What were you doing?"

"Vacuuming the Landie's floor. It's still full of sand and dye that keeps working out of the crevices."

"So you did not see, and you could not hear. I ask again, why did you come in?"

"Because -." She stopped, thinking about the question. "- I knew!"

"That is what I thought. There is a link between you, it is not very strong, yet, but it is there. Please go now, before he wakes, you distract him."

Chapter twenty-five.

Recovery.

About two months later, Joan telephoned to arrange a document swapping session, as she was acting as intermediary and buffer to protect Vince from the world until he was able to fend for himself. She arrived about four hours later, having got lost a couple of times on the way. Her little Metro clattered to a stop outside the cottage on the packed earth drive/garden. (George hadn't decided which it was to be, yet), the tiny engine subsiding with a crack as it back-fired.

Joan climbed stiffly out, and stood, stretching the kinks from her body that had been caused by sitting inside the confines of the little tin box for too long, while she took in the view across the fields, the little lake, and the hills. Used to the constant city noise, her ears were confused by the silence, and they started whistling and ringing of their own accord. "Damn it!" she muttered, then took a deep breath, ending up with a harsh cough. Her lungs, accustomed to the city stink and fumes, weren't ready for the fresh, clean air, the smell of grass, and the hint of salt from the sea, air devoid of the smells of chemicals, effluent, and sweaty bodies crammed in together. "What a dull, boring, place to live," she thought, "Miles from anywhere, nobody to chat with, no neighbours, nowhere to go, nothing to do. Talking of neighbours, where were they all? She wondered, as nobody had come out. They could hardly have failed to hear her arrive! She crunched up the gravel, shingle, and shell footpath, to the front door, and reached for the doorbell. There wasn't one. There was no knocker, either. She tried knocking on the solid door, her soft hand making a feeble "splat splat" noise that was barely audible. Nobody came, so she moved round the side, to a window, where she peered in. Apart from some shiny gym machines, the room was empty. Through the whistles and tweets in her ears, she thought she heard a giggle from round the back, and went to see, assuming a door or window was open.

478

She found the three of them lined up there, in the back garden, their backs to her. Tommy and Vince were performing what appeared to be a series of slow-motion karate moves, their motions smooth and flowing. George, at the rear of the line, was trying to emulate them, but only succeeded in looking like an escaped part from a threshing machine. Tommy and Vince turned their heads to the left, then made a downward- outward sweep with their left arms, step-turned left, at the same time their right arms bent 90" at the elbow, fore-arm held horizontally across the body, then rotated, from the shoulder, to bring the arm up vertically, to just outside the body-line. The right foot kicked forward, and returned, and then they leaned far over to the left, looking right, and kicked to the right.

George lost her balance, and fell over, lying on the grass, laughing, then saw Joan watching them. "Whoops, we've got company!"

"Hi, Joan." Vince called, without looking round.

"Stop chattering!" Tommy commanded. "Concentrate!"

"What on earth are you lot doing?" Joan was mystified.

"It's Chai tea." George replied, as she got up. "It's

supposed to be good exercise."

"Tai Chi." Vince corrected her. "Chai tea comes from a NAAFI teapot!"

"Silence! Concentrate!"

"Come on in, Joan, leave these two prancing about outside, and tell me some gossip."

They rather one-sidedly swapped tit-bits over a coffee and fruit-cake. Joan's talk was mostly city stuff, who was doing what, to whom, and in which hotel, while George's was more domestic, her experiments with a cook-book, at gardening, and such.

"Is this one of yours?" Joan indicated the cake.

"God, no! I use mine as paving stones. I bought this from a little bakery a few miles up the road. Mine always come out rock-hard, or dead flat, like pie pastry with currants in! My last attempt turned out to be a four-pound biscuit!"

"Let's give them a treat, then, what've you got in the cupboard?" They retired to the kitchen, where George displayed a thick, well-thumbed cook-book. Joan flicked through it, sneered, and threw it into the bin. "They're all wrong! Look! Do

480

this, and that, and that, and you have a basic sponge mix. Don't do all that fiddling with a teaspoon of this, a pinch of that. Flour, butter, sugar, eggs, and T.L.C. make a cake. It's not chemistry, its magic. Gas seven, no, make it six, I don't know your cooker. Middle shelf, and don't keep opening the door!"

Soon, the kitchen was filled with the smells of baking, and things cooling on wire racks.

Vince staggered in, drenched with sweat, gasping, to collapse into a chair, where he slumped, steaming gently, as Tommy came past, giving him a "You're hopeless" stare.

George entered the room, and plonked a frosted glass of fruit juice, and a still warm scone, next to him on a small table.

"Thanks, lover!" Vince eyed it cautiously. The last scone she had presented to him was still in the back garden, where it defied all attempts by the local wildlife to eat it.

"Don't worry. Joan baked them!"

"Ah!"

Joan came in, with two more coffees, and two more scones, on a small plate, and put them on a nearby table, while George took another, and a drink, in to Tommy, in the gym.

481

"I think George has offended Tommy." Vince mused, "Prancing about, indeed!"

"When you've cooled down, I'll show you those papers your solicitor has asked me to send. He was going to bring them himself, but has to appear in Crown Court, instead. He's read them through, and says they're all standard stuff. It's up to you to sign agreement, or propose a counter-claim."

"O.K. We'll look at them, later. Are you planning on staying for a day or three?"

"I wasn't planning on doing."

"It's no bother, if you do. I know George could use the company. Tommy isn't a very good conversationalist."

"And you have a year missing."

"Exactly."

"How are you getting on?"

"Me, or us? Us are doing fine. George isn't missing her flying, too much, and is enjoying living normal hours, She likes not having to get out of a nice warm bed, at unmentionable hours, just to go and sit in a tin box with a glass roof, for eight hours,  then finding that she is allowed to go to sleep just as everybody else gets up! I think she is enjoying the challenge of growing things in her own garden, although it does sometimes seem futile when the plant she has been cosseting and nursing turns out to be a dandelion, or a colts-foot, or something. She showed me one she nursed all winter, which was growing merrily, in a pot. She was most put out when I told her it was an invasive perennial weed, called Mare's Tail, which everyone else does their damndest to eradicate!"

Joan collapsed, laughing.

"And me. I'm well enough. I've no strength, or stamina, yet, but it's coming back, slowly."

George came back in, sat in a chair, and bit into a scone. "MM! I wish mine came out like this! What were you laughing at?"

"Vince was telling me about your horticultural activities."

"Oh? - - Oh! You rat! It's not my fault the damn things won't grow! I did have some good carrots, but the rabbits got there, first, and the caterpillars ate my lettuce faster than I could!"

"I hadn't heard about those, he was telling me about your

pot-plant."

"Which pot-plant? I don't have any."

"Your Mare's tail, lover-girl.'

'You didn't?" she glared at Vince.

"He did!"

"Right, you can sleep on the rowing machine, tonight!"

"But it's not intended for that!" he protested.

"It didn't stop you, though! Remember? I caught you asleep on it, the other day. Lucky for you it wasn't Tommy!"

The friendly banter continued for a while, until it had gone full circle, and they were starting to repeat.

"Joan says Betty is pregnant again."

"Really? It wasn't my doing this time, either! Joan, did you win your bet with her over the last one, that turned out to be twins?"

"Yes, and I got the red-head bit right, too."

"Apparently," George began, "His name's James Smith, - "

"Lancaster-Smytthe." Joan corrected, "and it won me a tenner, when she opened the envelope!"

"- and he's got a flash place near the park, with a Butler

and Chauffeur, even."

"She picked a rich one, this time, then." Vince shrugged.

"Don't you care?" Joan asked.

"No, just curious."

"I think so. He's got a kid of his own, Reginald, I think, and Joe gets on alright with him, or so I've heard. Anyway, that brings me to the reason why I'm here." She took some documents out of her bag. "Have a look through, and write in any changes that you want, and then sign each page. I'll take them back, or you can post them, to Fleecem and Leggett, then they can do their thing with Grabbit and Runne, etcetera. The less changes, the quicker they can be processed. I see you've already bought the wedding ring."

"Oh, no! That's the one I found in the wreck! I wear it to keep the local punters happy, and the prowlers off! It helps that I was here, alone, before, and I've encouraged them all to think we're newly-wed's, though what they thought, when they saw my stick insect, God only knows!"

"Tommy says I look like a Preying Mantis."

"What's one of those?"

"A stick insect that eats stick insects, I think." George replied, "It creeps up then shoots out a telescopic mouth, to bite chunks off things it fancies!"

"I haven't bitten any parts off you, yet!" Vince argued.

"Oh, no? What's this, then, a plum-skin?" George displayed a mark on her neck.

"Ah, well, that's different!"

"He's not all that weak, then?" Joan observed.

Tommy knocked, and came into the room as they all fell about. "Up, Vince. Time for work-out!"

"I've to read these papers, for the legal bod's!"

"They wait a year, another hour won't hurt! In!"

"Yes, Master." Vince climbed laboriously to his feet, and followed Tommy into the gym.


"Let us see how those cakes are doing, George. And who's cooking dinner, anyway?"

"Tommy will. He's feeding Vince a weird mix of his own, and proper food for us. It seems to work, as Vince is filling out, without getting fat."

"Tommy won't mind an extra mouth, will he?"

"No. It'll give him an excuse to show off! You're staying, then?"

"It looks like it. I don't fancy the drive back in the dark. Do you mind?"

"God, no! Your company is a welcome change to S4C, and that noise!" George waved an arm at the gym door, through which came raggedly rhythmic clanking and grunting noises.

"I see what you mean!"

"Vince said, when he's able, he'll put up a proper aerial, but until then, I'm using one taped to a pole, poked through a window. It works, sort of. The reception of S4C isn't too bad, Harlech is very spotty, and on a good day, I can get T.V. Aereann, but it's very fuzzy, and hissy."

"I've a few c.d. discs in the car, if you have a player."

"Ah, no. Cassettes, or L.P's, but the needle's worn out!"

"Not exactly high tech out here, are you!"

"I've had more important things to do, and as you know, I wasn't living here, regularly, until recently."

"Yes, I noticed. What did you do all day, until Vince came

back?"

"Like now. I broke my back all day, putting it right, and slept all night, like a corpse." The time interval between the clanks and groans coming from the gym were increasing. "It won't be long now, he's about done for. Listen for Tommy goading him!"

"Did you buy all that stuff in there? It must have cost a fortune!"

"No. A lot of it is Tommy's. He brought it with him, in his caravan. You saw it outside. He used to run a gym and karate school, at night, while his family ran the restaurant, but he's getting past the teaching, now, and his family has made him retire from the catering side of the business. As you know, Vince met him, years ago, and they've been friends ever since, so when I asked Tommy to help Vince, he came."

"What's his last name? I can't just call him Tommy, it wouldn't be polite."

"Just Tommy, and that isn't his real name, either."

They chatted on for a while, listening to the decreasing frequency of groans and clanks, and Tommy mercilessly bullying Vince into "just one more!"

Tommy emerged through the doorway. "He is useless! He thinks that making loud noises with his mouth, and pulling faces, will make him strong again." He stormed off out. George started to rise, but Tommy's voice came back in to the room, "Leave him! I told him three more presses, before I allow him out."

After a few moments, chopping sounds could be heard from the kitchen, and the odour of an onion drifted through the room, punctuated by a groan-clank from the gym. George took Joan on a quick tour of the house, instead. They were in the back garden, when Tommy called them in.

"You could always put a wire fence around the veggies." Joan suggested.

"I thought of that, but Tommy had a better idea. He's going to catch the rabbits, and cook them!"

"What about the caterpillars, though, I don't fancy having them in a soup!"

"Don't suggest it. He might try it!" They went in.

"What were those rocks, scattered around in the corner, for?" Joan asked.

"They're 'plants', when I find a pattern I like, I'll replace them with the real ones. It saves digging them up several times!"

"It makes sense, sort of."

As they went through the doorway, George's hand happened to brush against Joan's, and in the tiny transfer of energy, Joan saw something. She started to comment, then changed her mind. It would keep, for now.

Chapter twenty-six.

Realization.


In the morning, George took Joan on a quick tour of the area in her Land-Rover, ending up in Holyhead, so they could do a bit of shopping. When they returned to the cottage, Joan gathered up her few bits and took them to her Metro, ready for the trip home. When she opened the door, she stepped back sharply. "Whew! Something died in there during the night!"

George had a sniff. "It does pong, doesn't it? That's the normal city smell. You don't realize how bad it is until you've spent a few hours away from it! You will be appalled at the constant noise, too!"

They went into the cottage, to find Vince scribbling notes in the margin of one of the documents. "Hi, folks, have you spent up? Can't we persuade you to stay for a few days, Joan?"

"No, you can't. It's too quiet for my liking. There are no bars, no clubs, no nothing! I'll be back, though, now and then. Anyway, I've a club outing, tomorrow, a mystery tour, cost me three quid. I might even meet Mr Right!"

"Well, if you'd rather listen to a traffic jam, and sparrows with bronchitis, than a skylark, who are we to stop you? Those papers are alright as they are, but this one I've amended in a couple of places. I don't see why I should pay maintenance for a couple of kids that aren't even mine, especially as I have no income, and no Capital, either! I don't even qualify for dole money. They say I haven't been available for work, and as I was unemployed at the time of my accident, I don't get sick pay from work, either!"

"Where's Tommy? I've got those veggies he wanted." George asked.

"Either in the kitchen, his van, or having a digging session, on that patch of land you haven't touched, yet."

George took the vegetables through to the kitchen, and saw Tommy, through the window, leaning on a shovel, watching something across the fields. When it came into view, George saw a tractor, about a hundred yards beyond her boundary wall. "Tommy? Care for a drink?" she called, through the window, "Joan is leaving, soon."

He waved "no thanks," and continued watching the tractor, while prodding the ground, but his mind wasn't on the garden.

George made three coffees, and cut pieces of cake they'd made, yesterday. When she took them through, Joan asked - "What's up?"

"I don't know. Something is bothering Tommy, but there's nothing to see except a farmer, on a tractor."

"What's he doing?" Vince asked.

"Tommy?"

"No, the farmer?"

"It looks as though he's ploughing the field, over the wall."

"Again? They ploughed it last week. Something smells, and it's not manure!" He finished folding the document back into its envelope, put it with the others on the table next to Joan, then climbed out of the chair and went into the kitchen. In two minutes, he was back. "Definitely funny, the farmer is ploughing a ploughed field. Whose land is it?"

"I don't know. It wasn't used, last year, the same as the other one further over, and the ones either side. They're all weedy."

Tommy came in. "There is something funny going on," he began, "that farmer is -."

"Ploughing a ploughed field," the other three finished the sentence for him.

"I think it would be wise for your friend to leave, soon." Tommy decided. He turned to Joan, and do not stop for any reason, until you are at home. Do you have enough petrol in your car?"

"No, I'll need to fill it up. I can't help noticing that you have lost your accent, all of a sudden!"

"I have to keep up the image, but that isn't important, for now. It would be best if I follow you, for part of the way, until I am sure they are not trailing you. Tell me when you are ready. I need to telephone, first."

He made two calls. To the first one, he merely said, "It begins." The second, much more lengthy, was in Japanese, to

Oki, during which he made arrangements for a hand-over of Joan, to make sure she was safe, until they, whoever they were, showed they were either not interested, or were not following her. Satisfied, he cleared the line, and then went to check on his car.

Inspiration came to Vince, and he switched on his scanning receiver, programming it to hunt through the frequencies where he had found the tracking bug's signals, before. George, seeing what he was doing, had a similar idea, and went rummaging in a long dis-used box. She emerged, festooned with cob-webs, and clutching a couple of head-sets. Vince recalled her taking them off the group on the cliff-top. After a brief fiddle with one, she switched it on, held the ear-piece up, and listened. Apart from a faint electrical hiss, there was nothing. Vince was fiddling with the other one, until she pointed out that the battery was missing. She showed him the compartment, where a single AAA cell would fit. "It started to leak, so I took it out, and binned it." She gave him the working unit. "See if you can find the frequency, then we can save the battery. I never did get any that size!"

"It might be an idea to dust off that cannon, too."

"I already have. It's where I can get to it in a hurry, but out of harm's way."

Vince was still fiddling with the spare headset radio, and found how to dismantle it, then studied the miniature workings inside. He found what appeared to be the aerial, and measured it with a steel tape he took from a drawer. It gave him a frequency of approximately two hundred megahertz, so he cancelled the search programme in his scanner, and gave it new parameters, either side of the new setting, then began talking to the working head-set.

"One two, three, Mary had a little lamb," he spoke nonsense, watching the frequency display on the scanner, counting up and down the range. After five minutes, he had found nothing, and stopped to double check the components in the dismantled set. "Funny, I could have sworn that - Hello! What's this?" He'd missed something. "I could have sworn it was a dot of glue, holding it into place, but perhaps -," He muttered obscurely, then measured again. The length of fine wire on either side of the dot was identical. "I wonder if that's a choke? In which case, this is a stacked dipole!" He re-tuned his scanner to four hundred megahertz, then picked up the live headset. "Mary had -." He grabbed for the volume control as an ear-piercing whistle burst from the scanner's speaker. ""Ow! My ears!" He carefully nudged the tuning up and down, while talking nonsense to the headset radio, while he homed in on the exact frequency, then stored it in the scanner's memory.

"What was that noise?" George came back in.

"Only a howl-round. I've found the frequency." Vince turned the headset off. "Can you read what that tiny print says, there?" He pointed with the tip of a pin. George peered at it, then tried using the base of a tumbler as a magnifying lens, while Vince set up a scan programme either side of the 'prime' frequency he'd found. After a few more button-pushes, the radio was scanning both the bug and the headset frequencies. Satisfied, he turned the volume back up, then left it searching while he re-assembled the headset, then took the battery from the working set and tried it in the other, just in case. The howl came on the original frequency he'd set, so he now knew they were on the right setting. Before Tommy left, he gave him the old battery, and asked if he would get a new pack if he had the opportunity, then asked George if she'd managed to read the tiny print.

"Simple. It read - "Made in Taiwan!""

"That figures!"


Tommy's car crunched onto the gravel patch, rolled up to his van, and parked. The lights went off, the engine died, then he creaked stiffly out of the driving seat. He spent a few moments, stretching, then went over to his caravan, let himself in, then turned on the lights. After a minute, they went off again, and he headed towards the house, where George met him at the back door.

"Hello, again. Was there any bother?"

"No. Nothing happen. My friend meet her at place called Abergele, then I came back. Did anything happen here?"

"Not a thing. I hope we're not being paranoid."

"Confucius, he say, "Not to worry about things, until after!""

She chuckled. "Vince is incinerating something in the kitchen, if you dare risk it. The kettle's just boiled."

"What he destroying? Charcoal and cinders?" They eyed the blue haze creeping through the door-jamb that led to the kitchen.

"I don't really know. It's funny. In a tent, with a two burner propane stove, he can create a credible meal, but in a proper kitchen, with all the tools, he's a disaster."

They went in. "I got the batteries." Tommy passed her a plastic bag, "What they for?"

George explained, showing him one of the headset radios, and showing him Vince's scanner, still flipping through its programmed search.

"Ah, yes. Good radio. My people make them, in Taito-ku, Tokyo. One of my family work in the factory. There are a few things that can be changed, to make it better."

"You'd better see Vince about that, it's his baby. I am allowed to turn it on, and off!"

"I might discuss it, when he's finished destroying my kitchen. I have to send for the parts, anyway, they not commonly available.'

"I wouldn't know."

"There is a new model soon to be released, with more facilities."

"If you say so. What goes on inside them is a mystery to me. The kind of radio I'm used to, you dial up the channel, then either listen, or press a button and talk!"

Tommy chuckled, and went to see what Vince was doing.


Joan finished fuelling her Metro at that place near the Hotpoint factory/warehouse. As she came out of the shop, she saw Tommy similarly engaged, and noticed that he was keeping a wary eye on the surroundings, and passing traffic. The only other car on the forecourt was another Toyota, the driver apparently eating from a packet of crisps, but as it was parked away from the pumps, in a dark corner, it was hard to be sure. Tommy advised her to be careful, on her journey, and added that Ito would see her to her door. She gave him a quick wave goodbye, as she strapped in, then started her little engine, which sounded like a tin can full of marbles, in comparison with the one in Ito's car, which vroomed into life, and burbled quietly, as he waited for her to move off.

She bellowed homeward at a steady fourty miles per hour, ignoring with equal distain the de-restricted signs, and those calling for a thirty M.P.H. speed. Ito trundled resolutely along at varying distances behind, mostly in third gear, only getting into fourth occasionally, when other cars between them turned off, allowing him to catch up, before dropping back again.

Joan was first aware of the change of atmosphere in the car as she approached Queensferry. The previously warm, sunny day was disappearing into a grey murk as dusk approached. After another mile or so, she noticed that the clag was down to ground level, so she slowed to her usual bad-visibility speed of thirty-five. An enormous articulated lorry came barrelling past, it's air-horns blaring, as she did so, making her flinch and swerve. Ito cursed as he nursed his staggering Toyota along, behind, alternating between second and third gear, this speed falling in the range between the two.

A vague smell of rotten eggs was pervading Joan's car, so she clicked the fan onto its loudest setting, and cranked down the window, but the smell got worse. She suddenly missed the clean Welsh air, then laughed at herself as she recalled her words when she arrived at Llyn Hafodol Cottage.

She eventually trundled into town, dropped the documents off at Fleecem's a few minutes before they closed business for the day, and arranged to call in a few days, in case anything needed clarifying. She pulled away from where she had parked on the double yellow lines moments before the Warden strutted around the corner, only just failing to catch Ito's registration number as he pulled away behind her. Joan meandered around for a time, her intent being to lose anyone that might be following, with the exception of Ito. It was a waste of time, though, as nobody was. One of Ito's contacts had seen to that, bringing his Starlet to a staggering halt in the middle of a junction and creating instant grid-lock. Ito had seen him climb out of his car and open the bonnet, to peer bemusedly inside, as he and Joan drove away from the area.

Joan wound her Fiesta down the narrow cul-de-sac, parked up, and went into her flat. Ito received the 'high-sign' from another of his contacts, indicating that nobody had been near, then turned his Toyota, and took it for a fast run back home, to clear the valves and cylinders, after it's crawling journey.

The 'phone in the cottage rang. Vince happened to be nearest, and lifted the handset. A torrent of Japanese poured from the ear-piece. "Tommy, it's for you!"

"So." He ambled over."Aie?" He listened for a minute, spoke a short phrase, and then hung up. "She is home. No trouble."

"It took her long enough!" George commented.

"Ito, he say she very slow driver. Thirty-five all way. He can go faster on bicycle!"

Vince started to add a comment of his own, then stopped. George had her head on one side, listening hard. "I can hear voices!"

They all listened, then Tommy flowed to the door. Standing to one side, he gave it a firm push so that it swung open to bump against the wall. They heard silence, apart from a magpie, chack-chacking nearby, and Vince's scanner, which was hissing quietly to itself.

Tommy carefully poked his head around the door-frame, and checked the other room. "Nobody inside." He went in, to look through the window. Tractor man was chugging through the gate, on the far side of the field.

"I could have sworn - - perhaps I AM getting paranoid!" George muttered.

Vince went in, behind Tommy. "Perhaps you did hear voices. The scanner has stopped on a frequency." He twiddled a knob, so that the hiss became a harsh roar. "There's someone on this channel. It could be nothing though, it's too weak to tell."

George listened to the noise, hearing the faint rhythms of speech, but it was too weak to identify. Vince entered the channel into the memory bank, then re-set the squelch, and re-started the scan.

Joan had done the things people do after a long journey, and was busy trying to find the source of the horrible smell that pervaded the flat. She was rummaging in the 'fridge, in case something in there had 'gone off', when her neighbour called with a package left by the postman. "I see your friend has gone, again?"

"Which one?"

"The skinny one, with the Buddy Holly spec's, and the dead mouse under his nose."

"Oh, him! He's hardly a friend, he just wants to be. When was he here?"

"I saw him, yesterday, just as I was going in for 'Neighbours'."

"Well, I wasn't here. I was in Wales. I hope he had a nice long wait. Can you smell something rotten, in here?"

"Such as?"

"Rotten meat? I've been looking in the 'fridge, but it's not in there."

The neighbour did some deep-breathing exercises. "Air-freshener, bleach, your perfume, - No, nothing. Anyway, must dash, I've a pie in. Are you still going on the bus-trip, tomorrow?"

"I'll be there. Do you have any idea where we're going?"

"I've heard everything from Fingal's Cave, to Windermere."

"It'll be Windermere, then, and it will rain. It always does!"

"See you tomorrow."

George was woken by the noise of a helicopter thrashing past, about half a mile down the valley. She bleared at the clock, and then eased her way out of Vince's octopus-like embrace. Shivering in the dawn chill, she dragged some clothes on, and stumbled to the bathroom.

Ten minutes later, she went into the living room, carrying two cups of coffee. "Why didn't you wake me?" she asked Tommy, who was sitting in the darkest corner of the room. "It was my turn, from four."

"It doesn't matter. Us old folk don't need a lot of sleep. Anyway, you two didn't sleep for a long time!" He smiled as she flushed. "I know - you have a lot of catching up to do!"

"Anyway, I'm here now. It's your turn to put a few zeds in."

"Sorry?"

"It's an old military expression. They still keep popping up. It means, go to bed while you have the chance!"

"So". If George had known it, he had been asleep in the chair, the helicopter waking him, as it had her. He didn't feel guilty, though, because he knew the house was safely under surveillance by his own team, who could show the S.A.S a few things about camouflage.

The helicopter had turned, about four miles away, and was whacking it's way back again, after circling over Bryan Pabo, an empty, disused farmhouse at the far end of the lake. It suddenly turned north, and went over Carreglefn, zig-zagging and circling, as though looking for something, then disappeared in the direction of Amlwch.

George sighed, a vague desire to be up there, and not down here, coursing through her, and then she smiled, ruefully, as she realized that eighteen months had passed since she last tasted the desire, then she forced it back into the recess of her mind.

Tommy heard the sigh, and, following her gaze, guessed the cause. "When did you last go diving?"

"I thought you had gone to sleep. It will be over a year, now, when it happened. Why?"

"I think, perhaps, you need a change of routine. Is your equipment ready?"

She thought for a minute. "I don't know about Vince's. The

police returned the bottles and valves when they had finished with them. Mine will still be 'in test', but the valves will need a service. The bottles will need filling, of course." She paused. "But you're not supposed to dive alone, and I don't think Vince will be up to it, yet."

"I think yes. Where do you go, for a service?"

"I suppose the shop at Soldier's Point would do it. Vince might know. But servicing two valves, two life-jackets, direct feed, and maybe a bottle test, runs to about two hundred pounds, plus parts, and I'd rather not spend that money, just yet."

"Talking of spending money, we're getting low on stores. I make a list up for next time you go to town. It is by the radio."

"OK." The faint thudding noise of the helicopter became noticeable again. "That helicopter is returning."

"I hear it."

After a few minutes, they could feel it, as it thrashed directly overhead, seemingly just missing the roof.

"Noisy bugger!" She said, and then had a flash of deja vue, as she recalled her comment about the Phantom, when she first saw Vince at the camp-site. She listened. Instead of the

508

noise fading, it had changed to a harsh slapping sound, which told her the machine was turning tightly. Sure enough, it came into view again, banked over steeply, circling the cottage. George wondered what the Search and Rescue was doing, operating inland, then saw that the Wessex was lifting its nose, slowing, into the hover, just over the field from her back garden.

A hand grabbed her shoulder, making her jump, then Vince bellowed into her ear, "What's going on?"

"Beats me!" she bellowed back.

"What?"

"I said -. " she shrugged, then pointed through the window, to where the helicopter was settling on the field, sideways on to the house, it's door open. They could see the winch-man peering at them through a pair of binoculars, as he sat in the doorway with his legs dangling outside.

George said something Vince didn't catch, and then went outside, hanging on to the door, so it wouldn't thrash in the rotor wash. She shut it carefully, standing in plain view, her hair flogging in the down-draft. The winch-man spoke into his microphone, then waved.

509

George waved back as the machine settled onto the earth. The rotor pitch came off, and the draft and noise reduced to a bearable level. The winch-man un-strapped and un-plugged himself, then jumped down and walked across the uneven ground to the wall. George and he slapped hands together, obviously old acquaintances. They talked for a minute, then the man opened a zipped pocket, and gave her an envelope, before giving her a splayed fingers parody salute, which she returned, after the fashion of Harvey Smith, before he picked his way back to the machine. As he climbed in, the racket increased as the power came in, and it began to lift. George watched it scrabble upwards, then tilt forwards, and accelerate away. It then zoomed up, into an arcing turn, to roar back across her roof-top, before disappearing in the direction of R.A.F. Valley.

Chapter twenty-seven.

It begins.

George stood there for a few minutes, watching the disappearing aircraft, until it became a fading dot in the distance, then went out of sight. When she went back in, Vince was cremating sliced bread, and had made coffee.

"This for me?" she asked, picking up a cup, and tasting the contents. "Yeuk, no! Too much sugar!" She tried the other. "That's better."

"Yes, that one. Do you want some toast? You have an exotic line in postmen!"

She eyed the smoldering remnants on the wire rack, "No, thanks, I might make some for myself, a bit later."

"It's your funeral."

"That's what I'm trying to avoid. They were friends from Valley. They knew I had a place around here, somewhere, but didn't know exactly where. By chance, they recognized the Landie. Apparently, someone is looking for us."

"We already know that!"

"These two own a big ex-army truck, and go diving." She said.

Anger flared in Vince's eyes, and the cremated bread he was buttering snapped under the pressure of the knife. "Them!"

"Yes, them. They asked that this should be passed on, if the S.A.R. crew met us, somewhere." She produced a buff manila envelope, with a wax seal, and the embossed legend H.M.S.O. On the back, below the wax seal, was a stamped legend, H.M. Customs and Excise. "Perhaps they really are?"

"I'm still going to kick their nuts off!"

"Me first! I've had to wait longer for the privilege." She opened the envelope. Inside was a single sheet of headed, embossed, A4. "If this letter," she read out loud, "reaches the proper people, we need to talk. You know what about. We had been keeping an eye on V. until he left the place he had been staying, but we lost track, then. We haven't found where G. is. There is a third party involved. They are the ones you want. You will know where to find us. Please make contact. And it has 'urgent' heavily underscored. Signed P. and T."

Vince was peering over her shoulder, dripping melted butter down her neck-line from his cinders, whether deliberately, or not, remains conjecture. "It is fancy paper, anyway!" he commented, as she pushed him away. "It looks authentic, but then, I've never seen real C and E paper, anyway."

George passed the paper and the envelope to Tommy. "What do you think of it?"

Tommy glanced at the writing, studied the seal, and the embossing, then held the letter up to the morning light. "H.M.S.O. watermark, too. You can't buy this in Woolworth's! Regarding the words - only one way to find out."

George looked at Vince. "I think we should, too. I think they are genuine."

"They seem to think a meet is urgent, but they don't indicate to whom. I'd rather leave it a while, until we want to see them, but I seem to be out-voted."

513

"I presume the location - "You know where" - is the Valley of the Rocks?"

"That makes sense, and that gives me an idea. We can see them, but they won't see us. Depending on where they are, we can use these head-set radios to talk to them. They'll be looking for your Landie, or my Cortina, so if we go in Tommy's car, we can fool them, be in plain view, and unseen!"

"Better idea!" Tommy interrupted, "I telephone my friend in Bangor, He hire car, drive here. We go in it. He takes Land-Rover, follows us. Then, if they have friends too, they follow Land-Rover all over everywhere, round shops, until he gets out, and they see Japanese driver. Bring it back in two or three day."

Vince laughed, "Great! But what about the orange smoke?"

"I'll switch it off, and warn him not to fiddle, or else!"

"What is this orange smoke?" Tommy asked.

George explained about her smoke/dye/tear-gas booby-trap, then repeated the tale about the D.I. who had set it off, ruining his immaculate uniform, and ending up on his backside, in a puddle, coughing and retching.

Tommy, normally hard to amuse, started making a hee-haw noise, like a donkey. When they realized he was laughing, the silly noise set them off as well. Vince slid down the wall, ending in a heap on the floor, while George was doubled over, getting stomach-ache. "Stop it!" she gasped "S'not funny! Messed up my seats!" She slapped the table, "Stop it!" then she flopped into a chair.

"Never heard him laugh before!" Vince choked.

"Heee Haaaw!"

"Stop it!"

When they'd calmed down again, Vince asked, "Today, or tomorrow?"

"Today. Get it over with. Do you agree, Tommy?"

"Yes. I make telephone call to Bangor."

Vince dug out the old Ordnance Survey Land-Ranger map, number 114, and soon picked out a track which went round the back of the Valley camp-site, and around the back of the golf course. "It's a pity your name's not Penny!" he chuckled, pointing at a spot on the map.

George peered over his shoulder then gave him a jab in the

ribs as she read the name he was indicating, near South Stack. Pen-y-Bonc, it read. After a moment, she found an appropriate one for him, about half a mile north-west, and pointed it out. Foel.

Shortly after lunch, they were bouncing down a dual line of pot-holes, separated by two lines of ridges, in a rental Cavalier. Tommy was at the wheel, and clearly no respecter of other people's springs. George nursed the 'borrowed' Magnum, and some of her spare shells, and Vince had a headache, because, jammed into the back seat, the roof kept hitting him, when the side window wasn't. Just ahead was an indistinct three-way fork.

"Which way?" grunted Tommy, as they hit a rock with the front cross-member.

"Stop here. I'll nip out and have a look." George replied. She was back in a minute. "We've gone a bit too far, turn around, and park up by that lump of rock with brambles on it."

Tommy bounced them down to the fork, where there was room to turn, then jounced them round in a three point turn, with a few extra points thrown in for good measure, before backtracking to the indicated rock, where he turned the engine off. George slid out, and Vince fell out, suffering from a cramped leg. They were screened from the camp-site by a small ridge, topped by scrub.

"Do you think they heard the engine?" George asked.

"No, look. They've got four bottles hooked up to the compressor. I can hear it chugging, from here! There's no sign of your Landie, yet, but there's a white XR4I by the club-house, Geordie and Hopalong, perhaps?"

George chuckled at the nick-name as she recalled shooting the man in the leg when he thought he was hidden in a clump of scrub.

Pete clambered down from the back of the truck, where he had been monitoring the radio, stretched, yawned, and managed to take two paces towards the loo block, before the radio called "Head's up!" with Geordie's voice. Geordie was perched up on a rock face, on the south side of Porth Dafarch bay. "Looks like the Landie we're waiting for. - Yes, it's turning up P.D. road, only one in it, can't see who."

517

"Trev! Come on out. She's inbound!" Pete called.

"Yeah, I heard." Trevor emerged from the tent, and tied the flap open, so that the inside was visibly empty. "Leave the truck doors open, Pete."

"Good thinking. We don't want any more holes in it, if she still has that cannon!"

"D'you think she would have it?"

"I wouldn't take bets that she hasn't!"

"Nobody seems to be following." Geordie added, over the radio. "It's going out of sight round the bend, now."

There was a short pause, then "K'inell", aka Hopalong, came on air, "They've gone past, - No, wait. They've stopped a short way up. I can't quite see the cab. Shall I poke my nose out, for a look?"

A new voice came on the radio, then. "I wouldn't, unless you want a hole in it, to match the one I put in your leg! Everyone else shut up. Just Pete is to speak. What do you want?"

"I should have remembered you had our radios, too! I want your safety, for a start. Why not come in here, and talk, face to face?"

"You must be bloody joking!" George retorted, from behind her rock, on the far side of the camp, and across a small pond. "At least four of you, and I don't know where two of you are. I saw Hopalong's racing car, and I can see you, Pete, just at a nice perforating distance, so don't do anything silly to tempt me. I want to blow holes in all of you after what happened. So, I repeat, what do you want?"

Trev walked across, and stood near Pete. "I think she's bluffing." He whispered, making sure his headset didn't transmit. "There's no way she can see us, from there!"

"Ah! There you are, Trev." George scotched that idea. "Take two paces towards your truck, then I won't hit two birds with one slug!"

Pete wiggled his eyebrows, as Trev did as instructed.

"Hopalong. Get out of the car. Put the keys on the roof, in the centre, then sit on the bonnet! Now, that leaves Geordie to find. I know he's behind me, somewhere, so do not try creeping up on me, or you'll need major surgery, and not on a leg, either! I'm not playing. Now, tell me what you want, or I'm going."

"First of all, we need to apologize for - - "

519

"Apologize? Apologize?" George exploded. "You damn near kill us both. Vince is in a wheel-chair, and will never walk again! He's brain-damaged, and you dim-wits say sorry! I'm going. Don't come after me, unless you bring your own tailor-made box."

Vince looked at her, at his leg, and waggled it. She gave him an evil grin.

"No, wait! Please listen!" Pete called, "George, listen to me!"

She let him sweat for a while, until K'inell climbed into the XR4, and started the engine. "Freeze, Hopalong." She warned. "Pete, I call you that, because it's the only name I know for you that I care to use. I'm Miss Weastey, to you. You should know that you are about half an ounce away from a severe chest pain, probably terminal. Say your piece, quickly."

"Geo - Miss Weastey, we've got some documents here that you need to see."

"Do I?"

"Yes. They might help to explain what was, and still is, going on."

520

"I was set up as a patsy. What else?"

"Not by us. Honest! We were used, as well. It's in these papers."

"Why didn't you pass them to us, the same way you got the message you wanted to see us?"

"We had to be sure the right people got them, and not another group who are involved." Pete explained.

"Leave them at the Holyhead Post Office, poste restante, and I might pick them up, one day."

"O.K, if that's the only way. Don't leave it too long. They tell who we think is behind it, and who the third party is. You know the S.A.S. man is dead, don't you?"

"Yes. It was in the daily rag. What of it?"

"That was the third party's doing. After you had been taken out, they came after us. Luckily, we didn't use the cylinders we'd filled at the same time as yours, we had some twin-sets we sometimes use for deep dives, ready filled, or we'd never have come back from the Skerries dive. We still don't know when they sabotaged the compressor, but it had a radio-controlled valve fitted, with an extra bottle on the end of it. It isn't there,

521

now, of course."

"That was sloppy of you, not to have seen it when you checked everything. How long are you staying on the site?"

"Until the Boss pulls us out."

"Wait a minute. Nobody move." George eased down the rock, and moved to the car, to give them a quick resume, and ask "What do you think?"

"Smells of fish!" Tommy exclaimed.

"Perhaps they mean it." Vince argued. "It sounds feasible, but then they've had plenty of time to concoct a good story."

"You know these men, I don't." Tommy said, "If you half-believe them, get the papers, and read them, then make up your minds. Suggest you get in touch, again, in the same way, in a few days."

Vince seemed happy with the idea, having no better one of his own, so she eased up the ridge again, and turned the headset back on. "O.K. then. Leave the papers. I'll pick them up, and read them, then I'll get in touch with you again, like this, in a week or so, when I'm ready. I'm going, now. Don't follow me, or you'll need a Priest, and don't come to my house, either, you won't be leaving, except in a box."

"We won't follow. Guard your back. We're not the ones you need to watch out for."

George turned the headset off, and slid down to the car again. "Right, Tommy, tell him to go in five minutes."

Tommy picked up a hand-held c.b. set, and spoke into it in Japanese. It said something back, and Tommy gave a 'thumbs up'. George went back up the ridge, and joined Vince, who was watching the camp-site.


Pete stopped doing what appeared to be standing in the middle of a field, talking to himself, took the headset off, muted the microphone, and asked Trevor if he could see anything.

Trev had been studying the only likely place where both themselves and the XR4 could be seen, as had Pete. "No. Not a flicker. Nada. She's got to be up there, though!"

"Likewise, nothing. Do you think she would have shot me?"

"I don't doubt it. She has every reason. There's the Landie's engine." The rattle of it drifted across the site. "Hop into the truck and see if Geordie's following it."

"Yeah."

K'inell drove his XR4 round to where the truck was, climbed out, and stood with the other two. "I couldn't spot her, at all, but I didn't fancy my luck if she's kept that cannon!"

"Same here, and I believe she has." Pete added.

"She must have. She kept the headset radio."

"Vinny's in a chair, hey? Jeez, that's tough."

"If we meet up, keep well out of his reach, or you may go the same way as Green-top, whatever his name was, last year!"

"If I knew it, I've forgotten. It would be quicker than suffocating inside a plastic bag, though. Does it say whether it was suicide, or murder, in the doc's?"

"It was left open. We'll probably never know."

Pete ducked into the truck, and gave Geordie a call on the two-way, to see where he was being taken. When he came out again, Trev and K'inell had opened beer-cans, and had flopped into folding chairs. Pete snagged the can that Trev threw at him, swapped it for the one in the chiller, still wearing the plastic pack-loops, and promptly sprayed beer everywhere when he levered the ring-pull up. Trev and K'inell roared with laughter, then, as Pete sprayed them, dove for shelter.

"I'll get you for that!" Pete called after Trev's retreating back He ducked into the tent, threw his soggy tee-shirt into a corner, had a perfunctory mop-up on one of Trev's raggy ones, and then pulled on one of his own clean ones. Then he had an idea, took out his sewing kit, and sewed up the fly on Trev's last pair of clean underpants, put everything away, then went to the chiller, and got a fresh beer, one that hadn't been shaken up, Finally, he climbed back into the truck, to listen out for anything Geordie might say.

Vince and George watched all this from their vantage-point, on the opposite side of the camp. "If Geordie's fit, he'll be coming through the site entrance, - about now!" Vince muttered.

"Geordie, of course, didn't. He was being led on a circuitous tour of the back-roads of Holyhead.

"Then, of course, if they're smart, Geordie has another car, and is following your Landie."

"Do you think they would? Pete said they wouldn't follow."

525

"You told them I was a vegetable in a wheelchair! We don't know whether the S.A.R. crew gave them our location, or whether they'd believe it, anyway!" They slid down the slope, and told Tommy there was a third car to look for.

"So!" Tommy raised the c.b, pulled the telescopic aerial up to its fullest extent, and spoke into it, in Japanese. The radio spluttered and whistled back at him, so he tried again, this time hearing a broken acknowledgement. "He is almost out of range, but is looking for another car." Tommy folded the aerial down, and then turned the radio off.


Geordie followed the Land-Rover, at varying distances, letting it get ahead on the straights, and catching it on the bends. He followed it up to Holyhead, round the town centre, and back round towards South Stack. From there, it went through Trearddur Bay village, down to Rhoscolyn, back up the other side of the loop, to Valley, via the Four Mile Bridge. From there, it took the A5 to Llanfair P.G., over the Britannia Bridge, then back-tracked on the A4080 through Newborough.

"Where the bloody hell is she going?" He asked the

steering wheel. It didn't answer, of course. When they reached Llanfaelog, the Landie suddenly turned left, and went round by the Rhosneigr railway station, but before it went under the bridge it turned right, onto a little track. "Shit!" Geordie swore. This was a track appropriate for a Landie, almost a 'Green Road'. His low-slung M.G.B. was thumping and scraping its underside as he tried to keep up, while staying far enough back to hopefully remain unnoticed.

In George's Land-Rover, Tommy's friend watched the mirror with half an eye, while picking his way along the twisty lane, being careful not to get too far in front. Eventually, they bounced out onto the A4080 again, near the A5 junction. He went straight across, onto the B5112, and followed the road towards Amlwch. As they came through Rhosybol, he tried the c.b. as they were only a couple of miles across the fields from the cottage. Tommy answered immediately, and was updated on the car type, colour, and registration number. After a brief chat, they agreed to tease Geordie a bit longer, then dump him.

The Landie turned right, onto the A5025, and wound the

pace up. Geordie sighed with relief. This was his kind of road, and the Landie couldn't get away on an easy run. They bowled along for a while, past Moelfre, and came to Menai, across the bridge, left at the roundabout, and into Bangor. Instead of following the road round to the right, and into Conwy, the Landie turned left, onto a back road through a housing estate. Geordie closed up, a little, and started paying attention, ready to read the house number, but the Landie didn't stop. It bowled steadily on, right onto the sand, via a little slip-way, then it roared off, flinging wet sand up in a rooster-tail. Geordie tried to follow it, flooring the gas pedal, and taking a charge. The 'B' tried, gamely, but it was never designed for water-skiing, and bogged down after about a hundred feet, the rear wheels spinning helplessly. Geordie sat cursing, watching the Landie splash out of sight around the far side of a jetty, then got out to survey the problem. He promptly sank up to his shins in stinking mud. He was interrupted in the middle of a good cursing session by an Old Codger, who was sitting on the deck of a fishing boat which was perched lop-sided on the mud.

"Hey, Bhoyo! I wouldn't stay there too long, now. The

tide, she's coming in, and in an hour, you'll be under ten feet of water!" he cackled gleefully at the novel entertainment.

The salt and sand stained Land-Rover rolled up to the cottage and the driver climbed out. George invited him in. Tommy greeted him properly, and Vince made the bow to an equal. The Japanese spoke for nearly ten minutes, while Tommy went red, with the effort of trying to contain himself. Eventually, they wound down,

Tommy spoke to George, "You owe ten pounds for diesel, if you please. Sato put some in, on way back. I give to Sato, you give to me, later, o.k?"

"That's fine, but tell us what happened!"

"In a minute." Tommy passed over the Cavalier keys, and an envelope, receiving the Land-Rover keys, in return. Sato then left.

"He go home to work, now." Tommy said, and then told them what had happened to the M.G.B.

When George had her breath back, she said she regretted having missed it.

"Seconded!" Vince choked.

"Best thing, though," Tommy nodded, chuckling, "Nearest garage owe favour to Sato, so Sato fix that car will not be pulled out of mud until after tide comes in!"

"Tommy, you're priceless!"

"Have price. In bill, at end!"

"How about some food! I'm starving!" Vince put in.

"Later. Exercise machines, first!" Tommy ordered.

Chapter twenty-eight.

Contact.


Tommy looked up from the paper he was reading, sniffed, and asked "What burns?"

Vince, similarly occupied, looked up, shrugged, and wrinkled his nose,

George started, cried, "Oh God!" and dashed into the kitchen. There followed a clatter, then a sharp hiss, with water splashing, then she came back into the living room, carrying a smoking pan. "I emptied a tin of soup into here, lit the gas, and forgot about it!"

Vince took the charred wooden spoon from her, prodded the contents of the pan with it, making a crunching noise. "When I cook something, at least you can see what it was!"

531

Tommy shook his head in despair. "How will you children cope when I leave?"

"Leave? Who mentioned leaving?" George asked him. "You're welcome to stay as long as you wish."

"That is very kind," Tommy bowed, "but in two, three days, I go. You do not need me any more. Vince is well, and becoming stronger by the day. My purpose is finish. If you make him keep to the exercise schedule, he will soon be back to his previous level, but not so fat in the belly!"

"It wasn't fat. It was his chest, slipping down!" George argued.

"Fat! Too many cream cakes, and sitting down. Anyway, what you make of these?" he waved the papers they'd collected from the Post Office.

George looked at Vince, who shrugged, throwing the ones he held onto the table. George took the pan back to the kitchen, came back, picked up the paper from where she'd dropped it on the floor, and added it to the heap. "Not a lot! They don't tell us much more than we already know. It's all conjecture and supposition. It does say that the big guy, and 'green-top'," she glanced at Vince, "were who they said they were, S.A.S. and it confirms what they were doing. It doesn't give their names. It doesn't say who the person was that they 'removed' from the rocks, or why he was there, who sent him, or even what happened to him, after. It doesn't even say if they latched onto the right people in the end. There is more information in what they don't say, than in what they do!"

"That about covers it. Tommy?"

"No comments, just advice. Keep ears and eyes open, guard back, and don't trust these two with truck. Something not right, but I can't pin it."

Vince picked up a slim manila envelope that had been inside the larger, fat one. "What's in here?"

"I don't know, I haven't looked, yet."

"It's sealed." He looked a question at George. The documents were addressed to her, not to him. She nodded, so he slid a finger under the flap, tore open the envelope, and pulled out a single piece of stiff paper. George could see the reverse was blank. Carefully keeping his poker-face, Vince slid it back into the envelope, and passed it to her. "That's yours." Was all that he said.

Puzzled, she took it off him, and slid the paper out. It was a photocopy of a cheque made out to her bank, with her account number in the 'pay' space. Handwritten across the face of the copy, with an indecipherable signature, were the words, 'Without prejudice', and 'apologies'. The payee was Her Majesty's Government. Then her eyes took in the sum. The hand holding the copy twitched. Vince smiled as she drew in a ragged breath, then, with a tremor in her voice, said, "Well, that solves a few problems!"

"Without prejudice," said Vince, "that means it's a gift, in compensation, with no effect on any inquiry or court case that results from the incident, doesn't it?"

"I think so." Was all she said in reply.

"It's a cheque for a large sum, made out to George's account, from H.M.G." Vince told Tommy.

"H.M.G? - Oh, yes." He fitted names to the initials. "Good."

"I'd like to know where they got this account number. I'll have to change it."

"There's no point. If they can find that one, with no starting point, it won't take them long to track the new one down." Vince replied. "If they have the account, they also have your address, anyway."

"That's true, so why all the farce with the documents, why not just post them?"

Tommy jumped as realization struck, slapped his head, then walked his fingers across the table, mimicking a spider. "Don't know!" He pointed vigorously at the radio set with his other hand.

Vince caught on instantly, and mouthed 'Bugs!' then said "Anyone for a coffee?"

George looked puzzled, so Vince crooked a finger at her, and they went into the kitchen. Vince went to the sink, removed the plastic washing-up bowl, then placed George's burnt soup pan into the steel sink, with an oversize lid, upside down, on top, then turned on the cold tap. The jet of water hitting the lid made a loud splattering noise, and made the lid chatter. He gathered the other two in close, and whispered, "Talk low, the noise will confuse the bugs, and they won't hear us. Can anyone think if

535

anything was said, that might be useful to 'them'?"

"They know Tommy's, and Sato's names." George offered.

"If they understand Japanese, they know his home, too," Tommy added, "They also know how we fix M.G.B."

"That bit doesn't matter, they'd have caught on anyway, when the driver got back. The important thing is, to warn Sato they could be on to him, Tommy. First, though, we have to find the bugs. When we do, do we leave them, and feed them false information, or smash them?"

"I say, keep, and use. Better if we can switch on and off."

"I'll start with the 'phone." Vince went for his tool-box. In two minutes, he had the telephone dismantled, and showed them the little circuit-board that wasn't to G.P.O. specifications. 'That's one!" He whispered, in the kitchen, "I'd say it was an infinity bug that leaves the 'phone microphone live, even when the handset is down, so the other end can listen in. That also means the 'phone can only be used for ordinary stuff, shopping lists, or such, unless I take it off."

"Leave on, for now." Tommy replied.

George said nothing, but they could see she was furious.

536

"Don't worry, lover, they'll pay for this!" Vince told her. "Let us find others."

They started with the room they were in, and turned up nothing They were about to move into the living room, when George stopped, went back, and picked up a jar of stock cubes. She pointed at it, and held up one finger. In the jar were two cubes. The top and shoulders of the jar had a film of dust on them, as Tommy never used cubes. With careful inspection, they could see the ink on one of the wrappers was a slightly different shade, and the cube was a fraction larger than the other. George put the jar back onto the shelf, and they went next door. There, they found two more bugs, one under the table, and one behind the wall-clock. Vince held up four fingers, then pointed at the gym. There were two in there. While Tommy and Vince checked the equipment, George went to the loo, where she found another bug behind the cistern. She wondered what sort of person would listen to another's bathroom noises, and when she flushed, it went round the u-bend and into the sewer.

Vince found one in the bedroom, taped to the rear of the head-board. He removed it, and re-positioned it into the loft, next

537

to a nest two pigeons had built. Now 'they' could listen to two 'love-birds' billing and coo-ing all day! Tommy's caravan was last, and they found another in there, but as he only used it for sleeping quarters, and storage space, that one was of no significance. Finally, Vince checked the spare bedroom and found another bug behind the bed-head.

When they had finished, they gathered in the kitchen, again, where Vince set the pan-lid rattling. "That makes nine." He whispered.

"Ten, I flushed one down the loo." George added.

"Ten. That makes it an expensive job. I presume they are all on different frequencies, so that's ten channels to monitor. They aren't - no, nine! One's the 'phone. They aren't very powerful, because they only have little batteries, that means there is either a relay unit, or the listening post is very close, within half a mile."

"How big a thing, for post?"

"Probably two men, taking it in turns. Say, a transit van, or similar, in size."

"Have not seen one, but is covered farmer's trailer, in

field."

"That'd do nicely!"

"O.K. We fix, tonight, in dark."

George nodded, Vince made a thumbs up. "Anything else?"

Head-shakes all round, so he turned off the tap. Tommy went out to his van.


The man with the headphones on cursed again. One of the gadgets had gone off, one was just picking up bird noises, so all he could hear was "OO Koo Koo," over and over. One was just picking up a hissy, clattering noise, and the rest were doing nothing. He stretched, scratched an itch, broke wind, and then turned off the tape recorder, which was recording nothing useful. These surveillance jobs were boring. During daylight, you couldn't move about, and at night you couldn't use lights! He eyed the battery meter. The voltage was starting to drop, showing the first battery was used up, so he switched the second one into line, then turned the first one off, and transferred its plug to the third battery, ready for later. The clattering noise ceased, and he could hear cutlery clanking, and insignificant chit-chat. There were just the same three voices, two males, one non-British, and one female. Vaguely, he wondered if he would get anything worth-while, before the bug batteries died. It was lucky they had all gone out together, the other day. The batteries should be good for another twenty-four hours or so, before they needed replacing. He yawned. There were about two hours to sun-set, and another hour after that before his replacement arrived. His stomach growled and glugged, making him wish he had eaten something other than that curry for his last meal. He didn't even have a bucket he could use! Through the headphones, pots clattered, birds ooh hoo'd and static hissed. Then there was a thud, footsteps, and noises on the caravan bug, so he set the relevant tape rolling. Someone started speaking in a foreign language. Good, let someone else listen to hours of crap, too. He wondered who the foreigner was talking to, as there was no telephone in the 'van. More voices - all foreign, chimes sounded, then screechy music, oriental stuff, followed by a singer, in a thin wail, accompanied by the plink-plonk of some string instrument. When it ended, there was a sigh, then a twittering, whooping noise, trills, and warbles, "BONG! BONG! This is the B.B.C. - Now, the news - -". Headphones sighed, and turned off the tape. It was a bloody radio he was listening to!

The 'phone rang. "Hello?"

"Hi, George, how's lover-boy? You'll never guess where the mystery tour went! Bloody Menai! Then Bo-whatsits castle, and on round to sodding Holyhead for an hour, before bringing us back home again! I could have saved my three quid! Ah, well!" Joan gabbled on for another ten minutes, trading minutiae and gossip, luckily saying nothing of significance to the 'listener', before clearing the line.

"Was that Joan?" Vince asked

George told him the gist of her message, trying not to laugh.

"Fancy being taken on a tour of the place you've just come back from!" Vince chortled, "Poor girl! She must have been bored stupid!"

"Apparently, she passed the time by making eyes at her latest 'Mr Right'."

"That would help her pass the time, alright. It's her

favourite hobby."

"So I've gathered."

Vince clicked on the television, and when the picture came onto the screen, spent a few minutes fiddling with the broom-handle aerial pole, searching for the least spotty position. Having come to the conclusion that reception was best where it had been in the first place, they settled down to watch, After a series of adverts, and the News in Welsh, then more adverts, a play began, in Welsh. George tried Harlech, but that was just a hissy mess of dancing spots and lines, so she switched back to S4C, where they amused themselves by putting their own script to the activities on the screen.

'Headphones' listened to the rather steamy conversation his bugs were picking up, trying to figure out what was going on, while trying to piece together the spurious comments they were making. The man was saying - "Come into my bedroom so I can ravish you! What the hell are you looking for in that cupboard? Put that cricket bat down, my dearest!" while she was saying - "Oh, no! That is naughty! Mummy told me to - er - hit people who say that to me!" He said - "I think I'll use the -eh, what? Golf clubs? And a rugby ball? This time!" The woman started laughing, then there was a scuffle, followed by incoherent noises. One line the woman said was picked out, "Thank God it wasn't a rounders bat!" A short while later, he could hear rhythmic creaking and bumping noises, and smiled as he mentally pictured what they were doing.

Vince climbed off the rowing-machine and went for a quick shower while George made a cuppa for them both.

Tommy tired of the radio, not being particularly interested in how to make a sturdy garden gazebo from two orange boxes and a plastic bin-bag, and turned the radio off. He stood, stretched, then went outside, where he wandered down the garden and sat on a rock that was labelled 'rose-bush', from which he listened to the sunset chorus of the wild-life. Faintly carrying across the distance, the boom of the Holyhead to Ireland ferry echoed. A squadron of swifts whizzed about, snapping up insects and displaying their aerobatics skills. Across the fields a fox yapped sharply when a man sneezed. A faint clatter, then a

curse, confirmed it was a bipedal animal, not a quad. By his feet,
a scuffle drew his eye, and he looked down in time to see a
hedgehog waddle across the small space between two 'plants'
and disappear into the brambles. Something about the brambles
drew his attention, so he studied them. Yes, that one, about eight
feet long, was too straight! One end leaned on the wall, the other
end went to - -? There! That black bin sack, under that tangle.
Tommy stood, then picked a way through so he could peel a
corner of the sack back. Instead of dumped rubbish, a shiny grey
metal box appeared. This could be the relay that Vince had
mentioned.

Vince prodded the metal box with a toe, and then teased
more of the black plastic away from it. A black wire snaked from
a plug to the aerial. Another wire led through a gap in the stone
wall to a battery, barely disguised, on the other side. Two stiff
wires protruded upwards, and then bent in opposite directions.
"That's the receive aerial for the bugs." He said. "The box will
convert it to a lower frequency, and send it up this aerial, here.
Putting the battery outside makes it easy to change without

disturbing anything. When it goes dark, I'll help that piece of corrugated rust to fall across the terminals, then perhaps they'll send someone to find out why the thing went off, and we can 'bag' him, before we go for the trailer?"

'Headphones' could hear two animals having a serenading session, in the field, somewhere, and then there was a sudden yelp, and a tinny clatter, followed by silence. He scanned his panel of meters, which indicated that there was nothing being transmitted by the bugs. Funny! That one, which showed the incoming signal from the relay, was dropping down to zero. He clicked switches, and confirmed there was no signal. More switches clicked, a new dial sprang to life, and he picked up a microphone. Yes, they'd seen it go off. No, they didn't know why. They'd send someone to check, after dark. Until then, he'd have to pay attention, and monitor everything himself.

At three a.m. 'headphones' heard footsteps outside, and reached across, to open the tarpaulin 'door'

"Thanks, pal." Said the thin silhouette, "Anything

happening?"

"Nah. Two of them had a 'leg-over' a few hours ago, but it's been quiet ever since."

"Oh. Which two?"

"The woman, and one of the guys. The foreign guy was in the caravan, listening to the radio. He turned in. too, ages ago."

"Nothing to worry about, then. Come on out, then I can take over. I'll go and fix the box in a short while."

'Headphones' climbed out, and Vince fixed a solid karate chop to the base of his neck. 'Headphones' slumped to the soil.

"O.K. Tommy, pass me that string!"


At four a.m. a moped puttered up to the trailer and stopped. Vince put the headphones on, and slumped into the chair inside it. Footsteps outside, then the tarp was pulled aside. "Hi, pal. Anything doing?"

"No, everyone's asleep."

"Do I know you? Where's Steve?"

"Steve? Oh, rumble-guts. He's got the trots, and I had to take over."

546

"The silly bugger will eat that foreign muck. Move over."

Vince took the 'phones off, and stood, so they could shuffle round each other in the confined space. 'Headphones two' fell to the floor when Vince hit him.

Something was prodding Pete in the ribs. He squirmed about in his sleeping-bag, and settled down again. Prod! It wasn't something, it was someone! Prod!

"Buggeroff!" He mumbled.

PROD! Pete opened one eye, and peered at the slim silhouette with the golden halo. PROD!

"Whassamarrer?"

"Wake up, you lazy sod, and don't move a muscle!" George snarled.

Pete's eye focused on the loud end of a big gun, then his other eye opened, as well. " 'M awake, n' not movin'."

"Good. You are a lying sod. Nobody will follow, hey? Strange how I saw Geordie taking a mud-bath in his dinky-toy, in Bangor harbour. Why you bothered, I don't know, as you have my bank account number, and my address. I presume you pulled strings to get those. So, why did you have two bods, and loads of radio gear, scattered around my place while I was meeting with you, earlier?"

The noise woke Trevor, and as he started to move, the Magnum caught his attention.

"Don't!" George said to him. "I can see that the two of you are not quite as 'together' as you make out. That explains why I couldn't decide who was which, neither of you are. It's like everything else, a big con. Unfortunately for you, I wasn't taken in. I ask you again, like I did last time we met like this, is there any reason why I shouldn't top you both, now? I want to."

Trev shook his head, carefully, while thinking - "Where the hell is "K'inell?"

Pete said, - "One reason. It would make a mess in the tent! What bods and radio gear?"

"Oh, just a few radio bugs, a thing in the telephone, a remote relay station, a mobile recording studio, and two bodies to work it, plus a motorbike, and a load of batteries."

"It's nothing to do with us, honest!" Pete offered.

"Not ours." Trev said, in agreement.

548

"Well, I've made you a present of them. They're in your truck, along with Hopalong, who doesn't keep a very good lookout. In exchange, I've 'borrowed' his night-sight. It's a nice gadget, it's a pity it's Russian. Now, stay there for ten minutes before you come out, just in case my trigger-finger gets the twitches!" She backed out of the tent flap, paused, and came back in again, "Oh, and don't try sneaking into MY bedroom, you won't sneak very far! And if you decide to take the radios to bits, be careful. I've heard that they are often booby-trapped. I'm no booby, so I didn't look." She dropped the tent flap, and was gone.

"What bugs, relays, and bodies, is she talking about, Trev?"

"It beats me. They really aren't my doing!"

"And she took three guys out, on her own! Jesus. Maybe she's not the dumb blonde we thought!"

"What do you mean, WE?"

They dressed, then cautiously stuck Pete's head outside the tent flap. It didn't grow a hole in it, so the rest of Pete followed, followed by all of Trevor. They went across to the supposedly locked truck, and found K'inell and two others inside, well trussed up in thin nylon cord, and wearing duct-tape gags and blindfolds. On the bench seat were eight plastic things about the size of stock cubes, with trailing wires, one was in a stock cube wrapper. There was also a large grey box, with a rod aerial, a collection of receivers and tape recorders, without tape, a switching unit, and a heap of batteries.

"Bloody hell! Look at this lot!" Pete lifted a battery, and put it down again promptly. "How the hell did she get this lot here, on her own?"

Trevor ripped the tape from K'inell's face, taking most of his eyebrows with it. K'inell grunted, but didn't move.

"He's out cold."

K'inell had one hell of a headache, and his face felt scorched, too "Fuck!" he cursed, "Fuckin' 'ell! Ow, me fuckin' 'ead!"

"You may well curse, you useless sod! All your training and you're taken out by a woman!"

"Fuckin' 'ell, what woman?"

"George!"

"Fuckin' 'ell, I didn't see her coming!"

"What do you want, you prick? Written notice? All you had to do was sit there, and keep your eyes open!"

"Who the fuck're these two?"

"Guests."

"Fuckin' 'ell, my face is sore. What the fuck happened?" Trev showed him the gaffer tape with eyebrows on. "Oh fuck! Where's Pete?"

"He's gone to see if Geordie's still in one piece, you dumb sod. We don't like waking up looking down the dangerous end of a Magnum, when the person on the safe end wants to use it, badly!"

"Fuck!"

Feet scuffed, in the grass outside, then Pete's voice called, "Don't wet your pants, K'inell, It's me!" He pushed into the truck. "Geordie's o.k. He didn't know anything had happened. No-one came in through the gate, so she must have come in through that little gap in the fence by the small boggy bit.

551

There's nothing over the other way but a pond, with a barbed wire fence, then fields, and a golf course. It isn't possible for her to cart that lot across there, on her own!"

One of the 'guests' groaned, stirred, then his arms and legs moved against the ropes, before he uttered a muffled "Shit" into the gag.

"Yes, pal, whoever you are. Shit. That's what you are in, up to your neck."

"Aargh, mmph mg mmgmmh!"

"Save it til later."

"Mmmph gmmp mmfphg," he nodded carefully. "Umph!"

"Headache?"

"Mmm!"

"Good."




George, watching from the back of the ridge which concealed the track, saw Pete's head emerge from the tent. She made a gun with her fingers, took aim, and said- "BANG!" Trev went into the truck, while Pete went off towards the club-house, but stopped by a car displaying a 'Rent-a Car' logo on the side panels, and a local 'phone number. "Ah, there's Geordie! His petrol-powered skate-board must be poorly!"

"I wonder why?" Vince added, with a grin.

"Do we want to see where they go with the junk and the bodies?"

"Not particularly, do you?"

"No. I suppose, if we ask them nicely, later, they might tell us. Tommy, how about you?"

Tommy shook his head. "No need. My friends follow, and tell me, later."

"You have more friends than this field has blades of grass!"

"We Nips have to look out for each other, or you Gaijin's will stick in the knife."

"Talking of blades of grass, I'm ready to eat some! How about going home, for a second breakfast?"

"You're a gutsy sod!"

"I'm making up for lost time!"

553

Pete and Trev climbed into the cab of their truck, and after a brief delay, the engine started, in a fog of blue smoke, then they rumbled off down the track.

"Right, now we can go!" George ordered.

"What about Hopalong, and Geordie?" Vince asked.

"I presume Hopalong is still in the back of the truck, and Geordie is taking the hire-car out, now, see?"


An hour later, back at the cottage, Vince was cremating some cheese on toast, while George battled with the telephone. The first call was to her bank, to see if the cheque she had a copy of had been presented. It had, and had been credited to her account a couple of weeks ago. The second call was to Fleecem and Leggètt, to check on the whereabouts of the documents she had returned. She was advised that they were in order, and had been passed on to Grabbett and Runne, for the attention of the other party. She then asked for their guidance regarding the cheque. They briefly conferred, then she was told to use it, and enjoy. The 'without prejudice' bit made it a gift, with no repercussions, and no admission of guilt, on either side. She was advised to keep the copy in a safe place, and as photocopies tended to fade over time, was advised to photograph it while it was fresh, just in case. Satisfied, George cleared the line, then went to extinguish a small fire in the kitchen. Vince was snoring in a chair, while his cheese on toast was blazing merrily under the grill. She dunked a towel into the bowl of washing up water, pulled the tray from under the grille, and doused the flaming remnants with the wet towel. The sharp hiss woke Vince in time to see his breakfast being flung through the back door. Black smuts were floating around the room, ducking in and out of the pall of smoke. The wet towel slapped him in the face.

"Clean this mess up then get out of here!" George snapped. "You're banned from the kitchen from now on. Idiot!"

The telephone, in the other room, rang, so George dashed to answer it. A torrent of Japanese poured out.

"Sorry! Tommy's not here at the moment, can you say it in English?"

"Ah, Men, they go Bangor, - (japanese) how say, Station of coppings, you know?"

"Police station?" she offered.

555

"So, P'lice station. Change to dry-clean truck, down track. Dry-clean go Bangor, Army go Holyhead. Follow dry-clean. o.k?"

"Yes, that's fine. I'll tell Tommy as soon as I can."

"O.K. Is all."

"I heard that. It sounds as though they really are Customs and Excise!"

"Get scrubbing! I want that kitchen spotless, before you eat again!"

"Cruelty, and torture!"

"Wait until I tell Tommy what you did!"

"Ouch!"

Chapter twenty-nine.

Piece of the jigsaw.


Pete brought the truck to a halt. "That must be it!"

"Looks like it. Are you sure this is a good idea?"

"No, mate, but someone has to go first, and we owe them that much!"

"If I don't come back - -."

"You've been K'inelled! I know!"

Trevor sighed, and climbed down, then began the long walk along the drive to the cottage. He was wearing an old pair of tight cropped-off jeans, and a tight tee-shirt that didn't meet the waistband of the pants, thus demonstrating he was not a walking armoury, while remaining covered in the manner society

557

dictated. Nobody was in sight as he trudged round a slight bend, where the scrub-covered dry-stone walls hid him from view of the truck. The cottage looked deser- BLAM! He was face down, in the dirt, with his arms rammed up round the back of his neck, in an agonizing Aikido lock.

"Struggle, I snap them!" a foreign voice said. "Where you go?"

"Who the hell are - OW!" Trev strained against the pressure, but couldn't gain an inch. His shoulder joints were screaming. A hand hooked into his hair, and pulled his head backward. Jeez, this guy was strong! He had both of Trev's arms locked, only using one hand!

"Where you go?"

"To the cottage, to see Miss Weastey."

"She know you come?"

"No."

"She want to see you?"

"I don't know - OW!"

"Not to struggle, hurt self! You friend stay in truck?"

"Yes."

"Better he stay there." The hand released his hair, then explored all the places a weapon could be concealed, with no concession given to modesty.

"I'm carrying noth - OW!"

"Speak when tell, not until! I let you up. Do not be stupid."

Trev felt his arms released, then climbed to his feet, immediately launching a strike at - an ancient old man, in a kaftan, who must have been eighty, at least, and a good foot shorter than Trev, who merely stepped sideways out of the way. The man, Japanese, or Korean, made no attempt to counter, just stood there with a quizzical smile on his face, arms folded. Trev danced forward, fired a punch from the hip, and missed. The follow-up blow missed, as did a round-house kick. It was like attacking fog. The old man just swayed, ducked, or stepped aside, still smiling, still with his arms folded. Trev tried the bulldozer method, and rushed him. The old man flicked aside, giving Trev a tiny tap on the genitals which made him flinch. The message was plain - "I can drop you, but it's too easy!"

Trev launched another punch, which the old man avoided by stepping aside, putting him up close to the brambles and the stone wall, as Trev had intended. His next blow had to land. It slammed in, launched from the back foot, with the hip-thrust that gave it all the power Trev could muster. Instead of ducking, the old man caught it, in one hand, and twisted Trev's arm round and down, to bring the elbow up and out, killing the power. From there, the arm would be taken up his back; the best counter was a hands-up forward flip, without touching the ground. As his arm reached the danger point, Trev somersaulted, to find that his arm had been released, and, as he hung, upside down, in mid roll, the old man gave him a clip on the ear!

"Too slow!" the man said.

Trev finished the roll, his feet slapping onto the tarmac, then spun to face the old man, flinching as a hand snaked out, and flicked the tip of his nose.

"Terrible! Fast no good, strong no good. What next?" The Jap smiled, and stood there, arms folded again.

Trev sidled in, in a semi-crouch, arms half-extended, with the hands straight, like axes.

"Good! Now you thinking with your head, not your -." The man pointed south.

560

George heard someone yelling, outside, and went to see what was happening. Vince was sitting on the garden wall, by the gate, watching with total concentration. She'd seen that look once before, when Green-top came at him with a knife. A short way down the road, Tommy stood facing them, as a big man moved in on him. She drew breath to shout, but Vince snapped "Quiet! Don't distract them, or someone will get hurt!"

The big man launched a flurry of chops and jabs, none of which landed, as Tommy ducked, weaved, and swayed, avoiding them all, except the last one. The big man gave a yell of triumph which changed to agony as the chop was blocked by a sharply raised elbow which struck into the wrist.

The big man jumped back and turned to one side, the damaged hand to the rear, its fingers limp He then made a fast double shuffle, and snapped a very fast kick to Tommy's head. Tommy merely leaned way over backwards, and then stood there, holding the leg in the cross of his arms, and waited. The big man wobbled, recovered, then wobbled again. Tommy raised his arms, forcing the leg up, until the man fell over. The big man landed on his back, legs curled, and bounced back to his feet using a back-spring. As he came upright, Tommy pounced, raining a hail of light blows, which did no damage whatsoever. Starting with single hits, then going to doubles, every one of which was blocked, until Tommy took them into multiple combinations, eight out of ten of which landed, but without any power. George belatedly realized that Tommy was playing with the big man, sparring, although the man wasn't!

Trevor was gasping, now. The rain of feather-light blows totally outclassed him, and he realized he was up against a Master of the art, who was giving him ample warning to back off - and a lesson in karate, at the same time! At first, he had blocked all the taps, but as the speed and complexity increased, very few were stopped, despite all his efforts. The Japanese could have minced him if he had so chosen. Trev learned, backed off, drew himself loosely to attention, and bowed, watching the old man, who wasn't even breathing hard, while Trev was panting, and dripping with sweat.

"Enough. I am defeated." Trevor acknowledged. "If I continue, you might hurt me by accident."

"True. And I was just getting warmed up. Is your wrist damaged?"

"I don't think so, sprained, maybe."

"Let me see it."

Trevor cautiously extended the arm, and the Japanese took it, feeling the bones and tendons with steel fingers, then gently flexing it. "Is O.K. Not broken. Sore for week or two."

Only then did George realize who the big man was.

Vince sighed, and said. "It's o.k. It's all over. I wonder where Pete is."

"Sod Pete! What happened?"

"You saw, but didn't see! Trev's gone from potential assassin, to pupil, in less than a minute. Tommy was in command from the first moment, but Trevor hadn't realized it, and was trying to defeat Tommy. Barring an accident, he had no chance of touching him. If Tommy doesn't want you to touch him, he just goes away. It's like punching air. I got one through his guard once. I really hit him, dead centre, and it STILL didn't land! It's as though Tommy can make a hole in himself! It's weird! It should have hit him on the sternum and pushed it clean out between his shoulder-blades!"

Trevor and Tommy were coming up the lane, so Vince put on a silly face, and as they came close, said "Hi, feller, do I know you? I see you've met my tutor, Tommy."

Trev looked puzzled, for a moment, and then recalled the conversation over the radio, a few days ago. "Yes, we met a couple of times, last year."

"He come to see George." Tommy added.

"He's seen me. Now he can go." George snapped, her voice cold. "You weren't invited."

"I've been instructed to tell you who the men were." Trevor began, "We took them to Bangor -,"

"No, you didn't, you took them to Gwalchmai, then transferred them into a dry-cleaner's van, which went to Bangor nick. Tell the truth."

"- in another van, and turned them over to the Plods. They turned out to be Special Branch!"

"Specials? What the hell's going on? Why us? All I want is to be left alone to pick up the pieces of my life after you

564

destroyed it. I'm just getting it sorted, and you lot turn up again. Why?"

Vince just sat there, looking puzzled. "Last year?"

"Yes, darling. Just listen, I'll explain it, later." She played along, not sure of his plan.

"Alright. Who's special?" Vince knew that as long as Trevor thought him a non-entity, he was the hidden ace.

"You are. Hush, now."

Trev said, "Sorry Geo - Miss Weastey. I don't know. I can tell you that we're all on the same side."

"Sides! I'm on my side, you aren't! You make it sound like a football match, and I think you mean you won't tell me, not that you can't. You will, either voluntarily, or Tommy will persuade you!"

Trev looked around, as Tommy had been behind him, but no longer was. Angry at the bullying from this slip of a girl, after the Nip had shown him up, he made a terrible mistake. He reached for her shoulder. George spun, very fast, her arm pulling his straight, so that her shoulder-blades banged into the back of his elbow, bending the joint the wrong way. Instinct flung him forward and sideways, to save the joint, then, too late, he realized she had changed her grip, so he was flung up and over the stiff arm by his own weight. The shoulder joint was forced to rotate far beyond its designed limits, and snapped out, with a nasty crackling noise. In the same instant, over the wall to the field, came the sound of a sudden scuffle, a splat, a thud, and a yell of dismayed despair, then a body was flung over the wall to land with a thud on the road. Pete managed to turn his arrival into a roll, and landed on his shoulders, saving his neck, then fell heavily on top of Trevor, who had gone grey, and was sweating with the agony from his shoulder. Tommy bounced over the wall, carrying a rifle, with a telescopic sight. "He came to join party. Stupid man has long gun, and came in close! You want it?"

"No, do you?"

"For what? Grow beans up?" Tommy flicked a catch, withdrew the magazine, worked the action, caught the ejected round, put it back into the magazine, and tossed it to George, who caught it. Tommy then withdrew the bolt, removed the springs from it, put it back, destroyed the springs, and threw them into the field, thus demonstrating he was no stranger to fire-arms. George recalled doing almost the same thing with the other Magnums she had confiscated, only she had flushed the springs down a loo. Tommy threw the now useless rifle at the two men.

Pete untangled himself from the rifle and Trevor, then rolled to his feet. Trevor came carefully to a sitting position, then using his good arm, carefully lifted the damaged one, turned it the right way round, then folded it across his chest. Fresh sweat, and a deep groan, burst from him.

Only then did Tommy realize Trevor was injured. "He give trouble?"

"Not really. He reached for me, and I stopped him."

"He not make same mistake."

"Keep the ammo," Pete said, "It fits the Magnum."

"Right, then, you two dog turds. Start explaining. Who are you, really? Why all the fire-arms? What else is there in the truck? Rocket launchers? Grenades? Semtex? Cordtex?"

"I told you, we're Customs and Aargh!" Trev got a prod in the shoulder from her toe.

"Tommy, take Pete up there, to the truck, and make him

drive it back here. I'm going to strip it, and then we might get the truth out of these two!"

"O.K."

"Can I see to Trevor, first?" Pete asked.

"No, he won't die just yet, and it will keep the pair of you quiet. Move!"

"That man's arm looks funny!" Vince hammed it up.

"Yes, darling. It doesn't matter. Forget about it."


An hour or so later, George had four heaps of gear on the floor, provisionally labelled truck junk, diving kit, dangerous, and whatsits. The whatsits were mostly electronic gizmo's, a few walkie-talkies, four more head-set radios, the big transceiver, and a few things she couldn't identify. The dangerous pile contained four concussion grenades, several smoke bombs, another rifle and scope, four rocket-like things she couldn't find a launcher for, three Magnums, boxes of ammo, and a tin of pink plasticene-like material. "Where are the detonators?"

"In Geordie's 'B'." Pete answered.

"These," she indicated the rockets, "look like mortars,

where is the launcher?"

"In that pile." Pete indicated one.

She looked at the 'truck junk'. Spanners, tools, wheel-brace, jack, filler, rubber tube, tin of odd nuts and bolts, fuel can, an odd length of bent pipe with battered ends, the wrong bore. The jack! She fitted its handle, and pumped a few times, but nothing happened. She turned the handle, and something in the body went 'snap!' She looked at the ram mechanism again, and then pulled the axle stand out. That left her with a short, fat, tube. She cautiously tried a rocket for size, and it fitted perfectly. The rocket, and the jack, went into the dangerous pile. She eyed the heap, then said: - "I've known Mercenaries to go into the field with less kit. What do two C and E's want with it all, I wonder? They can't possibly, so they aren't C and E. They are pally with the cops, and can call up disguised transport, at the drop of a hat. They are H.M. Government, the cheque said so, and the Bank liked it, so it was real. And they can parade around the country in a mobile armoury, and no-one bats an eyelid. They are also incompetent, because they keep making the same silly mistakes." She picked up a Magnum, weighed it briefly, in her hand, worked the action, and then pointed it at Pete. "O.K. Geordie, Come and join the party, carefully! And bring Hopalong with you!"

"Shit!" Geordie stood up, behind the other lane-side wall, and then climbed over. "Jeez, Trev, who hit you, a charging rhino?"

"I did. Where's Hopalong?"

"He's at base, honest. He's got 'flu, the sweats, the shakes, everything."

"Shut up, and sit down. If you're lying again, you'll all wake up with holes in you. I'm sick of you trying to sneak up on me. Tommy, would you telephone for the Police, and an Ambulance, please, tell them we caught some burglars, and one got hurt."

"Will do!"

Geordie's foot scraped as he gathered himself, ready to make a lunge at her. The Magnum snapped into line. "Don't even think about it!" George snarled.

Tommy came back. "Is done, Police in ten minute, Ambulance in maybe twenty. Further to go."

"Thanks. Right then - you, Geordie. Empty your pockets, carefully!"

Geordie hesitated, defying her.

"Do it, Man!" Pete hissed. He could see her trigger finger going white, as she increased pressure.

Cigarettes, lighter, flick-knife, hand-cuffs, keys, handkerchief, a condom, a few coins, a wallet, and a couple of bits of paper formed a heap.

"Watch them, Tommy." She picked up the wallet and papers. They proved to be petrol reciepts, one local, the other from Kensington, she couldn't quite read the blurry name on the cheap paper. "You get around, don't you? London, indeed." She flicked open the wallet, to see money, plastic cards, and an I.D. card, complete with photograph. Albert Keith McGillighan, aged 37, was employed by Her Majesty the Queen, in a non-specified role. Should there be any difficulty, dial 01 -. "Alright, Albert, add your pop-gun to the pile." He did. "And the Sgein Dubh!" The Magnum she held shifted aim slightly, drawing his eye. He was sweating now, either from rage or fear, but he held his face emotionless, before twitching up a trouser leg, and sliding a slim knife from its ankle sheath. He tossed it into the pile.

"And the other one!"

The patches under his arms grew larger, and a drip fell from the tip of his nose. Unbidden, the words of a long-forgotten instructor drifted through her mind, - "Watch the ones who have hot flushes, they're nasty bastards!"

Geordie didn't move, so she applied the last gram of pressure to the trigger, the sear tripped, the hammer fell, the pin struck the percussion cap in the waiting cartridge, which obediently detonated, igniting the main charge. The expanding gases forced the copper- jacketed lead slug down the rifled barrel. As the slug erupted from the muzzle, a small portion of the expanding gas reset the hammer, ready for the next release, and rotated the cylinder by one chamber, bringing a new round into line. Geordie wet himself as the slug slammed past his ear, and then buried itself in the wall behind him.

"You're lucky! These sights are way out, high and right." George moved the gun slightly, "The knife!"

It was added to the growing heap. It had an ornate hilt, with a large gemstone balancing the blade, complemented by a basket-weave grip.

George picked it up. "Very nice. Antique? Family heirloom?"

Geordie nodded yes.

"Well, you just lost it. Now you, Pete, put everything onto the heap." She dropped Geordie's wallet, but kept the I.D. card and the jewelled knife.

Pete tossed his wallet, a few coins, and a bunch of keys onto the heap, and then hitched up his trouser legs, to show he was 'clean'.

George picked up his wallet, but there was nothing in it, except some cash, so she tossed it back. Faintly, in the distance, the 'hee-haw' of a siren made itself heard.

"I don't imagine they will be able to keep you for very long, but this lot will take some explaining away. Don't call again without a personal invitation, and in that unlikely event, don't come armed, and don't come mob-handed, or else you will be going away in a box, like you have already been warned, do you understand?"

They nodded yes.

573

"I'll keep these few items, and Vince can have the radios, he likes playing with them, - You!" The Magnum pointed at Albert, "will NOT attempt to reclaim your pencil-sharpener, nor will your pals, they aren't daft enough. Now, just sit there, like good little kiddies, it will save on the paperwork."

P.C. Jones screeched to a halt in his patrol mini-van, (all Bedford mini-vans screech to a halt!), and climbed out of the cramped cab. He took in the scene in a sweeping glance, and under the pretext of putting on his hat and tugging his tunic straight, thought, "What the hell do I do, now!" His duties since leaving training school, eighteen months ago, had mostly consisted of making the tea, brushing up, going to the chip-shop, or car park duty at the various fetes. It was unfortunate for him that he had been on an errand, making the canteen run in the only transport the local nick had available, apart from a bicycle, circa 1935, and had been diverted to see what the heck was going on. Armed burglars, indeed!

Well, somebody had been armed! Hiding safely behind the two-millimeter thick steel of the van door, he said, in his best

574

'Dixon of Dock Green' voice, "Alright, what's going on here?" It was a pity that his voice came out as a thin squeak, as his nerves gave it a pre-pubescent falsetto.

George flicked a glance at the pimply youth, and suggested he use his radio to call for reinforcements.

That seemed to be a good idea to P.C. Jones, and he was soon gabbling his story to H.Q.

Pete shifted uncomfortably. His pants were thin, and the gravel was sharp. George's eyes moved, but the Magnum didn't. It continued its unwavering stare at Albert, whose shirt was now totally sodden. Another 'hee-haw' siren made itself heard, and shortly afterwards an ambulance zoomed up. P.C. Jones waved it down and had a brief discussion with the driver, who shrugged, talked to his radio, lit a cigarette, and put his feet up on the dashboard. The crew-man got out, and started forward. George cautioned him to keep back, as nobody had been shot, yet, the only injury, so far, was a painful, but not lethal, dislocated shoulder. The crew-man went back to his flask of coffee and a sardine sandwich. After all, the girl had the gun, and that definitely put her in charge!

575

After a delay, another car, a private saloon, roared up and halted behind the ambulance. A grizzled sergeant, also a Jones, climbed out of his own car, a Metro, and took in the situation. He vaguely recognized the girl, as she had called in at the station, once, to discuss locks, security, alarms, and such, and recalled that she was the owner of the cottage behind them, as he'd called round to see the situation for himself. The old chap in the nightie, and the one sitting on the wall, he didn't recognize. The three on the floor, - His mental rolodex flipped rapidly through, and came up with trouble. They'd crossed swords, when was it, fourteen, eighteen? months ago. Yes, that was it, when a crime-wave had landed. The I.R.A., the S.A.S, dead bodies, a riot on the parade at Holyhead. More trouble in one day than in the previous year! The girl, what was her name? held a hand-gun, a big bugger, too! He smiled at 'Pimples', hiding behind the van door. If she fired the thing at him the thin tin wouldn't even slow the bullet down! Western, was it? She seemed to know what she was doing with the gun, anyway, she wasn't waving it around at random. It held unwaveringly centred on one man's head. No, not Western, Westey, something like that. Sergeant Jones sighed, he had six hundred and seven days to go before the fancy clock and the golden hand-shake, and he wanted to enjoy every last penny of it! He looked at the three on the floor, again, as something else popped into his memory. The old chap could be the home-help, and the chap on the wall, her disabled, live-in partner. Yes, that fitted. Weastey, Joe? Nearly right, was it? The other three looked pretty pissed off, one sat lopsided, and grey-faced, clutching one arm in the other, and one dripped hate and sweat. He looked to be the nasty one, and the girl knew it. The cannon pointed steadily at him, although her eyes watched all three, constantly alert. What were those black specks on his face? Powder burns? That made sense. Her score went up several points in his estimation. Grey-face, on the floor, his name began with a T. Terry? No. He looked hurt, but not shot, there was no blood. Maybe a broken arm, the way he was hunched up. Who did it? Grand-pa? No, he was a stick-insect, and wouldn't have the strength to break a match! The one on the wall, no, he lived in a wheel-chair, which seemed to be missing at the moment. It must have been her, then. It wasn't that difficult, if you knew how, and she seemed competent with that cannon, so she

577

probably knew how. Her score went up even further. Trevor! Trevor someone, and - Pat! Or was Pat the one they had been looking for? It would come in a minute.

'Pimples' Jones finished inhaling, "Hello, Sarg! I think we'll need more than two of us!"

"Alright, son. Let the wood see the trees, is it?" He eased forward, keeping to the side of the woman. She flicked a glance at him, and he stopped. "Alright, Miss, I'm here now! You can put that down before there's an accident, is it?"

"In a minute, Sergeant. Get this guy chained up first, for his own safety." Her voice was cool as cucumber.

"The other two?"

"They're pussycats. This one's the one to watch, he's short fused, and stupid. Then I'll tell you what's going on!"

"Alright, Miss. Can I go round behind him?" Sergeant Jones knew better than to argue with a gun-person!

"Yes. I won't shoot you." Her voice was as steady as her gun-hand.

"I'm glad about that." Sergeant Jones scooped up the handcuffs, from the little pile of other bits, on the road, saw they were standard issue, and went to the sweaty man, carrying them. "Come on, son, you know the routine!"

Hate poured from Geordie in waves, but he knew he was beaten - for now, anyway. There would be another time. Carefully, making no sudden moves, he rolled onto his stomach, and placed his hands behind his back, wrists close together. Sergeant Jones ratcheted the cuffs tight, and then gave them an extra squeeze, for good luck, before stepping clear. George lowered the Magnum, but didn't un-cock it.

"Right Miss, - er, Weastey, is it? What's this all about now?"

George gave him a fast run-down, starting with the man in the field, the radio bugs, (her version almost tied in with theirs), and on to the three on the floor. Sergeant Jones looked at the various pieces of ordnance, as she described them, the truck from which she had removed them, from where she knew Pete and co, and what had happened to Trevor, (Trevor nodded agreement), and on to the present, where she ended with who they claimed to be, and that she wanted them out of her hair before she got angry and really hurt them! All through it, she was

579

coldly neutral, in control, but with that last, he felt her iron will, just for an instant, and knew they would get no mercy if they crossed her again. P.C. 'Pimples' Jones was scribbling furiously in his note-book, trying to record everything. Sergeant Jones felt like he had been briefed for a Military exercise, then another file popped into his mind. She was ex R.A.F. and not a paper-shuffler, either! 'Pimples' finished scribbling, just as two other P.C's crunched up, in a taxi. "Jacko's car wouldn't start!" was the offered explanation.

Jacko eyed the arrayed hardware. "Christ! Where's the war?"

"You missed it, son. Give 'Pimples' a hand to shove that lot into his van, carefully! He can take it back to the nick, and we'll catalogue it, there. What's the jack for, is it?"

George emptied the Magnum she held of ammo, and handed it to 'Pimples', who was now hiding behind Sergeant Jones, then described how the rockets fitted into it, as it was a disguised launcher.

"Are they fused?"

"I don't know - the same goes for the grenades. I haven't

580

found any fuses that might fit. Pete, there, says they're in Geordie's car, an M.G.B. I don't know where that is."

"Jacko. When you've done that, take these two back, and lock them up until I get back. Separate cells. Take the cuffs off that one at your peril! If Paddy's sobered up, you can chuck him out, is it!"

"Right, Sarg."

"Doc, come and see to 'one-arm' here. The panic's over." George called.

"On my way!" The paramedic swallowed the last of his coffee, and picked up his bag of miracles. It didn't take him very long to realize that there wasn't much he could do, here. "O.K. Pal. We can put it back here, and listen to you scream, or we can take you to Clwyd hospital, where they will put you out, it's badly twisted, as well."

"Hospital, do it right." Trev groaned. His eyes met George's, "It'll teach me to keep my hands off, won't it!"

"Yes." She glared at him.

"Right, then, you. P.C. Morgan can go with you in the meat-wagon, and stick with you like glue until he's relieved, or can bring you to the shop. I'll try to find out what's going on, and here seems to be a good place to start, is it?"

"Yes, Sarg."

The various vehicles moved off, after a bit of backing and filling in the narrow lane, to depart to their various destinations.

The Sergeant invited himself into the cottage for a cuppa, before getting down to serious investigating. He was about to offer Vince a hand, but his flabber was thoroughly ghasted when Vince stood, and went inside, followed by Grandpa in his nightie, what were they called, Kimmo's? No, Kinmel's? Not that, either, that was a bay near Rhyl! He turned, and followed the girl through the garden gate, eyeing the straggly plants that were nearly growing, there. "That ground needs some horse-muck!" he commented."

"Yes, I know, but I can't get any. Plenty of sheep, or pig, pig's too acid, and sheep won't rot down. I've got a ton of cow maturing at the local dairy farm, but it's too young, yet. Mind your head on the lintel, as you come in."

He ducked under it, and fell up the step, instead. "Booby-

582

traps, is it?"

"Everyone else bangs their head while avoiding the step!" She parked him at the dining table while she made tea, but found the process was under way, guided by Tommy. "Don't put those scone-biscuits out. Open a packet of Chocolate Digestives, instead, please"

"So!"

"Your baking is getting better!" Vince commented, "At least, the scones snap, now, not your teeth!"

"At least I don't need to call the fire brigade out, when I cook!" She retorted, thinking of his cheese on toast.

"Ah, now. Remember the soup!"

Over tea and biscuits, she repeated the story, filling in the background and the details, but still overlooking one or two things. At the end, Sergeant Jones was no better informed than before, but he sensed that she was as baffled as he was.

"Why do you play at being confined to a wheelchair?" he asked.

"Simple. I'm the ace up the sleeve! I very nearly was in a

chair, and it seemed a good idea to continue. That's for your ears and eyes only, mind! To everyone else, I'm in a chair for the rest of my natural, until this is over, o.k?"

""Providing you don't try it on with the D.S.S., I'll let it slip for now. Who's the Chinese fellah?"

"I wouldn't let him hear you call him Chinese! He's Japanese. Tommy's an old friend, who used to be a Restauranteur, now retired, and he's helping out, and chauffeuring, while I get going again."

"So." Sergeant Jones recapped, "This Trevor, with one working arm, his buddy, Pete, Geordie, who is really Albert McGillighan, and one other, who isn't around, are supposed to be Customs and Excise. The two bods with the snoopy kit were Special Branch. Two guys who both met mysterious ends were S.A.S. Another man, name unknown, was taken out by one or more others, names unknown, for reasons unknown, present whereabouts unknown. That lot has access to R.A.F. helicopters at short notice, and their edited report found its way into the hands of Trevor and Pete, via their Boss, name unknown, who also sent you a copy, reason unknown. You two met, by chance, while on holiday, separately, and took to each other. You both met Trevor and Pete at the same camp-site, when they offered to take you out on their boat for a dive, which you all seem to do for fun. On the way back, you were answering a call of nature, and found a funny pipe. Then you both end up nearly dead in a diving accident that wasn't an accident. Miss Weastey recovered quickly, but Mr Birtwhistle was in a coma, until recently, when he woke up, and after a while, came here to recuperate, bringing this Tommy. Then the Specials turned up, followed by Trevor and Pete, is it?"

"And Geordie, yes. In a nut-shell."

"So you beat them up, searched their truck, which they happened to have brought to you, and pulled a gun on them. I suspect that you discharged at least one round at one of them, is it?"

"Yes, Geordie needed a bit of persuading!"

"And you don't know why any of this is going on?"

"No, do you?"

"That's not for me to say, is it? You seem to have missed a bit out, how the snoopers found their way to the Valley of the

Rocks camp-site, and into the back of the truck, trussed up like turkeys. Yes, I know about that."

"Ah, well, we managed."

Sergeant Jones looked at them for a minute. "Yes, as you say, you managed! I think there is more to this story. I think that the mud-bath Geordie tried to give to his car before today was your doing, that's why he's so mad at you.. I also think you had something to do with that fracas in Holyhead, last year, when there was a gang-fight on and in the harbour, when one of the punks went to meet his maker, rather unexpectedly. That investigation is still open. Then there are the deaths of the two S.A.S. men, who really were S.A.S, by the way. One went for a swim beneath the Dun Laoghaire ferry. Amongst other things, he had a broken neck, two broken arms, and a leg that was never recovered. The other, a big gorilla, like the one you winged earlier, Trev, had a ragged hole in one ear, remarkably like a gunshot wound, and was found wearing a plastic bag hat, tied firmly around the neck."

"That lot is nothing to do with us!"

"Maybe not. It is interesting, though, that a Land-Rover

like yours was seen in Bangor, when the 'B' went paddling!"

"There are lots of Land-Rovers about."

"True. But there are not many green ones with orange upholstery! I find it interesting that this Geordie was apparently chasing this particular one!"

"Perhaps he was carved up at a junction. He gets angry very easily! We certainly weren't there. We were here. Your Specials should be able to confirm that!"

"Unfortunately for me, they did!"

"Well, then?"

"One thing. How did you find out that Geordie was Albert?"

"I borrowed his I.D. card. It claims he is Albert Keith McGillighan, in the employ of Queen Liz, duties unspecified. There was a 'phone number on it. I'll show it to you, unofficially, but you can't have it. I'm going to send it to Security, at the Air Ministry, and let them sort it out. I'll tell them that I think he's a Russian spy! That will keep them all busy for a while."

She produced the card, and the Sergeant wrote down the

details on a scrounged piece of paper, with a borrowed pen. "I should confiscate that, as evidence, but, as you don't have it, I can't, can I?"

"It would be difficult."

"I also noticed that when you gave 'Pimples' that cannon, earlier, you managed to keep the ammunition. I won't ask if there happens to be another one lying around somewhere, then you won't have to perjure yourself, will you?"

"No, Sergeant." It was about three inches from his foot, in her bag.

"Likewise, I won't ask where you got it, or whether you have a license, then I won't have to take it off you, in case someone else needs 'persuading.'

George nodded, non-comittally, the same thought was in her mind.

"That brings us to the incident, just now. With a bit of stretching, I could say that the lane belongs to you, therefore -."

"It does. I have sole access. My land starts at the edge of the road, so, technically, you were, and are trespassing, as were all the other vehicles, the taxi, the private cars, the ambulance, the van, the truck, - "

"- the fact that you were waving a fire-arm about, - "

"It wasn't waving about!"

That was true, it had been very steady! "- could be construed as 'reasonable force', considering the arsenal the others had with them, and that nobody had any holes in them - ."

"Geordie's lucky the sights were twisted. I was aiming at his head!"

"I didn't hear that! - there is no proof it was discharged here. I suppose, if I looked hard enough, in the right place, I would find a fresh bullet, but as I don't know where to look, and I can't be bothered getting dirty, it would be a waste of time doing anything about it."

"Yes, it would." Vince tossed a mangled scrap of metal onto the table.

"So, I will merely give you an unofficial warning. Call us out, first, if there is a next time. Let us do the 'sorting out' and 'persuading', o.k. is it?"

"I did call you out. But the circumstances were such that, if I had waited for you, it would have been all over before you arrived. At least, I saved you the effort of looking for evidence, and more bodies!"

"I have to agree with you, unofficially. Just how did a slip of a girl like you put that gorilla's arm out?"

"Stand up, and I'll show you. - Reach for me, that's it. I deflected the arm, like this, and then turned, to take it round behind, like this, but he thought I was going for the elbow, and threw a forward roll, leaving the arm behind, and did it to himself, really, with his own body-weight."

"Mmm. Is that that Japanese ninja stuff?"

"Karate, you mean? Not really. R.A.F. self-defence course."

"Is that why Tommy's here? What's his full name?"

"No, of course not! I don't know, just Tommy."

Sergeant Jones thought about that, for a moment, mentally separating, and connecting, the answers. "Just Tommy, and he just happened to be here?"

"Not quite. As we said earlier, Tommy is cooking for us, at the moment, and has been helping Vince back to fitness."

"With that karate stuff'"

"No, with Chai Tee!"

"Tai Chi. You always get it backwards!" Vince spoke for the second time, "Tai Chi for suppleness, and the gym machinery, in there," he gestured, "for strength, plus the vitamins and stuff, in his catering."

"Mmm. And Tommy's name is?"

"Tommy. I never knew any other name for him. I can always ask him, but everyone knows him just as Tommy."

"Alright. I'll leave it at that, for now, is it? I trust that none of you are planning on leaving the area, in the next few days?"

"This is our home, Sergeant. Tommy was talking of going back home, now his work here is finished, but other than that, the furthest we are likely to go is shopping!"

"I'd prefer it if he were to stay around for a few more days, in case I need to talk to him. The recovery crew will come and remove that truck a bit later, maybe tomorrow."

"That's alright. If we need to go out, we can get around it."

"Watch yourselves. There's something very funny going on. I shouldn't say this, but while we are talking unofficially, there are rumours of trouble filtering up from the local villains,

591

and they are all keeping their heads down."

"Thanks for the warning." George rose as Sergeant Jones did, and saw him to the gate. As they reached it, the' phone rang, so she excused herself, and dashed back.

Vince put the handset down as she entered. "That was Joan. She says to watch out. She can feel trouble brewing, nothing specific, but she keeps getting rivers, bridges, big cranes, and an arrow over a map - pointing northeast."

"North-east, rivers, cranes? Tyneside? Geordieland? She's a bit late!"

"That's what I said, but she insists it is future, not past."

"Well, unless he's murdered the copper, and legged it - !"

Meanwhile, over on the Valley of the Rocks camp-site, a motorcycle leaned drunkenly on it's side-stand, next to an orange pup-tent, and a couple in a tatty V.W. camper-van were looking for a level pitch, as the place they usually occupied was already claimed.

In a small room, behind a locked door, a telephone rang

once, twice, and then the answer-phone machine kicked in.

"Jimmy? Er, I hate these bloody things! Ah, it's - the job's laid on for tonight. It won't go wrong this time! It cost more than we bargained on, though, twenty gee's, and two ounces of stuff. He said if we want the best, we'd have to pay for it! er, - I think that's it."

Several miles off-shore, a Spanish registered fishing boat chugged casually along, its nets up on deck, ready for deploying. A Royal Naval mine-hunter shadowed it, indirectly, using the beamed down-link radar picture from a Nimrod surveillance aircraft, which was circling in a holding pattern at thirty-two thousand feet altitude, and a hundred miles south. They had been watching the boat, in shifts, ever since it had been 'handed on' to them from the Gibraltar sector as it crossed the Bay of Biscay, two days earlier. A diesel electric 'Fleet' class submarine lay waiting on the sea bottom, near the likely target area, listening.

The sonar operator was using hydrophones - underwater microphones - to listen for the fishing vessel. At the moment, all he could hear was the whining of outboard motors, the slapping

593

of wind-surfers, some dolphins chattering in the distance, and the heavy throbbing drone of a passing cargo vessel. He sighed, scratched at a sweat-rash, and fought down the desire to scratch his itching haemorrhoids. Most of the crew were 'turned in', making the sub seem vast and cavernous, unlike the sardine-tin conditions of 'Action Stations', as there was little chance of action before dark. On the intercom panel, in front of him, a light flicked on. He turned a knob, switching his headphones from hydrophones, to intercom. "Sonar."

"Duty Officer, anything happening?"

"No, Sir, just background noise, and a freighter, to the south, medium distance, at a guess."

"Very well. Keep a sharp lookout!"

"Yes, Sir. Of course, Sir." He switched back to the hydrophones. "Three bags full, Sir! What the fuck do you think I can see, from here?"

"What was that, Eddie?"

"Nothing, Hookey, just that sprog Subbie telling me to keep a good lookout! Will you have a listen while I go for a jimmy? And while I'm there, I'll open a fuckin' window for him!"

"Yeah. Hurry up, though, I've got to monitor the broadcast from Rugby in ten minutes."

"Cheers."

"Oh, use the bow head, the aft one's backed up, again!"

"I thought it was a bit ripe in here, today!"

"That's Shagger's socks, he's taken his boots off!"


Inside the Nimrod, the radar op finicked with the range dial, then picked up a microphone. "Foxtrot three, this is Picket, he's slowed down again! Once that tanker has cleared, turn left to north, and make ten knots, over."

"Fox three, ten and north behind the tanker, copied. Out."


Near Llyn Hafodol, two hikers waddled along the road, almost buried under enormous ruck-sacks, dangling and clanking below the bags was a ring of pans, kettle, and utensils. The hikers paused, leaning their burden on a wall, while they consulted a map and compass, then went on their way to the Standing Stone, at Brynddu.

The noise they were making distracted Tommy from his reverie, and he watched them pass out of sight, shaking his head at the behaviour of these crazy Gaijin's. They lumber along, making an awful racket, he mused, then complain that there is nothing to see! He went back to his favourite pastime. At the moment, he was engrossed in trying to persuade a wren to take an insect from his fingers. This involved sitting quite still, an exercise he enjoyed more with every passing year. The wren hopped up onto a branch in the nearby shrub, cheeped at him, and hopped down again, watching with its little black eyes.

Out of sight of the cottage, the clanking hiker on the left, with the big frying pan dangling, said to the hiker with the kettle: "That's the place marked on the map. I couldn't see very much of use, it's too far from the road."

"I think I got a glimpse of the girl, through a window. No sign of the one in the wheel-chair. Who was the old geezer in the garden?"

"Don't know. He's not on the list. I suppose, if he's still there, we'll have to do him, as well?"

"Seems like. It's a nuisance, though. He's one more to

watch out for when we go in."

"Only briefly. Two or three seconds, and - thppp" Frying pan made a squelching noise with his lips.

Kettle smiled. "I hope she's pretty. That last one was an ugly cow, and didn't struggle either, she just lay there, and took everything, until I couldn't get it up again. It was a relief to top her, not like the one in France, last year!"

"Is that the one you kept for a week in that tumble-down old farmhouse, out in the sticks?"

"That's the one!" kettle licked his lips, at the memory, "She fought like hell, too, every time. After a week of her, I was shagged out. Although I could get it up, I was dry. I couldn't raise anything more. If I hadn't cut her throat, I'd still be shagging away, maybe I'd have sucked myself inside out, trying to raise another squirt!"

"I heard that was not all you got from her, either!"

"Nah! The dirty bitch gave me a dose of clap!"

Frying pan chuckled. "I've never been caught, you want to use noddys"

"Bloody things. I can't get on with them."

597

"You might have to, if the new tests they've come up with, work!"

"What tests?"

"Haven't you heard? They think they can take a sample a hundred years old, and tell you which man put it there!"

"You're kidding!"

"Straight up! They can take a dried flake, and do something with it, and it makes a pattern, each one's different, they say, like a snowflake. Dee and Hay, or something, they call it."

"Clever buggers." They trudged on, for a distance, "But if they haven't got the man, how can they tell who did it?"

"Dunno, but if he's been spreading it around, they can say he did that one, and her, and that one, but not her!"

"Nah. I don't believe it!"

Chapter thirty.

Trouble.


At some time around four a.m. Tommy came awake. Something was wrong. He listened hard, but heard nothing other than silence. That was it! It was too quiet - all the normal night noises were missing. The crickets that lived in the stone wall weren't chirping. All the little scuffles, and the odd squeak of alarm, had stopped. Tommy eased from his bed in the caravan, and dressed without using the light, then slipped the latch on the door and opened it an inch, to allow him to hear better.

A stone clinked against another. Gravel crunched, as the intruder trod on it and hesitated. A few tiny clicks as particles dropped from a lifted shoe, and then a faint swish of grass followed. A shadow that was slightly blacker than the black night eased along the rear wall of the cottage. Faintly, at the upper register of the limits of his hearing, Tommy heard a bat change from its search chatter to a scream of warning, then the flutter of leathery wings as it departed. Little clicks and scratches, then the snick! of the kitchen door latch. The door eased open a bare foot and the shadow slid through the gap. Tommy ghosted across the grass, barefoot, and went into the kitchen cautiously. He heard a muffled thud, and a bong from the gym room, as someone nudged a guy wire. Tommy drifted over, and through the door, and then stood, waiting.

Vince woke when the latch snicked. He listened, knowing that it wasn't Tommy - he wouldn't come in during the night, as he respected their privacy. A faint slithering sound of cloth on wood came from the living room, followed by a muffled clang from the gym, as someone walked into a steel guy wire. There were two of them, then. George's eyes snapped open as he put his hand over her mouth, so she couldn't speak. She nodded, and slid her hand under her pillow, then withdrew it, clutching the

Magnum. She eased the hammer back, cocking it, and lay waiting. Vince slithered out of the bed, and stood behind the door.

The doorknob wiggled gently, and then turned very slowly.

Tommy's intruder made a circuit of the gym, finding nothing of interest. Hoping his partner hadn't heard him fall over the damn machine, he turned to try the next room. Shock surged through him at the sight of the old man standing there in the doorway, a quizzical smile on his face.

The intruder moved swiftly in, and smashed a chisel-like hand at the old man's larynx. It missed, somehow, and the man tapped him on the back of the wrist with one finger. Searing agony lanced up the intruder's arm, drawing a sharp hiss of indrawn breath as the hand went limp. The old man stood waiting.

The bedroom door swung open an inch, and the latch was carefully released. The top hinge groaned slightly as the door moved, and a person came in. He saw the woman lying there, with a duvet pulled up to her neck, her long blonde hair scattered

601

on the pillow. Lust surged through him as he looked at her. God, she was a beauty! He studied her oval face, the dainty ears with crystal studs in the lobes, her blonde eyebrows and long lashes. In a minute he would look whether she was a real blondie, or from a bottle - in a minute! He savoured the moment.

She stirred slightly, lifting a knee beneath the duvet, and leaning it sideways. She was begging for it! Vince slid out through the door without the intruder noticing him, as his attention was focussed on the girl in the bed, his mind filling with thoughts on what he might do to her. Out here in the middle of nowhere he could enjoy it, right here in her own bed. No need to find a place to take her. His anticipation built, his breathing grew faster.

Vince flowed round the table and across to the gym room, where the faint noises were coming from, easing through the door just as the man in there took a swipe at something. Vince took a pace forward as the man jumped back, hissing. Perfectly positioned, Vince mashed him one in the kidney. Reflex arched the man's back, and he let out a deep groan, then staggered forward and banged into the wall.

The man in the bedroom heard the thud, and smiled. His partner had obviously found the crip, and would probably toy with him for a while before seeing him off. He reached out a hand towards the duvet, then paused. Draped over a chair next to the bed was a nightie. Was she naked beneath the cover? Joy chased desire around, inside him, as he gently lifted the bottom corner of the duvet. Bare legs gleamed whitely on the pink sheet. She was! He took a better grip on the duvet as her eyes opened. He ripped the duvet off her as he looked into her eyes, expecting to see the fear leap into them. Instead, HE felt his own fear as her icy cold gaze met his, his eyes failing to register what he saw for a long instant. The blonde curls at the join of her legs framed gleaming blued metal.

She spoke. "I hope you enjoyed it!"

The Magnum slug slammed him through the doorway, to land sprawled on his back on the floor.


Vince jumped forward, double-footed, and mashed the man again in the short ribs, as he hung there, leaning on the wall.

603

The wall shook, and a decorative plate fell to the floor. Someone else! Vince whirled, and block-punched, then checked it, before it really started. Tommy! Tommy lifted an eyebrow. Vince winked, and held up two fingers. Tommy nodded yes, two. Vince took one pace towards the door, then the Magnum spoke the other man's death knell. The man was flung through the bedroom door and crashed to the floor. He twitched a few times, said "but - - ", then died.

George slipped into her nightie, then stepped over the body, and went to the 'phone.


"Well, there's no point creeping about, now!" Vince turned on the main light, then stooped to pull the balaclava off the dead man. "He's made a mess on the carpet!"

"He was planning on raping me, but I had other ideas. Thanks for leaving him to me!"

"I knew you could cope, and I wanted to get the other one before the noise started."

"What other one?"

"In the gym room."

604

"Is he -." her voice was beginning to quiver, as shock set in.

"No, just having a rest!"

George took a deep breath, focussed, and clamped down on her emotions. The shakes stopped. "Right. Let's talk to the bastard, then. We might find out what is going on!"

"Tommy's in there, too. Don't shoot him!"

"The way he moves, it would go right through without making a hole!"

"There could be more truth in that than you realize. Have you seen this one before, anywhere?"

She studied the startled face. "No."


The other man was still sprawled against the wall, groaning. Tommy was still standing just inside the door. "I imagine the other one will not run away?"

"No, he's gone to meet his maker. We think this one might like to talk to us, with a little persuasion!"

"Perhaps." Tommy was doubtful. "We can try!"

Sergeant Jones, unshaven, bleary eyed, wearing his uniform jacket over a 'deck-chair' striped pyjama top, looked at the mess lying on the floor. "There's no point in cautioning that one! Where's the other one?"

"In the gym. Tommy and Vince are 'talking' to him."

"Has he said anything?"

"Apart from 'AAARGH', not that I've heard."

"Do me a favour, lass, and put the kettle on. My brain doesn't work without tea in my belly. 'Pimples'! Get on the radio, we'll need a camera-man, and a Quack to officially tell us that he's dead. He sat down in a chair, by the table.

"UUURP! Right Sar -UUURP!"

"Chuck up outside, and stay out, if you can't handle it!"

"UUURp" 'Pimples' dove out, white-faced, and sweaty.

"One day, he'll be a copper!" Sergeant Jones shook his head, "God help us!"

"Sorry if I got you out of bed, but I didn't think this would wait until office hours! Two sugars?"

"Make it three, until I wake up. That's one reason why the wife moved into the spare bedroom, no 'phone in there!"

George placed a freshly loaded teapot in front of him, together with a huge cup, a spoon, and sugar and milk, in containers. "Fancy a scone?"

"Why not? I'm in no hurry, and he's going nowhere."

"What about 'Pimples'?"

"I wouldn't bother, he's feeding the weeds."

Half an hour, three cups of tea and two buttered scones later, Sergeant Jones sighed. "Right, I'm officially here, now. What happened?"

George gave him a resume.

"And you shot him, with his own gun?"

"Yes, when he ripped the duvet off me, it snagged, somehow, and fell onto the bed. When I grabbed it, it went off!"

Sergeant Jones looked at the pea-shooter she had offered up. It was a dinky little MAB Brevette automatic, of .22 calibre. One round had been fired. "I won't ask how that little toy made a big hole you could put a wine cork into, it will save you making up another silly story!"

"Most of it is true. He did break in, he did go into the bedroom, he did rip the duvet off me while I was lying there in bed, and he did get shot!"

"And he was dressed like that?"

"Yes, plus a balaclava. I don't know him."

"What time was it?"

"I didn't look, some time between midnight and five a.m."

The Sergeant compared the size of the hole in the man's chest, with the tiny gun, and sighed. "You know, Miss, You're lucky I believe in fair justice, as well as the law. You killed a man, making a half-inch hole in him with a three-sixteenths bullet. If you had really shot him, there, with that, - "

"He'd have said ouch! and carried on with his plan to rape me!"

"You've got it." Lew sighed at the thought of all the paperwork. "The way I see it, if he hadn't broken in, he wouldn't have got himself dead, so it's his own silly fault, is it?"

"Yes!"

"Right, then, if your man and his pal have left anything of the other one, let's go and see if he has learned to talk, yet."

They went into the gym.

The man was stripped of his head-wear, and was lying on

the floor, face up. There was a trickle of blood running from his chin, up to his nose, and a matching smear on the wall, at head height, where he had collided with it, earlier. The Sergeant studied the man, his mental index cards flipping. He looked a bit greasy, with a long, thin, and bent sideways, hooked nose. The skin was brownish, and the hair black and crinkly. He was not Caucasian, and too dark for a Greek. Arab maybe? An Italian? "Alright, then is it! Has he got a name?"

"Aaagh, pissoff, I think" Vince supplied an answer

"Hmm. Is he marked anywhere?"

"Only slightly. I hit him twice, at the beginning, Right kidney, and left lower ribs. He banged his head on the wall, there, fell to the floor, and crawled to there. I took those off him." Vince pointed to a weight-press bench, where a big Bowie knife, a yard of shiny wire with a wooden toggle handle at each end, two slim knives, with blades and handles of the same length, a bunch of lock-picks, and a torch, were lined up on the padding.

"He likes to cut them, strangle them, or both, is it?"

"Oh, yeah, and these!" Vince picked up a packet of three

from where they had fallen, and put them back onto the bench.

"Maybe they were going to take turns with your lass."

"It looks that way."

"Nothing else?"

"No, no wallet, no keys. They must have stashed them, somewhere, until after."

"That makes them pro's!"

George came in. "The Doc's arrived, and there's an ambulance just turning into the driveway."

"Thanks, lass. Show the Doc the body, and tell him we're waiting for the photographer, please."

"Will do."

"Right, you!" Sergeant Jones prodded the not yet dead intruder with a toe, his pyjama pants protruding below the blue serge uniform ones, at the ankle. "You're nicked. Anything you say, blah blah, you know the words, and I can't be bothered reciting them all, at this time of day!"

"Uuurgh!"

"What did you do to him/"

"Me? Nothing!" Vince exclaimed, "Tommy was holding

610

his hand, so he wouldn't run off, that's all!"

"You. Have you got a name, is it?"

"Uuugh, fuggoff!"

"Tell the Policeman your name, or I will hold your hand again!" Tommy warned.

"Fuggoff!"

Tommy picked up the man's limp hand, near the wrist, between thumb and first finger, then applied some pressure. The man jerked, and squirmed, sweat beading his brow anew. His whole arm and shoulder were jumping spasmodically, and an animal howl erupted from his mouth.

The Doctor peered around the doorway, to see what was making the noise. "The one out there is certified deceased, at -" he glanced at his wrist, "- Damn, my watch is on the dresser at home, at whatever time it is now! Cause of death appears to be a gunshot wound to the upper left chest. The autopsy will probably confirm that. Does that one need me?"

"Not yet, Doc, but if he doesn't learn to talk, he might well do, is it!"

"I hope you are not assaulting a prisoner!"

611

"I haven't laid a finger on him, Doc! You know me, would I do a thing like that?"

"Yes, unfortunately, I do, Lew, and Yes, you would, if you thought it appropriate!"

"Well, then?"

"Is there any tea left in that pot?"

"You can try it and see, if not, I'll make a fresh one." George offered.

"Are you hurt, Lass?"

"You're the first to ask! No, but I would have been, if I hadn't stopped him!" she pointed at the corpse. "He was preparing to climb into bed with me, uninvited!"

"More fool him, hey! Ah, I mean, - er."


In a locked room, the 'phone rang, and was 'picked up' by the answering machine. "Er, it's me. Something's gone wrong, they didn't come back to pick up the envelope, er, When I, er, find out, you know, I'll let you, er, know, you know, er, ah, soddin' things!"

In an office, some hours later, the 'phone rang.

"Fred's." The voice sounded like a ton of gravel sliding off a tipper-truck.

A cultured voice spoke, "I've a job for you. Somebody is becoming a nuisance, and I want him stopped. Are you interested?"

"Usual terms?"

"Of course!"

"Post box three."

"O.K."

"Twenty up front, used and small, for expenses."

"Done."

"It will be."


Later still, the 'phone in the small, locked room rang. "Jimmy, it's me again. It looks like Alberto got himself dead, and Tony's been - Hey, Get out! I'm making a - NO!" Crash! The line went dead.

Later, P.C. Plod, trudging around his patch, saw the vagrant, asleep on the park bench, a bottle clutched lovingly to his chest. Next time round, three hours later, it was drizzling steadily, and the P.C's 'milk of human kindness' had been washed away. He was freezing his nuts off! The tramp was still asleep, on the bench, so he went over, and applied his truncheon to the man's chest. "Come on, now! You can't stay there, you'll freeze to death, in this!"

The arm nursing the bottle dropped to the floor, then the body slid sideways, disturbing the cap it wore, and revealing the little black hole in between the eyes.

"OOH SHIT!" The P.C. groped for his soggy radio with numb fingers.


Everyone had gone, or been removed, leaving the three of them studying the stain on the carpet. They had worked on it with a wet-and-dry vacuum cleaner, and reduced it considerably, but it still looked like a bloodstain.

"We can try a steam cleaner on it, or we can buy a scatter-rug, and chuck it over the top."

Vince suggested.

"Or the Government can buy us a new carpet!"

"It might be wise to wait a while, though, in case there are any more intruders, their pals might come looking for the first lot."

"Now, that's a cheering thought, and we STILL don't know what is going on!" A van crunched to a halt on the gravel outside, and George reached for her purloined Magnum. Tommy sighed, and went into the kitchen shaking his head.

"Oh, put that away! It's Jones the Post." Vince went to the door, had a muttered conversation, someone laughed, then he came back with two boxes, as the van drove away. One box measured about 2" x 18" x 24", and the other was around 18'" x 18" x 56". "What on earth have you sent for, now?" he asked.

"It's a sort of present, for you!"

"Sort of?"

"Yes, do you recall last month, when you were watching the seagull thermalling, and you asked how it stayed up, I said

I'd show you later?"

"Vaguely."

"It reminded me of a conversation we were having, before, when we were out walking, and I drew airflow sketches, in the dust, do you remember that?"

"When you were trying to explain how gulls could fly along the cliffs without flapping?"

"That's it, well, if they've put in the extra bits I asked for, this is the final part of the explanation."

"I'm glad you know what you are talking about, I don't!"

"You will have to wait a little while longer, then you will understand."

Vince read the label, saw the dispatch address, "Solar Sailplanes? It's not a toy plane, is it?"

"No, it's not a toy." She half-answered, then added "Treat it gently!" as he gave it a vigorous shake.

"There's not much in here, it's too light!" he put it on the table, "Fancy a coffee?"

"Yes, please. I'll be in the garden."

Halfway to the kitchen door, the 'phone rang, so Vince

616

made a 180' turn, and went back to the table. Ten minutes later, he took two steaming cups outside, one for George, and sat on the wall, watching her. She was engrossed in the business of trying to make weeds die, and flowers grow, and not the other way around, as seemed to be the case.

"That was our G.P on the 'phone. He wants to come and give me an M.O.T. The hospital has been on to him, and as we haven't seen him, he couldn't give them an answer. So, he'll be here at about four."

"That's fine by me." She was chopping at the brambles with a spade. "I wish these bloody things would die!"

"You could always go and get your Magnum, and shoot them!" he suggested, unhelpfully.

"Fun-ny, Ha Ha!" The spade hit a rock with a loud clang, and drew sparks. She dropped it, shaking her wrist. "Ouch!"

"It's your own fault! You're thrashing at it, like a wild thing. Anyway, who's going to teach you to fly the toy aeroplane, when you've built it?"

"No-one, and it's not a toy. I learned to fly them when I spent eighteen months at Kinloss, in Scotland. I put in more

617

hours flying models than I did the Nimrods. It was either that, climb mountains, or be rude to sheep!"

"And you don't have the fittings for that!"

"You have a one track mind, I wasn't meaning the bit with the wellies!"

"You've tried it, then?"

"No, I have not!" she declared, vehemently.

"Then there must have been something in the toy plane thing that kept you amused!"

"Drink your coffee, I put bromide in it."

"If you don't collect yours, sharpish, I'll drink that, as well."

"Or was it arsenic?"


The G.P. arrived and took Vince through to the bedroom, where he checked the things that G.P's check, Weight, blood, heart, lungs, cough!. He was sitting in his car, writing up his notes, when George came round the corner of the cottage, carrying her spade.

"Well, Doctor, will he live?"

"I'm astounded at his progress, Miss. Whatever it is that you are doing, it is working marvelously. Vincent has more than doubled his body-weight in the last three months, and none of it is fat! You knew him before the – ah - accident. Does he seem any different, to you?"

"It's funny that you should ask that, he does. Before, he was passive, subservient, even. A bit like a lump of plasticene, but now, he's positive, vibrant, aggressive - "

"Violent?"

"No, that's the wrong aggressive. He's never laid a finger on me, I mean 'Go for it' aggressive, not 'let's leave it, and see'. He's the same, but he's different. I can't really explain it."

"Is he angry about what happened?"

"No, not at all. It's as though it happened to someone else. At first, he was very frustrated, when his body wouldn't follow his wishes, but that is over, now. He seems to be more aware, and knowledgeable, than before, and is always looking to learn more."

"Like, maybe, he has discarded the bad bits of himself, and made room for more of the good bits?"

She thought about that for a moment. "Yyyyes, something like that!"

"That isn't a new thing, you know. It usually happens to survivors of some brain damage accidents, and occasionally coma people, too."

"Oh."

"Don't worry about it." The Doctor hesitated, something about her eyes, and her stance, caught his eye. "Tell me something, are you and he - lovers?"

"Yes, why?"

" Ah, it's none of my business, but have you felt a bit off-colour in the mornings, recently?"

"Now and then, why?"

"Have you missed any periods?"

"Yes, but I always was erratic, and if you knew what had been going on around here, you'd know why. - Oh! You mean -." She patted her belly. "No way Jose, he told me he went to the 'Vet' years ago!"

"When you add two and two, and insist that the answer is not four, buy a calculator!"

"Eh? Oh, alright, but it will be negative."

"Come and see me, when you've done the test, hey?" He finished jotting his notes, dotted 'I's, crossed 't's, and started the car engine. "Next week, some time."

"Yes, alright, if you insist. I'll see you. Thanks for calling."

The G.P. shuffled his car round a thirty-six point turn in the narrow lane, waved, and drove off, leaving George leaning on the spade, adding two and two, and getting four.

Vince found her sitting on the garden wall, gazing across the fields, with an odd expression on her face, a mix of amusement, surprise, and horror, overlaid with confusion. "Hey! What's up?"

"Hmm? Oh, nothing, really. Just something the Doc said."

"Good, or bad?"

"I don't know, yet. If he's right, and I'm wrong, it means a change of plans! Is there a late night chemist in Holyhead?"

"I don't know. There will be, in Bangor, but I don't know where, why?"

"Oh, I just need some things, and I forgot to go today."

"Well, let's get the Landie out, and go and find one. I'll ask

Tommy to stay around, not that he goes anywhere!"

"I've noticed that, too. I'm starting to think he's fallen in love with the area."

Chapter thirty-one.

Surprise!

George peed inaccurately into the little bottle, splattering her water everywhere, but captured enough for the test. After a quick sponge down and mop dry - to repair the damage - she washed her hands again, then took the little spatula from its packet and dunked it in the urine, then watched in amazement/horror as the chemical impregnated onto its tip changed colour. "Four!" she muttered.

"Are you playing golf, in there? Vince demanded, hurry up, I'm bursting!"

Ten minutes later, she was sitting across the table from

Vince, wondering how to tell him.

"Alright, I give up. What did the test show?" he asked.

"You guessed?"

"Well, when a woman talks to a Doctor, then suddenly decides to call in at a chemist's shop, it's either thrush, or a test kit."

"The test says that I'm pregnant."

"Good! Who's the father?"

"You are!"

"Me? No way! I told you, I was snipped, years ago, and I'm firing blanks!"

"I hope you will believe me when I say I've been with nobody else."

"Not even once?"

"Not even once!"

"Then either I'm Daddy, or it's a miracle! And if it's the first option, it's still a miracle!"

"Perhaps you aren't as sterile as you think."

"I am, or was, rather. When Joe grew into a bump, I had myself re-tested, and scored zero. Anyway, an Angle, or a Saxon, doesn't make a frizzy haired child with a built in sun-tan!"

"That's true."

"I knew then that she was available to anyone she fancied."

"This one," George patted her belly, "won't be chocolate, or yellow. It really is ours, you and me."

"There is one thing left to consider, no, two."

"Termination? I don't think so. I wasn't planning on being a Mum, but I couldn't end it, unless it is damaged. It might be our only chance!"

"We agree on that, then."

"What's the other question?"

"Pink, or blue?"

"Pink or blue what?"

"Decoration, in the nursery!"

"How the hell do I know? What nursery?"

"It's the guest room, right now."

"I thought maybe you might like to shove it into the old coal-shed, and then you won't hear it crying for its feed at three a.m.!"

624

"Now that's a thought!"

There was a mutual pause, then Vince asked, "What was the 'fore' for?"

"Not 'fore', as in golf, four as in two and two. The Doc said, if you add two and two, and deny the answer is four, buy a calculator."

"Eh? - Oh, I get it, calculator, test kit!"

"Two and two's four."

Tommy tapped on the door, then came in. "Meal in five minutes, please!"

"Thanks, Tommy. Have we any wine in?"

"Think not, just sparkling grape juice."

"That'll do, we're celebrating, tonight."

"So?"

"George and I are going to be parents!"

Tommy looked puzzled, then made scissors with his fingers.

"Yes, I was, but I seem to be un-snipped!"

"Crappy nappies, and screaming fits, and you both look pleased! Ah, well!" he shook his head, and returned to his pans.

625

"Should we ask him to be Godfather?" George giggled.

Vince choked back a snort of amusement. "There are worse people!"

"Aren't you going to deny you put it there, because - ?"

"That would be a waste of breath. You said there has been nobody else. I believe you. I don't know why you DIDN'T find someone else, but as you said you didn't, you didn't."

"I didn't, because I wanted you! While there was a chance, I waited. I was tempted once or twice, but I didn't succumb. If you'd been dead, then maybe things might have been different, but you weren't, so I cried myself to sleep instead."

Tommy tapped on the door, and came in, carrying a candle in a glass, and some dandelion flowers in a jam-jar that he had decorated with kitchen tissue. "Instant posh restaurant!" He went out again, and returned with a bucket, inside which was the bottle of 'fizz', wrapped in a bag of frozen peas.

"Will you join us?" George invited.

"Not this time, Miss, I running in and out to cook, change of plan, something extra-special!"

Afterwards, with the dandelions wilting, and the candle flickering as it burned low, the bottle lay 'dead' in it's nest of half-thawed frozen peas, used in lieu of ice-cubes. George sighed. "I don't know how he managed to turn sausage and chips into an exotic meal, but he did!"

"MM. More magic! Do you want to sit outside for a while, and feed the mossies, or do you want the telly on? I'll put the aerial up."

"Neither. It's been a long day. Take me to bed, and cuddle me to sleep, I'm shattered."

"Alright." He stood, walked round the table, picked her up in his arms, and carried her into the bedroom, where he stripped her, kissed her, thoroughly, and then lay her down. They were both asleep in less than a minute.

Once they had settled, Tommy came into the main room, cleared the table, washed up, then retired to his van, where he dozed, keeping a listening watch while they slept. You didn't need to be psychic to know there was a storm in the offing, and they would need all their strength to overcome it.

Sergeant Jones was in a foul temper. He had finally finished all the paperwork at midnight, and managed to get to bed at one thirty, only to be rudely awakened by the telephone. Jacko had the night shift at the station, and had barely settled into the routine when he was deluged with 'phone calls from higher echelons. He had successfully fielded them all - until this last one. The Commissioner, himself, wanted Sergeant Jones, and everyone else involved in this mess, at Bangor nick at eight-o-clock. Constables do not argue with Commissioners!

At ten to, they were all in the largest interview room, in their best uniforms, waiting. Eight came, and went, as did nine. At ten-thirty, the little Martinet strutted in, glared at the assembly as though they were something a dog had rejected, and slapped his thigh with his cane. His stare skewered each man in turn, making them look away and fidget, except Sergeant Jones, who was sure he could still see orange dye in the deeper creases of the man's face. The Martinet strutted out again, and marched off down the corridor.

"Was that it? 'Pimples' Jones queried, "What a waste of time!"

628

"Hush, son," responded the Sergeant, "That's just the prelude, is it!"

Footsteps sounded outside, and the Martinet strutted back in and stepped smartly sideways, to leave the door clear, then snapped to attention. The Commissioner strolled in behind him, with all his gold braid sparkling. "Relax, lads, this Gentleman wishes to speak to you. Remember, this meeting has not taken place. It did not happen. He stepped aside as well, to allow access to a pear-shaped individual, in the city uniform of three-piece pin-stripes, bowler hat, and brolly.

"Right, men. I know who you are, and you don't need, or want, to know who I am. It is sufficient for you to know that I swing a much bigger stick than you." He looked at the Martinet, who cringed, and fiddled with his malacca cane. "I have been kept informed of the activities of various sections in this area who are all involved in tripping over each other while the criminals go about their nefarious business unchecked. The latest cock-up ended with a dead body. The one before that caused three Customs and Excise men, one injured, to be arrested while under-cover in the field, - where are they?"

"In the cells, Sir!" The Martinet snapped.

"Well, get them in here, you silly man! I don't intend saying this all, twice over!"

"Do you want those two Specials in here, as well?"

"Do I have to repeat myself? I understood that you were ready for me. Really! If you waste any more of my time - !"

The Martinet left, not tick-tocking, but hurrying smartly! He was back in a few minutes, and five more men crowded into the room, leaving the Martinet stuck in the doorway with two more P.C's lurking behind his shoulder.

"Is everyone here, this time?" The suit asked.

The two Specials glared at the three Customs men, one of whom had an arm in a sling.

"As I started to say, before - you don't know me, and don't want to. There has been too much back-stabbing and inter-departmental squabbling, and no results, because you have all been watching the wrong people. There have also been a lot of cock-ups, and a large amount of unauthorized equipment has been in circulation.

Now, enough is enough, and I have had more than enough.

630

You are now all one team, commencing immediately, like it or not. MY team. You stay in your same groups, because you know each other, but you will all, and I mean all, co-ordinate through Sergeant Jones, who is the only person who seems to be successfully in charge of anything, and has made useful connections. He reports directly to the Commissioner, and he, to me. Instructions will flow in the reverse direction. Nobody else is told. Nobody else gives orders. Nobody, and I mean nobody, will have fire-arms, bombs, rockets, funny radio sets, spy kits, or any other such gadgetry. Nobody will go off half-cocked, because they are playing at being S.A.S. hit squads, you aren't good enough! You!" he pointed at Trevor, "were crippled by an eight stone female." Trevor drew breath to respond.

"Shut up! I'm talking, and you are listening. Then there's you. Those specks on your face aren't black-heads. I believe you are lucky to have a neck under your mouth, which is drooping disgustingly open. Now you! You were supposedly on watch, and despite the fact that your private bugging system was installed, you were taken out like a two-week apprentice being sent for a long wait! Your partner was worse. He walked into it, with his eyes wide open, and even exchanged pleasantries with the person he was supposed to be spying on, or rather, NOT supposed to be spying on, as you were watching the wrong people, again, even though such actions had not been authorized. You," he pointed at Pete, "had a private armoury stashed in your truck, and seem to have mislaid certain pieces of radio equipment. I think I know where they now are, and there they will stay, consider it a gesture of compensation. A document will be prepared, stating that the possessor is the owner, and it will be delivered by Sergeant Jones. I do not normally condone 'borrowing' from my staff, but such events seem to have become standard practice, I refer to a particular mislaid hand-gun and a quantity of ammunition for it. As no record of its issue can be found, I cannot say for certain who lost it, or where it is, but I do know that a body in the mortuary is a silent witness as to its location, despite the record stating that he was killed with his own pea-shooter. Therefore I cannot press for its return, and can only hope that the present owner is more careful with it than the previous one! You," he pointed at Geordie again, "were foolish enough to give away your I.D. card. That it was a false one is

632

irrelevant. As for your partner, the only intelligent thing he has done so far is go off on sick leave! I know how he received a hole in his leg, last year, who put it there, what with, and why. I also know that you tried driving across a tidal mud-flat in a sports-car, though heaven only knows why. As it was your own car, I cannot do anything about it, but I do not expect to see any bills regarding the cost of its repair or rescue passing across my desk. They will not be approved! You two, hovering outside the door with your ears flapping, have just been conscripted as paper shufflers, form fillers, and telephone answerers. I don't care what you were supposed to be doing, if you have the time to hang around listening to private conversations you have too much time to spare, and I can see that right now you are doing nothing at all! That leaves you!" he pointed at the Martinet, "I have a very thick file on you, detailing all your conniving, ducking, diving, and maneuvering. You have contributed nothing at all. You are a waste of space. Go away. If I see you again anywhere near my team, I will have you scrubbing out the drunk-tank in your pretty orange uniform!

Now, the first thing you are all, and I mean all, going to do, is put in individual reports, including all the little details that you carefully left out of the previous ones. Start from when you were originally given the mission. Dates, times, who said it, anything you have in writing - everything. The reports are to be on Sergeant Jones' desk, at nine a.m, complete with copies of all documents, photographs, video or audio tapes, and such. In your cases," - he indicated Pete and Trevor, "I will accept a rough draft, as you have a lot of material to collate, with the full report to follow in a few days. Until everybody else has put in a full report, none of you are to leave this building under any pretext, Sergeant Jones is exempted, as he has a previous commitment, and other work to complete. If any of you has any sensible suggestions, put it in your report. Are there any questions?"

"Yes, Sir, with respect, I am booked in at the hospital in the morning for a follow-up x-ray on my shoulder."

"Very well, get straight back here afterwards, no diversions, side-tracks, or private missions! Anything else? No? Right, then, the largest room with tables, here, is the canteen. Cup rings, breadcrumbs, grease blobs, jam smears and chocolate fingerprints on the reports will be severely punished!

Commissioner, Sergeant Jones, remain here, please, the rest of you, move it!"

They went.

"Sergeant Jones, I want, from you, a rota that ensures that there are always two of your five men, including those two I commandeered just now, but not yourself, on duty in this building. You are to be available, twenty-four hours a day, seven days. If you are not here, you will be in radio or telephone contact, so leave the numbers of all the places you are likely to be, understood?"

"Yes, Sir."

"Right, off you go. Close the door, behind you, and keep that idiot with the little stick out of my way, or I may be tempted to insert it into a place that will make sitting down very uncomfortable for him!"

"Sir!"

Chapter thirty-two.

Another piece.


The interphone on the Commissioner's desk buzzed.
"Have we wrung anything from that man in cell six yet?"

"No, Sir. We are still waiting for the Norwegian
Ambassador's representative. I think the best we can expect is a
P.N.G. and a ticket home, for him."

"P.N.G?"

"Persona Non Grata, Sir."

"Yes, of course, I should have known that one! Call me if
you get anything."

"Yes, Sir."

"Excuse me!" the Commissioner's Secretary broke in,
"I've just heard that the Diplo is being flown to Valley, courtesy
of the R.A.F. He should be landing about now."

"Thank you."

"Is someone meeting him with a car?"

"Sergeant Jones sent Tick-tock, in the Granada."

"Who?"

"Tick-tock, Sir, the prick with the stick!"

"Ah, yes!" The suit chuckled, "That's about all he's good for, a chauffeur!"

"If he doesn't get lost! I'll call if we get anywhere."

"Right."


George was feeling distinctly dreadful, this morning. They had decided that she was no more than eight weeks gone, and she was trying to decide if she was really ill or just thought she was ill, because she knew!

Vince was watching her poking a spoon at a few corn-flakes that were floating in a dribble of milk, while he surrounded a bowl-full. She suddenly bolted for the loo, and he heard her calling into the porcelain telephone for someone called 'Hughie'. He resolved to keep out of the way for a while. Tommy had gone into town, being a tourist for once, not shopping, or maybe he was keeping out of the way, too!

"Oh, god!" she groaned, as she resumed her seat, looking

distinctly green around the eyes, "I hope this isn't going to last another seven months!"

"You're seeing the Doc at three. Perhaps he can prescribe something for you. Try a dry cream cracker, and a glass of water."

"What did your ex do?"

"Betty ate like the pig she was, salmon and whipped cream sarnies, and chucked up!"

"No bloody wonder!"

"Then she had a spell of custard and pickles, on toast, and chucked up!" The last bit was shouted, as George was on the way to call on the telephone, again.

She came back with two tumblers of water.

"Two?"

"One's for you!" She threw it over him. "You rotten sod!"

"Greasy bacon, dripping with fat! Fried eggs swimming in lard!"

."UUUrp!" she barely made it.

Vince went into the bedroom to change into some dry clothes.

638

The Coroner's report on Sergeant Jones' desk stated that the deceased had died of a gunshot wound to the upper body which had severed the Aorta. Death was almost instantaneous. There were hypodermic marks in all the usual places, some of which were infected, or abscessed. There were traces of amphetamines in the blood. The liver showed signs of heavy alcohol abuse, indicating the early stages of jaundice. There were also signs of another blood disorder, possibly Weill's, or syphilis, but the tests were inconclusive. Samples had been dispatched for better analysis. The Coroner concluded that the deceased had only been shortened in his life-span by six to nine months.

"Good riddance!" Sergeant Jones mused, as he added his copy to the file.

Trevor had writer's cramp. As he massaged his aching fingers, trying not to jar his aching shoulder, he watched Pete doodling on the acquired blackboard, trying to link up the various names and actions with coloured lines, hoping for a pattern to emerge.

"Who is Jimmy?"

639

"I'm buggered if I know! It's a name I've heard, or read, somewhere, but I can't find it in this lot." Pete waved a hand at a precariously wobbly stack of papers. "But it's come from somewhere. I've got a hunch that he's the spider in the centre of this web of deceit. Somewhere, I've read, or heard, someone saying 'Jimmy'll fix it', or 'Jimmy'll sort it'. Something like that!"

"And this dead guy, in the park?"

"I can't tie him in anywhere, but somehow I think he was this 'Jimmy's' fixer, and he was 'retired' because he failed to fix it."

"Hmm. It feels right. So you think that 'Park bench' sent 'Norway' and 'dead one', and because they failed, he was -- Hey! Maybe he sent the previous ones, as well, and because they ALL failed, he was taken out! Which means --?"

"There's another team involved. They may be harder than the previous ones, and with a different controller." Pete scribbled 'Park bench' into a box on the line connecting 'Jimmy' to 'Norway' and 'corpse', then linked 'Park bench' to 'Other mob, and to 'Watcher', added a new line to a box, labelled 'Control 2', and 'New mob', then took a pace back, to study the mess anew.

Trev picked up the 'phone, and dialled an internal number, "Sarg, can you spare a minute? I think we've stumbled onto something!"

Sergeant Jones studied the spaghetti on the green blackboard as Trevor took him through the thought processes, and it felt right, somehow. "Right. Tidy it up, put it onto paper, and I'll pass it on up the line. I think a warning to Miss Weastey, and Mr. Birtwhistle is in order, too."

"How about putting a bouncer on their doorstep?"

"No, I don't think so. That would just tell the opposition that we are waiting for them, and so far they've done alright on their own! You, Pete whatsits, have you got an operating manual for that radio you lost?"

"It's not lost, it's on permanent loan!"

"If that makes you feel better about it, just don't try borrowing it back!"

"No, thanks. I don't want any holes poked into me from that cannon she hasn't got that is stashed away somewhere!

There's a hand-written supplement to the manual, too, why?"

"I want them. Yesterday."

"I've just had a thought. She's got a radio, we've got a radio. If we arrange a frequency, they want us, they yell, we turn up, pronto, and we can talk to them, direct, if anything develops."

"Yes. Do it!"

"I'll put it with the manual. Give me a minute to dig it out of my pile of junk, now the truck's been confiscated."

"You see! We all know little bits that on their own don't go anywhere, but when you put them all together --! Get me that manual. I'm going to see 'The Boss' in a few minutes, and I'll drop it off, on the way back."

The 'phone rang, and Pete answered it. "The gate says 'Tick-tock' just brought the V.I.P. in."

"Right!"


Geordie was up to his armpits in filth and grease. He was just about finished with the dismantling of his beloved M.G.B, and ready to start cleaning all the salt, mud, and green slime

642

from it, following it's dunking in the harbour. As he worked, he was cursing steadily. Cursing the garage, who appeared to have dragged his car through every bit of smelly muck they could manage as they hauled it back to the launching ramp. Cursing the old man who had sat on the fishing boat - which was well afloat by then, laughing his rotten socks off and jeering. Cursing the recovery service which had taken until today to carry his "B" the eight miles from there to here, leaving it exposed to the ravages of the salt that was rotting the body-work. Cursing the sharp edges hidden under the filth which persistently cut his knuckles and chewed lumps out of his fingers. Cursing this stupid job which sent him off on a wild goose chase following the wrong Land-Rover, while the people he thought he was behind were safely in their cottage, the tapes from the bugs proved that. Cursing again, because they were the wrong people, anyway! And cursing, because he felt thoroughly pee'd off because he had been publicly whipped by an amateur, again! The spanner he was wielding slipped off the nut buried in the greasy muck, and another rivulet of his blood joined its fellows, and a particularly vicious epithet was flung into the delicate ears of the

643

passing V.I.P.

Tick-tock strutted up. "Mind your language, Constable!"

"Piss off, dick-head! I'm not a bloody P.C." Geordie
snarled, waving the mud, grease, and gore spattered spanner
under the Martinet's nose, "Or I'll wipe it on your pretty suit!"
His phrasing was less than eloquent, as he was rather stressed
out.

"Really! I will be forced to report you to your superiors!"

"Good. Then while you are doing it, I'll be left in peace.
Sod off!"

Sergeant Jones, leaning through an upstairs window,
having a sly cigarette in the no-smoking office-block, called
down- "If I were you, I'd give that man a wide berth. He's been
beaten up by a slip of a girl, and his precious baby's poorly, is
it?"

Tick-tock looked up, saw the owner of the voice, not that it
needed identifying, and saw the blue plume appear as he spoke.
He decided to make the enforcing of the no-smoking rule his
personal crusade. Geordie sneered at him as he strutted off,
guiding the V.I.P. to the hospitality suite, aka the canteen.

Sergeant Jones sighed, and continued enjoying his cigarette.

Geordie broke the seal securing the carburettor to the manifold, and successfully emptied half a pint of petrol-smelling salt-water into his left shoe. The air became bluer than Sergeant Jones' breath.

"I hope," the Sergeant called down, "that you will have that disgusting mess cleaned up by tomorrow morning, and all that scrap disposed of properly!" He retired to the dubious safety of his office as the courtyard rang to a fresh string of Anglo-Saxon dockyard phrases.

The two 'bug-men' Specials were in the canteen, in the darkest recess they could find. Their department head, from whom they had been sequestered rather abruptly, had given them a comprehensive chewing out, then sent them on their way until they were returned to their normal duties. He was not so much worried by the unauthorized bugging, but by the way they had been caught, so easily! He wasn't exactly delighted by the lack of useful information they had gleaned, either. What little there was only served to indicate the innocence of the people they were watching, and also gave them an alibi for another occasion, to boot! The two had roughed out their report, then had it typed for them, as they were one-finger typists. On re-reading it, they realized how lame it seemed. How lame THEY seemed. What the report lacked was the name of the person who had given them the mission. They had tracked down the original written instruction, but there was a corner missing, now, that hadn't been, before. Someone was covering his back. No other copies had come to light, other than a photocopy of the one with the missing corner. Forensics had been at it with the fluorograph, and come up negative. There were no other useable marks on the paper, which was a regular sheet of A4, of which there were many reams in the store-cupboard. There were no useable fingerprints on it either, not even a partial, it was a solid mass of overlapping prints, and was a total mess. The missing piece had been subjected to excessive torsional force - in other words, torn off.

Vince opened the box. Instead of there being a body and a wing to fit together, there was a large sheet of paper, printed with a mass of criss-cross lines, and obscure notes. Beneath it there lay a bundle of assorted thin sticks, and some thin planks of wood, again with printing on them. In one corner was a plastic bag with some odd-shaped plastic pieces, a few screws, and some bits of bent wire. He studied the wooden pieces, but couldn't see anything he recognized as being part of an aeroplane. The other box was no help, either. There was a black plastic box, with two levers on ball-joints, a switch, and a volt-meter, on its top surface, assuming the volt-meter went at the top! Below, and to the insides of, the two levers were four little knobs that could be pushed up and down slots. There were also four little caramel-coloured rectangular boxes, with a square knob on top, and another box with a thin wire at one end, and a row of sockets at the other. There was also a folded-down telescopic aerial. An 'Operator's Manual' lurked in a corner, so he pulled it out, and studied it. After two pages of apparent gibberish, he gave up, and put it back. For all the sense it made, it might have been written in Serbo-Croatian. Tucked into an un-used space in the box were a few tubes of different adhesives, and a sheathed scalpel.

George came out of the bathroom, hesitated, and went back in, just as a siren 'dee-dahh'ed' briefly, outside, and a police van turned into their driveway. "George! He called, we've got company!"

The only reply was a strained "Bleaaagh!"

He sighed, opened the door, dodged into the kitchen, put the kettle on to boil, and was back in his wheel-chair, before the visitor reached the door.

Vince waved Sergeant Jones to a chair, abandoned the wheel-chair, and went to brew up. When he came back, the Sergeant had the plan unrolled, and was studying it. "Hope you don't mind!" he said "I had a go at this game, a couple of years ago, It kept me busy for a while, but I never mastered the steering bit, is it? I could build them, no problem, but they wouldn't stay up for more than a few seconds, so I got lots of practice at re-building them!"

"I've never made one. It's George's idea. I've only just opened it, and I can't make anything out at all. I was expecting a few parts to clip together, like those kid's plastic ones, but --!"

The Sarge chuckled, "No! It isn't that easy. Look, now, this piece goes here, and this, here, -" he put a few sticks onto the plan, along the printed lines, "Then these go here, across these first pieces. Those are the spars, and these, the ribs, just like your backbone and ribs." He slotted a curved piece of plank with notches cut out of it, taken from one of the printed planks, over the sticks he'd already laid out. The sticks fitted into the notches. "See! The big one here, and tapering down to the smallest one, at the other end. Then some more spars on top. This rounded bit goes here, and this triangular piece at the back, like this. There are a few more bits and pieces, but that's half a wing. Simple, is it"

Vince studied it some more, then the patterns on the paper clicked into place. "Aha! I see it, now. This other lot of lines is the other half, printed overlapping, to save space! "

"You've got it, boyo. Once you know what you're looking at, it's straight-forward. The hard bit comes later! Has your lass made any?"

"She says so. With luck, she'll be out in a minute, she's not feeling too good, this morning."

"Oh, something she's eaten, is it?"

"No, rather something she hasn't eaten, she's got morning sickness."

"Ah, that's nasty. My wife swears by pickled eggs, and coal-dust butties. It doesn't work!"

"The funny thing is, she wasn't sick until she found out!"

"Psycho - er - whatsits, in the head."

"The tea will be done, by now, do you fancy one?"

"Now that's what I call a good idea. I knew I came here for something!"

"George, Cup of tea?"

"Bleaagh!"

"Perhaps not!"

"Got it bad, has she?"

"It seems so." The 'phone rang. "Excuse me a minute." Vince picked up the hand-set. "Oh, hello, Joan. Yes. No. No. Of course, any time! Yes. That's right. Oh? We have, too. Yes. O.K., see you later. Yeah. Bye!" - "George? Joan's coming down, later today."

"Bleagh-cough!" The loo flushed, then the sound of a tap running, and water splashing. George came into the room, her face wet, white, and pasty. She flopped into a chair. "Oh god!"

"You'll get over it, my dear." Sarg put in.

"When? Eight months?"

"No, dear, a day or two, then your pipes will get used to the idea, and settle down. Forget food, just drink gallons of water, so you don't get dehydrated, and you'll be alright. Some will come back, and some will go through."

"I see you've made a start on the balsa bird."

"No, not me!" Vince denied it, "I was baffled. Sarge - er?"

"Llewellyn, - Lew."

"Lew showed me how it fitted together. I can see it, now, though."

"You've forgotten the wing joiners. It will be tricky getting them in, now."

"No, lass, nothing is glued. It's just sort of resting together."

"Ah, good, urp, scuse! I presume you've made a few?"

"As I was saying, Miss, I can build them, but they won't fly for me."

"Call me George. I can see I shall have to start a flying

651

club, there are three members, already!"

"Come to think of it, there's one I never started, in the cubby-hole. I could be tempted."

"Have you ever tried scuba-diving?"

"No way, lass, the bath's quite deep enough for me!" He poured the last of his tea down his throat, "Ah! Thanks for that! I must be on my way, now!"

"Before you go, Lew, what did you call round for?"

"Bloody hell! It's a good job you asked, Vince! I've got a letter for you. I was going to ask Jones the Post to drop it in, but I had to go to Llandyfrydog, just up the way, where is it?" he patted various pockets, "ah, there!" the produced a crumpled manila, and passed it over. "Must be off, now. There's detail of a call-up arrangement, in there, and a few other bits and pieces. He let himself out of the door, and went to his van. Vince watched him drive off, then turned, to see George sample a few drops of tea, followed by a feeble 'urp!' moments after.

"Can you take yourself to the Doc's? I'll have to stay in for Joan, unless Tommy comes back."

"Of course I can, I'll have to - urp - drive, anyway, as you aren't insured!"

"That's a mere technicality!" he slid a finger under the envelope flap, and tore it open. Inside was a dog-eared manual for his recently acquired radio, with hand-written notes detailing some modifications, plus instructions on how to call up the unofficial transmitter frequencies. There was also a tatty receipt, for the purchase of the radio set. The serial number tallied with the one on the case, when he checked. It was dated three years ago, and bore his signature. The shop which appeared to have 'sold' him the set had been a business that had 'gone bust' very publicly, two years ago.

"Just look at that!" he exclaimed, showing it to George.

"What do you expect? They could hardly knock on the front door, and ask for their toy back!"

"I'll have to get a proper aerial for it."

"Won't that bit of wire you use for the other one, do?"

"For listening, yes, it's adequate for that, but not if I want to use the transmitter. If the wire didn't melt, the transmitter would go bang!"

"Why?"

"It's all to do with resonant lengths, matching wavelengths, and stuff. I could explain it, but I'd just blind you with science."

"In other words, you don't know, either!"

"No, you're wrong. It's just difficult to explain, like - er, - putting this 'plane together. Words are all well and good, but until someone shows you, it's just a mess of sticks. You know how the B.B.C. describes its stations as so many hundred metres long wave, and I've used ham frequencies of eighty, ten and two?"

"Yes."

"Well, that's the wavelength. How long one radio wave is, and how long the aerial needs to be, to work properly."

"But my trannie hasn't got an aerial, at all, and that works, although it isn't very good in this spot, for some reason. It works in the garden, though!"

"It does have an aerial. It's a very thin wire, wound up on a special metal bar, inside the box."

"Oh." She thought about it, "but what waves?"

"The electric current in the aerial wire. You know how mains electric is A.C, alternating current?"

"Er, sort of, I've heard the name."

"Well, the generator at the power station sends pushes and pulls of electric down the wire, the push sends the electrons one way round, and the pull sends them the other. Are you with me, so far?"

"Just about."

"Right, then. At the point where there is neither push nor pull, that's zero volts. Imagine a straight line, with a start point." Vince sketched a line in the air. "Call that zero volts, too. Now, the generator starts to push. The power builds up to a peak, then sinks down to zero again, as the push stops. Then there is a pull, so make another peak, but on the other side of the zero line, so you have a shape like a stretched out 'S', with the zero line through it, like a dollar sign. That's one wave, or cycle. Mains electric is fifty cycles, or dollars, in each second of time."

"So what's the 240 volts bit?"

"That's how far up from zero the wave comes up, before it starts back down."

"If you say so. But if the electric is pushed, then pulled, the same bit keeps wiggling back and to, why doesn't it get used

655

up?"

"It does, and it doesn't! The electrons go so fast, that they go all the way round in an 'n'th' of a second, so the used ones get replaced with new ones, from the generator."

She grappled with the mental imagery. "Alright, but what's the Megs I've heard you talk about?"

"That's just a quick way of measuring big numbers of cycles per second. There was a big row, a few years back, about who discovered electrical waves. In the end some guy called Hertz got the blame, - -"

"The car rental man?"

"No! A different Hertz! Long before him! - And what was called cycles became called Hertz. It's still the same thing, but with a different name. So, Hertz, cycles, waves, or wiggles, per second is long, slow, stuff. Kilo, or thousand, Hertz, is a bit faster, then it's Mega, or million, faster still, then Giga, or million million. So, long wave is about 250 Hertz, or waves, per second. Radio One, for example, is around one point two Megs, or one million, two hundred, Hertz per second, that's in the medium wave band. Eighty metres is equal to about three point

656

five Megs, Ten metres is around twenty-eight Megs, two metres is one hundred and fourty-something Megs, and a microwave cooker works at around one centimetre wavelength, up in the Giga range, along with radar, and stuff like that. Do you still follow me?"

"Just about, give me time to absorb it." She sipped the cold tea. "Urp! Damnit! So why does the length of the wire matter?"

"That's the easy bit, follow me, and I'll show you." He crooked a finger, and led her to the back garden, where he unhooked the nearest end of the clothes-line from the wall. It hung in a slack arc from his hand to the post about twenty feet away. "Right, here's the aerial wire, or half of it. I'm the transmitter, o.k?"

"It's not wire, its rope!"

"I know - its pretend wire. Right now, I'm not transmitting anything, so there is no wave coming from me, and the rope aerial isn't moving. Now, watch!" He jerked his hand up and down again, sharply, making a ripple run along the length of rope to the post, where it 'bounced' off, and came back, making his hand jerk. "That was a wave being reflected, because it was the wrong length. Did you see how it made my hand jerk, when it came back?"

"Yes."

"If I had been a radio - that would have been a jerk of power going the wrong way. Now, watch this." Vince waved his rope hand, slowly from side to side, and after a bit of experimenting, had a long, thin 'S' shape in the rope, with the two curves swapping sides, in opposition, while the centre bit barely moved, his hand just moving a fraction to keep the 'wave' going. "There, that's one wavelength. See, there are no stray lumps or bumps, and I'm hardly doing any work to keep it going." He changed the tempo of his hand movements, and had four loops, or two 'S' shapes, along the rope. "Now, that's twice the resonant frequency, but I have to work a bit harder. I could get four times, and have eight 'S' shapes, but that's difficult. Or -" he slowed his hand movements right down, and had a single loop flipping from side to side, "That's half a wavelength. If you imagine another rope, of the same length, coming from the back of my hand, and going to a post behind me, with the same 'S' shape, you can picture an aerial working with radio waves."

She took the rope from him, and sent a ripple down the length. It bounced back off the post, and tugged the near end out of her light grasp.

"You just blew up! He chuckled, then rescued the end of the rope, and re-hooked it where it belonged.

"But, your wire doesn't wiggle about, nor does the telly aerial, unless the wind blows them."

"No. You're confusing the electrical wave with a mechanical wave. The rope was making a visual representation of the electrical voltage in the aerial, like I said before, from zero, to full power, and back to zero, then full reverse power, and back to zero. Have you realized that while we are messing about with this, you aren't feeling sick?"

She paused, brows furrowed. "I'm not, am I - UURP! Thanks for reminding me! Anyway, the telly aerial isn't a piece of wire, it's a squashed porcupine!"

"It's an optical illusion, too. Really, it's a short, stiff wire, this one, here, folded into a squashed 'O' Inside the plastic bit, there's a gap. The square pole doesn't connect to the 'O' Then there's this 'H' section, at the back, called the reflector. Just the crosspieces matter, the upright bits just support them. These in front are called directors, and they don't connect to anything, either. They direct the radio waves to the aerial, and these reflect them. It's done that way, so the aerial works like a torch, only backwards. The style is called a 'Yagi', invented by a Japanese scientist who was trying to make a death-ray! It will ignore radio waves coming from over here, but the ones from here," he moved around, "will be steered onto the aerial. Microwaves are fussy little buggers, and they get lost easily as well. They'd rather bounce off things and play, than go where they're sent. That's why radar works."

"Ah! That bit I understand. That's why radar can't see a plane that's behind a hill, or a tree!"

"Yes, that's it."

"And why VHF is 'line of sight'. Two people on the ground, using radios, can be out of range at two miles, yet an aeroplane high up, a hundred miles away, can talk to them both."

"That's right. VHF and UHF will go to the moon, but not down the street, yet with low HF, you can talk to Australia, but not the moon. There are layers of reflective gas, called the

660

Ionosphere, way up high, that reflect the long waves, but not the short ones."

"I've heard of that, somewhere, and something to do with sunspots."

"Yes. The more sunspots, the brighter the 'mirror' is. It is caused by radiation from the sunspots hitting the outside of the atmosphere. It's a radio mirror, don't forget, not a light mirror like in the bathroom!"

"I'd guessed that, or it would be dark all the time!"

"Clever clogs!"

"We did that in ground school, way back in nineteen tiddley-plonk."

"Nineteen when?"

"Tiddley-plonk. Pre-history, irrelevant. So why does the length of the wire matter?"

He sighed. "You've not followed it, have you? If the wire is too long, or too short, for the wavelength, the power bounces back, and fights the power coming out. That makes the transmitter work harder to achieve the same power level, and it can only do so much work. Work makes heat, too much heat, and bang! The poor little transistor gets mad-hot, and melts. If you take the mis-match to extremes, the reflected wave can be at exactly the same timing as the new outward wave, so 100% out combined with 100% in, ends up as 200%, or, if the two waves are in opposing polarity, or phase, you get zero out, despite the efforts of the transistor, and you get an even bigger bang!"

"What's opposite phase?"

"Imagine the wave in the rope - again, two peaks, one either side of zero, three zero points, start, middle, end?"

"Yes."

"Put a second wave on top of the first one, with the three zero's in the same places, but with the two peaks on opposite sides, like two ovals."

"Yes."

"What's the result?"

"Er!"

"Alright, do it mathematically. One hundred, add minus one hundred. What's the answer?"

"Nothing!"

"Exactly. One hundred percent work, no result."

"Oh. So, why doesn't your radio blow up when the wire's the wrong length, then?"

"That's because it's working on a slightly different principle. The radio isn't exciting the aerial, the aerial is exciting the radio, so it isn't so critical. If I had two wires, one the exact length for a particular frequency, and one that wasn't, you'd hear the difference in quality. The 'wrong' one would be noisier, and the 'right' one would give a stronger reading on the meter."

Tyres crunched on the gravel, round the front. "Here endeth the lecture, that's either Tommy, or Joan."

It was neither. Sergeant Jones met George at the gate. "I had a package for you, somewhere!" he muttered, "Where the hell is it?"

"You gave it to us, earlier." George reminded him.

"No, not that one, this is another. Oh, yes. It's in the back!" he went to the van, and took a supermarket plastic bag from the rear. "Pete said you might need this. It's cut to size already, whatever that means!"

"I think I know, thanks. We were just discussing that! Do you have time for another brew?"

"Not now, thanks. Must push on. Duty calls, etcetera, is it! See you!" Lew ducked into the van, shunted it around, and drove off.

George looked into the bag, and saw two coils of gleaming copper wire, some glass bits, and a coil of black wire, with a plug on the end. She took it to Vince, who was keeping out of sight, just in case, and told him it might be his aerial. "I wish I could figure out what is going on! One minute they're spying on us, and the next, they're helping us!"

"I don't think its Pete, Trevor, and co. It's whoever's at the top of the heap, pulling the strings."

The 'phone rang. George went in, and picked it up. "Hello? Oh, it's you. Yes, we got them, thanks. No, not yet, we've only just got it. Yes. Who? No, I don't think so. No, hang on. - .Vince?" she called, "Do you know anyone called "Jimmy"?"

"Jimmy? No, I don't think so, should I?"

"Pete thinks that Jimmy could be the string-puller."

"Jimmy? No - yes, maybe! James, Betty's new man is James - somebody, er -, Lancaster-Smytthe. He lives in a big house near the park near my ex-flat. I don't know his address, but Fleecem and Legget might, if that's any use."

George relayed the comments, and Fleecem's address. When she came out again, she added that it was unlikely to be relevant, as it was too much of a coincidence, but you never know!

"Well, he's rich enough! Vince was studying the cottage roof, what he could see of it, from the ground.

"What's doing?"

"I'm wondering where to put the centre-pole of the aerial, what to fasten it to, how to get up to it, in the first place, and where to run the coaxial cable."

"Hmm. Where's the pole, right now?"

"Your telly aerial's on it."

"Hey! That's my broom handle! You can't have that!"

"Have you any better ideas?"

"Yes. Leave it for now, and I'll see what I can arrange."


Three hours later, a short while after George had left for her medical appointment, the S.A.R. helicopter came thrashing over, zoomed round a couple of times, then came to a hover a few feet up above the field, just over the wall. The half-open side door was pushed fully open, then the crewman slid a few scaffolding poles out, gave a thumbs-up, and shut the door. The machine climbed higher, dipped its nose, and thrashed away. When it had gone, Vince climbed over the wall and dragged the poles back. One had a small sack taped to one end. Inside were some pole couplings, and a note, which read "Will these do?" signed by E.P.K.

Vince was rummaging in his tool-box, looking for a spanner to fit the clamp-bolts, when another car arrived. This time it was Joan.

Over a coffee and biscuits they made small talk, all the stuff people with nothing to say, say, while waiting for the main event. Joan was looking for a way to let Vince invite her to stay overnight, and Vince was looking for some hint that Joan wanted to stay.

"What were you doing, anyway?"

"I was putting up a radio aerial. Do you mind getting your hands dirty? I could do with some help."

"Isn't Tommy around, or George?"

"No, Tommy's off sight-seeing, and George has an appointment in town, they'll both be back later."

"The Doctor will say its positive! Give me a few minutes to put on something more suitable." Joan was wearing a white lace blouse, a short skirt, and a pair of stilts.

"O.K. Have you anything with you?"

"Always, just in case!"

When she came out again, more suitably dressed, Vince was untangling a coil of stiff yellow wire. One end of it was fixed to a thing on the end of a builder's pole. Another coil of the yellow wire was sprawled across the grass, with its other end trapped under a brick. Some black wire ran down the pole from the lump at the top, and went to a big tangle near the house wall. Strips of plastic loosely held the wire to the pole. A clothes line was also tied to the pole in a funny knot, just below the lump with all the wires on.

"I'm nearly ready." Vince said. "I just need to put the telly aerial on the top of the pole. If you want, you can thread the telly aerial wire down the pole, through the ties, like the other wire, starting at this end, and take the spare wire across to the house.

Won't they get mixed up? They're the same colour."

"No, they have different plugs on the ends. Ah! Got it!" With a twang, the yellow coils separated, and sprang apart. Vince took the loose end a few feet away, and trapped it under another brick, as he had done with the other coil. Then he lifted the end of the pole and propped it on a rickety old saw-horse that looked like a cast-off from the Roman invasion. After fiddling with a clamp-thing, he put the t.v. aerial on the top of the pole, pointing at his left foot. "That should be about right. I can turn the pole a bit, once it's up."

Joan, who hadn't a clue what he was talking about, agreed.

Vince made a loop in the two wires, close to the top of the pole, and then put another plastic strap round it, and them. When he pulled it tight, it made a noise like a zip fastener. Then he worked along the pole, positioning the wires and zipping, but left the bottom few slack. Finally, he went along again, snipping off the spare ends of the zippers.

"Right. Now comes the hard bit!" Vince gave Joan the end of the rope that had been flung across the grass. "Stand close to the wall, and when I tell you, pull on that! I'll push from this side, and with luck, the pole will drop into that hole, and stand up. If it keeps going, get out of the way. Don't try to catch it! O.K."

"This wall?"

"No. The house wall!"

"Oh!"


When George drove up, she saw Joan fiddling with a coil of the copper wire, while Vince was holding a fourty foot pole upright, near the garden wall.

"Aha!" He called. "You're just in time! Can you get that other coil and take it down the back, Every time I let go, the damn thing starts to topple!"

"This one?" George asked.

That's it."

"Where'd you get the poles from?"

"Your whirly-bird pals brought them, there's a note inside, for you, too signed by E.P.K.

"Oh! Paul Korderley!"

"Maybe. I'll give it to you in a minute. A bit further, that's it! You too, Joan. Trap the wires there. Right. I'll let go, and see what happens. Nothing did. The pole stayed upright, swaying slightly in the light breeze.

"Is that my clothes-line?" George had seen the rope.

"Yes, you can have it back in a minute! Now, if you'd back your Landie down here, I can stand on the roof-rack, and tighten these braces up."

"You're pushing your luck! First you steal my clothes-line, and now you want to tap-dance on my car roof!"

"If you'd stop moaning for long enough to notice things, you'll see your telly aerial is on the top of the pole, so no more snow-storms in the Sahara, or whatever! You love me, don't you?"

"Once too often, I think! But, if my telly works now, I'll forgive you!" She maneuvered the Land-Rover into position. "Will that do?"

"Perfect. What did the Doc. suggest?"

"Abstinence, in future!"

"I meant for the sickness!"

"Oh, a change of diet, and a few motion-sickness pills, to tide me over. I thought you'd never ask!"

"Ask what?"

"Exactly!"

"Well, - He was only confirming what we already knew!"

"Have you told Joan, yet?"

"He didn't need to. I thought maybe, last time I was down, and I knew, when I came in earlier." Joan replied. "Who did it?"

"Vince."

"But, I thought -!" She made scissors with her fingers.

"So did we!" Vince said, wryly.

"I took a sample of his - with me, for a double-check. The Doc's going to send it to the lab, and let us know. Has Vince fed you, yet?"

"Sort of. He was too busy playing with his pole."

"Well, come on, then, we'll get organized while he plays with it on his own!"

They both sniggered at the other implication, and went in.

Chapter thirty-three.

The light at the tunnel's end.


The Commissioner sighed, slapped the folder shut, and added it to the pile in his 'out' tray, before taking off his reading glasses then kneading his forehead, and the bridge of his nose. "Damn!" He spat the word at the print of a daisy in a jam-jar, hanging slightly off-square on the wall opposite his desk. "Damn, damn, damn!" He buzzed through on the desk intercom, and asked for a fresh coffee to be brought through to him, then stood, walked round his desk, and adjusted the picture. Then he turned to stare, unseeing, through the window at the water of the bay, while his brain assimilated the material he had ploughed through. The coffee came. "Take those with you, please." He waved at the files. "No, not that one!" He indicated Sergeant Jones' resume of all the other files. When the door snicked shut, he sighed again, and broke wind, vaguely wondering why everything the canteen offered up as substitutes for food nowadays made him flatulent. The unpleasant odour made him wrinkle his nose as he caught sight of a portrait of Queen Liz staring down at him. Feeling guilty, he opened the window, vaguely recalling a comedy film clip with Peter Sellers in a crowded lift. He resumed his seat, and sampled the coffee, which was too hot. Now the damn daisy was leaning the other way! "Sod it!"

He opened Sergeant Jones' file. It took a while to wade through the report, and at the end, he had not altered his own conclusion. Sergeant Jones had successfully condensed all the documents, and even resume'ed his own resume, reducing it down to a pair of pages, skipping all the trivia, and highlighting all the parallels. Basically, all the different departments had been directed down the same blind alley. As none of them had had common management, the initiator was further up the chain of command. No direct mention was made of this mysterious Jimmy, although there were vague references to him, in third and fourth hand comments made by the Special's 'bug-man', who had written the team report. Unfortunately, the report didn't record who had mentioned him!

The intercom chimed, discreetly. "Sergeant Jones, on line two, Sir."

"Sorry to bother you, is it, but I think I've stumbled on a link to this Jimmy character. I've been given a contact who has a contact that may part with the address, if it is the right Jimmy."

"Excellent. Keep me posted."

"Will do, Sir."


"I saw Betty in the park, the other day." Joan was saying. "We chatted for a while, but she avoided saying anything, if you know what I mean. She had the kids with her, all fighting and screaming, like they do. Apparently James whassname is in the middle of a big deal with someone. Mysterious 'phone calls at funny times, and I think she said he has a locked room off his 'office' room and only he has a key. Even the butler can't go in there, to clean."

"Is there a telephone in there?" Vince asked.

"There must be, unless he was communing with the dead, from what Betty said, but I leaned a bit too hard, and she shut up."

674

"That's a pity, but you did well. It could be a useful snippet to help unravel the tangle." George mused, "But you didn't come all this way, just to tell us that!"

"And it's too soon for Fleecem and Leggett to be responding." Vince added, "So you must be here for some other reason!"

"Did I tell you," Joan hedged, "that when I got back home, last time, I spent two days trying to find the source of the horrible smell in the flat? I thought it was rotten meat, at first. Then when that coach trip brought me here again, I realized that the smell was of the town, and not something going off! I also noticed just how noisy the place is! It never bothered me before, or maybe it's gradually got worse, and I hadn't been aware of it until I came out here! So, I've been thinking, maybe it's time to move house. So, could I use your spare room for a few days, to give me chance to see what's on offer, and how much, around here. I don't want to be this far out, but maybe one of the bigger villages might suit."

"Certainly! I'd be glad to have you! I'll take you into Holyhead tomorrow, you can get a road-map, and call at a couple of Estate Agents for a few pointers, and then you can take yourself off to look around. In return, you can teach me how to bake!"

"Do you mind, Vince?"

"It's George's cottage, and she already has two guests, Tommy and me. If she can put up with all of us, it's her choice."

"That's a careful non-answer!" George glared at him. "Speak up, or I'll chuck you out!"

"Aar! And after I've put your telly aerial up, too!"

"Who got the poles for you?"

"I did the hard bit, pulling that rope!" Joan said.

"And whose car roof has dirty great boot-prints on it?"

"They are nice boots, aren't they? But they aren't dirty, -well, a bit muddy, from the field, perhaps. Seriously, I've no objection. Perhaps Joan might like to keep me warm at night, when your belly gets too big!" He ducked under a flung half-biscuit.

"Men! Only one thing on their minds! He's not even hitched, yet, and already he's off looking for new conquests! - or, were you first in the queue?"

"No, we never got that close, but when you're finished with him, I could do with a bath-runner, and a bed-warmer!"

Don't ask him to do any toast. It's always flambé!"

"Nicely crisp, I'd describe it." Vince argued"

You weren't asked. Shut up!"

"That's telling him! Yes, shut up!"

Vince made a zip across his lips, with two fingers, then immediately made a liar of himself when he opened his mouth and fed a piece of biscuit in.

"How long have you known him, Joan?"

"Oh," she waved an arm, "since forever. I think we've always been around each other, but I didn't 'meet' him until Betty introduced him when they were courting."

"She did the courting, I was taken along to pay the bill - I know, shut up!"

"Yes, shut up!" in stereo.

"I'll just finish this coffee, then I'll go back to my clog-dancing, then."

"Hurry up!"

"That's just like you two, preventing me from hearing the

677

juicy gossip!"

"It would damage your ego, after all, it's frail enough. Now, where were we?"

"Telling me to shut up!"

"Shut up! No, we never went out together. Before Betty, I hadn't seen him, and after Betty, she was always there, like a Siamese twin, so I never had the chance if he'd wanted to."

Vince held his lips shut with his fingers, and semaphored with his eyebrows. "OW!"

George had kicked his shin. "Go and play with your phallic symbol, outside!"

"Yes, Boss!" He tipped the last of his coffee down his throat, and collected another biscuit on the way  past, wondering if he'd heard right. Was George offering him on loan? Then again, did he want to be loaned? Joan's comment about being kept warm in bed was said in jest, or was it?"

Over on Holy Island, on the Valley of the Rocks campsite, the bike and the orange pup-tent were waiting for their owner to return. The biker was in the Scimitar, trying to drink the cellar dry. He'd come all the way to this god-forsaken dump, on a one day turnaround, only to find that the boat was two days late, because it's supplier had been delayed by the French Customs, and hadn't been able to collect it's cargo.

Pat and Trevor, in their camper-van, were also cursing for the same reason. They had passed the word along previously that this site wasn't a good one for them, because as non-divers, they stuck out like the proverbial sore thumbs. The message had come back from on high, "Learn to dive!" That was hardly appropriate, Pat mused - Trevor had a phobia about water, and wouldn't walk through a puddle. Any container of water larger than a cup had to be securely capped, in case he fell in. In her case, well, it would spoil her hair-do, wouldn't it?"

In an office, inside the port of Holyhead, a teleprinter finished chattering out a message about the Spanish fishing boat OKEAN CONQUISTADORE, explaining, in French, that it was under suspicion of being a drug-runner, but the Douane had failed to find anything, and had to let it sail. The duty operator ripped the message off, glanced at it, and tossed it into a tray.

679

"Anyone read Froggese?" he enquired of the rest of the watch, receiving blank looks, so he tapped out a new address on his keyboard, then ran the perforated paper tape copy through his 'reader', sending the message onward to another department for translating. The operator there ripped that copy off, and added it to the pile in an overflowing tray. Unfortunately, that day, the French/English translator had 'phoned in sick, and due to the cut-backs, there was no other one available. The Russian translator admitted to knowing a bit of schoolboy French, and would have a go when he had time, but not to hold your breath, as he had a wobbly stack of his own to work through, first!

The first printer op removed the re-directed copy of the message from his printer, and placed it with the first one, then, duty done, forgot about it.


The French AWACS patrol tracked the target, from its race-track orbit west of Gibraltar at thirty thousand feet. As the boat sailed out of the Mediterranean, into the Atlantic and then north, across the Bay of Biscay, it was 'handed over' to the R.A.F. Nimrod that was circling off Lands-End, on a similar mission. The radar op, naturally, knew nothing of the significance of the target, as the relevant message lay, un-translated, in the 'in' tray. So, when the fishing boat CONQUISTADORE passed very close astern of a Liberian registered freighter, which had come to a brief halt, ten miles from the Channel Isles, nothing was thought of it. After all, Liberian freighters were always breaking down. Most of them had been rescued from Greek scrap-yards, and the Greeks were renowned for running a ship until it was practically sinking beneath their feet before selling it on, and there were a lot of ships crammed into a small space in the busy lanes, as well.

Because the Nimrod crew was not in 'eyeball' range, they couldn't know that the 'fish' being netted had neither gills, nor fins, and were shaped more like torpedoes, remarkably like those being heaved over the side of the Liberian freighter, in fact. Having 'caught' it's load, the CONQUISTADORE carried on up the channel into the Thames estuary, where it placed it's nets, then dutifully chugged up and down all day, catching very little, as what fish hadn't already been removed by the over-fishing had been poisoned by industrial pollution. Several hours after

681

dark, it rendezvoused with a small inshore boat, and some 'torpedoes' were transferred, in exchange for some little bags of shiny stones. A while later, another transfer took place - and another - throughout the night. The Skipper added some engravings of South African Presidents to the growing collection in his safe, joining the little stones, some yellow metal bars, and bundles of printed portraits of Queen Liz, amongst others.

At first light, the CONQUISTADORE was chugging west, passing between the Isle of Wight and Portsmouth. At noon it was off Plymouth. Having called in at the Dart estuary, leaving a 'torpedo' on a line attached to a two pint plastic milk-bottle 'float' in a pre-arranged spot, it was off on its travels again. By dusk it was rounding Cornwall and heading up towards the Irish Sea. During the night several more exchanges took place off the Severn estuary. At sun-up it was off the Dee, making the last of its drops. By this time the Nimrod crew weren't even watching its track. They were more concerned with looking for a light aircraft which had been reported missing. It had filed a flight plan from Southend to Le Touquet, and failed to arrive. No Mayday calls had been heard, no distress beacons were being received. After making countless descents to 'eyeball' debris in the water, or steer searching boats to potential targets, it was found that the pilot had cancelled his trip but the Control Tower had forgotten to cancel the flight plan! Cursing the folly of amateur chairborne aviators, the Nimrod Captain climbed his aircraft back to patrol height, with the Engineer anxiously watching his fuel gauges, which were reading a lot lower than they should have been after all the downs and ups. His co-pilot was talking, via the UHF radio, to the co-pilot of a VC10 tanker that was climbing out of Brize Norton, in Oxfordshire, to bring them an urgently required top-up.

In the Customs office, in Holyhead, the teleprinter finished chopping out another message. The duty operator typed in his redirecting address, and sent the message off to keep the previous one company, thinking that there seemed to be a lot of messages from France this week.

On board the OKEAN CONQUISTADORE, the Skipper was putting the final payment into his safe, this lot was in the form of tubes of yellow coins, printed with the words SUID AFRICA, and bearing the likeness of a gent with a goatee beard. The plan now was to fiddle about, fishing the Dee estuary, work around to the Mersey, and then head off homewards. If they actually caught something, other than Pneumonia, the better it would look, but the truth was, the profits from this one trip would pay more than a years-worth of fishing, and there was no mess to clean up, either!

In the Nimrod, the co-pilot was yelling, in his best Gentlemanly fashion, at the pilot of the VC10 tanker, telling him to get his backside up here, pronto, before the Nimrod was transformed into a large tin glider! The engineer was struggling to find a way to route the last ton of fuel, located in the port inboard tank, round a stuck valve, to the centre-line main, and thence to the thirsty engines. "Skip, I think the only way is to pump it backwards, to the port outer gravity feed, and then run it to the main via the backup feed. The thing is, it'll take ages, because the outer only holds thirty gallons, and we could end up venting some of the gas to waste through the overflow. I'll have to squirt a bit, and then pump it back, and squirt a bit, it'll play havoc with the trim!"

"Do it, I'd rather fly lop-sided than go for a swim!"

In the Customs office, in Holyhead, a telephone started ringing, and went unanswered. Eventually, it stopped, but began again after a short pause. "Oh, soddin' 'ell!" The Supervisor again put down the cold grease-burger she'd been trying to eat for the last hour, and answered the 'phone. "Yeah?"

A torrent of vituperative French burst from the ear-piece - making her jerk it away from her head. When the flood eased, she cautiously brought it near again, and said "What?"

Another torrent erupted. "Does anyone speak Frog lingo?" she hopefully asked of the room, getting no offers of assistance. "Er, nyet sprechen sie frankaise!" she offered to the 'phone - "English?" Another torrent of French was the response. "English, damnit, English! Inglayzee!" there was a pause. "Oh sod off, then!" she slammed the 'phone down. The grease-burger made it halfway to her mouth, before the 'phone rang again. "Shite!" she put the food down yet again, and lifted the hand-set, "What? -- What? -- I can't hear you! Oh, hang on! Heads up!"

685

she spoke to everyone, "does anyone know a Dwayne, from Callies? Is he one of yours, Rosie?"

"Who?" Rosie put her Mills and Boon down, I don't know a Dwayne. No, hang on. Dwayne! Is that Douane, from Calais, French Customs?"

"Oh, yes! Of course!" To the 'phone, the Super said, - "Go ahead."

On the other end, the co-opted brickie, who happened to speak some English, tried his best, "Avec vous, - er - 'ave you - er, getted uno - one ah, massage, regardes vous OKEAN CONQUISTADORE? Ah, what is - er, transportes le heroin?"

"What?" the supervisor replied, "Heroin, you said? What's Okkin Coheestawhore?"

The brickie spelled it phonetically, "O K E A N  C O N Q U I S T A D O R E!"

"Oh! Okean Conquistadore! Why didn't you say that? What about it?"

"Pardon? Not quickly!"

"Oh, god! What - about - Okean - Conquistadore?"

"Are you getted massage?"

686

"No, I don't want a massage! Is that you, Joe, stop messing about, I'm busy!"

"Non! Non! Es Importante!"

"Who's impotent?"

French swearing came out of the earpiece.

"Did you say Okean Conquistadore? The Telex op asked, I saw something about that, a couple of days ago. He leafed through his back copies. "Yes, here it is, in French. I relayed it to 'translations', and heard no more about it."

The Super glanced at the smudged carbon copy, and read out the serial number, "Is that it?"

"Oui -Yes! Is. Why not you - ah - do no things?"

"It's in Fro - French! We can't read it!"

"No Anglais?"

"Yes, no we can't read it. Non comprende!" A flash of school french lesson.

French discussion in the background, then "What do with?"

"Eh? Oh, we passed it on to the translations dep't."

French conversation, then - "Pissed on Trains lashings?"

"Almost. We gave it to translations,-trans-lay-shuns"

French conversation, "Why not do no things?"

"About what?"

"Le massage - er - the massage of Okean Conquistadore?"

"Okkin - Ocean Con - we heard no more about it."

"Not getted trans lay shun?"

"You got it!"

"Non, we not getted it!"

"Nor did we." This conversation was going round in circles!

"Eh? Non! We send, you getted!"

"Oh, god!" The supervisor held her aching head in her spare hand "Yes, you send, we get, we send, we no get, comprende?"

"Ah, Oui! Is cock-up!"

"Yes, it's a cock-up!"

French conversation. "O.K. you read, you un-cock-up. O.K.?"

"Yes, ok, I'll chase it up!"

"Pardon?"

688

"Er, I'll sort it out. I fix cock-up!"

"Ah, Oui! Bye-bye!"

"See you!" she put the 'phone down, and then turned to the telex operator. "Right, send this through again, and stick on the end that the Frogs are getting uppity because nothing has happened!"

"Right. Will do!" The telex op propped the carbon up on a stand, and began rattling his keyboard. Paper tape spewed from its perforator, then was fed into the reader, and fired off down the wires.

In 'Translations' the teleprinter chopped to the end of the message, then the copies were ripped off and dumped into the heap that totally buried the 'in' tray, after which the operator, strictly unofficially, clattered keys, sent an acknowledgement, and explained that there was nobody there TO translate.

In Customs, the op read the inter-departmental note, and told the Super that Joe said the translator was off sick, and there was a pile of messages on the desk, two feet high, waiting for processing.

"Jeesus! Is there no-one else that can do it?" The Super

689

picked up her 'phone, and began dialling, and yelling.

Vince slung the two cable ends in through the open window, then walked round, went in through the door, turned the t.v. to face the window, switched it on, plugged in the aerial, and went out again, taking the remote control with him. George looked at Joan, who shrugged, and then they carried on swapping gossip.

Outside, Vince looked in through the window, then turned the aerial pole a little, looked, turned, the picture went spotty. He turned the pole the other way, looked and so on, until he found the best angle, then changed channels using the remote, before going through it all again, until he had finalized on a direction. S4C was pin-sharp, Harlech a bit fuzzy. BBC had a good picture, with a slightly hissy sound, and the Irish station was better than usual, although still poor. Satisfied, he climbed back up onto the Land-Rover roof, and tightened up the last nuts, locking the mast into position.

K'inell showed his face for the first time in over a week,

and wished he hadn't, because he walked into a load of hassle. Geordie had started to rebuild his car, carefully stripping, cleaning, and repainting or greasing each piece, including the nuts and bolts. Pete was checking over the diving kit, stripping the regulators, and checking the o-rings, diaphragms, valves, hoses, and fittings. Trevor was wishing his damn arm would stop aching, and heal up. He was sick of making the tea, running errands and being duty gofer, but while he was lame, that was his allotted task.

Vince took the loose end of the curly copper wire, and stretched it towards the clothes-line pole, then tied a length of nylon line to the glass insulator, and hung it slackly up. After collecting the free end of the other coil, he looked for something roughly in line with the clothes pole, and the mast, eventually settling on a forked branch in a tree, across the wall from the gate. He was trying to throw a weight fastened to the end of a length of string over the fork, when Tommy rolled up. He watched a couple of abortive attempts, one fell short, and one bounced off the fork, because the string kept snagging on smaller branches.

"Wait a minute, Is easier way!" he levered himself out of his car, and creaked into his caravan, to emerge with a crossbow, and a bolt. "Tie string to arrow, I shoot it over!" he began to crank the bowstring back to the sear. When he was ready, he seated the bolt, aimed high, and squeezed the trigger. The bolt, towing the string, arced over the branch and dropped, to dangle just clear of the ground on the other side. "Easy, yes. What it for?"

"It's a radio aerial!" Vince tied the string to the nylon rope, then drew it over the branch, and let it hang down, on the other side, then passed the crossbow bolt back to Tommy.

"How many time you throw stone?"

"I don't know, a couple of dozen. Joan's here, again!"

"I see. She park in my place. Why is Land-Rover down there?"

"I was using it as a step-ladder so I could put the mast up!"

"Ah! George know?"


The Nimrod eased up behind the VC10, and stabbed its

refuelling probe into the trailing basket on the end of the hose. "Slicker than the Bishop and the Whore!" the co-pilot commented, crudely.

"Fuel is flowing inboard!" the engineer sighed with relief, clicking switches.

The tanker Captain called, via the radio, asking how much fuel was required.

"Keep pumping! We were sucking fumes on all tanks!"

"Cutting it a bit fine, eh?"

"You won't believe how close we came!"

The engineer called, on the intercom, "That damn valve has opened, now!"

"Right, we'll burn that tank first. I don't care what the book says!"

"Right, Skip."

Eventually, the Nimrod Captain called, "Complete, thanks!"

"You're welcome. I can go back to not watching the cricket, now!" The basket pinged off the probe as the Nimrod eased back, and then dipped its nose, while the VC10 powered away in a climbing turn to the right. The Nimrod gave it a couple of minutes to get clear, then called on the intercom, "O.K. Resume work, continue tracking. Radar on! He clicked master over-ride switches returning control to the operator's consoles, then spoke to the radio. "Base, picket three, refuelling complete, back on station in a few minutes, over."

"What you really need," said Tommy, "is small pulley on tree branch. Take line from wire, through pulley, down to weight, then when wind blow, tree sway, line go up and down instead of pull and snap, or break wire."

Vince smiled. "Over by the house, just outside the door, there is a strop with a pulley, on it. I tried to find a way up the tree without climbing it, but now I've a rope over the branch, I can rappel up."

"If need help, shout!"

"If I shout, I've fallen out of it!"

"Probably!"

Chapter thirty-four.

The beginning of the end.

The OKEAN CONQUISTADORE was going home, its task completed, when the Leander class Frigate surged up alongside and matched speeds, very professionally. A man wearing a white cap, on its bridge, picked up a microphone, and a bull-horn bellowed "Heave to! Customs inspection!"

"Fuck you, Sailor-boy!" The Conquistadore's Captain roared back, "I go home, you no stop!" and punctuated it with an internationally recognized one-finger sign, before shoving his throttle lever up for maximum rev's. Black smoke belched from the diesel's exhaust, the hull shook and rattled, and the boat went about two knots faster.

"Okean Conquistador, this is Her Majesty's - . " The Conquistador Captain visibly leaned over, and turned his VHF marine radio off. "Heave to, at once!" The bull-horn repeated.

The trawler Captain repeated his one fingered sign

On the Frigate, the quartermaster's mate emerged onto the wing. "Excuse me, Sir, the radio room says - "

"I know, I saw him switch it off!"

"Sir!" the seaman converted a salute into a grab for his cap as the breeze threatened to remove it, went in, came out again, "Sir, the Captain says to try -"

"Plan B?"

"Yes, Sir!"

The Sub-lieutenant reached into a covered box, from which he pulled out a six inch long orange stick, a shade under an inch thick, lit the blue touch paper at one end, waited for the jet of sparks, then threw it across the narrow gap of water, onto the fore-deck of the fishing boat. Two crew-men shot out from behind the deck winch, and ran aft, yelling.

The thunderflash detonated with an earsplitting crash and a cloud of blue smoke, as it was designed to do, being nothing more than an oversize firework banger. In retaliation, the trawler Captain fired a red Verey light flare at the Frigate. It bounced off the hull, and fell into the water.

The Subbie sighed. "I always get the awkward bastards!"

"Alright, I'll handle this one." The Captain was standing behind him, a walkie-talkie in one hand. "Guns? What's the port Oerlikon loaded with? Tracer? One short burst across that boat's bow, NOT into it!"

Up on the lifeboat deck, just aft of the funnel, a rating slapped the breech closed on a belt of gleaming copper ammunition, pulled back the cocking lever, hooked his shoulders into the butt-frame, took brief aim, and squeezed the trigger. The gun spoke with a sharp KAKAKAKAK! Five orange streaks flashed past the trawler skipper's nose, just outside his bridge window, causing him to say some words you won't find in a Spanish/English dictionary, and then turn his helm hard right. The Okean Conquistadore swung round, right at the frigate.

High up on his bridge wing, the Frigate Captain snapped, into his walkie-talkie, "Collision alert! Full astern both!" A siren began whooping the 'Action Stations' alarm as the Frigate performed the nautical equivalent of an emergency stop. "Stop both. Hard port the wheel, starboard engine half ahead. Guns! Uncap the .45's.and point them at that dinghy! Wheel amidships. Half ahead port! Starboard Oerlikon, fire one short burst across

697

his bows. Full ahead both. Wheel port ten.

The fifty tons of Okean Conquistadore waltzed across the bows of the frigate, as it continued its starboard turn, and the two thousand tons of Tyneside-built steel dodged and weaved, using its twin screws and enormous power reserves to avoid trampling the fishing boat into oblivion. The starboard Oerlikon fired its short burst. Six rounds bored into the sea, as intended, but due to the gyrations of both vessels. The seventh one hit the fishing boat's anchor chain, and 'spanged' off at an odd angle, doing no further damage, but giving the young gunner a fright, as the only thing he had fired at previously were empty fifty gallon oil cans.

The Skipper of the Okean tried to put a new cartridge into his Verey pistol, and spin his wheel to port, at the same time. Below, the chef, cum fish salter cum greaser, caught his pot of curry sauce as he hopped past it on one foot, off balance as the deck changed from leaning steeply to the left, to leaning steeply to the right. He was also using phrases you won't find in a 'linguaphone' course!

On the frigate, the Captain said, "Guns, have we any of those saluting blanks for the .45 handy?" On the stepped fore-deck, a bell started a plaintive 'tang - tang' note as the gun turret turned to bring the twin barrels into line with the fishing boat. A rating in anti-flash gear ducked out of a hatch, and ran across the red cross-hatched area on deck, then fell onto his backside when the Frigate leaned over, and turned the other way, his feet skidding out from beneath him on the salt-wet deck.

"Come on, Sonny boy! Stop lying down on the job!" Gunner 'T' roared over the general noise. The rating scrambled to his feet, rescued his tin hat as it rolled towards the scuppers, then ran to the front of the turret to remove the crested barrel stoppers from the loud end of the two guns, glanced hastily up the 'spouts', looking for stashed beer cans or cleaning cloths, then ran back with the caps, and ducked back into the hatch. As the hatch clanged closed, the ammunition hoist fed two blank rounds to the two breeches. Hydraulic rams pushed them home, the breeches closed, and the guns were ready. "Two blank rounds loaded!" Gunner 'T' reported. The frigate continued its turn to port, at a moderate helm angle, and full power.

At thirty-six thousand feet, the radar op in the Nimrod

reported- "Skipper, there's two ships off the Lizard, having a dance!"

"Roger. Keep an eye on them. Nothing's been reported, yet."

⚓

The radio op finicked with the tuning of his radio, tuned to marine band channel sixteen, the general calling channel. He thought he had heard a naval ship calling someone, but it had been buried in all the chatter and hash, and was indecipherable. He heard someone calling that a ferry was crossing behind someone, and someone else asked someone to put the kettle on, they'd be in dock in five minutes. Someone else was blathering on about has anyone found anything to catch in area something or other, and "I'm just inside the breakwater, where's the bloody tug?" Then cutting through, and creating radio silence, "Pan Pan Pan! This is S.S. Gigant! I see someone firing red flares about twenty miles north of my position, which is crackle screech, can anyone assist?"

There was a brief pause, then "Pan call, this is Golf Mike Whiskey Tango, Royal Navy vessel. Disregard the pan call, it's a

Spanish fishing boat getting stroppy with Customs. Repeat, - disregard the red flares. This is Golf Mike Whiskey Tango. Out"

Another voice came on, a distinct south-western Cornish drawl, "Go get 'em, Jack! Sink the thieving boogers!"

After another short pause, the normal hubbub built up again, as everyone resumed talking to everyone else, simultaneously. Breaking through the noise came a final, parting comment. "Who, the Spicks, or the Snatchers?"

On the frigate, they were preparing to launch the Wasp helicopter, and in the radio room, a coded message was being prepared - about shots fired, etc.

In Holyhead customs, the shift supervisor was still cursing the translations dept., who in turn was cursing the translator for being off sick, and frantically hunting around for a French speaker who had security clearance!

Vince finished hanging his aerial tensioning weight, and wandered up to the other end of his new aerial, to adjust the tension on the end that was attached to George's clothes post.

701

Satisfied, he went into the cottage, plugged the aerial into the set, switched on, consulted the hand-written notes, set a few switches, saw the frequency display change to a very non-amateur frequency range, and tried the transmit button, then paused, uncertain what to say. He settled on the simple option. "Pete, this is Vince, how copy, over?"

Nothing happened.

"Pete, this is -." he let go of the button, said to himself, "you silly sod!" then he changed the set from c.w. to n.f.m., and tried again. As he pressed the 'transmit' button, a red light illuminated, and a needle on the power meter rose to just over 100 as an in-built automatic aerial tuning unit chattered. "Whew! A hundred watts out!" then he spoke again, "Pete, this is Vince, how copy, over?"

"Hi, Vince. I was wondering when you'd come up. You're booming through. How me, over."

"Bending the needle. Thanks for the extra bits, over."

"We'll bill the tax-payer. I suggest you give us a call at about ten, daily, in case we've turned something up. We'll be listening all the time, just in case. Does that suit?"

702

"Fine by me, Pete. What about after?"

"We'll worry about it then, over."

"Suits. I'll clear, now, and speak to you tomorrow, over."

"Rog!"

George poked her head through the kitchen doorway. "I guess it works, then?"

"Yes. If you want assistance in a hurry, just pick up the mike, and yell, the cavalry will be around, hot-foot! What are you lot doing?

"Joan is teaching my oven how to bake things."

Tommy manages alright!"

He never uses it, just that giant frying pan of his, what's it called, a wack?"

"Wok. What did he roast that chicken in, then?"

"Don't split hairs! He chai tea'd it!"

Vince sighed, and went back to fiddling with his scanner. He'd set the frequency of the local amateur repeater into its tuner, and was listening in to an intermittent conversation between two stations until he understood that the topic under discussion was about an obscure fault on a photocopier!

The frigate was still playing dodgems with the fishing boat, which was still hammering along at its top speed of twelve and a bit knots. The Skipper loaded his last flare, leaned out of the wheel-house, and fired it at the frigate. The flare slammed dead centre into the bridge window, as the Skipper dove hastily back inside, slamming the screen door behind himself." Main armament, just above the target, one blank round, FIRE!" He commanded.

A twenty feet long tongue of flame leaped out of the barrel, closely followed by an ear-shattering BOOM! and a cloud of smoke. The Okean reeled drunkenly out of the cloud, its Skipper choking on the cordite fumes, and dancing a jig, hands raised in a two finger salute. He was bellowing, in Spanish "You missed! You silly bastards!"

On the frigate's bridge, the Officer of the Watch was frantically trying to keep the daily log up to date, and muttered, "This bastard's got a death-wish!"

"Moderate your language on my bridge, Lieutenant! The Captain snapped, followed by, - "Stop port. Wheel hard a-port.

Half astern port. - Where's the silly bugger going? Sub, try the

loud-hailer again. Bunts, grab hold of the Aldis, and flash

'STOP' at him a few times! Midships. Stop port. Is the Wasp

ready to deploy? Half ahead port. Main armament, when the

target bears, fire the other blank at him!"

"Sir! The O.O.W. interrupted. "At him? That will - "

"Break his bridge windows, yes. It might get his attention,

too! Starboard ten the wheel!"

"Wasp's ready, but the crew can't start engine in the

hangar, with the rotors folded, Sir!" a rating reported.

"Tell them, after the next .45 round, to spot the helo, and

start up ready for a rapid departure."

"Copied, Sir!"

The Okean bashed across the wake of the frigate, pitching

and heaving violently in the foaming water

"Midships the wheel. Rev's for twelve knots, please."

"Target is too far astern, Captain." Guns reported.

"Not for long, Guns, He's about to get run over,

backwards. Be prepared for him to break to one side, probably to

port." The Captain went out onto the bridge wing, to enable him to see the antics of the trawler. "Yes, he's chasing us, with half a knot advantage!"

The Okean had dodged round the stern of the frigate, with a deckie in the bow, preparing to heave an old net over the side, in the hope of tangling the frigate's props into a snarled mess of old rope. With his Spanish blood riled, the skipper didn't realize he was being suckered. He closed in, slowly, to about a hundred yards, and only then noticed that the frigate's big shiny bronze props weren't turning. Then water boiled along the flanks of the frigate as it went astern! The peseta dropped, and the fishing boat skipper screamed more insults as he flung his helm hard to port - too late. The suction from the big props was sucking his little boat under the frigate's counter. Before he was sucked into a collision, though, the Frigate reversed its engines again, going full ahead, blowing the Okean away like a cork from a pop-gun. At the same instant, when the frigate was stationary for a moment, four burly Marines hurled their Gemini inflatable over the side, leaped into it, and blasted away in a tangle of arms and legs. Once clear, they sorted themselves out, then came creaming back in a huge half circle. The other .45 barrel roared as it came into line, belching a long flame at the bridge of the Okean, the shock-wave blowing in the already cracked window, and cracking the rest, as well as giving the paint-work a thorough toasting. In the resulting confusion the Gemini zoomed in, disgorging three Marines onto the Okean's after deck, the fourth remaining in the Gemini, holding it clear of the still turning fishing boat, its Skipper temporarily blinded and deafened by the muzzle flash and the bang. One Marine darted onto the bridge, glanced around, found a switch, and flicked it. The radio came on, and started hissing. Another switch activated the deck lights. Another turned on the wheel-house light. He tried a lever, and the siren 'baarf'ed. Then he saw a key, in a switch on the wheel-post, and turned it. The diesel engine coughed, spluttered, and died. The dazzled and deafened skipper was groping for him, and received a swift jab in his ample gut to keep him quiet.

The other two Marines dove down a hatch. The rest of the motley crew promptly spilled out of the other and onto the deck, yelling and shouting, and tossing bottles, cans, and cellophane wrapped packets overboard, which were promptly scooped up by the Marine in the Gemini who was using an angler's landing net.

The chef appeared, waving a ladle at a Marine, while the other searched the cabins, below.

"Slow ahead both, port ten, the wheel! The frigate Captain commanded, bringing his ship round again, in a big circle.

"Wasp deployed, and ready to go! Someone called, from the rear of the bridge, as he replaced a telephone handset. They could all hear the screech/whine noises of a gas turbine coming from the flight deck on the frigate's stern.

"I think she's stopped, Sir! A lookout reported.

"Marines say they've boarded, Sir" Bunt's called, from his corner with the VHF radio.

"Train main armament fore and aft. Oerlikons to safe. Mid-ships the wheel, Stop both. Starboard five the wheel. Slow astern both." The Captain ordered. The hull began to bounce gently, as the props bit into the water. "Mid-ships the wheel. Stop both!"

"Not responding to the helm, Sir!" the wheelhouse called, on the intercom. "Wheel's mid-ships. Both engines stopped."

"Launch the Wasp!"

The screeching reached a crescendo, and then the little helicopter threw itself into the air, rotor blades battering, its

708

spidery undercarriage supporting the four, free-castoring wheels which pointed in random directions. Thirty feet up, it sidled sideways until it was clear of the ship, then dipped its nose and thrashed off. The Frigate drifted slowly past the fishing boat, about fifty feet clear to starboard.

"Slow astern, both!" the hull began bobbing again. "Stop both!"

"Guns safe, fore and aft." Gunner 'T' reported. "Main guns breeches empty. Oerlikons loaded, un-cocked, safeties on, Sir!"

"I presume I can discontinue flashing "STOP" now, Sir?" the signalman asked.

"I thought you already had, flags!"

"Using my initiative, as you keep saying, Sir!"

"Five days number nines punishment, for smart-arsing an Officer~"

"Sir!" aggrieved.

"Suspended indefinitely."

"Message from C in C Fleet, Sir. A radio op came onto the bridge, bearing a sheet of paper.

"Read it, sparks."

709

"Sir, it says 'Imperative use minimum force necessary to apprehend suspects considering International Diplomacy.' Sir."

"As usual, Our Lordships are half an hour too late to make any difference to the outcome! Are you laughing, Officer of the Watch?"

"No, Sir, sneezing."

"Sneezing used to go "ah - choo, ah - choo", not "hahaha, er, choo", when I was at Dartmouth."

"Yes Sir, sorry, Sir!"

"Min of Ag Inspector is crossing, in the cutter, Sir." A lookout reported.

"Very good. Bosun's Mate. Now would be a convenient moment for coffees, I think."

"Yes, Sir!" A spotty junior seaman stopped hiding in a corner, out of the way, and nearly ran down the passageway.


"It looks like the Navy's got the Spick, er, the Spaniard, Captain" The radar op in the Nimrod reported. "There's another track appeared, could be a helicopter, low and fast."

"If the Navy's a frigate, it's probably a Westland Wasp, or

it could be one of the new Lynx, if they're a Destroyer. But it's a tight squeeze!" The Captain pressed his transmit button connected to the UHF radio that was tuned to the 'guard' channel of 243 Megs. "Navy chopper, south-west of the Lizard, this is Picket Three, you on the guard channel?"

"Er, Pickup tree, was that? Navy Zero Four. What can I do for you, over?"

"Navy, this is pick-ett th-uree, Nimrod on station, we've been tracking the Okean Conquistadore for days. If you're pulling a drugs bust, you're too late, she's unloaded, and on the way home, over!"

"Picket three, Navy. Sorry, these things are a bit noisy with the doors open. Going home, you say? Typical! Late again! I suppose the gen. will come through, later! We're on our way to Portland, but our HF. is bust, can you keep an eye on us, until we're in UHF range, over."

"Portland? Playing war-games?"

"Neggo! Playing Postman!"

"O.K. Navy, will do."

711

While all this was going on, the Commissioner was holding a meeting with all, except Pete, who was on radio guard.

"Right, then. Silence! Settle down, is it! QUIET! Thank you." Sergeant Jones got their attention, and then passed the 'chair' on.

"Right, lads. We've been chasing our own tails, so far ---"

"That's not what I saw 'K'inell' doing!" someone muttered.

The Commissioner glared at the offender.

"It was a WPC's tail" the voice offered, in defence.

"If you don't shut up, I'll send you back to beating your feet!" Sergeant Jones warned him.

"--chasing our tails. You lot," he indicated the Specials, "were following Pete and Trevor, instead of Pat and Trevor! Those two gentlemen were given slightly different instructions, they were watching for a blonde woman, and a skinny man. Unfortunately, they picked the wrong couple, because their dates were off, and ended up running surveillance on Miss Weastey, and Mr. Birtwhistle, who just happened to fit the description and times, and by sheer chance, met and paired off on the camp-site! Then you two, McGillighan and pal, rolled up, and stuck your oar in, but only succeeded in getting your arses kicked by a pair of amateurs who were merely defending their right to privacy" Trevor, massaging his aching shoulder, noticed that 'K'inell' was rubbing his leg. "You were lucky, because two more people turned up dead. One by the hand of Mr. Birtwhistle, who was protecting Miss Weastey, when the man went berserk for as yet unknown reasons. The other one was shuffled off by persons unknown. There are at least five more civvies involved. Who they are, and who sent them, is unknown. Miss Weastey bumped one off with a hand-gun which appeared from nowhere, and has now disappeared again. The deceased's partner has been spirited away by the Diplo's, and we can't touch him. The person we suspect of sending them has turned up on a park bench, with a third nostril," that raised a snigger, "So they are all dead ends, in more ways than one" He waited for the laugh that didn't come. "Yes, well, any comments so far?"

Trevor spoke. "Sir, you've missed out the man who was whisked from the rock cave, by the apparent Search and Rescue

713

guys."

"And what about the Scousers you had a punch-up with, on the sea-front in Holyhead?" One of the 'bugmen' asked.

"I think they are an irrelevance, just a bunch of punks who chose the wrong time and place for a party. Are you going to tell us your names?"

"No."

"O.K. then. So why did Jim Bond one, and Jim Bond two, turn up, and run a covert surveillance on the cottage belonging to Miss Weastey?" Trevor asked.

"We'll come to that, later." The Commissioner said. "Just bear in mind that you two got whipped by them, as well, so don't get smug! The only people to come out on top, are Miss Weastey and Mr. Birtwhistle, and to a lesser extent, Sergeant Jones, who is, forgive me, Lew, an ordinary Plod, with no special training, no fancy gadgets, no rockets, bombs, rifles," he looked at Trevor, "or funny radio's." The two 007's received a glare, in turn. "Unfortunately, although Sergeant Jones collected two of the bad guys, one was dead, and the other a foreign national, so we've gone full circle again. Now we come to these two anonymous, ah, gents. Over a year after the start of this, just after Mr. Birtwhistle comes out of hospital following a nasty accident which wasn't an accident at all, these two turn up at just the right place and time to carry on from where you left off. Who sent them? Nobody is saying. We have a copy of an anonymous fax with the heading cut off. I presume the heading would identify you?

The 007's nodded yes.

"So it would appear that even I am not to be privileged to know who you are?"

007 no 2 nodded yes, meaning – no!

"So be it. As I am not to know your identities, or who you work for, or what you are here for, - Sergeant Jones."

Sergeant Jones opened the door, to admit four very large plods, who trooped in.

"I have here two arrest warrants, made out in the name of John Doe, for you two gents. You will be held incommunicado, at Her Majesty's Pleasure, for the duration. Will you leave voluntarily, or do you require assistance?"

Number two left voluntarily. Number one needed

assistance, and was very much the worse for wear when he was eventually carted off.

The Commissioner continued. "Right, then. Someone, somewhere, will eventually start yelling for the return of their men, and maybe we will find out who they really are. Trevor, have you got any further with this 'Jimmy' character, yet?"

"No, Sir. We keep getting baulked, so we've passed it on to the legal department, who are wrestling with the Solicitors at the other end. Once we get past them, we might get somewhere."

"Hmm. Perhaps we need a bigger club to swing. I'll see what I can arrange. Has anyone else anything to add?"

"Only that the comm's link set up that I suggested is up and running." Trevor added.

"Good. Anything else? No? Right, then. Meeting concluded at whatever time it is. I'll be in the bar, across the street, in half an hour, if anyone is thirsty."

Someone knocked on the door, then opened it. "Ah, there you are, Sir. We've received a confused message on the printer that concerns you. It seems that the Navy has apprehended a Spanish fishing boat off Cornwall, the name's garbled, and apparently they were running drugs. It seems that the French Douane told our lot, in Holyhead, days ago, but Holyhead just chucked it into a file, and forgot it. That means the Spaniard has been swanning around our coast for days, and nobody has been watching them."

"Damn! No, not you, son! Thanks. Carry on. Trevor, we got you from C and E didn't we? Take McGiddywillie with you, go and breathe down their necks, find out what happened, and fix it so it doesn't happen again."

"Right, Sir! Come on 'K'inell', your car is quicker than my truck."

"Er, I meant -."

"Yes, Sir, but Geordie McGillighan has his car in pieces!"

"Oh, yes. Alright."

Outside, Geordie asked, "What about that free drink the Boss offered?"

"We're in Wales, you berk! The pubs are shut on Sundays!"

"Oh yeah!"

"Hey! The Navy's having a scrap with a Spanish boat!" Vince called, to anyone who cared to listen.

"What?" George was in the kitchen, "eggs, flour, butter, where's the bloody currants? Ah, there. Cherries? Cherries? I had some this morning! Vince, have you pinched my glace cherries?"

"Yeah, I ate them while you were - OUCH! What was that for?"

"Eating my cake before I've cooked it!"

"It's more economical, that way! I can't eat it after you've cooked - OUCH it OUCH! Come here, you minx!"

"Careful, I'm in a delicate condition!"

"Well, don't run away so fast, and then I won't have to chase you!"

"Gerroff!"

"Mmmm!"

In the kitchen, Joan muttered something along the lines of "I guess she's out of cherries!"

In a small, locked room, off a locked office, a telephone rang, briefly, and then the answer-phone cut in. Ten miles away in the exchange, a relay snicked, tape was drawn past magnetic recording heads, and a suddenly awakened monitor grabbed for his headphones, scattering coffee and chocolate raisins everywhere.

"Ay, Jimmy, you might like to know they're on to you. The Navy's got your Spick boat, and the nets are tightening. It's time to pack in, and move shop. See ya."

The monitor's partner was using a piece of equipment not normally found in telephone exchanges. Based on line impedance, the gadget could sometimes tell where the call was being made from. This device had been modified, though, by the addition of a highly illegal 'infinity loop' circuit, an inclusion that meant that once the telephone line it was connected to was 'opened', when the call had ended and the handset had been replaced, it was still 'live' and could still pick up any sounds in the room the hand-set was in. It also prevented the line from 'clearing', so it could be more readily traced.

"One end's a call-box, sounds like a shopping centre. Is it

worth tracing?"

"No, but stay on it for a while, in case he uses it to make another call."

"Yeah."

"What's on the other end?"

"A bloody ansafone. I can't hear a damn thing, so either there's no-one in, or the mike's disabled."

In the submarine, still parked on the sea-bottom, the sonar operator had reported on, and was listening to the chase, trying to work out what was going on, based on the surges of engine and propeller noise carrying through the fourty miles of water.

The sub's Captain continued his waiting game. This wasn't his problem, providing the Navy won!"

Pete was in the back of his truck, feet up, eyelids down, headphones askew on his head. Trevor reached over, and sharply turned up the volume control, turning the subdued hiss into a roar. Pete jerked up, ripping the 'phones off.

"Wake up, you lazy sod! 'K'inell' and I are going to the

Holyhead office to gee up the paper-shufflers, because they've cocked up. Keep an ear on the VHF!"

Pete bleared at him. "I've only got one ear now, thanks to you! You've ruined the other!"

"Serves you right, kipping in the H.Q's back yard. You're lucky it was me, and not the Boss!"

Pete made a two finger sign, which, roughly translated, means "Go away!"

'K'inell' fired up his XR4I, and bipped the horn

"Keep out of blondie's way, in case she tickles your other shoulder!"

Trev gave Pete a glare. "You'd better watch out for her chef!"

"Ooooh!"

'K'inell' leaned out of his window. "Come on, or it'll be tomorrow before we get there!"

"The way you drive, it'll be yesterday!" Geordie yelled across the yard.

"At least, I stay on the tarmac!" 'K'inell' revved the engine as Trevor climbed in, then dropped the clutch, pinning him to the seat and shutting the door with a bang. The tyres shrieked and spat gravel, wagging the back end of the car as they gripped unevenly.

The monitor and his mate, using their electronic gizmo, had located the extension, and passed it on to H.Q. While the troops were gathering, ready to 'bust' this 'Jimmy', they carried on listening, just in case. Two people had tried to use the supermarket phone, but found a dead line, and given up, so the team released the line, rather than risk warning the 'Jimmy' caller that the line was traced, but considering the content of the message, it was unlikely he would call again. Their spare 'phone rang, and the team leader said they were all ready to go when this 'Jimmy' turned up.

Everyone waited.

The Navy had made a lightning search of the Okean, and found nothing of significance, merely a couple of dodgy-smelling dog-ends, and a pinch of white powder. The Fisheries man fared no better, the fish-hold contained only a few dozen non-descript fish, not covered by the laws, and a couple of buckets of cockles, which were in the process of being 'cleaned' by the simple process of frequent water-changes.

"Fishing no bluddy good!" the mate kept saying, in between "que?" "non comprende", and "why you no pissoff!"

"Right, lads. Best thing we can do is to take her home, and search her properly, we're getting nowhere!" The Marine who appeared to be in charge, spoke. The cutter puttered away with the Min of Ag man, and returned with a scratch crew of a killick and two seamen, who set about starting the engine, shutting hatches, and pointing the boat in the general direction of Plymouth. The Marines herded the original crew below and made sure they stayed there, to allow the new crew to get on with it. The Marine in the Gemini whizzed off, back to the frigate, whose siren cut loose with a series of short whoops, warning a lumbering freighter to keep away. (A lone crewman poked his head out of a hatch, rubbing his eyes, and then ran for the bridge so he could spin the wheel, and go around the frigate and fishing boat. A dog barked frantically at them, from the bridge-top).

"Get the name, Number One, if you can make it out, through the rust-streaks, and we'll report it, crew one man and a dog, with the dog on watch!" The frigate Captain ordered.

"Sir". The First lieutenant was already doing just that, studying the ship through binoculars. "What the hell IS that flag? It looks like a dirty floor-cloth!"

"I thought it was a dirty tea-towel!" Bunts replied, only half-joking.

The rust-pile trundled past, and curved back onto course.

"It looks like "Z - IT 99." The O.O.W. read the name, through his binoc's, as the stern came into view.

"Very appropriate, zit. It's certainly a blot on the sea-scape. I wonder if it will reach its destination, before it sinks!"

The Captain watched the floating stain pass. "I wonder if we would be doing the world a service, if we 'accidentally' sank it?"

"It's probably stuffed to the gills with Italian toxic waste that no-one will allow in, so it is doomed to wander the oceans until it founders." Number One was still trying to read the name. "No, Zit 99 it is!"

"Captain, sir, the cutter's on the falls, and the boot - sorry, Marine and his dinghy are on the quarterdeck."

"Engines, slow ahead, steer west, for now. Officer of the Watch, resume the patrol. I will be in my day cabin if I'm needed."

"Sir! I have the watch."

The Captain glanced at his bare wrist. "You would think the Government could allow us one each!"

In the sub, the hydrophone operator tweaked his volume control, and fiddled with the filter controls, listening hard. He had heard the frigate move off, in between the tweets, squawks, and whistles that normally filled the headphones with noise. Yes! There! The rumbling whoosh, with the funny 'tweet' of the nick in the prop blade that was making it 'sing' as it revolved, was fading in. He pressed the mike button.

After a minute, the sub trembled, stirred, and angled gently upwards as feet pattered, and the crew took up their stations again.

In Whitehall Commcen, a teleprinter chattered, spitting out a curly length of paper. Ratings passed the message on to others, who clattered keyboards, or tapped on Morse keys.

In the frigate, Morse beeped irregularly, and teleprinters chattered. Picket three received a verbal message, and began trying to fit the data to his radar tracks.

On the frigate's bridge, the signal-man read the message just handed to him, and then did a double-take. "Sir! This message appears to relate to that rust-bucket, astern of us!"

"Really? Let me see! Yes, how long have you had it?"

"About thirty seconds, Sir!" the rating replied, while thinking "Can't you read the time printed on it, you dim sod?"

"Wheel, ten to port, steer zero seven five! Messenger, take this to the Captain's - Don't bother, he's here. Captain, Sir -."

"I heard, carry on."


'K'inell' and Trevor roared into the staff car-park, and came to a tyre-shredding halt in the only available space. Startled out of his doze, the attendant belatedly closed the single pole barrier before heaving out of his chair, to lumber ominously across.

"OY! YEW! YEW CARN'T PARK THAT, THERE!" he bellowed, after the fashion of all Petty Officers, Gunnery, retired.

"The kraken awakes!" Trev quoted, as he rolled his window down. "Why not?"

"That space is reserved!" the standard uninformative reply.

"For whom?"

"The Boss!"

"And when will the boss be back?"

"Two weeks tomorrow, he's in Tenerife!"

"Then we have two weeks and ten hours to conclude our business. Where's your i.d. card?"

"Who are you?"

"I asked first. If you had been doing your job, you would have asked before you let us into the car-park! Show me your i.d."

"I saw you coming down the street. If you'd been going at the right speed, I'd have put the pole down."

"It should have been down! Did you see the artic in front of us?"

"Of course, d'you think I'm blind?"

"What company name was on it?"

"Er, - Stobart, why?"

"So, if I look in your gate-log, it will show Stobart, just above the entry for us?"

"Er, yes."

"That's clever, because there was no truck, we came in behind a coach. Where's your i.d. card?"

"Ay? Er."

"A Belfast registered coach, with just two occupants, who left on foot."

"Er, I've got to -."

"I.D. card. NOW!"

"It's in my jacket, in the hut."

'K'inell was trying not to laugh as Trevor baited the non-security guard, there had been no coach, either. He locked the car up and leaned on the rear corner, waiting for Trevor. A ginger head poked through an open window, attracted by the noise.

"Hi, Josie! Put the kettle on, love!"

"Up yours, "K'inell"." The window banged shut.

"She loves me, really!" he said, to no-one in particular.

When Vince was hunting for a spare mains plug, earlier, he'd found a forgotten tea-chest, buried under all the other spare-room stuff that accumulates. He'd had a quick look inside, and found two long-abandoned sets of diving gear. Bored with the radio, he hauled it out, and sorted his gear from hers. Everything was there, except his wet-suit. Her knife was a lump of rust in a sheath. He gave the handle an experimental tug, and it sheared off from the blade, leaving the rusted steel behind. He glanced at her demand valve. The chrome-plated parts seemed alright, but the hoses were perished, as was the 'O' ring in the 'D' clamp. He put it with the knife. Her stabilizer jacket seemed intact, although it was sparkly with salt, and the hoses ruined. Its brass fittings were green but salvageable. Her mask was undamaged, and the fins and schnorkel, being of a rubbery plastic, were fine. Her wet-suit was sparkly, and streaked with dried salt. Her gloves were on the ragged edge of being useable, the neoprene feeling tacky, but still sound. One boot had the sole hanging off, and the other had the two sides stuck inseparably together. Her

729

weight-belt was, well, a weight-belt, brass fittings, lead weights, and nylon webbing. The battery in her dive computer was long deceased. The two cylinders were empty. He knew that because her pillar valve was open, while his only managed a feeble 'psst' that stopped almost as soon as it began when he opened the valve. The 'O' rings were done for, of course, but there was no visible damage to the harnesses, apart from a missing strap.

His main knife was stuck in its sheath, but some determined waggling broke it free of its dried-up grease coating, and it slid out. Apart from a few flecks of rust, the blade was perfect. The secondary knife sheath was there, but empty. His a.b.l.j. had all the straps cut, and a ragged tear in the back of the collar, rendering it useless. His mask, fins, and schnorkel were useable, although one of the fins had a strange curl to the blade, from where it had been trapped under a cylinder. It might relax back into its proper shape now the stress was removed, given time. The demand valve was salty, but the hoses looked sound, and the gauge glasses were intact. In his lone boot, he found his watch still ticking away happily, albeit an hour and a half slow. He reset it, and put it on. Both his gloves had cuts up the full length of the back, but were repairable. He puzzled for a minute over how they'd got his fingers out of the glove, when he wouldn't let go of the strap, then forgot about it, it was unimportant. Absently, he pressed in the purge button, on his valve, and it clicked in, and sprang out again, as it should do. He took the valve through, and picked up a screwdriver from the tool rack near the radios. After a brief struggle, he cracked the screws free and dismantled the unit. The diaphragm was perfect, and the exhaust valve just needed a quick rinse. There was a trace of verdigris on the valve seats, but nothing that couldn't be rectified in minutes. He took the parts through to the kitchen, but the sink was cluttered with pots, so he back-tracked, and went to the bathroom to wash the valve parts under a running tap, then dried them with a few squares of tissue off the roll. He then went back to the table, and re-assembled the valve. He was finishing just as George came through with a cup of coffee for him.

"I see you found the stuff, then."

"Yes. What happened to my wet-suit?"

"They had to cut it off you, and I binned the bits."

731

"Oh. My a.b.l.j's ruined, too. Your gear seems o.k. It just needs some minor bits and pieces."

"Did you dismantle it?"

"No, I only gave it a look over the externals. I thought you'd prefer to have it professionally serviced. Your cylinder needs testing, anyway, it's out of date. Mine has about six months to run, but as I don't have major parts of my gear, it's academic, really. I will have to find some employment, soon, won't I? It was more of a statement than a question.

"I suppose. What will you do?"

"Beats me. I have no clothes that fit, no transport, and no finance. There isn't any thriving industry around here. I suppose I will have to go to Holyhead, or Bangor. How about you, have you anything under consideration?"

"No, I was going to worry about that when the time came. At least, we haven't got a mortgage to worry about. This place," she slapped a wall, "is mine. Ours, really, as most of your possessions went into the pot."

"Yeah."

"You can strip my valve, if you like, to make sure there are no desiccated shrimps in it, but somehow, I can't see me using it again."

"You will. You just need an excuse. I'll clean up your suit and jacket, as well. You should really have washed them off."

"I know, but I had more important things to do, and it didn't seem to matter, then they just sort of got forgotten."

"Your computer needs a new battery, too."

"Oh." She was disinterested. "I might get a new one. I'll have to send it off."

"I don't know why, it only clips in under that hatch. I imagine it is a standard lithium button cell."

"I wouldn't know, but if you take it to bits, you void the guara - ah!"

"Guarantee? That's long gone, unless you took out an extension?"

"Er, no!"


The monitor heard a faint clatter in his headphones, picked up by the ansafone handset, which had been kept live by his gizmo. "Here we go!" He pressed down on the 'record' and 'play' keytabs on the recorder, setting the tape rolling, while his partner said "Stand by" to the other telephone.

A faint jingle of keys sounded, then a scrape followed by a sharp snick, was heard over the speaker. Somebody coughed, making the record level needles wiggle across their meter scales, then a loud crash/twang/whirr noise. After a moment, the monitor recognized the sounds of the ansafone tape being wound back to its beginning. Another crash/twang sounded. Hiss, beep! "Jimmy, it's me again. It looks like Alberto got himself dead, and Tony's been - HEY! Get out! I'm - no! - NO! crash. Click. Beep. Click , "Ay, Jimmy, you might like to know they're on to you - "

"That's it! GO, GO, GO!"

Two sledgehammers swung, and a splintered door wavered open, the team rushed in, up the revealed stairway, to another door, which got the same treatment, then a third, to reveal, an empty room, three blank walls, no doors or windows. On the floor, in a corner, a dusty cardboard box stood, wires leading from it to a mains socket, and a telephone socket, both on the wall, and to another, metal, box, with a telescopic aerial.

"Shit! It's a blind exchange!" Someone swore, and

prodded it with a toe.

BEEP! BIP. BIP. Numerals lit up, counting down from 9. "JEEZ! IT'S A BOMB! GET OUT!"

3, 2, 1, the room lit with a brilliant flash, the following concussion bowling the last man out, down the stairs, and into his preceding companions, knocking them down as well. There wasn't much damage to the main structure of the building, but everything in the room was reduced to white powdery ash. The resulting uproar as the building emptied gave 'Jimmy' ample time to be elsewhere, if he had been there at all, and not some adjacent place.

As the raiders sorted themselves out, the Officer in charge asked 'toe prodder', "Roughly what range do you think that transmitter had?"

"Dunno, Sir. I barely had time to look at it. It had plenty of power available from the mains, so several miles, I should think."

"And how many offices and flats around this area?"

"In a three mile circle, at a guess, couple of thousand, maybe as high as four."

735

The first fire engine came bellowing up.

"You're too late, lads, it's all over! The O.I.C. told the Fire Chief.

"You fucked up, then?"

"Yeah. It was a booby trap! Sarn't. Show the pyromaniacs the site, so they can check for embers."


The frigate easily caught up with the rusty freighter, provisionally named Zit 99, and rolled along a few hundred yards astern, while they endeavoured to check with the sub. that they were shadowing the right ship, struggling with the unwieldy delay via Whitehall Commcen, and Rugby VLF radio, the submarine's broadcasting station, Eventually, they gave up, and tried the unauthodox, direct route, on VHF channel 16.

"Earwig, this is Jacko" The radio-man sought a middle ground that was sufficiently obscure to the many listeners, and clear enough to the people it was meant for.

"AY! Youse C.B.ers! Booger orf the shipping channel!" A Cornish voice demanded.

"Er, if Jacko's who I think, can you go to channel 97

upper, over?"

"97 upper, going up"

"Booger orf. These channels're for sailors!"

"What you on it for, then?" Another voice butted in.

"I'll see you in the bar, tonight, Frankie!"

"You bloody won't! I'm off to the Hebrides!"

"No fish up there, Fingal's et em!"

"Who?"

"Fingal, him wi't cave!"

"OO ar!"

"Albert?" called a female voice, "You comin' 'ome tonight?"

"Ar, I am lass, about seven. Where are you?"

"I'm in the lifeboat watch-room, wi' Jessie. I'll have something warm ready for you, then!"

That started a fresh round of crude banter as the small boats worked their nets, pots, or whatever.


Trevor, tired of hassling the un-security guard, went to look for 'K'inell', who he caught in mid-cuddle with Josie. "Put him down, Carrot! I know where he's been, and you don't!"

"I can guess where he'd be, though, if I gave him half a chance!" she fended off an exploring hand.

"Take it easy, Trev. It's sorted out already. They've found someone who can read French, and they're translating the stuff, now. There's about two thousand messages for doing!"

"Two thousand? Is there no-one here regularly?"

"There used to be three, on each shift, but, - Get your hand out, you letch! - but now there's only day staff, one for each language, sometimes they can double up, if they know another." Josie replied, "But about a month ago, the body we borrow for holiday cover - retired, and went on a world cruise to see all the places she's read about for fifty years. If that hand, yes, that one! Moves any further up my thigh, I'll use these scissors on a certain dangly bit of yours! "

"But-".

"If you want more than that, you'll have to marry me!"

"Before, or after?"

"It seems that the Douane'rs have a similar problem. The person that 'phoned us was some sort of builder that happened to walk past. They've no-one there speaks English, and we've no-one who speaks French, result, non-communication. These scissors are about to communicate with you, 'K'inel'l!" She rocked her pelvis against the exploring fingers, sighed, and stepped back while she had the will-power to do so.

The door opened, and another radio op came in with a piece of paper. "You alright, Carrot? You look a bit flushed? According to this, the Okean Conquistadore is bringing in a ton or three of 'H', packed in six foot plastic tubes. They think the destination is, or rather are, various estuaries, round the south and west, Mersey to Solent, areas, But the date is five days ago. The Duane stopped, and searched, and found nothing, so think the stuff is being trans-shipped, in the channel, somewhere." She read aloud.

"So, the O.C. will be empty, now. No wonder they are laughing at us! I wonder if the freighter is the one the Navy's been watching?" Trev picked up the nearest telephone, and began dialling."

The radio op. came in again. "This one's the same, but

with the prefix, "Have you seen this? - Urgent!"

"Thanks."

"We'd better send one back to the Frogs, apologizing for the cock-up! 'K'inell' suggested. "I'll go and draft it, with the translator." He ducked through the door. In a minute, he was back, looking shocked. "Christ! The translator is a school-kid!" he exclaimed.

"Yes, my neighbour's daughter offered to help us. She's taking H.N.C's in two years, and wanted to practice on some real French, not the text-book stuff. She does Spanish, Italian, and some Russian, too!"

"Clever clogs!"

"I don't think she'll come here for a job, though, the pay's too low!"

"Tell me about it!" 'K'inell' went through again.

"Are you and 'K'inell' serious?" Trev asked Josie.

"About seventy-five percent." She replied, "He wants my body, but doesn't want to settle down. He says he has itchy feet. As far as I'm concerned, there's no-one else and I hope he hurries up and realizes it, I'm getting hungry!"

James Lancaster-Smytthe emerged from his inner sanctum and went looking for Betty. He found her sprawled on a chaise-longue at the pool-side, doodling in a notepad. "Hello, lover, you look happy today!" she glanced up at him.

"Yes. That business that has been niggling has been satisfactorily concluded, and I fancy a break."

"Let me change, then, and we can get the car out, and go somewhere."

"Rhodes is nice, now, I believe"

"Rhodes? I thought you wanted a break, not a holiday!" She put her notepad down.

"I'm in no hurry to get there, and I can see that you are getting nowhere with that programme. How does - take the car to the airport, internal hop to Southampton, and a Cunard Mediterranean cruise appeal?"

"Commercial, or the Cessna 310?"

"Commercial. The landing fees at Soton are crippling!"

She smiled at the thought of him paying thousands for a cruise, and quibbling over a hundred or so, for parking their aeroplane.

"The children aren't back from camp for a fortnight, and Harry can cope. They spend most of their time thrashing him at squash, anyway! I'll ask Nanny if she will have the babies, full time, while we are away. I don't think she will object." Betty said.

"It is decided, then, I'll just call to confirm the tickets."

"I have some news for you, as well!"

"Oh, no. Not again?"

"No, no! I've instructed my lawyer to accept Vince's offer. I think I have dragged it out long enough, and sucked him dry. It's not as if he can walk into another job, is it?" She smiled at her own joke, "So, he's not going to have any significant income, in the future."

"Personally, I think you are being rather harsh on him."

"Harsh? No! I've let the insufferable fool off lightly!"

James momentarily hesitated at the acid in her voice. This was a new side of Betty that hadn't shown before. He would have to watch her more closely, in future.

Chapter thirty-five.

The end of the end.

Sergeant Jones had tired of piddling around with the computers because he was getting nowhere, and resorted to the method he knew best. He was plodding around every office in every station, with a sheaf of the mystery messages, asking every typist and secretary he found if they recognized any of them. Most faces returned blank looks, but now and then one person recognized one or other of the messages, but couldn't recall where or when. He tenaciously followed these vague threads, losing them, and finding them again, using his years of fine honed intuition. The threads all led to one place, the telex room. After a pause for a mug of tea, and a cheese toastie, he began nibbling again. Security wouldn't let him into the telex room, no matter what. Undaunted, he dialled a privileged number.

Within ten minutes, a courier rushed up to him with a

special one-day unlimited access pass, courtesy of the

Commissioner, and a note which read 'Do not abuse it.' This

pass opened the door for him. Inside, he worked round each

printer op. in turn, with his sheaf of copies, drawing a blank. He

finally tried the shift co-ordinator, who tried to fob him off with

vague nothing statements. As they matched ranks, that way was

out. As they stood in impasse, Lew read the other's name-tag. A

tiny bell rang with a memory from many years ago, and his

mental rolodex started flipping. Yes! "Henry Peterson." He said,

slowly, "nineteen fifty-eight. Padgate. The Senior Training

Officer's trousers, on the flagpole at colours, instead of the flag!

April. Passing out Parade! Cadet - cadet - Hanson? Yes, Hanson

was booted out. But you and I both know it wasn't Hanson's

doing, don't we, Harry? Yes. I didn't find out until later, because

I was in the sick-bay, with appendicitis. When I found out, it was

too late for Hansen. Although he was invited back to pick up

from where he'd left off, he declined. I can't remember why. It

doesn't matter, now. It was your word against mine, and you

were the number one in class, while I wasn't there at the end,

and had to drop out for two months, and our paths never crossed again, until now. So, Harry, you either tell me where these came from, or a whisper will start circulating - about nineteen fifty-eight!"

"You wouldn't. It is still your word against mine!"

"Oh, I wouldn't say a word myself, but you know how rumours spread, and have a habit of being embellished! Someone sees a memo on someone's desk, and happens to mention it to someone else. Mud sticks, Harry. I've been chasing this person for a long time, and I'm getting close. A worm like you cannot stop me. I have a lot of clout behind me. How do you think I got in here so easily, Harry? Give me a name. The real one, and I will go away, hopefully to never meet you again. What is it to be, Harry, the name, or the mud pie?"

Sergeant Harry Peterson was caught between the proverbial rock and the hard place. He knew, but didn't know whether Lew Jones knew, that mud was already sticking. He had managed to lose three prisoners a while ago. The fourth one in the group hadn't tried to escape, because he was dead. Since that incident, he had managed to get himself enrolled in trials for the Armed Response Group, and while practicing on the indoor range, had successfully shot out two room-lights, and the Range Officer had managed to lose a middle left finger, thanks to an experimental, cowboy style 'fast-draw' that accidentally discharged a round. That ended THAT line of advancement. There was also a Rover 3000, with a very low roof, a few years earlier, when he had managed to roll it on a motorway. He had managed to avoid admitting he was seeing how fast he could go, in reverse.

Harry groped for a chair, and sat, defeated. He sighed. "The name," he croaked, then cleared his throat with a nervous cough, "The name is -." He named the Member of Parliament responsible for the overall running of the Police Force, amongst other job-titles.

"Thank you, Harry." Lew said. It was time to pass the baton on. He picked up the nearest 'phone, and dialled that number again. The Commissioner answered. "Tell him, Harry!" Lew passed over the handset.

Harry repeated what he had said, then went white, at the response.

Lew had already left. He had two new friends who had a

right to the knowledge, and he couldn't trust his minions with this particular hot cake.

The Navy persuaded 'Zit 99' to heave to, but not before a Robinson 22 two seat helicopter fluttered up from somewhere on the upper-works, and buzzed off inshore. Radar tracked it for a while, until it crossed the coast, and it disappeared into the ground returns.

The boarding party found the Captain, who greeted them with "No spikka da Ingelishk, bye-bye."

"Who does?"

"Bye-bye"

"Habla Espagnol?"

"Nyet."

"Parles Francais?"

"Bye-bye."

"Er, Sprechen sie Italiano?"

"Pianissimo, Pasta, bye-bye."

"Perhaps he speaks Brazilian." The other Officer had seen the small flag on an overhead stanchion.

The first Officer looked around, and spotted it. "Brazil?"

"Eh? Ah! Ayreton Senna!" The 'Zit's' Captain made a cup from his hands, at groin level. "Mucho Cojones!"

The Navy Officer looked baffled, his delicate upbringing didn't cover this situation.

"Ayreton Senna has big balls!" Navy number two whispered, "He must be a motor-racing fan!"

"Ah! Nigel Mansell!"

"Emerson Fittipaldi!"

"Er, Graham Hill." Navy was struggling. Cricket was more in his line.

"Nikki Lauda!"

"Stirling Moss." He dredged his memory desperately.

"Juan Fangio!"

"Jack Brabham."

"Mike Hawthorne!" The 'Zit's' Captain seemed to be enjoying this exchange.

"Er, ah, Colin Chapman."

"Hooo?"

"Sir, Chapman isn't a racer, he's a designer!" Number Two

whispered.

"Hoo Chap-man?"

"You've never heard of Chapman? The Officer bluffed, "He's got ten points, this season, already!" The other officer flinched, resigned to his fate, now.

"Eh? See-zon she no star'. Two month! You lies. Bye-bye. Go!"

"Enzio Ferrari!" He knew it was a hopeless cause now, he'd 'blown' it.

"Bluddy things. Go. Bye-bye."

Someone waved a machete, and the two officers found themselves standing on the waist, where the rope ladder had been, but no longer was.

"Go! Yump!"

"He means jump, Sir." Number two swung his legs over the rail, and stepped into space, clutching his treasures in one hand, his hat in the other, then plopped neatly into the water, demonstrating his past experience of rapid departures from hostile vessels. The first officer followed, with an ungainly sprawling fall, ending in a mighty splash as he landed on his back, star-fish fashion.

Even the Commissioner had Superiors, and he was now
waiting to see his. For three hours, now, he had been holding his
bombshell, knowing that the short fuse was burning. Once
Sergeant Jones had given him the key it hadn't taken long to
open the cupboard, and all kinds of nasty skeletons had fallen
out. They ranged from secretaries who took sudden long leaves,
to dodgy business deals, - one of which clearly showed that the
M.P. had sold a company that he owned, to himself, at a quite
considerable profit, then, a while later, had sold it back to the
original owner, himself, for another considerable profit.
Naturally, his name never appeared, except as a minor share-
holder. It did not take very long to discover that he really owned
40% A Miss K. Rodenberry held 30%, an unknown held 3%, and
the other 27% was in the possession of a W Ferrigolde. Some
deeper digging revealed that Miss Rodenberry was the maiden
name of the M.P's wife. W. Ferrigolde was a pseudonym used
by their son, who had a police record longer than a giraffe's
neck, mostly for drink/driving, speeding, disturbing the peace,

resisting arrest, and other fairly minor offences. Towards the end of the list, were three counts of possession of class 'A' drugs, in small quantities.

The secretary, who was busy doing nothing, seated behind the vast oak and leather desk, suddenly looked up and said "The Director will see you now." No little lights had flashed, no discreet buzzer had beeped, and the word 'Sir' wasn't used, either, so either she was psychic, or had been instructed to keep the Commissioner sitting there for three hours.

The Commissioner stood, tugged his tunic straight, and marched into the office, via the indicated door.

The Director was seated behind another leather and oak desk. On one corner, one of those silly 'executive toys', five steel balls suspended on thin wire, from a frame, stood, swinging gently. A faint odour of expensive Scotch permeated the atmosphere, although no decanter or glass was visible.

"Yesh?"

The Commissioner told him the bombshell, watching the Director go red, then white, then back to red again, as the tale unfolded. He sat, soaking it up, for a minute, then slid a silent drawer open to enable him to press a concealed button. "Have my car ready in ten minutes!" A piece of shrimp fell from a fold in his clothing as he moved, to drop untidily onto the immaculate desk. "Come with me. If you care to step through there, you can 'freshen up' first."

The Commissioner did as suggested, and found himself in a private bathroom. In moments, he was standing by the appropriate piece of porcelain, sighing with relief. A brief use of the wash-stand followed, and then he returned to the other room. The Director re-entered, via another door, his breath now smelling of mint, as a chauffeur came in from the reception area.

Chapter thirty-six.

Loose ends.


George and Joan went off on a tour round the Estate

Agents. Tommy had gone off with some friends, doing the

tourist thing. Vince was pottering around doing nothing

significant, and was deeply engrossed in examining the backs of

his eyelids for pin-holes when Lew's car rolled up, with a brief

'Dee-dah' to announce his arrival.

Over a brew of tea and a slice of Joan's cherry-less fruit-

cake, Lew dropped his bombshell again.

"Why?" Vince asked. The only reaction he showed was his

suddenly white knuckles.

"We're still working on that, but it looks like a massive

piece of mis-direction, to ensure that his record stayed lily-

white."

"Yes, I can see that, but why George, and me?"

753

"As far as I can tell, just sheer bad luck. You happened to be in the place and time he gave, and you fitted the vague descriptions that he appears to have invented."

"But, even the names were close. That's more than chance, surely! Perhaps there are another couple who look like us, using that camp-site, - - wait a minute! Come to think of it, there was a couple, who turned up on that last day, in a van of some sort!"

"A transit, is it?" Lew's instinct was prickling again.

"No, one of those, whatchacallem's, like the hippies have, Yeah, a Volkswagen, with a round front, and the engine at the back, It had an awning on one side that unclipped, so they could drive off without packing it away!" The memory crept back, "Red and green stripes, I think, faded. What were their names?"

Lew sat, silent, mentally recording every word. He knew that if he interrupted, the thread of thought would be broken, and perhaps gone forever.

"K registered" Vince muttered, "Cream and purple." His eyes looked through the window, but his thoughts were in the past. "Tatty old thing, it was, nearly as rough as my Cortina, Pat and Trevor! They had a water-barrel like a garden roller. Didn't look like divers. He was skinny, and cod-belly white, like I was, a few weeks ago. She had a fancy hair-do. Bleached blonde, black roots. Looked like a tart!" he was quiet again.

Lew's mental index files were flipping. That last had triggered a memory of a report from - somewhere. He would find it.

Vince sucked in a deep breath, and came back to the present. "Perhaps you know!" He decided. "I meant to ask George, before she went out, and forgot. This flying machine, the drawings don't show it but the instructions keep on about an angle of incidence, but I can't find it. What, or where, is it?"

"Where's the drawing?"

Vince unfolded it on the table.


The Commissioner, and the Director, waved their I.D. cards at the totally underwhelmed Commissionaire manning the reception desk.

"Do you Gentlemen have an appointment?" he asked

"Unfortunately, no. The matter is most urgent, though."

The Commissionaire lifted a telephone, pressed buttons,

and said, "I have two Gentlemen here who wish to see the man, on a matter they claim --He isn't? Where? Until when? Thank you, is his Deputy -- In Yorkshire? Ah, well, thanks." He replaced the handset. "I regret, Sir's, that the Right Honourable Sir Jeffrey Pallbearer is on holiday, he caught a flight to Crete, this morning, and isn't due back for a fortnight. His Deputy is in Yorkshire, pressing palms."

"Damn!" The Commissioner cursed.

"It would appear that 'Jimmy's' done it again!" The Commissionaire commented.

"Jimmy? I thought you said his name was Jeffrey?"

"I should not have said that. It's a nick-name we have for him, a play on words. Jimmy, Jimmy riddle, widdle, take a leak, He always finds a hole to escape through, when he's painted himself into a corner!"

"Yes, I see the connection. Was this holiday taken at short notice, by any chance?"

"It is funny that you should ask. He left a list of cancelled appointments a yard long."

"Do you have a forwarding address?"

"No, sorry. His Deputy might, but I cannot imagine you prying it out of him."

The 'phone was ringing. Vince fished under the drawing that spread over the table, and found it. "Hello? Yes, speaking. Fleecem's, yes, what can I - you have! They have? It has! Great! Yes, tomorrow's fine! Yes, thanks. No, you will find that a bit difficult, sorry, Mrs Willis is down here, with us. Yes, bye for now!" he put the 'phone down

"My ex-wife has signed the Divorce petition." He told Lew, "and the rich guy she's with is footing the bill for a quickie. It's going in today, and they're sending me the document tomorrow!"

"Good. I'm glad for you. For both of you!"

They had sailed around several of the islands, calling in at some, where they had toured Greek ruins, World War Two ruins, and the far-flung markers of the Hilton Empire - in the shape of some of his hotels. They were cruising towards Crete when

James Lancaster-Smytthe emerged from his cabin, wearing striped pyjamas and a monogrammed dressing gown, to meet the Steward hurrying towards the electronic summons.

"Have you seen my wife, anywhere?" he was asked. "She went on deck, for a breath of fresh air before turning in, and I haven't seen her since."

"Please wait in your cabin, Sir, It's a bit chilly, and you aren't dressed. I will see if I can find her."


Pete was reading a two-day old newspaper, while he waited for Trevor to come out of a departmental meeting, then they were going to Holyhead on a diving trip. "Mystery Explosion sinks ship in channel!" he read. Skimming through the article, he saw that some old Liberian tramper had suffered an engine-room or boiler explosion, and sank in three minutes. A nearby R.N. frigate had picked up a few survivors, although some of the crew remained unaccounted for.

Another small headline drew his eye. 'Overboard'. The wife of a passenger on a cruise shop was believed to have fallen over the side during a night passage to Crate. The bereaved husband, a Mr. J Lancaster-Smith was inconsolable. Pete smiled at the typos, then the name registered.

Georgina became Mrs Birtwhistle in August. Sergeant Lew Jones gave her away. Joan nursed the, thankfully sleeping, baby for the duration of the ceremony. A surprise Guard of Honour met them outside, with an arch of borrowed radio aerials and diver's fins. Pete, Trevor, 'K'inell', and Geordie held the aerials, while the Valley S.A.R. crew held the fins. The expressions on their faces when Vince walked out of the church were indescribable, as they still believed that he was wheel-chair-bound.

'Pimples' Jones drove the wedding car to the cottage, with the sirens blaring and the blue lights flashing all the way. His excuse was; - it was the Commissioner's car, and he couldn't find the switch to turn them off! Lew and the Commissioner followed up, rather more sedately, at the rear, in George's Land-Rover.

Tommy took charge of the catering for the reception. No-one dared to refuse him. He had also tracked down a couple more people, so Ginger Jill, and Mary O'Flaherty, from the hospital, were there, with their partners.

The Right Honourable Sir Jeffrey 'Jimmy' Pallbearer never returned to face the charges lined up against him. The value of the shares in his companies crashed, and his whole house of cards came tumbling down. A Greek entrepreneur - who'se name was withheld - was left teetering, his foundations showing.

End of book one, more to follow...........

If you enjoyed this novel, you might like to read -  by this Author -

Tea Break Tales.

Isbn 78145094226

Rick and Rosie

Isbn 9781451549300

and coming soon – book two of the 'Vince' series.

Made in the USA
Charleston, SC
23 May 2010